The Stones of Yemen

J. Michael Jones
Mount Erie Press Anacortes Washington

This edition was first published in paperback in the United States in 2023 by
Mount Erie Press
Anacortes, Washington
thestonesofyemen@gmail.com
Copyright ©2023 Mount Erie Press
Identifier: ISBN: 978-0-9977591-9-8

CONTENTS

For the children of war; 2 million killed, 4-5 million disabled, and 12 million left homeless, in this decade alone.

Thus, I do not see what use there is in those millstones of the gods said to grind so late as to render punishment hard to be recognized, and to make wickedness fearless.

Plutarch in *Moralia circa 100 AD*

CHAPTER ONE

Yemen seeps through the chinks in your soul, her healing sand deposited in the narrowest clefts of your deepest marrow. The country leaves your life furrowed, tormented, never to be the same again. It makes you a casualty and then a hero, both unsought.

The Yemenis were like a lost branch of my family, becoming dearer to me than those who shared my own country and DNA. The closest of them, Jabbar, like a long-lost brother, nearer to my heart than the two I had grown up with. I, a dearer brother to him than the one that suckled his own mother's breasts. I loved him, yet he was the only man I ever plotted to murder—and with good reason.

Those haggard mountain people barged into my personal life on an otherwise quiet summer day. I was more than halfway circumnavigating the world in my sailboat, a Farr 45. The "45" stood for the length, 45 feet, and 13 feet wide. She was a racing yacht, built for speed not comfort, and ready for retirement if not the scrapyard. After saving her from her Himalayan blackberry interment on her previous owner's estate, and a bit of restoration work—new electronics, and an updated galley, I wanted to take the old girl for one more spin—around the whole damn world.

After almost a decade of working as a physician associate in neurosurgery in Seattle, the trip was my sabbatical, my gift to my tired, stinky feet and depleted brain. I never wanted to don a surgical mask again or go to a compulsory six A.M. meeting to listen to a hospital executive—a blood fainter, nonetheless—lecture us on the latest paradigm shift in medicine. At thirty-four, it was time to call all my scattered thoughts home and reconsider what my future should be, rekindling my love for medicine from the remnants that remained, if there were any to reclaim.

I came to sailing in an odd way. My sister, Angie, nine years younger than me, called me one day from New York. She had an intuition that something was out of kilter in my soul. She was right. I had a great job, working with an excellent neurosurgeon, and we were doing good work, fixing broken spinal cords, and removing brain tumors. Still, I felt empty. Few friends, no loves, just work. I couldn't imagine bringing other people into my jumbled inward sanctum. There was a big, ugly crater in the middle of our family, filled with twisted steel girders and broken concrete, papers, and dust; it was the footprint of the 9/11 attack. Inconceivably, a hand-wrought human catastrophe. It took my dad, a medic, climbing the south tower, leaving only his bag, a couple of burnt bones, and his watch. He was my best friend in the whole world.

I was sixteen when I lost Dad, Angie just seven. My twin brothers, Hank, and Wayne, nineteen. My mom and brothers became emotionally catatonic. Not good conversationalists. Angie, on the other hand—while the youngest—became our family's anchor.

My little sister had dated into sailing. Her boyfriend, Joel, was from a sailing family in Annapolis. Joel had taken us down to Sandy Hook Bay on a beautiful July morning in his 1987 Pearson 39-2 Sloop; it was a hand-me-down from his grandfather. Sailing hadn't left a big impression on me that New York morning, but I spent the whole time talking to Angie while Joel handled the lines, tiller, and sails. Having a shared traumatic experience—although to her, just a hazy memory—Angie had easy access to my internal space.

One crisp morning, the following April, Angie called. She had just returned from their longest trip under sails. Four weeks down to the Caribbean, calling me twice from ports along the way just to share her joy. But this land-based call from her apartment seemed more formal.

"Bryan, you've got to take up sailing. Joel says the Puget Sound is one of the best places in the world to sail, and then you have the entire west coast of British Columbia to explore."

I listened to her but said little. Maybe that's why she fell off her chair—literally—when I called her eight weeks later with my news.

"Angie, I followed your advice. I took a sailing class, sooled in a daysailer, put in a bid on an old Far 45, I'm quitting my job and going to sail around the world. Could you possibly come with me while I crossed the Pacific?"

I heard a crash, then mumbling and finally her clear voice, "What? What are you talking about?"

"Angie," I said. "I've found peace on the water. No purposeless chatter around me, just the wind and sails. So, I'm sailing around the world! It was your idea."

"I said nothing about sailing around the world, just taking up sailing. Why Bryan are you so damn impulsive!"

I didn't have to reply, she knew the answer. That's the way I cope. I wasn't sailing away to find myself, but with hopes of losing the world, which no longer made sense.

Two months later, Angie took a four-month leave from her job in New York to sail with me from Seattle to Thailand. Joel was so kind to join us for the Seattle to Hawaii leg, then he had to get back to work. Once I had my sea legs, I said goodbye to Angie at Bangkok's Suvarnabhumi Airport. For the next six weeks, I alone crossed the stormy Bay of Bengal, the steaming Arabian Sea, and then moved into the Gulf of Aden.

The Gulf of Aden is beautiful water, an ocean painted in blue pastels, the thin edges like crystalline peridot cutting deep into the rugged tan Al Hajar mountains. As I sailed along the Omani coast, I was alone with my thoughts of pirates and the blistering early-August sun. Heat stroke in such an isolated place would be a real menace.

As the winds pulled me toward Africa, my worries were soon supplanted by my preparations for transiting through the Suez Canal, just a couple of weeks away. With calm seas and a good close-haul wind, a big smile took up residence across my sun-scorched and peeling face. It was the first time I had tasted serenity since I was sixteen. Taking advantage of my privacy, save a few nomadic birds, I plugged my ears into my phone's playlist and danced barefooted across my salt-stained deck. I'm a private dancer, never having graced a public venue with my gauche movements. My stuttering moonwalk scared away even the small flock of white-cheeked terns that were hitching a ride on my bow. Sailing through the Mediterranean would be the highlight of my one-year journey. Then downhill across the Atlantic and back home to New York. Seattle just a reverie. What was coming next in my life? I hadn't a clue, but I felt the sea was making me a better man.

As I approached the Bab al-Mandab Strait, that narrow river of sea that cuts between the southwest corner of Yemen and the northeast corner of Djibouti, I had no choice but to think about the bloody civil war just beyond my starboard. It came to me unsolicited. Gray Saudi Arabian patrol boats were out in force, attempting to prevent "conflict contraband," such as drones and bombs—as well as food and medicine—from slipping through the cracks of their otherwise iron embargo. They pushed the shipping lanes farther to the west and away from the Yemeni shores, slowing us all to a crawl.

I could see the sun reflecting in brief flashes off the Saudis' beady binocular lenses, as they watched my every move, including my exclusive dance steps. I added a sudden turn toward them and extended middle fingers that they could focus their damn binoculars on. Not a lot of love lost. After all, those bastards had killed Dad.

I'm sure most Saudis are good people. I would've forgotten my Army Arabic if it had not been for Dr. Khan, a Seattle vascular surgeon and a Saudi national, who insisted I speak only Arabic with him, for my benefit. A true friend and a good man. But I had to focus my rage somewhere. If not at God, why not the Saudis?

Two years after 9/11, a couple of my buddies and I went down to the military recruiting office. One of them had lost an aunt, a dishwasher in the Windows on the World restaurant, in the north tower. The other, just pissed. They wanted to put bullets between the eyes of terrorists. I, in respect to Dad, a pacifist, asked to be a medic. We all got our wishes. My buddies both died in Fallujah while I was patching up people in Afghanistan. I came out of that conflict more conflicted. Yet, I knew I loved medicine, completing a pre-med curriculum at Columbia, and then Yale's Physician Associate program.

That evening in my sailboat, I was mesmerized by Yemen's coast, the shore veiled behind a brown dust cloud with spiky bronze mountains rocketing into the clear air above, as if the Alps had been hung there to dry. Squinting through my own binoculars, I saw lofty crags sparse of trees. Leaning over my starboard gunwales for a better view, I saw a mysterious highland resting among summer's tall cumulous clouds. Despite knowing that a civil war was ravaging through its lower valleys, I found it enchanting. The suffering, unimaginable. I had to turn away—but I couldn't.

It seemed to me that war had been shadowing me my entire fucking life. I had added another eighteen years since losing Dad, and those wars were still raging. I swallowed hard what spit I could muster. I wanted nothing to do with fighting anymore, yet I was enthralled by this land of struggle of which I knew almost nothing. I kept putting my binoculars away, wrapping the neck strap around them and tucking them into a drawer in the cabin, only to go back every few minutes to retrieve them for further study of the coast.

I moored my boat near the Hanish Islands as darkness was settling across the Red Sea. While the Hanish were Yemeni, they fell outside the Saudi blockade of the mainland. The islands were nothing more than an archipelago of camel-colored rocks floating upon the translucent blue waters. The largest of the islands, with its elongated tail pointing north and its jutting head on its south end, lay on those waters like Jabba the Hut lounging on a waterbed, wearing a lighthouse as a hat. I chuckled with the comparison. The water-swept rocks were inhabited by hundreds of war-weary fishermen, along with tens of thousands of seabirds who really didn't give a damn about any man's war.

Following one of the colorful fishing dhows draped in nets, I found a relatively quiet bay of liquid jade, a safe harbor to drop my anchor. A colony of stone houses covered the tan bluffs above me. The peaceful waters were soon interrupted when three small rowboats piloted by thin, dark-skinned boys donning dirty faces approached my portside. One child stood in the center of his boat and screamed, in English, through a big white grin, "You buy, okay?" Then he and his friends held up long sticks with trinkets, bracelets, and combs dangling on strings. One of the boys held up a stained blue-and-white baseball hat that read "I [heart] Yemen." Apparently, I wasn't the only transient boat that had stopped there to moor for the night.

I rifled through my pockets and tossed the scrawny boys what money I had on me—a few Omani rials, leftovers from a brief resupply stop in Muscat a week earlier. One coin fell into the water. A scrappy boy, so thin that you could see his ivory bones through his mahogany skin, dove in after it. In a minute he came to the surface with a big smile, the water draining from his black hair, the curls quickly popping out of the mat, and the coin between his teeth. My jaw dropped. A ripple of giggles spread across the children.

The little boats were immediately multiplied by a factor of five, one piloted by girls, seeming to come out of nowhere as if the stones themselves were bearing children. With a stunned look I quickly pulled up my—just deployed—anchor while yelling back at them, "Lays ladaya almali. Yabtaeidu. [I have no money. Go away]." To my surprise, as I'm sure they were in want, they slowly rowed back toward shore, their little shoulders slumped. Looking over my own shoulder for one more glimpse, I saw them climb out of their boats, stand on the beach—oars in hands—and give me one last stare with their rusty brown eyes. Eyes like pairs of peepholes on exotic doors, behind which a mysterious world loomed. The life of Yemen's sweet-smiling children of war—an enigma.

I re-anchored my boat farther from the shore to discourage more visitors. I was too tired to sail through another night, and the shipping lanes were becoming too crowded for my autopilot while I dozed.

I went into the cabin, cooked up a good meal, and opened a beer. I had a foot-long sharkha, an Omani lobster, which I'd bought from a fishing boat three days earlier. I'd tried to keep it alive in a bucket of sea water, but it had become quite docile since that morning. If I failed to consume it that night, it would go to waste. As I sat inhaling the meat of my crustacean in garlic butter, I wished I had given the little trinket-selling kids some food. Only two hundred yards away, they were likely eating their last dreams.

My satellite dish was well positioned for a good internet hookup. While I should have been sleeping, I spent most of the night reading about the war, so close that—despite the dark—I could sense its presence, smell its oily smoke, and hear its faint rolling thunder on the mainland, preceded by flashes of light. The star-spangled sky told me this wasn't just a summer's storm. Out of curiosity and before retiring to my hammock, I searched online for opportunities for physician associates in Yemen. Fat chance, but what if? Rubbing my chin stubble, I focused intently, my face drifting so close to the small font, my eyes began to blur, and my breath fogged up the screen.

By the wee hours of the morning, the pursuit had landed me on the International Rescue Committee's (IRC) website, where a job was posted for an "Advanced Practice Clinician, NP or PA" in a refugee camp in the mountain village of Haydan. Interesting. I brushed my teeth and fell into my hammock, knowing that a few hours of slumber were required before another busy day of sailing.

Having fallen asleep while my brain was so engaged, a chain of odd dreams about Yemen's war haunted me throughout the morning, like Dickens' Christmas ghosts. But it was predawn when the most upsetting and vivid dream occurred. It came in that twilight time, between deep sleep and awake when the boundaries of reality and illusions are indistinct.

I made the teak decking in the open cockpit my bed during the night, escaping the previous day's heat that had refused to dissipate from the cabin. The early morning's redness was leaking over Yemen's craggy peaks in the east. My eyes, half open, I heard a soft whisper, a child's voice in Arabic, coming from across the dark water. "Bryan, help us."

How do they know my name? I sat up, the muscles in my legs tightening like ropes, and answered in a sleepy whisper, "Who's there?" Then quickly repeated in Arabic, "*Min hunak?*"

With the silence, save the distant booms, I lay down again. I felt a chill flush over me as I wrapped my chest with my arms, tucking my hands into my armpits for warmth. My jaw quivering, I unzipped my spinnaker's storage bag and pulled the corner of the crimson sail through the opening and over me like a makeshift cover. My trembling spread. I didn't want to return to the cabin until my encounter with the voices was finished.

Before long, the child's voice was followed by dozens in harmony, in Arabic and English. "Bryan, please help us." Finally, the voices of thousands of children.

I flinched with each petition. I rotated on the hard deck, one ear down and the other covered by my arm and the sailcloth. Still, the voices softly penetrated my ears. *A solo-sailor's hallucination?*

Sitting up, I rubbed my face with my hands, moist from a cold sweat. I shook my head and stood. A milky air had filled the space around my boat and across the sea rendering the Hanish islands invisible. However, mainland Yemen's mountainous silhouette to the east stood in the glassy space above the haze, the mountains' sharp edges becoming more pronounced as the sun's rise was imminent.

The application for the IRC position in Yemen asked for a current photo. I went into the head to take a piss. In the dim light afforded by the overhead LED, I studied my face in the stainless-steel mirror under the brilliant white light. My cheeks were cherry red and marked by patches of flaking and peeling skin. I was overdue for my weekly shave. My unkept hair, normally the color of coffee, was sun-bleached on the tips like a cosmetologist's experiment gone awry. Additionally, I had been a stranger to a barber's chair since leaving Seattle six months earlier, and my shoulder-length locks couldn't have been crustier from the buildup of sea salt. Maybe if I were applying for residence in a homeless camp such a "current photo" would have been helpful but in every other instance should have put an end to my prospects of employment. But it didn't.

Two weeks later, when I reached the southern tip of Egypt's

Sinai Peninsula where I should have been turning to the northwest to Suez, I instead turned to the northeast toward Eilat's harbor in Israel. After forty-eight hours spent corresponding with Dorothy Edwards, IRC's Yemeni country director, via e-mail and one satellite phone conversation, I had agreed to take the position in Haydan, my background check pending. *What the hell was I thinking?*

My degree in Arabic from my Army days must have impressed Dorothy, especially when she asked me a couple of questions in the Yemeni dialect, adorned richly in a British accent but understandable. I must have answered to her satisfaction. I didn't explain to her that I had studied Arabic, not as an Army requirement—Afghans don't speak Arabic—but because I wanted to read the Koran for myself. A Muslim will tell you that you must read the Koran in Arabic. I wasn't a Muslim, but I wanted to know why the hell the 9/11 terrorists had slaughtered so many innocent people that morning, including my dad. I never figured it out, even after resorting to an English translation of the book. My Muslim friends were as perplexed about it as I was, except that hate has no boundaries, no nationality or religion.

For the next six days, I lived on my boat moored in Eilat's quiet harbor. The Israeli city was flanked by lovely white beaches peppered with dark-skinned, half-naked tourists. Behind them, the well-lit storefronts were full of more modestly dressed shoppers. Once the IRC paperwork was processed, a two-year contract signed, I dry-docked the *Protagonist* in the marina and took a bus to Tel Aviv's airport. Then a convoluted flight to Geneva, where I waited a week for a Red Cross flight directly to Sana'a's international airport, a strip-mall looking facility, squarely in the crosshairs of both the Saudis and the Houthi rebels.

I was greeted on the tarmac in Sana'a by Dorothy. A tall woman, about my height, five-foot ten, with auburn hair, but gray sprouting here and there like weeds, all well sprayed to hold its bold form even in the mountain breezes. She reminded me of old videos of the late Margaret Thatcher—same red lipstick and string of pearls but with a schoolgirl's giggle. I would guess she was in her early sixties, but her skin was a smooth as a twenty-year-old. Her sense of humor may have been her way of coping in a very stressful environment—it even calmed my own nerves; her humor was so dry it could ignite a fire.

We approached her snorkeled Land Rover where her Yemeni driver was sitting on the bent-up hood in his button-up tan shirt, hands folded, legs crossed, a smoking cigarette between his fingers, and staring off into the distance as if he was wishing he was doing anything else but this. Suddenly, the rear door opened, and a woman stepped out. A gorgeous woman with a pale complexion and coils of shoulder-length blond hair. My attention was drawn to her irresistibly. I watched her in my peripheral vision over Dorothy's left shoulder. I glanced now and then to see her directly, not believing what my peripheral vision was telling me. Meanwhile, I listened carefully to Dorothy as vital information about the country and my job poured from her fluttering bright red lips into my curious ears.

As we approached the car, Dorothy paused and looked at the woman. "Oh, Bryan, this is Sheila, uh, Dr. Emory, whom I was telling you about."

I reached out my hand and took hers. It was soft and strong. A dimpled smile erupted on her freckled face. Her natural beauty left me speechless. Perfection. I blushed as if my sailor's cheeks could get any redder.

"I'm so glad you're here Bryan. I've been in Haydan for a year with no rest. I've worked my buns off," Sheila said with a silly laugh.

Stuffing my sweaty hands in my pockets, I responded, "I don't, uh … I mean, I don't know why, but I assumed you were a man. I mean, on the phone when Dorothy told me, 'Dr. Emory is alone in the camp,' for some reason I was thinking of a man. Maybe I didn't expect a woman, especially a woman of your beau—I mean, uh … I mean a woman alone would feel safe enough to take this job."

Her dimples reappeared, "Oh, I can take care of myself.

Besides the people in Haydan … well, they love our work. They'll watch your back."

"You're so … like, I mean young," I said with a staring squint, "I mean you look so young. When did you complete your residency?"

"I didn't," she said. "Came here straight from medical school."

"Really?" I said in a tone of disbelief. "You're one brave woman."

"Well, I don't know if I'm 'brave,' maybe I am. Some would say, 'foolish.'"

Dorothy interrupted her. "You two will have plenty of time to talk as it's a six-hour drive to Haydan. It's not that far, but the infrastructure of this broken-down country makes you work hard for each mile gained. If it's not for the dissolving roads, it's going through countless checkpoints and dodging Saudi bombing raids." A big smirk crossed her face. "Oh … hmm, or you could take the bullet train I suppose and be there in an hour."

Her face—then straight as an arrow—left me stunned. I grinned. "Sure. Made of real bullets, I assume."

Dorothy giggled as she wiped an unruly tuft of hair off her face.

As we pulled out of the airport and into the chaotic streets, I clinched my jaw and fists. It was the same feeling pulling out of Bagram Airfield into the bustling streets of Kandahar. The streets were crowded with people and animals. Many of the men had AK-47s slung on their shoulders. Others, holding big, curved knives, sat in circles around tables sipping tea from small clear glasses. Street vendors quickly washing out the empties and refilling them for the next customer. The women, some with their faces covered by burkas, some not, all carrying something—babies, big blue water jugs, bundles of bedding, or straw—were constantly crossing the street and dodging the chaotic traffic. Amid all of it was a menagerie of animals, beasts of burden, sources of meat or fiber, or both.

I didn't know how big Sana'a was until Dorothy said, looking out her side window, "Sana'a has over four million residents … and it looks if they're all out on a summer's stroll today." After a reflective moment, she added, "With so many people crowded into such a small mountainous space, during such a vicious war ... you know, it could get quite dangerous." She glanced at me over the back of her seat and winked. "Don't you think?"

I was speechless so I just stared at her.

"Sitting ducks," she added. "What were they thinking ... starting a bloody war here? Must have run out of khat and needed something to do." Then she turned and looked over the seat again wearing her smirk. Sheila chuckled. I saw our driver squinting at Dorothy through the rearview mirror. I flashed him a perplexed look.

The poverty around us, was all encompassing, from the worn-out clothes of the adults to the skinny arms and potbellies of the children. People with missing limps, or patched eyes dotted every block. All their faces weathered by war. My mouth went dry and stayed dry for the next two years.

We dropped Dorothy off at the IRC office, and Sheila moved to the front seat, while I remained in the back seat alone.

"I get car sick easily on winding roads," Sheila said, "And, as you'll see, Yemen is quite mountainous." She closed her car door and fastened her seatbelt.

Having the back seat to myself, I wanted to close my eyes, calm my nerves, and sleep. Only two time zone changes since Switzerland, but our flight had left before dawn, and I'd had a sleepless night with a head full of worries before that.

As my eye lids gently closed and I focused on relaxing my muscles and taking deep, long breaths, Sheila turned and spoke to me over the back of her seat. "Bryan, I have a lot to tell you about life in Haydan and how we practice medicine there. It's busy right now. I hope you can be in the clinic first thing in the morning. With me taking two days off to come to Sana'a to pick you up ... well, we'll be swamped tomorrow for sure."

We navigated through the chaotic streets of Sana'a and out of town. I leaned forward and put my face closer to hers, so she didn't have to turn around to speak. It also put me within the spell of her delightful ambience and the cool stream of the car's air conditioner, which was struggling to reach me. Maybe it was the smell of her hair that enticed me. Possibly strawberry shampoo mixed with something organic. Since stepping off the plane, all I had smelled was a rotten kind of smoke. Her smell was a pleasant change, distracting from the ill feeling I was having about being in this place. She was the familiar. American. As I listened to her sweet voice, I studied the back of her head and noticed the spectrum of colors of her hair. Each hair a different shade. Certainly, a natural blond.

I watched Sheila's expressions, dimples, smiles, and grimaces, all from a side view of her face. I noticed how she wrinkled her nose whenever she spoke about something unpleasant, like children dying from cholera or Saudi bombing raids. I looked at her freckles and tried to count them when I should have been listening to what she was saying. I lost my place at forty-four. I saw a translucent chicken pox scar on her left temple. I imagined her as a little girl, covered in sores, in bed, golden locks around her head like a mane. I would have brought her ice cream. Meanwhile, she, ignoring my stares, continued talking in earnest. Me, trying to ignore the images behind her on the other side of the Land Rover's window. But soon those images took control of my senses.

My mind was not able to keep up with the visuals along the road. The farther we traveled from Sana'a the greater the impact from the war. More people on crutches or homemade wheeled chairs, some with bandages from recent injuries. The children dirtier and thinner with each mile gained toward the Dammaj Valley, the war's epicenter. Each scene of misery passed by my car window like a fast-forwarded dystopian movie, streaks of color but silent. With each mile, I felt us going deeper into the country and farther away from the possibility of escape. Panic material.

We traveled through several towns—Raydah, Khamir, Huth, Alamashya, and Sa'dah. The images beyond the glass came out of its blur and sharpened as we slowed down to pass through those congested towns. Vicious horrors and signs of violence written in the rubble of what had been homes and scrawled in the scars on the bodies of the people—on their skin or in the haunting expressions of their faces. But seated on my side of the glass was the most gorgeous woman I had ever seen, lecturing me on how to survive in that world. Entranced by her beauty and distracted by the humanity outside our car, I heard few of her words. Yes, her hair did smell of strawberries, and she had a little body odor. But who doesn't sweat in Yemen's summer?

As we passed through the town of Sa'dah, Sheila lowered her window and then stuck her finger outside, pointing at a white-washed stone and brick building, and identified it as the Doctors Without Borders hospital. "They take our difficult cases," she said. As we left the hospital behind us, she added, "I'm dating Michel, a doctor from France who works there. He's smart."

"Damn!" I mumbled under my breath while collapsing into my seat. I was just starting to think that Sheila was the one woman I could allow into my life. Now, just a fantasy.

"Are you okay?" she asked. "Car sick?"

I nodded. "Yeah, and a little tired."

With my back resting against my seat, I turned my head to stare out my window. I had to reprogram my mind, like making it colorblind but beauty-blind instead. Sheila would be a colleague and nothing else. Too many weeks alone at sea had left me vulnerable to an attractive woman, especially an American. She was out of my league, as most women were. What woman would want a man as muddled as me? I had no dreams, no life plan, and set adrift. Rudderless. I would also have to ignore Sheila's American familiarity and embrace the Yemeni peculiarity if I was going to adapt to this place.

Soon we passed a row of massive trees lining the road, looking gnarly and old, like they had witnessed a thousand seasons of peace and war. Pointing at the trees, Sheila said, "The legend behind those olive trees, those big ones over there, is that they were planted by one of Mohammed's nephews ... yes, that Mohammed. We're right on the old frankincense trail that ran from Mecca to Oman. The story goes that the trees were planted almost fifteen hundred years ago and promised protection for everyone who stands in their shade until the final hour or day of judgment. You'll see believers congregating there, especially during bombing raids. But myth or no myth, the trees are old."

I watched men, women, and even goats high in the strong arching branches picking and eating its green fruit and spitting out the pits. Then I must have dozed, being overtaken by my exhaustion in the moment of silence. As I drifted off to sleep, I could hear the Land Rover's squeaky brakes engaging and disengaging, my head going forward or backward with each squeak, and the seat rising and falling in sudden jerks as we navigated bumps. Muffled by the window, I heard distant voices in the crowds outside. Then dark silence ensued.

"Bryan! Hey, Bryan, we're here," came her soft voice.

I opened my eyes to a blurry world, the car still moving. I rubbed my eyeballs and looked again. I sat up. Where the hell was I? People were walking in long lines. Like leaf-cutter ants, they walked in straight rows on the road's shoulders carrying bundles on their heads. The short, brown-teethed men had turbans or scarfs wrapped around their heads and wore white or brown thoobs (long robes) under sports jackets. Others wore silky wraparound plaid skirts of ashen blue. Several of them had highly ornate curved knives in the front-center of their belts. Others were wearing shirts and pants, much like in the western world. I saw children, many carrying loads too. Little girls were in brightly colored dresses and grimy faces and boys in thoobs with sticks in their dirty little hands. The boys pausing to aim their sticks at one another like guns.

The bundles appeared to be straw, wheat, or possibly khat leaves. While khat had no nutritional benefit, I quickly learned that because of its monetary value as a drug, it could be exchanged for food or consumed as an escape from hunger. The users of this drug were obvious from their single protruding cheek, like lopsided chipmunks. I soon found my nose pressed against the car window — eyes wide to take in the full view of my new town.

The Land Rover was slowing down to avoid the people and because the road had become quite bumpy. I looked down at the pavement, which had dissolved into dirt and rubble. Little campfires dotted the roadside, women cooking circles of—what looked like wheat—paste spread across pieces of hot hammered metal on bricks above the fires. Behind the marching lines of people were adobe and concrete buildings, all in shades of brown, most with white accents around windows and doors, and many a ruin. Concrete buildings were broken into large pieces, like a Lego city after a toddler's tantrum, but with tangled rusty and bent rebar sticking up into the air. The adobe ruins appeared like dirt that had returned to its natural state of piles.

High on the hills in front or west of us were five- and six-story buildings, precariously perched on massive rock outcroppings. The old adobe buildings, so tall and wedged side by side, some rows leaning, reminded me of a colony of giant mud dauber nests.

Turning left, we pulled through a stone wall's metal gate, four panels painted red and green, looking as if it had been cobbled together from pieces of cars and other war debris. The compound sat on the eastern edge of the village where the old mountain road leveled off, catching its breath after a steep climb from the Dammaj Valley. Beyond the clinic, the gorge's flat bottom was covered in a deep green, orchards flanked by fields of grain. Back the way we had just come, the green continued in stacked terraces, down the ravine until the water petered out. It was the same going up the mountain, west of the village, where green patches climbed the mountain like a carpeted staircase for Titans.

"We're here. This is the clinic's compound. Home!" announced Sheila.

All I saw was a dilapidated, partially destroyed, old stone structure, with shiny—obviously new—corrugated steel roofing over wings going north and south.

As we stepped out of the car, Sheila turned to me, rested her warm hand on the back of my shoulder, and explained, "This was previously a private hospital built in the fifties by a local doctor.

Then it was taken over by Médecins Sans Frontières—you know, Doctors Without Borders—until the Saudis bombed it three years ago. Some locals patched it up, at least the north and south ends, but MSF didn't have the personnel to return to Haydan. IRC had a refugee camp here"—she pointed to her right— "to the north of the village, and they got a permit from the Houthis to reopen the clinic. The clinic is on the south side of the old hospital. Our personal quarters and … oh, and the commons … are here in the salvaged northside. The commons has a kitchen, two restaurant booths, and an informal area with a couch and coffee tables. It's a nice place to hang out. Personally," she added pointing at herself, "I prefer to eat dinner out in the garden on the south side. It's a grassy area with nice shade trees where the patients line up in the mornings. We close the south gate after the last patients leave, so we have the area to ourselves. At the end of a busy day, I close my eyes and pretend it is … well, Pawnee Park back in Nebraska."

"Nebraska?" I asked.

"Yeah … west of Lincoln. And you?" Folding her arms to wait and listen.

"Me … uh, New York. The Bronx, to be exact."

"Hmm," she said. "Didn't hear a Bronx accent."

"Oh … I lived in Seattle for ten years since. Before that Kandahar."

With the word, "Kandahar," her brow furrowed. "Really?"

CHAPTER TWO

It took me a few days to get settled. I tried out the small indoor space for my quarters for three nights but soon decided I preferred to sleep outside in a pup tent. I found the tent in our supply room left over from when the first IRC survey team stayed in Haydan for a week prior to starting the clinic. Not only did I love sleeping outdoors, but it was much cooler than the indoor space, especially by morning, when it was almost cold, even in summer.

The survey team had set up an outdoor shower and toilet, which I preferred to the indoor bath shared with Sheila. Once my sister Angie turned eight, she took over our single bath for two hours each morning. I wasn't sure if Sheila would need the same, but I wanted to give her the personal space if she did.

The next morning, I joined Dr. Emory in the clinic as promised. It was busy, but we were able to see patients at an amazing rate. The good pace was set by our nurse, Mazen, who kept the whole clinic running efficiently, and with a broad smile on his boyish face the whole time. Never frazzled. Humming some strange Swedish grunge tune as he worked.

Mazen had grown up in Sana'a and then immigrated with his family to Stockholm at age twelve. His older brother stayed behind and eventually enlisted in the Houthi army, perishing in the Battle of Sana'a in 2017.

In Sweden, while picking up fluent Swedish and English, Mazen also finished nursing school. Then he heard the same faint children's voices I had. However, for him, they were not just imagined words in the dark. He was intimately acquainted with the world of growing up Yemeni, at least before the war. While he was well into his twenties, he could have passed for one of those children himself, and it wasn't just his short stature.

For the first few weeks, I was nervous about my medical skills. I caught myself constantly rubbing my face and combing my hair with my fingers, like a nervous tick. While I had been a medic in the Army and had a good education in Yale's PA program, having spent most of the previous decade in surgery, I wasn't sure I was up to general outpatient medicine, especially in the developing world. But Sheila was a great mentor, helping me to resurrect my dormant skills. I watched her make critical judgements that saved many lives, and it was beyond what could be taught in four years of medical school. In turn, I helped her hone her surgical skills.

In my third week in the clinic, a man about my age, Jabbar, was carried in by his two wives and two small children, one at each of the corners of the taut blanket. He was in bad shape, barely conscious, mumbling something in Arabic, which I could not understand. But I could understand his wives, who spoke clearly in Arabic. He had a high fever and coughed continuously, sounding like a whale's blowhole when it first emerges from the water. But instead of seawater, he blew yellow and green sputum with each cough, leaving clumps of it sticking on the blanket beside his face.

Jabbar was a sick man, lungs full of fluid, which we could hear but could not image without a working x-ray machine. We started IV antibiotics, assuming it was a typical bacterial pneumonia. Cultures were sent down to the MSF hospital in Sa'dah, but it would take a week for results. Sheila contemplated sending Jabbar down, along with his sputum, to be cared for in a real hospital, if he could survive the trip. But when she called her boyfriend Michel on the radio, he told her that they were so busy dealing with another Saudi bombing raid in the valley, they would probably have to let nature take its course with poor Jabbar. Either he would respond to the antibiotics and live or he would die. But they didn't have the eyes to watch him. I volunteered to stay with him overnight in our clinic.

I never imagined that sitting with Jabbar would carry on for the best part of a week. But I was already used to nights of catnapping thanks to the times I'd had to tend my tiller and sails. As Jabbar started to recover—and he did recover—he started to talk. On those first nights, between his rudimentary English and my rapidly improving Arabic, we were able to communicate remarkably well.

He could sense the gravity of his illness, the death angel encamped outside his door so close we could smell her musty breath. He began sharing things that his family had to know in case he died, such as where he had hidden money near his old house in the fishing village of Al Hudaydah. Three thousand American dollars in a jar, tied on a string, dangling inside an abandoned well of an ancient mosque. The string had been covered with mud and no one could find it without knowing exactly where to look and he told me. "Just inside the well, between a white rock and a red rock is a deep groove. Dig out the clay and you will find the string there. Don't let it slip out of your hands, but carefully pull it up."

This money was his and his extended family' life's savings. He insisted I tell his wife Ghada about it but not his other wife, Mona. The reason, as he explained, was that Ghada was his son's mother. He felt that in the case of his death, all money should be channeled toward his only son, Alam, his family's name bearer.

When Jabbar became too tired to talk, he would listen to me. I shared things with him that I had never told anyone, even the fact that I was falling in love with Sheila. It was the first time I had experienced love at first sight. But she was taken. He listened attentively to me, talking about a silly grade-school crush despite his own plethora of things to worry about.

Jabbar also gave me the space, despite his own dire circumstances, to spend most of one night talking about losing my dad. I cried when I told the story of that horrible day.

With me sitting in a chair beside his bed and tears starting to drip from my chin I said, "Jabbar, I'm so sorry for crying so easily. It seems like my tears are always sitting at the threshold of my eyes, never going completely back inside to rest. On the other hand, my brothers, who experienced the same loss but older than me, never cry."

He reached over with his right hand, the arm that was taped to a green IV board and grabbed my wrist. Raising his head from the pillow with great effort, he looked into my eyes and said, "In Yemen, loss is your daily bread, uh … *masa* [tragedy] the hourly markings on your life's clock, men cry … uh, until they are dry." He chuckled, adding, "It's poetry in Arabic too, *tabki hataa tajifa*. Don't be ashamed of your tears, Bryan. The Koran says, 'And that it is He, Glory to Him, who makes [one] laugh and weep.' It is Allah who dribbles the tears in your eyes as from the tip of his merciful finger. Never shun them … knowing that he is also the one who brings the laughter too."

After Jabbar recovered, he spent his last two, more energetic days telling story after story about his adventures at sea as a fishing boat captain. We shared our love of the sea and boats, but I lost count of how many times he was almost killed. A dozen? Honestly, I kept him in the clinic for an extra day because I wasn't done listening to his stories of the sea. My one thousand Arabian nights of storytelling needing just one more night.

We drank tea throughout the last night to stay awake, laughing so hard at times, we blew more tea than snot out of our noses. The next day, Jabbar was given over to the care of his wives and children. By the time he walked out the clinic door—bushy-haired, frail, thin as a rail—I had come to see him as a long-lost brother.

The Yemenis taught me to love their country. The stony land had shaped this mountain people over millennia. It was as if the baren hills had instructed them in kindness and hospitality. They had learned a long time ago that if they didn't help one another, they would perish. The long, narrow springs had pulled the people deep into their ravines, closer and closer together, their waters a spiritual adhesive.

War made hospitality even more necessary. There wasn't a day that went by that I was not invited to someone's house for tea or food—if they had food. I attended weddings and home birth celebrations on a regular basis and, sadly, too many funerals to count. Those we laid into the cold earth were far younger than those in America. Often little children.

I played soccer with the boys after work several days a week, when they weren't distracted by chores. We had balls made from rags and bottles wrapped in bandage tape. I sent notes to my sister Angie to mail me a real soccer ball, but with the embargo, nothing got through.

I hung out with Jabbar a lot that first year, helping him with his apple and pomegranate harvesting. We stood side by side on rickety bamboo ladders picking fruit, him talking constantly about his days on the sea. I could tell that he had lost part of his soul when he had to move into the mountains. He wanted so much to take me to the fishing village where he grew up. I agreed to go, but we both knew it would be wise to wait until it was safer. Al Hudaydah was highly contested and bombing raids were routine. But if we couldn't go to his village, another—safer—village on the Red Sea would suffice.

All things were well in Yemen, as well as they could be in a hellish place of conflict and loss. The more I came to love the people and the country, the more I hated the war and killing. I grew sick of the smell of death. But we had found a rhythm in the clinic, and despite working virtually every day and most nights, I had never been more satisfied as a physician associate, or as a human being. I also rediscovered my love of medicine, sometime about my sixth month. It was hidden all along in the "*shukran* [thanks]" of my patients, in their handshakes and kisses on my cheeks. Once again, I had a purpose.

While I saw so much good in the country, I was also a realist. Sheila and I soon became the last Americans in the Dammaj Valley after three American missionaries were evacuated. We knew they were Yemenis who wanted to harm us, maybe not residents of Haydan, but farther down the valley. We represented America, their enemy's closest ally. Convenient targets. Near my one-year mark in the country, when things were just starting to go so well, our life clocks, as Jabbar called it, struck thirteen.

CHAPTER THREE

The sun, like a showman, performs magnificent rises for each of earth's inhabitants, whether in New York, Kandahar, Seattle, or in Haydan. It was my favorite time of day. The displays of colors and light, infiltrating the eastern sky, lift the moods and instills hope to the hopeless. The new day a carte blanche on which the observer can once more sow their measly dreams in the bleakest of places. Even the Yemenis who bed with misery in the evenings, dirt in the creases of their hands and under their nails, empty pits for stomachs, and crusty sweat clinging to their sagging brows, awaken with the shallow hope that the fresh sunrise will bring peace. But not on this day, one year deeper into the country.

On the morning of the anniversary of my arrival in Yemen, the orange walls of my tent were fluttering around me as the cooler mountain air seeped in to replace the rising warmth of the dawn. I slid up and stuck my head out of my tent to look straight up into the beryl blue sky. I felt I was home—oddly—more so than in Seattle or the Bronx.

I watched the thermals giving loft to the peregrine falcons as they spiraled upward on their gray wings above our village to the best vantage point for obtaining a rodent breakfast. With my hands interlocked behind my head as a pillow, my elbows pointing up, and a grin on my face, I watched the raptors that morning swirl and glide. Peace amid chaos, the eye of the storm.

But then I noticed, in a layer above the birds, puffy streaks of white contrails, like slices from a knife in an otherwise perfect demin sky leaving a frayed white line. The only jets around there were machines of war. My smile went tight, then folded into a pucker. It was unimaginable that before that day was over Yemen's war would visit us, then spread across the entire friggin' world, like flying sparks in a whirlwind over a world of dry tinder. And that somehow—I alone—was the only man to stop the coming inferno.

My morning eyes were still adjusting to the rising sun's illumination, its heat quickly overpowering the soothing effects of the nocturnal mountain air. I slid back into my tent with a sigh, hoping to escape whatever was coming. Inside my sleeping bag, I looked at my cellphone, which in that country's infrastructure—or lack thereof—was useful only as a time teller and music player. It was a quarter to six and I still had time before I had to get up. I closed my eyes and pulled my sleeping bag further over my head to block the meager light and savor a few more moments of rest before facing reality outside and who knew what tragedies walking into our clinic.

I stretched my tight muscles. The stench of smoke filtered through my bag and filled my lungs as I took a deep breath. I coughed. The stink was of a grass and plastic fire. Day and night the penetrating aroma found my space, my hair, my clothes. It lingered on my tongue and in my morning mucous as a bitter taste. I'd grown used to it, except with that first deep morning inhalation. I gagged and spat the bitterness out the tent's door.

When I first arrived in the valley, I searched to find the source of that morning smoke in the hope of putting an end to it. But the smoke was the product of a thousand cook fires fueled by weeds and garbage in this deforested and poverty-infested land. Subsistence smoke for many. Let it be.

I couldn't rest any longer with the intrusive smoke and my anxious thoughts. I was fidgeting, rapping my sternum with my fingers like a drum. Slipping on my scrub pants, I made my way with my red daypack over my shoulder down a dusty path to our outdoor shower.

As I walked, I paused and looked around our high valley, my anniversary date rousing a meditative mood. Our valley was most beautiful in the mornings when the air was clearest—the smoke more smell than substance. After that, the traffic would stir up the dust.

The narrow beams of sunlight that morning, angling around a few puffy clouds and illuminating the countryside in shades of amber, was nothing short of a piece of art, like Joos de Momper's famous Mountain Landscape, in oil on canvas. I loved fine art, a beautiful place even better. My mother was a painter and tried to teach me to have an artist's eye, before she lost her desire. The scene shifted my mood, giving me a sense of morning's hope returning. I took a few more steps toward the shower.

The green of our orchards—contrasted with the drab mountains surrounding them—looked artificial that morning, like they had been sprayed with the same dye Chicagoans put in their river on Saint Patrick's Day. The patchwork plots of grains in the field beside our compound were golden, like the silky fur of a lion, a million stems leaning to the right in unison, then the left, and back again, whipped by morning breezes into mesmerizing ripples. The kernels of the wheat and millet rarely made it to maturity without being plucked by the locals' dirt-lined and calloused hands to fill the hollow bellies of the pickers' families. In the dim light of that day, I could see vagrant harvesters already at work. Despite the gleaners, landlords still carried the hope that some of their crop would survive to ripeness, when they could collect the heads in baskets and take them to the old stone mill at the west end of our oasis. I could see the mill up the valley from my viewpoint. No one in line, no harvest to grind.

Our mill's two thick stones, the runner stone atop the bedstone, etched with spiral grooves like a giant vinyl record, were relics from centuries of plenty. At the center was a square timber rubbed as slick as brown alabaster by years of turning, attached via a large wooden gear to a yoke. There, camels, or donkeys would walk in a small circle, sweat dripping from their mandibles, the driver's wounding sticks on their scarred backs. Sometimes the mill would be turned by women, whose desperation to feed their children empowered their drudgery. On occasion, I had stopped and put my back into the effort when the women seemed overwhelmed. No camels, donkeys, or women that morning. I continued walking to the shower.

The outdoor shower had privacy walls of corrugated steel that came down to my knees and old wooden pallets as floors to keep one's toes out of the sticky ginger mud. After ten in the morning, touching the metal walls could cause a burn. But I never showered later than seven, because the heat turned my domed tent into an oven.

While washing, I took in a deep breath of the mountain air, flouting its smoke, and slowly released it. It was a communal air that filled our oasis and our lungs, a gift of the mountains and the green crops.

I loved those mountains. I had bought a dirt bike from Jabbar's cousin and rode it hard along the highest ridges, and through the boxed canyons, besides wadis that returned our summer's rains back to the Red Sea. Woven within that rugged place, sewn among the high green patches, are primeval cultures as in Haydan, rich as any on earth and with no better people. There are none who yearn for peace more or despise war less. I knew the land better than New York's gridded streets. If not for its ruinous war, Yemen would be a top tourist destination, a banner across Expedia's main webpage. It was my air, my breath, Yemen—the Colorado of the Arab world—my new home. Sheila and I were the only Americans left who knew Yemen's secret.

On that morning, I was showering before six because Sheila was driving to Sa'dah to pick up supplies. Our Sana'a office shipped intravenous fluids to Sa'dah for our clinic. The semi truckers wouldn't drive the treacherous mountain road to Haydan, making the Médecins Sans Frontières Hospital in Sa'dah their route's end.

Dressed again, towel draped over my arm, I began the walk back. I heard voices in the streets, motor bikes, yelling, and gunfire. A starving hunter shooting at a pigeon? Or a family dispute and quick justice in this otherwise lawless land? Haydan was awakening, its roosters heralding the morning like feathered town criers.

I paused and took it all in. I survived my first year! I inhaled deeply again and looked up at the sky. The contrails gone, blown away like dust, discarded like a sad thought.

Walking the dirt path to my tent, I paused again to do another survey of our stunning world. Looking up the rising valley, I could see all of Haydan. My eye caught a figure coming down the street. It was Mazen, walking at a brisk pace, a joy in his step, earbuds in his ears.

"Hey, what's up?" Mazen said, pulling out his earbuds, my standing stare grabbing his attention.

"Sheila's taking the truck to Sa'dah for supplies," I said, "It'll be just us in the clinic today."

"I'll keep that in mind as I set up," Mazen said. "How many exam rooms do you want?" he asked, breaking eye contact, then looking at the ground.

"Can you handle three?"

"Sure," he said in a quiet tone, head still down.

"Then keep three going, as our friend cholera is back in town. How many did we see yesterday?" I asked.

He frowned. "How many cholera patients?"

I shook my head, "No. How many total?"

"Oh … hmm … one hundred and five, but that was a normal day, you know, you and Sheila both working."

Mazen resumed his walk along the same trajectory, then suddenly pivoted back, a scowl now on his face. "Why does she have to go? Ahmed always picks up supplies. I could go if he can't."

"Mazen, you know what happened last month. Our boxes arrived full of dirt. Black marketeers, I'm sure. If they're empty this time, Sheila will need to stay and negotiate with the MSF folks for an emergency loan of fluids. We're out."

He appeared unconvinced, so I added, "Besides, I need you here. You're the most indispensable of us all."

Mazen just stared into the distance with an empty look, "Yeah … right," he said in a disbelieving tone.

Should I say it?

"Oh, the other reason she needs to go … well, she has a

honey at the MSF hospital."

"Who?" he asked, jerking his head back.

"You know Michel, the doctor?" I asked.

"Him? Since when?" he asked with a chuckle. "Doesn't surprise me, though. He's a confident man. A real 'doctor without borders' ... womanizer."

"Mazen, she told me about dating him when I first met her a year ago," I said.

"I worked with him in Sa'dah before you guys came, but I've never seen his face in Haydan."

"He's never been here, as far as I know. Because they're so busy, they see each other only once a month or so. That's where Sheila goes when she's away."

Mazen was squinting due to the rising sun behind me. But no words.

I turned to leave but then quickly added in a louder voice as he was walking away, "But if I were dating Sheila ... well, I would treat her better." I bit my tongue so I would say nothing else.

Mazen shook his head as he continued his walk across the compound to the clinic. The earbuds back in his ears, and a spring in his step.

Back at my tent putting on clean scrubs, I thought ahead to my day. Cholera! I felt my chest tighten each time the word wandered through my head. We thought we had tamed the infection after sinking a ninety-foot well into the aquifer, breaking Haydan's dependency on surface water for drinking and shitting. With the constant influx of refugees coming to a big camp just outside the oasis, the contagion surged into the local population and camps in waves. The refugees preferred drinking from the springs and stone-lined water channels that had irrigated the orchards for thousands of years. But they shit in them too, thinking that shitting downstream was okay. But downstream to them was upstream to someone else.

After I had finished dropping my things off at my tent, I walked through the commons, hoping to catch Sheila before she left. Just as I reached for the door handle, it popped opened, and she stepped out. I took a giant step backwards to give her space.

"Good morning," I said with a smile.

"Hey, good morning ... I overslept," she said in a rushed voice. "I wanted to get back by the afternoon so I can help in the clinic and— Oh, shoot!"

"What?" I asked.

"Oh, Ahmed made me a breakfast sandwich." She turned to go back into the commons and then suddenly stopped. She placed her hand on the back of her neck and rubbed it. "Forget it. I'll find something to eat in Sa'dah." She turned back in the direction of the parked truck.

I kept my distance but watched her every move, hands in my pockets. A natural beauty. She showered twice a day. In the morning, she said, to wake her up. At night, to wash off the sweat and dirt before climbing between her relatively clean sheets. After she showered in the morning, she shook out her curly blond hair like a poodle after a swim, and then she was perfect. On her fair and impeccably freckled Nebraskan skin, makeup would have been a mar, lipstick over her paprika lips, vandalism. I was beaming. Could she tell?

She threw her backpack over her shoulder, her lab coat draped over her arm.

"What's with the lab coat," I asked.

She looked at me and then at the lab coat. "Oh, Michel wanted me to observe him making rounds in the hospital. He always has something to teach me. It won't take long."

"I bet he does," I said in a whisper, a smirk on my face.

"Huh?" she asked, staring at me with a simpered grin.

"Nothing," I said, shaking my head.

I had thought my infatuation with Sheila would dissipate after a year, but it had only intensified. She hadn't a clue how much I wanted to be Michel.

"Damn," slipped from my mouth in a whisper. She glanced at me.

Opening the door of the truck and looking inside, she turned to me and asked, "Have you seen the truck keys?"

"Huh? Oh, yeah … should be in the glovebox."

She crawled over the driver's seat, butt sticking out the door. I turned my head to look away as not to ogle.

Besides the fender bender injuries, the truck had several bullet holes across its rusty door. I didn't know how it had earned those. Perhaps in the war. Maybe it was still in the war as a new bullet hole appeared each week.

The Dammaj Valley, our imperfect home; Sheila and I jokingly referred to it as the Damaged Valley. Everything in it was broken. The buildings, roads, trucks, and most of all, the people. I fit there very well.

I shouted as she was digging in the glovebox, "Be careful and hurry back. You know how hard it is to run this place alone." A sheepish grin toyed with my stubbly face. When she didn't respond, still digging, I added, "I guess I went fishing for a week with Jabbar, didn't I?"

She turned and sat in the driver's seat, keys in hand, blowing her bangs out of her face with a puckered mouth, She smiled, closed the door, and said through the missing driver's side window, "That's right, you did." Leaning out the window, she added, "You owe me one, buster." She winked.

My heart fluttered. I lost my breath. Then I smiled, "You're the only person I know who still says, 'buster.'"

"But I'll try to be back by lunch to help," she added, as she started the truck.

As she was driving through the gate, I shouted, "Say hi to Michel!"

She raised her head and looked at me through the rearview mirror. I could see only her squinted blue eyes and the shaking of her head.

As I was turning to walk away, her brake lights suddenly came on. I paused. Two bearded men jumped into the back of the truck right outside our gate. Typical hitchhikers. Routine in Haydan where most people didn't own cars.

I went into the commons and ate a quick breakfast to quiet

my stomach. A date pastry and two scrambled eggs prepared by Ahmed our fifty-year-old cook and handyman, who'd been chosen from the locals because of his work ethic and command of English. He worked tirelessly, perpetually in tune with his surroundings, ahead of any needs that might arise on the compound; instructions or work orders were never needed. Between his IRC chores and caring for his family, I don't know when the man slept. While malnourishment surrounded us, the IRC made sure we were supplied with food from Sana'a to keep us healthy. Ahmed made the food go as far as he could and then took leftovers home to his two motherless daughters. I suspected that he often went hungry so his girls would have plenty. He was a good man and the best father I've met.

I had a hunch this crisp morning would melt into a bad day. Maybe it was just the contrails I had seen. But something was stirring in the crater of my stomach like a wambling snake. It wasn't just hunger. The eggs and pastry didn't satisfy it.

CHAPTER FOUR

The last bite of a date pastry, baked to a perfect golden brown, the dates caramelized into a divine sweetness, was in one hand, and a mindless romance novel in the other. I was enthralled in the story, a kind of book I would never pick up in America. The paperback was salvaged from a box of books donated to the local refugee camp. With no TV, movies, or radio, and only spotty internet, the only entertainment we had, besides our own conversations, were those novels. The senders may have had good intentions, but the refugees couldn't eat them, although some hungry ones may have tried. The books were all in English so even if the people in the camp could read them, they didn't have the time, as they were too busy looking for things they could eat. They left the box out in the elements. Most were missing pages, used to start cook fires or to wipe their choleraic asses. So, not a complete waste.

I tucked my book under my arm, a cup of tea in each hand, one for Mazen and one for me, and walked through our garden to the clinic. Our garden wasn't of the vegetable or flower variety but was simply a flat space with sparse grass overgrazed by local goats plus a few shadowing trees.

I entered the south wing of the dilapidated complex, a long hall flanked by patient exam rooms—six rooms total, three on each side of a central desk. Behind the desk were a couple of storage rooms and a makeshift operating room. At the end of the hall was a larger storage room with a small window that opened to the outside, which we used as our pharmacy. The outer walls were of the original stonework, the inner walls were of cinder blocks painted white. Above, the ceiling arched to a peak formed by the simple corrugated steel roof, painted white on the bottom. In those high places was a microenvironment inhabited by bugs, lizards, birds, and the occasional snake hunting for the others.

Mazen was in the second exam room on my right, crouched on his knees beside a cupboard inventorying our supplies. His head was bobbing and there was a contorted look of horror on his face, stirred by loud music emitting from his earbuds.

Poking my head inside the exam room's door, I said, "Mazen, good morning." It was the formal greeting I had omitted with our previous encounter. "Here's some tea," I added, setting his cup on the cabinet.

He looked up; a smile having found his face again. As the earbuds were still in his ears, I was surprised he had heard me. I could hear the bass two feet away, "boom … boom … boom." "Good morning to you too, Doctor Bryan. It looks like everything's in order." He stood. "I've all the exam rooms set up to your preferences." He reached for the cup. "Thanks for the tea."

I asked, "Hey, what time is it?"

"Where's your watch?"

"You know … someone knocked it down the well," I said speaking into my teacup as I drew a sip.

"Of course, but I thought you got a new one?"

"Where?" I asked with a quick shake of my head.

"They sell them on the street in Sana'a, … or Sa'dah … out of trunks of cars everywhere," he said with a sigh as he stood up.

"Okay, I'll look the next time I'm there. I keep hoping someone will find mine … but what time is it?"

Glancing at his watch, he said, "We have twenty-five minutes until we open. Oh … I saw Jabbar in line outside with Mona and I let them into the garden. He said it was nothing serious, just he needed help with something. I thought you would want to see them out of courtesy before we open. You need a new watch."

"I didn't notice them on my walk over. Too busy juggling books and tea." Swallowing, I asked, "What does he want? I saw him in the village yesterday and he said everything was fine." I finished my tea and quickly added, "Hey, that watch, by the way, was my dad's. Mom got it fixed for my birthday. I keep thinking that someone will pump it up when they get their water. It was waterproof."

Shaking his head, Mazen said, "Yeah, in Sweden, we call that 'magiskt tänkande' which means 'magical thinking.' A metal screen at the bottom of that pipe will stop anything from coming up bigger than dirt." With intensity in his voice, he added, "Should I bring Jabbar back? He wouldn't tell me what it was, just that it was something 'nushir [private]' … just between friends."

I stared up at a spider closing in on a beetle on the ceiling. "Hmm."

"Should I go get him?" Mazen asked again in a louder voice.

Dropping my gaze to look at him, I said, "Did I ever tell you that Jabbar was a fishing boat captain in the Red Sea? He comes from a long line of fishermen. Only moved here to farm because of the war."

Mazen sighed. "Yeah, about a hundred times." He looked up at me with a scowl. "Now can I bring him back? We have just twenty minutes until we open. I'm sure he's not here just to talk about fishing … if he brought Mona."

"You're right! Sorry, but he's a dear friend and I just didn't expect him. I'm puzzled."

"You seem a bit scattered this morning," observed Mazen.

"Sorry, I guess I am. Woke up with a bad feeling I'm trying to shake. It's my anniversary day here, did you know that?"

Mazen didn't answer, just rolled his eyes as he quickly exited the room, mumbling, "Maybe I should've baked you a damn cake."

Mazen's gift as a nurse was his organizational skills. He kept things running smoothly, even during chaos. However, I had always been spontaneous. I would get distracted by talking with patients and their families while more grave cases waited. In ways we complimented each other's style, yet not without moments of frustration, especially for Mazen on busy days.

I put my book down and tilted my head back against the wall. I always read in the morning, to calm and focus my mind before the onslaught of a busy day. Then I usually pitched in to help Mazen set up, but he had beaten me to it this morning.

As I waited, my mind floated to Jabbar and our recent fishing trip. Yemen has no rivers, only wadis—streams that appeared during brief rainy seasons, buckling under the weight of monsoons, then disappearing like Brigadoon. That year had been more drying than most. Proud anvil-shaped thunderheads had formed, towering black toward space but possessive in their rain.

I had read the novel *Salmon Fishing in the Yemen* while waiting for my flight out of Switzerland. I had a dream of fly-fishing in the salmon stream mentioned in the book. Jabbar told me, speaking through a chuckle, "The book and movie are fiction. But the Red Sea is the greatest place on earth to fish." It took a month of planning, waiting for a lull in the Saudi bombing runs, but we were finally out on the sea in an adze-carved wooden boat.

My reminiscing was interrupted when Mazen came through the clinic with Jabbar and Mona, a little taller than her husband, walking behind him. Jabbar was wearing a white thoob under a gray sportscoat; Mona, wearing a flowered orange dress under a black hijab. They passed my open door walking briskly. The scent of jasmine perfume followed in her wake and infused my room. I walked to the open door and stuck my head out, my gaze following them down the hall. My medical exam always started by watching the patient walk in. Though Mona was walking with a stoop, her gait seemed fine. Mazen took the couple into an exam room and closed the door.

Soon Mazen reappeared, looked at me, and nodded.

As he was walking past me, back to the outside door, he said, "It's his wife who has a problem."

"Yes, I assumed that, like you said, otherwise Mona wouldn't have come."

I opened the door to their exam room, a spontaneous smile erupted across my face. I found Jabbar sitting next to the provider's desk, his back to me, and Mona on a blue plastic chair just inside the door. She avoided direct eye contact with me as I entered, studying her sandals, which were planted on the floor. Typical for a Yemeni woman.

Jabbar stood, gave me a quick kiss on my cheek with his cardamom-infused, wet mustache as I passed and sat down in front of my desk, me behind it. I could see Mona in my side frame of view, over his left shoulder, still studying her shoes as if they had a secret message from Allah inscribed on them.

Jabbar, while having put on a few pounds since his scare with pneumonia a year earlier, was still quite thin. He carried his thick black mustache above an otherwise cleanshaven face. His lips were thin, disappearing when he smiled. He smiled a lot, being easily humored, and as he had said before, believing that laughter was from Allah.

Though Jabbar was just one year older than me, his face— sun-damaged from being at sea, wrinkled and leathery—made him appear years older. I had also spent time at sea, six months in my sailboat before stopping in Yemen. The wavy steel walls of the shower, my makeshift mirror, wouldn't tell me, nor did I care, if my face was aging like Jabbar's. When he was angry, crow's feet would clutch the corners of his intense russet eyes. I tried not to anger him.

"I was just thinking about our fishing trip. That was fun. We should do that again," I said.

"Yes, Bryan, I hope so. But today … uh … well, I have a problem," he answered while pinching his Adam's apple.

He continued speaking in his imperfect English. I assumed it was because Mona wouldn't understand. "I want to bring Mona here because she hasn't been pregnant since laboring our daughter."

"'Giving birth.' We usually say, 'giving birth.' We call it 'labor' when a woman is in the process of giving birth, but we call it 'giving birth' when they are born."

Jabbar stared at me, brows furrowed.

I raised my hands and said, "You said you wanted me to correct your English … that's what I'm doing."

Jabbar continued, "Oh, giving birth, uh … giving birth to Maritza … who is now eleven. Mona worries about this. Ghada has given me Alam and Nadira. Alam is the only heir left in my family. We don't count girls. I have one brother, Salim, who has two daughters, and he has a boy that became dead five years ago."

"'Had,' you know, in the past. The boy died, so we say 'had.' I'm sorry about that, you know, that your nephew died. That's very sad."

Jabbar's crow's feet appeared on the sides of his eyes. I stopped interrupting him.

Jabbar sat quietly.

Leaning toward him, I said, "Okay, let's talk about Mona. Why is she worried?" I took off my stethoscope and laid it on my desk. I flashed Mona a reassuring smile, tilting my head to listen to her husband.

"Mona's afraid that if she doesn't birth to me a son, I'll divorce her or take a third wife. But that's not true. I won't divorce Mona. I love her. Uh … I could never afford a third wife … I can't afford two." Jabbar started rubbing his Adam's apple again.

"How can I help?"

"I've heard that in America you have treatment to cause women to birth boys. Can you help us?"

Leaning further toward him and putting my elbows on my desk, I answered, "Jabbar, I have no training in what we call infertility treatments. I could guess ways to help. If I prescribed a birth control pill to Mona for a few months, then took it away … well, it might increase her chances of getting pregnant. It appears that some women become more fertile as soon as their birth control pills are stopped. That's what a couple of studies have suggested. I'll ask Dr. Emory and see what she thinks. I know all about brain tumors and how to remove them, but infertility isn't my area of expertise. And I'm sorry, but there's no way to choose the baby's sex."

Jabbar nodded, then turned to Mona and said to her in Arabic, "He wants you to take birth control pills, and that will make you have a boy."

I shook my head, poised to say something but Mona spoke first.

"Jabbar, this makes no sense," she said with a sigh. "Birth control pills are the opposite of what I need. I'm not taking them!" She turned to face the wall.

"Mona," Jabbar said loudly, "I don't understand either, but I trust Doctor Bryan. He knows what he's doing. Remember, he saved my life. He's my best friend."

I closed my eyes and savored his comment, like it was music.

"I'm not taking them!" Mona said in a loud voice that startled my eyes open. She stomped her sandaled foot, folded her arms across her chest, and looked back toward the wall.

"You are!" he said, pointing at her. "If you want me to keep you, you'll do as I say." He stood up, his back to me. "And Bryan says if you don't do this … you might get a brain tumor."

I strangled on spit. "Now, Jabbar—," I said.

He turned and gave me a hard frown.

Mona pulled her scarf away from her pouting face but remained quiet. Since the argument had burned itself out, I asked Mazen to escort them to the pharmacy for a supply of birth control pills.

As he was escorting Jabbar and Mona out, Mazen remarked, "I was going to let the other patients in as I return but the social worker, Prisha, is here from the camp. She's doing one of her surveys about vaccinations and wanted to talk to each patient first. It will be another ten minutes." He groaned and added, "This is going to be a really long day."

Shaking my head, I picked up my novel and sat on the exam table. I was going to read a couple more pages, however, seeing Jabbar provoked wonderful images of our fishing trip, and those images obscured the words on the page.

I tossed my book in a drawer and closed my eyes again, my head resting on the old stone wall, waiting for the onslaught, reflecting on Jabbar calling me his best friend. No, I didn't approve of the way he handles his wives, lying to Mona for example. But that was so engrained in their culture. He treated his family better than many local men who beat their wives. But I knew he could do better. He was a good man. I felt a wave of contentment surge over me, pushing away the remains of the morning's omen.

Two weeks earlier, I had borrowed the bullet hole–ridden pickup and taken Jabbar on the 130-kilometer trip to the coast, most of it on gravel, over the dry mountain's crests, and the rest on broken asphalt. The road cuddled up to the war front in several places, tilling our nerves from the back of our minds to the surface, muting us for the entire ride over. Once to the port in Al Luhayyah, our spirits were calmed by the sea, and we began to talk. We were only fifty miles north of Jabbar's boyhood home, but in a much safer place. The bombs fell in Al Luhayyah on a monthly schedule, in Al Hudaydah—daily.

Our week at sea was fantastic! Jabbar brought his seven-year-old son, Alam, a good boy with thick dark hair; as thin as his dad; and, like all seven-year-olds, full of energy. He was very inquisitive, more so than the average child. He was studying English in elementary school and was eager to try his limited vocabulary on me. Alam called me *Eami*, which means "my uncle." He loved Greco-Roman wrestling. I had twenty matches a day with him—and let him win them all. Every ten minutes, whether on the beach or at sea, I heard, "*Eami*, let's wrestle." Even if I didn't answer him right away, I would suddenly find his arm around my neck and my head in a headlock.

We caught plenty of bonito and dogtooth tuna. When Alam reeled in his first fish, a masked puffer, he squealed and danced from one end of the boat to the other. Total hysteria. His dad had to yell at him to settle down and to come and watch the fish deflate in the bottom of the boat. We threw it back, knowing it would be dangerous to eat.

We caught so many fish that we cleaned them in Al Luhayyah and packed them in sea salt. We hauled two hundred pounds of fish back to our inland oasis and the hungry mouths of Jabbar's extended family, sprinkled by war across the Dammaj

Valley.

My daydream was quickly interrupted when I heard Mazen shouting, his voice growing closer and babbling. I couldn't understand a single word.

I stepped out of the exam room and saw him running toward me in a full sprint, a yellow two-way radio in hand, a static-infused voice spewing from the speaker, only a word or two understandable. Sheila's voice.

While panting, trying to catch his breath, he said, "Something's wrong. She's asking you to come quickly." He bent at his waist, hands on his knees, breathing hard.

"What?"

I grabbed the radio, pulled out the antenna, and stepped outside the clinic door, followed by Mazen. "Sheila, this is Bryan. What's up? Over." I stared intensely at the radio's speaker as a sweat broke out on my forehead.

A piercing scream suddenly cut into my eardrum like a razorblade. I jumped.

"Bryan, come quickly! Grab the trauma bag. This is awful. Hurry ... my god ... hurry! I'm in Sa'dah! Main road, by the old olive trees. I've got to go."

"Sheila! Sheila, what the hell's going on? Over."

Nothing but static.

Slamming the radio on the doorframe, I shouted, "What happened? Over." Silence. "Dammit!"

My mind raced through plausible scenarios. Mazen grabbed the door and yanked it open and dashed inside. Soon he returned dragging a big brown duffle bag marked in red paint with the word "TRAUMA."

"We have only my bike. Are you coming?" I asked.

"Hell, yeah!" he said with a gasp of breath.

I snatched my stethoscope from the clinic, then the key to my bike from my tent. My heart was beating fast, my palms so sweaty that I dropped the key twice. Mazen, still panting, was at the bike with a red jerrycan putting gas in its tank. I jumped on, turned the key, and gave it a quick kick start. Mazen jumped on as the bike was rolling away, wearing the duffle like a big backpack.

As we tore out of the compound, red dirt flying from my knobby tire, Ahmed held the gate open for us. He always knew what was going on, even without us telling him.

We flew past a line of patients who had queued for the clinic. Mostly women in long black abayas, with black hijabs around their heads. Prisha, the Indian social worker, was sitting at a small metal desk in her long blue dress and matching scarf. I saw the bewildered look on her face as we passed.

Among the queued, were an assortment of children, all thin and sullen-eyed, occasionally pulling away their mother's murky robes revealing their brightly colored and embroidered long dresses beneath. When it was clear that we were going right past the line of patients, their grim, sad faces watching us leave, their jaws dropped. One woman raised her hands, waving them in the air, and shouted *"ma hadha* [what is this]?"

With a full throttle, I headed down the steep graveled road toward Sa'dah leaving a dust cloud in our wake. Mazen had ridden on my dirt bike before but never at breakneck speed while holding on to the large trauma bag. I handled the bike around potholes and stray goats, navigating around slow cars, and a legless beggar crawling across the road, his shirt covered in the ginger dust. He threw his hands over his eyes when we barely missed him. We maintained our speed at over eighty kilometers per hour as I left our verdant oasis, descending into the dreary desert valley below.

I tried to recreate a mental image of the two men jumping into the truck outside our gate. I knew who they were and did not consider them a threat … but maybe I should have.

I leaned hard into my handlebars, gripping them as tight as I could bear, gritting my teeth. Perhaps Sheila had come upon a terrible car accident on the way. She'd said it was by the row of olive trees. That was just four blocks from the MSF hospital. But a car accident, she could handle by herself.

"Oh Lord," I mumbled too softly for Mazen to hear above the

noise of the bike and the wind. "Help us."

CHAPTER FIVE

The stream of pedestrians dispersed the farther we got from Haydan. I twisted the throttle until it wouldn't turn anymore. Down the old road we shot with Mazen's fingers gripping my ribs like a bear's claws. The whistling wind around my helmet was deafening. Sheila's lingering shrills in my ears pulled me off the mountain, leaning into the handlebars with gritted teeth.

"Dammit!" I screamed. Chickens in the road. Around the next curve, goats. Fifty minutes of broken asphalt passed under my knobby tires before the Sa'dah's paved streets began rolling beneath us. I saw nothing unusual in the litter-lined lanes, typical amblers weaving in and out of traffic. I let off the throttle to merge with the cars, trucks, and animal-pulled carts. I sat up straight, swallowed hard, and looked to the left and right. Nothing.

Then I felt Mazen's hand poking my right shoulder. I leaned my ear in his direction, and he shouted over the sound of the bike. "Look up!"

My eyes drifted to the tops of the dusty tan buildings, then to the palms and to the celadon sky. I saw a funnel of smoke—a thick, dark plume—towering above the city like a black tornado. I felt a sharp pain in the pit of my stomach. I stood up, straddling my seat to see what was ahead.

I screamed toward the traffic in front of me, "Get out of the fucking way!"

A pedestrian shook his fist at me and yelled, "*Allaenat ealayk* [damn you]!" when I almost hit him.

We traveled a few more blocks toward the smoke. There was a spooky restlessness—people running either toward or away from the fume. I fidgeted on my seat, standing, sitting, turning, and looking.

The traffic suddenly came to a stop. We waited for a minute, but nothing moved. I steered the bike onto the sidewalk. Dodging people, we kept moving ahead. Over and around mud bricks, tires, garbage, and a bloated dead dog encased in a swarm of yellowjackets, I steered toward the epicenter of hurt.

Mazen yelled, "Take it easy! You about threw me off!"

I looked over my shoulder at him and shouted, "Sorry!"

As we got closer, we were met by a dense forest of human forms, pushing, screaming, ripping their ragged clothes. Some ran by us with their hands over their ears, looks of terror contorting their tear-soaked faces. My own skin went clammy. I squeezed the handles as hard as I could while maintaining a very slow throttle, pumping the brakes before each new obstacle.

I came to a stop, unsnapped my chin strap, and took off my helmet, hanging it on the handlebars. The surrounding chaos was fully visible, smellable, and audible. With my feet on the ground, straddling my seat, I screamed, "What the hell's going on?" Then in Arabic, I repeated, "*madha hadath!*"

The crowd was rumbling like a rolling thunder, babbling, no one making sense. Not one word decipherable.

"This smoke smells awful," said Mazen over my shoulder.

"Yeah, if you could aerosolize highway death, it would smell like this. Dreadful." I rubbed my face with my hands, then grasped the handlebars again, gave the bike's throttle a slight twist, and clicked it into first gear. I meandered at such a gradual pace that I had to slide the soles of my shoes across the concrete.

The first victim we saw was in the arms of a man running toward us donning a soot-covered thoob, veering to go around. He was carrying something crimson. A blood-soaked child. A young boy wearing the remains of an ankle-length *qamīṣ*. The boy's right arm was missing, blood dripping from the stump like a tap.

I hit the brakes, squealing to a halt. We jumped off the bike and Mazen grabbed the old man by his salt-stained shirt. The man stopped, stumbled, and looked at us with round gray eyes. He was as pale as an albino. His victim, paler.

"We're doctors!" Mazen yelled. The man took one step in our direction, terror permeating his dirty face.

Mazen dropped the duffle to the ground—I stooped and unzipped it. With my left hand I firmly squeezed the boy's stump, his tepid blood running down to my armpit. I opened the bag and grabbed a tourniquet. I looked at the child, who was limp at the neck, and noticed he wasn't breathing. "Damn!"

I felt for the carotid artery beside his windpipe. His skin was soft and moist as is typical for a child but cold. I felt nothing. I repositioned my fingers. No pulse. To confirm my dreaded thought, I laid my head on his blood-soaked chest and listened. Complete silence. My ear now wet with the dead child's last lifeblood, I looked at the old man and shook my head.

In America, we would attempt to save this boy—but here? No hope. I grasped the man's shoulders, looked directly into his downcast eyes, and said, "*Hu mayit* [He's dead]."

The man peered at me with a harsh, opened-lipped stare. Through the gnashing of his teeth, he whispered, "Allah." His weeping quickly became uncontrollable. He jerked away and ran again, as if driven by hollow hope. Mazen yelled after him in Arabic, "What happened?"

I understood the man well enough to make out the word *qunbula*, meaning "bomb." The term, *Bas almadrasa*, meaning "school bus," soon followed.

A bomb hit a school bus? "No, God, no!" I screamed. I bit my lip as I felt my own blood drain from me.

Cars stood at a standstill while between them crazed people darted in all directions, some carrying injured children. No path for a motorbike. "Grab the bag, Mazen. Let's go on foot."

Stuffing the tourniquet into my pocket, I carried one end of the duffle by a strap, Mazen the other. In single file, the bag between us, we weaved—pushing, shoving, and stepping over people who had dropped to the ground in anguish. Mazen was oddly quiet.

"Allah! Allah!" came the unanswered calls for help from

throughout the crowd, like a full-voiced chorus from inside Hell—just as the gates were closing.

As we got closer, the walkers were at a standstill. Impermeable. People were pushing in the fire's direction, but no one was moving. I could see the burning bus and a destroyed market next to it. The bus was wheelless in the front, its rear wheels on fire and its shell gone, leaving only a crinkled frame and a few of the roughed-up seats still in place. The market was a skeleton of its former self, the overhead signage reduced to a twisted metal frame. A couple of traffic cops were trying to tame the chaos without success. The merchandise of the market had spilled into the street and had mingled with the burnt and bloodied clothes of the bus's occupants. I could only gawk, as if I were observing the scene from a timeless dimension.

During my first trip to Haydan, I remembered Sheila pointing out the big olive trees, beneath which now sat the ruins of the bus. According to Sheila, the trees were strong and had stood as centurions guarding the remains of Sa'dah's broken road for centuries. However, this morning they looked feeble. They stood squat and gnarly, their twisted limbs, tipped in boney fingers, with leaves that looked like long waxy nails. Derelict in their duty on this day, now draped across their gray-barked branches were bits of plastic and long strings of skinny sausages, dark and pink, hanging like Spanish moss, glistening and dripping. That couldn't be children's entrails—could it? God, I hoped not! The flies had descended upon them. Crows sat on higher limbs. We'd gotten here in under an hour and the birds were already feasting? "God help us all," I whispered audibly, heard only by Mazen, he too impassive.

Becoming cognizant, I whispered to myself, "What do I do?" This wasn't my first civilian bombing. There had been many in Afghanistan from Taliban suicide bombers or collateral damage from our own attacks. But I was disoriented.

The sounds of sobbing and yelling continued to fill the air, grief consuming its oxygen, scattering my thoughts as soon as they formed. About that time, Mazen suddenly emerged from his eerie silence and began yelling in Arabic, "Let us through, we're doctors!"

He began pushing harder and people started parting.

"Sheila's in this mob," I mumbled. Somewhere deep within this forest of dilapidated souls, she was at work.

The sight of the next victim made me suddenly focus. A little boy, no older than six, wearing dirty and torn clothes. Thick congealed blood matted down his dark curly hair. He still had his tiny blue UNICEF backpack over his shoulders. He was holding the hand of a woman, whose brow was crumpled by worry. The boy's dark eyes were wide open, looking straight ahead. No tears. Shell-shocked. I stopped them and looked at his injuries. He had a large scalp wound, but nothing was penetrating his brain. His pupils were big but equal and responded to my small flashlight. The wound was no longer bleeding. I directed them to the MSF Hospital where someone would stitch him up. I couldn't imagine what it was like there.

The vapors were suffocating as we got closer to the catastrophe's epicenter. I stretched the neck of my Henley shirt over my mouth, and Mazen wrapped his keffiyeh around his face. The flaming bus was sending out waves of burned oil fumes, thick soot floating in the air.

As I approached the bus, my usual dry mouth was wet. I was salivating. I realized that one of the smells drifting into my subconsciousness was that of grilled meat, like in a steakhouse. I had been ignoring it, assuming it was the locals cooking their lunches. I suddenly recognized the odor's morbid source, the cooked flesh of the precious children. I stopped and bent over facing the ground, forearms on my knees. I dry-heaved, and then vomited the remains of my date pastry. I felt Mazen's hand on my back. I looked at him. "Where are the wounded? Where the hell is Sheila?"

He shrugged his shoulders. "Are you okay?"

"Yes, Mazen, are you?"

"Not for a minute," he said, shaking his head. "This is horrible. But where are the victims? All I see is the aftermath."

"I think we're too late. We better find Sheila, if she's still here, and then head to the hospital."

We walked a little farther and saw that on the dirt street beside the bus the witnesses had lain dozens of bodies side by side, all with mortal wounds. Bloody mud surrounded them. People were weeping and screaming as they grasped at the corpses. One man was punching the air, swinging his arms like he was battling a swarm of invisible bees, ripping off his shirt, and screaming in Arabic, "Why?"

I had smelled blood a thousand times before in the operating room. Even the whiff of burned flesh, which the surgical cautery can leave hanging in the air and penetrating our surgical masks—is part of the OR's ambience. But this smell of death was overwhelming. So many sources at once. I groaned.

The bodies on the street had missing limbs, disfiguring facial and head wounds, and penetrating shrapnel wounds. One child was only a chest and head and another missing his head. All of them were burnt beyond looking human, like industrial waste. I had to look away to regain my composure.

Pieces of limbs and other organs were scattered around the bus. In the old olive trees, hung blue backpacks and clothing—and I was now certain it was strands of intestines upon which the crows were already pecking, fighting among themselves for the tastiest pieces.

I studied the bodies. Were there any signs of life? One man was lying on his side, chest rising and falling. We rolled him over. Protruding from his left eye was a piece of the bus's window frame, surely penetrating deep into his brain. Hopeless. I gave him morphine in case he could still feel. My hand was shaking as I drew it up. Never in surgery had I had a shaking hand. "Paradise, please come for him … and please be swift," I mumbled as I pushed the plunger on the syringe.

As I stood up, my eyes found Sheila. I wouldn't have recognized her if it were not for her hair. Blondes standout in this swarthy country, but she was filthy, her lab coat covered with the maroon mud, red blood, black ash, and yellow-green coolant from the bus.

I pushed my way in her direction. She was attending to a

child, held by a woman sitting on the ground with a worried look. A deep smile warmed Sheila's face but was quickly overtaken by a frown and hollow squint. The cavalry had arrived but could bring little comfort to a disaster of this magnitude.

"So glad you're here. This is awful," she said. With her hand still on the child, her thumb below the girl's eye and her index finger above, forcing it open. Sheila's chin began to quiver, and her blue eyes filled with tears. She continued talking to me, with her eyes focused on the child. "I was a hundred feet away when the bomb hit. I was watching the bus, a little boy looking out the back window making faces at me and me waving back to him. He was so adorable. Then suddenly I felt an incredible thud in my chest and there was black smoke everywhere. My ears popped. I never saw the bomb." Her hand fell away from her patient. The woman holding the child watched Sheila, now distracted by my presence. I pulled Sheila's ear against my chest and wrapped my arms around her.

I felt her shaking, sobbing into my shoulder. I put my mouth down against her hair. I whispered, "We're here. What can we do? Are we too late? I don't see any survivors." She didn't answer, so I asked, "What's wrong with the girl?"

"Oh, I just removed a foreign body from her cornea. She'll be fine. Go check by the bus and see if there are any other injured."

I continued to the smoldering bus. I stepped inside. Just my weight on the first burned step caused the ramshackle frame to lean in my direction, as if it was ready to fall over. I encountered waves of heat radiating from its floor. Once fully inside, I saw that only the first few bench seats were still attached, but they were blackened, and the vinyl had burned away leaving only their metal frames.

In the back of the bus, there were six or seven burnt bodies—skin cooked black, five white skulls protruding at the top, the flesh burned away. The sight, not to mention the heat, was making me ill. I dry-heaved again.

I ran out and punched the side of the bus with my fist, shouting, "Son of a bitch!"

A man who had previously been lying in the grass beside the market, heard my shout and limped over to me. "Are you ... doctor?" he asked in his limited English.

"Yes. Are you injured?"

He pulled back his brown shirt to reveal something protruding from his belly. I checked the rest of him. No other visible wounds. I felt his gristly wrist and his pulse was a surprising eighty beats per minute, I'm sure much slower than my own. While a serious injury, he was stable and therefore not urgent. I had him sit on the sidewalk and did a simple field dressing to keep dirt out of his wound. I asked another man to escort him to the hospital where he would need surgery for sure.

I looked at Sheila, who was working on another child twenty feet away. She pointed to the right of me. A woman wearing a black abaya, only the top part, the part below her waist apparently had been blown off by the blast, leaving her standing on scratched up legs, her red panties showing. She was saying loudly, "I can't hear! I'm deaf. The bomb ... it deafened me." She pointed down and leaned over a little boy on the ground in front of her.

The boy was in distress, blue-faced, and with a bloody torso. A dirty towel was draped over his little body. I removed the towel and cut away his gray qamis beneath a huge blood stain, to expose a four-inch slit on his right side. It was gurgling frothy blood. The child was dying for lack of oxygen—a collapsed lung, I was sure. I needed a chest CT scan to know what was wrong inside his lung. He might get only an X-ray at the hospital—if he made it.

I stood up and looked all around. "Where the hell is Mazen?" He heard me, as he was just ten feet away, and looked up.

"I need the trauma bag!" I shouted.

"Settle down. I'll be right there with it."

I knew the boy was dying, so I worked expeditiously. My first task was making sure he didn't have other life-threatening injuries. Sheila came over and stood beside me. As I finished my assessment, Mazen returned and clipped a pulse oximeter on the child's finger. "Seventy-two percent."

"Are you serious?" My heart started to race again.

From his color I had been expecting a pulse ox of 85%, whereas normal would be above 95%.

"This kid's dying," said Sheila. "Nothing we can do. I've had several die on me this morning."

I looked at Mazen, "Get me a chest tube!" I added, "Are you sure his dirty fingers aren't messing up the readings?"

"Hey, I'm ahead of you, Boss. I've been looking for the chest tubes but can't find them." Mazen pulled out a wet wipe from the bag and cleaned off the child's limp finger and placed the pulse oximeter back on. "Seventy-seven percent." Then he dumped the trauma bag's contents on the ground.

"Mazen, get me a scalpel, Heimlich valve, and stylus too," I shouted.

"Of course," he said as he rifled through the sterile packets of medical supplies now piled on the dirt.

Mazen paused and stood up, looking down on the pile, one hand behind his head, "There are no chest tubes—child or adult!"

Sheila put her hand over her mouth and said, "I'm sorry, but maybe this is my fault. I took out the expired stuff a week ago. Ahmed was going to sterilize them and put them back. I don't know what happened."

"Dammit!" I yelled as I stood. I looked around. My eye was twitching. Then I caught sight of the terror in the boy's mother's face. I had to do something. I stooped beside him again.

I held my hand over the wound, feeling the suction with each feeble draw of a breath. The life was draining from him, each attempted breath another step down the abyss.

"We've got to get this kid to the fucking hospital!" I shouted to whoever was listening.

I looked at Mazen, "Give me that plastic bag of gauze … oh, and tape."

Mazen tossed me the items. I cut the tape into strips, sticking them to my thigh and then cut the plastic bag into a square. "This is something I tried in Afghanistan," I mumbled. "It didn't work there but it's our last hope here."

I cleaned off the wound with a piece of gauze after wetting it with my spit, then dried it with more gauze. Placing my mouth over the hole, I waited for the child to rest between breaths and sucked as hard as I could. Frothy blood filled my mouth and splattered down my windpipe, causing me to gag and cough. With my fingers, I pinched the wound's slippery surface to pucker it, preventing air from leaking back in. I spat out bloody saliva. I slapped the plastic over the wound and taped it, then let out a slow breath, closed my eyes, and relaxed my muscles.

Mazen stooped beside me. I looked over at him and mumbled, "Sorry for being such an asshole."

"Don't worry about it. We're all stressed."

During the five minutes we waited for help from the hospital, the child's color changed from blue to a dusty violet. The pulse oximeter was now reading eighty-four percent. A couple of medics from the hospital were returning with a stretcher. I jumped up and grabbed one by the wrist. Pointing at our child, I yelled, "Take him next!"

"That was reckless," Sheila said, shaking her head. "While I respect your compassion, you know that blood exposed you to every pathogen the child harbors. If we lose you, we'll lose a lot more of them."

I nodded.

The chaos was slowing down. The thick forest of mayhem filtered down to a few standing—a few fallen. The crying and wailing, while no quieter, had dispersed into echoes from every desperate street and alley. Random gunfire pierced the empty heavens. People cursed at the jets, which were long gone and petitioned Allah for help. One woman pulled a fistful of hair out of her scalp by its roots as she buckled to the ground. A victim's mother, I assume.

I felt something cold against my elbow and turned to see Mazen touching me with a cold can of Vimto Fizzy soft drink.

"Where did you get that?" I asked. His other hand held an open can, Sheila sipping her own.

"The market's cooler was blown all to hell … cans are lying around."

I chugged mine, feeling the icy liquid cutting through my parched throat like a knife.

There was nothing left lying in the streets except corpses and little bodies in pieces, awaiting their families to claim them. A police officer was keeping the stray dogs away with a crooked stick and throwing an occasional stone at the crows in the olive trees. The site secured; we went to the MSF hospital.

The three of us, walked slowly, our shoulders slumped. The two-story stone building that housed the hospital seemed sad, its grimy windows drooping. Faded peeling paint and rust stains ran down from its metal roof and gutters like sorrows. A tattered banner read "MSF Hospital." Below that written out in French and English, "Médecins Sans Frontières / Doctors Without Borders."

Even if those walls could talk, they wouldn't. Grief would mute them.

The crowd now displaced to its door—no less restless.

CHAPTER SIX

"*M*ustashfaa, [hospital]" accentuated every conversation I heard. Those walking toward us, all recipients of bad news, some physically supported by family members and friends. Those walking in the same direction as we were, seemed carried along by the angst written on their faces, their grief held in suspense until they got the news, good or bad.

We arrived near the hospital's old double doors, which led directly into the trauma ward. Outside the mob, a hundred or more agitated souls, had gathered, pushing, yelling, and throwing rocks and bricks at the handful of security guards near the doors, screaming, "*Daena nadkhul* [Let us in]!" Chicken wire had been embedded in the glass of the entrance's windows, making the panes virtually unbreakable. The fronts of those doors were armored with sheets of steel. This wasn't the first grief-riot to have played out here.

The security guards—sweltering in black woolen suits, long rifles hung over their shoulders by a canvas strap—were trying the sort out the chaos. Their uniforms had been confiscated from a Yemeni national army barracks when it was taken by the Houthis. I suspect they were intended for winter use. Sweat was beading across the guards' foreheads, soaking their dark hair, and white salt stains showed in their pits when they raised their arms to push the crowd back.

A guard recognized Sheila as a doctor from Haydan. Blondes really do stand out in this dark-complected land. He motioned for us to come to the front. I was stunned to see Ghada, Jabbar's second wife standing on the opposite side of the crowd, her burka pulled down below her chin. She was howling and mascara tinted tears ran down her puffy face, her eyes just slits between swollen lids. She was hitting her face with her fists as I had seen others do. I froze in my tracks. Sheila and Mazen had not seen her and continued walking in through the door. The guard behind me was pushing me to follow them.

My jaw hung open as I stared at Ghada. *Why is she here?* I didn't see Jabbar until he stood up from a stoop. He was right beside her, wiping his narrow almond-shaped eyes with a dirty handkerchief and screaming that familiar question, "Why?"

An ill-defined fear gripped me as I watched them. The guard kept pushing me, but I stood my ground. I shouted across the mob, "Jabbar!" He didn't hear me. Again, cupping my hands around my mouth, I yelled, "Jabbar! Ghada!" No response. Too many people screaming.

Then I heard Sheila calling my name.

I turned to look at her. She was inside, holding the big door open, her face behind the chicken-wired pane. Mazen was further inside, beyond my view. "What?" I asked, my palms turned up.

"Are you coming or not?" she shouted.

"Sheila, my friend Jabbar is in the crowd."

The guard behind me mumbled in Arabic, "Move. You can't stop here."

"Jabbar!" I yelled again. No response. The guard gave me a shove. I looked at his face with a sulk, "Don't push me! I'm moving."

I joined Sheila inside the door, and we squeezed into the crowded room.

"What was that all about?" she asked.

"My friend Jabbar and his wife Ghada are outside. I just saw Jabbar and Mona in the clinic right before you called me on the radio. They don't have a car. Someone must have given them a ride. But why are they here?"

"I haven't a clue. We'll figure that out later," she said as she motioned with her head for me to follow her.

As the door closed behind us, I watched Jabbar and Ghada through the wired glass, but then a guard shoved them out of view.

Suddenly, the noises inside became all-encompassing. It was the high squeal of children's voices in consonance with their parents' unbridled wailing. A chorus of Perditions. Their sorrows—enough to fill the Grand Canyon—were now confined to a room about the size of a tennis court. There was a cacophony of screams, yells, wailing, and sobs, accompanied by putrid odors of, blood, scorched hair, melted plastic, diesel, and burned flesh. The air above the beds was buzzing with large black flies, that must have tracked the scent in from the streets.

Metal beds with thin black mattresses stood in rows holding their capacity in broken children. Protruding from beneath green sheets were small limbs with burned skin drooping from them like melted wax. Other limbs ended in tourniqueted stumps. For a minute I couldn't move, but only stare. *Where do I even start?* I wiped sweat from my eyes with the tail of my shirt and calmed my breaths.

Every patient had someone working on them. I spotted Michel, an accomplished physician from Normandy and the apple of Sheila's eye. I felt my muscles tighten. He looked up and nodded from where he was stitching a child's face. The three of us from Haydan stood in our place, waiting for his direction; we were on his turf.

Soon, Michel took off his rubber gloves, dropped them to the floor, where for the first time, I noticed piles of blood-soaked gauze, pieces of cut clothing, small shoes, along with many pairs of bloody gloves. Blue UNICEF backpacks were scattered about the room. The unzipped ones appeared to be empty, except for a single pencil or coloring book inside, mirroring the poverty. It was like the room was carpeted in the rubble of tragedy.

Michel swaggered in our direction. Crimson blood covered him from his chest to his ankles. He flashed a smile that quickly morphed into a deep frown, as he came up beside Sheila and gave a peck on her cheek. "What a damn mess. Horrible," he said. "Someone should execute those fucking Saudis!"

Sheila asked, "How can we help?"

"We've checked and stabilized those patients," he said, pointing to his left. "We are assessing the others. Some need x-rays, or surgery." His face lightened and then he looked at Sheila and asked, "Do you wanna stay this afternoon and first assist in the OR?"

"Sure," she answered with a soft smile.

"I can stay too," I quickly added. "It's been over a year since I've been in a real operating room but I'm sure—."

Michel interrupted, "That's okay. We don't need your help … uh, I'm afraid you'll just get in the way."

Rolling my lips tightly to a pucker, I responded, "Say what?"

He grinned, and for some reason, winked at Sheila, then responded, "We have an OR tech. Only doctors first assist here."

"I would like to get in his fucking way!" I whispered in Mazen's ear.

Our Haydan crew got to work. Sheila set a man's dislocated shoulder and then secured it with tape and a sling. We each, including Mazen, stitched wounds. I must have closed six or seven.

Sheila and I cared for another child who had lost an eye. The blast had burned it and the cornea was white like a fried egg. The child was awake and aghast in fear, screaming and thrashing his arms and legs as hard as he could. His parents were trying—without success—to console him. The mother kept mumbling in Arabic, which I doubted Sheila could understand, "Help him! Why aren't you helping him?" I translated for her. She then put lidocaine drops in his burned eye and patched it for comfort. She finished, then turned toward another table.

My eyes followed Sheila across the room, then caught sight of a girl lying on the bed in the corner. A thin gray man was beside her, green curtains pulled around them. Through a crack in the curtains, I could see his wiry figure leaning over from his chair toward the bed, prayer beads rotating mechanically through his fingers. I shuffled closer, but before going through the curtain's gap, I paused and surveyed the room once more. No sign of Jabbar or Ghada.

Mazen walked by in a hurry. I grabbed his shirt. He turned and frowned at me. "Hey Mazen, I saw Jabbar and Ghada in the crowd outside."

"So?"

"Why are they here? They got here as fast as we did."

"How in the hell would I know?" He scratched his head, "I know Ghada has a sister in Sa'dah. Her sister has three girls, maybe one of them was injured."

"Damn, I hope not. But why didn't they come inside?"

"They're only letting immediate families inside. They wouldn't let them in because they wouldn't be the girl's parents. If the child was killed, she wouldn't be here anyway. They've turned the dead ones over to their families to be washed. Gotta go."

As Mazen marched off, I looked down at the messy floor, shaking my head. Poor Jabbar and Ghada. Poor damn country.

About that time an MSF nurse, Maria from Sicily, walked by. I grabbed her arm. "Excuse me," I said. Nodding in the direction of the girl and the old man in the corner I asked, "What's her story?"

"Uh … well, we put her over there to die. Brain injury. Non-responsive and fixed pupils. She was in the market with her grandpa." Shaking her head she added in a whisper, "*Pietosa* [pitiful]."

"Holy shit!" I walked through the parted curtains, and to the girl's bedside. The man beside her had tears filling his old sagging eye sockets. The dark bags beneath them pulled his lower lids down and away, revealing his cherry mucosa as red crescent moons. He rocked back and forth as he rotated his amber prayer beads between his gaunt fingers. Seeing me, he stood up in a wobble, then placed his hand on my shoulder and pleaded, "Can you save her? Please have mercy on us. We're poor people … but I'll give you what we have."

I motioned for him to sit, and followed him down, stooping beside his chair, my arm behind his back. In a quiet but confident voice I said, "Maybe. God willing, I can try to save her." The words surprised even me. While neurosurgery was inside my wheelhouse, in this place it was almost unthinkable. Yet I knew she might be salvageable. What did I have to lose?

I turned my attention to the listless girl in the bed. A green sheet covered her up to her chest. Her right pupil was as wide as a dime and fixed, her left pupil reactive. This could be consistent with a right brain subdural hematoma, blood between the brain and its outer covering. I pulled the sheet away and tickled her feet, right, then left. She had subtle movements on the right side of her body, on the left, not so much.

I jogged over to Michel and asked, "Hey, did you get your CT scan running?"

Michel looked up at me with a glare. I watched what he was doing. He was placing a chest tube into the boy I had seen at the bomb site, the one I had sucked air out of his lung. I interrupted him before he could speak, "Hey, I took care of him ... uh, out in the field."

"Really? Well, he had a pneumothorax." Then he added, as if I didn't know what a pneumothorax was, "a collapsed lung."

"Of course," I said.

"We x-rayed him and saw a piece of metal in his lung. Right middle lobe." He looked up at me and added, "We have a doc who's done a little thoracic surgery. He'll take that lobe out but not until tomorrow. You asked something about a CT scan?"

I was standing, hands in my pockets, trying to say only what I had to. "Is it working?"

"Hell, no! Of course not. We have parts ordered, but you know with the embargo, nothing's getting into the country."

I returned to the head-injured girl. I picked her up and carried her gently to the x-ray area, talking to her in English, to calm my own nerves, "Sweetie, you're going to be alright. We're gonna take good care of you." I added, in Arabic for her sake, in case she could hear me, "Kulu shay' sawf yakun ealaa ma yurami [Everything is going to be fine]." I laid her on the table.

Ansh, a very dark man from Hyderabad with straight black hair, walked in my direction. "Did you need something?"

"Could you get a skull x-ray and go light on the exposure? I'm looking for a cracked skull ... and blood."

The technician from India could work magic with antedated

machines. The best I had ever seen.

Soon I had the x-ray in my hand and held it over a grubby, chicken-wired outside window. With careful inspection, I could see a skull fracture on the right parietal bone. It looked linear and not depressed. I looked with a magnifying glass and became confident that just below the fracture was a line of blood between the brain and its covering. Or was the blood just my imagination? You needed a CT scan to see blood. The bleeding had to be on the right. That's where the metal struck her. It was obvious by the bruising above her ear.

I thought of another question for Michel. I walked slowly in his direction, took a deep breath, and asked, "Do you have any equipment here for doing a bur hole in a child's skull?"

He stood up, waved the cloud of flies away from his alarmed face with the back of his hand, then pointed at me with his bloody No. 11 scalpel. "Nope." Shaking his head he added, "Why in the hell would you ask me something like that?" A close-up staring match ensued.

After I didn't answer, just stared at him, he sat down with his back to me. I heard a buzzing sound. I looked at the bed beside us. Another MSF doctor was standing over a little body and Maria was using an electric drill to put an IO (intraosseous needle) into the child's tibia for hydration.

When she was done, I asked her if I could borrow the drill.

She nodded as she was hooking up the fluids to the freshly placed needle.

With the drill in my hand, I asked Maria for her longest IO needle. After she got the needle, I walked back across the room, passing Mazen who was sitting and suturing a boy's arm. He looked up at me. "What's wrong?" Had he sensed my annoyance?

"Mazen," I asked with my finger against my lips. "What's Michel's problem? He's a bitch to deal with. I've only worked with him a couple of times, and he's always disrespectful."

"In Sweden we would call him an 'arrogant *skitstövel*.' Notice that *skit* rhymes with shit." He chuckled. "But when he gets stressed or angry, he becomes condescending. Don't take it personal. It's about the kids."

"Do you think he's jealous of me, you know, with Sheila?"

Mazen finished his suturing, cut the threads, and stood up. "No, I don't think so." Cocking his head, he asked, "Does he have a reason to be jealous of you?"

"Oh, lordy, no. Only in my dreams," I said with a grin.

"No, I can't imagine Michel jealous. He usually keeps a harem of his own," Mazen said with a wink.

"What?"

"Never mind," he said. "What are you up to?"

"I'm getting ready to drill into a girl's skull ... wanna help?"

"Sure," he said without flinching.

Maria walked by and asked, "Don't you need an IV set up?"

"Just the tubing, empty IV bag, and a three-way stopcock."

She halted, folded her arms, and gave me a stunned look. "Empty? For what?"

Pointing to my head with a smile, I explained, "I need to drain blood from a child's skull."

Maria shook her head and walked away, but soon returned to the bed where I was standing over the girl, the tubing, and an empty IV glass bottle in her hand. She whispered in my ear, "Michel's gonna be pissed. He's the only hero around here."

I nodded.

Mazen soon joined me behind the curtain and explained to the girl's grandfather, "The doctor is putting a needle into your granddaughter's head to drain the bad blood."

The old man nodded as the tears brimmed and then overwhelmed his eye sockets once again, dripping down his crinkled face, as he continued to rock in his chair. He prayed in an Arabic whisper, "Allah save her!"

Mazen interrupted his prayer with the warning, "The treatment could kill her."

The old man nodded and said, "She's in Allah's hands."

As I set up the space for the procedure, the old man

explained, "The Saudis killed her parents and brother with a nighttime bombing. My wife, her grandmother … she died for reasons only Allah knows. She became thin and died. We had no doctors like you."

As he spoke about his wife, tears swamped his cataracted eyes for the third time. Pointing at the girl, he added, "Elmira … she's the only family I have left. I will pray to the merciful Allah, while you work. If it's Allah's will … he will save her."

We pulled drapes tight around her space to block out flies and rubberneckers, such as Michel. If Michel caught me, he would probably tell me to let her die. Not salvageable in this environment. If I had been working from my head instead of my heart, I would've let her go.

Mazen knew his way around. He ran and came back with a razor, always one step ahead. As he shaved away the girl's coal black hair, it fell to the floor, mingling with the spent gauze, bloodied bandages, and gloves. A small butterfly clasp fell to the floor with her hair still within its grasp. We scrubbed off her scalp, and I set up a sterile field around the work area so as not to introduce bacteria into her brain or spinal fluid.

Based on the girl's body size, I predicted her parietal bone was six millimeters thick. I had never drilled an IO needle into a child's head. As I placed the needle's tip on the center spot, my hand was shaking. Sweat dripping into my eyes again, I wiped my face with my shirt sleeve in order to see what I was doing.

After reaching the six-millimeter depth, I nodded at Mazen. He aspirated with the syringe. Nothing came out. If blood came out, it meant I was either in the right place, pulling blood out of the pool around her brain, or that I had inadvertently punctured a cerebral artery. If I hit her artery, the little girl would have a hemorrhagic stroke and die. Right in front of me, she would die, and it would be completely my fault.

I took the tubing off, replaced the stylus and twisted the needle with my hand to advance it slightly more. We repeated the process. I concentrated on the needle each time, my gloves so lubricated on the inside with a cold sweat, I thought they were going to slide off.

Mazen drew back on the syringe and blood came out. I watched the girl's response as Mazen removed almost thirty milliliters of dark blood, a good sign. If the blood had been crimson, it would mean I had hit an artery. We paused and waited. She didn't die. I left the needle in and attached it to the bottle sitting on the floor. Blood slowly dripped into the bottle. I began to breathe again. Then, she squirmed. Her left arm and leg becoming more animated. Her grandfather began shouting "*Allah 'akbar* [God is great]!" He fell from his chair onto the floor and wept. I sat flat on the dirty floor beside him, my legs extended. I wept too, from relief. The odds of me saving her, with an interosseous needle, blindly, had been one in a hundred. In a day defined by misery and hurt, I'd had one moment of elation. I smiled so hard I thought my face would cramp. But I knew we weren't out of the woods yet. I left the girl to her grandpa's watchful eyes and worked around the room, suturing, setting broken bones, and removing pieces of debris from eyes and skin.

Later, Michel and Sheila came over with tea. I looked at the analog clock on the wall. Four P.M. The chaos had settled down. The staff were working on cleaning up the mess on the floor. Mazen was across the room starting an IV.

Sheila handed me a cup, "It's time for tea. You like yours with one sugar, right?"

I nodded, and asked, "So, how's it going?"

She opened her mouth to speak, but Michel answered for her. "Sheila was helping me do an ultrasound on a man's abdomen. I'm not so good at reading those. She was a big help. He smiled at her, putting his hand on her back, rubbing the flat spot between her shoulder blades.

"Oh, he's getting the hang of it," she said with a wink. Even when she was dirty, sweaty, and exhausted, I could see why Michel found her attractive.

Michel pulled up two chairs and a small round table. He sat on the bed's edge, Sheila and I in the chairs. After sipping his tea, he looked across the room. Then looking at me, he said, "I heard those damn planes before sunrise. They were circling overhead. When I hear jets, they do something asinine like bombing a village. Do you know how those jets can stay up, coming all the way from northern Saudi Arabia?" He stared at me with a scowl.

I knew the question was rhetorical, so I shook my head to set up his response.

"Because your damn tanker planes keep their petrol tanks full. Not only that … you Americans do the scouting and reconnaissance for them." He started to sip his tea but then added, "This was probably your bomb."

Is he blaming Sheila and me just for being Americans?

"How do you know that?" I asked shaking my head.

"How do you not?" answered Michel.

"But this bombing … it must have been an accident."

"Hell, no!" Michel angrily raised his arms, sloshing tea out of the cup in his right hand. "This isn't my first damn war. These bastards, both the Saudis and you damn Americans, pick soft targets, thinking they will break the people's will. Generals know the quickest way to demoralize an army is to kill their babies."

I was dumbstruck. I stared into my cup of tea.

About that time, Sheila stood up and said to Michel, "Let's check on our patient." There were still dozens in the room.

Michel mumbled, "Thanks for your help, Bryan, but we have things under control. Sheila's going to stay and assist us in the OR. You can leave … and take your boy with you."

Maybe if Mazen and I had tits, he would have asked us to stay.

I checked on Elmira, the little girl with the needle in her head. It had been draining for an hour. Her eyes were now open, and she was moving all four limbs, and whispering to her elated grandfather. He stood and shook our hands, sandwiching my right hand and then Mazen's between his two. The blood was no longer dripping, so I pulled the IO needle from her head. I asked Maria to make sure they watched her in the hospital for a couple of days.

Mazen and I loaded up our gear and made our way back to

the bombing site. Seven hours later, mourners were still standing nearby, staring into the rubble. I heard their sobs, not as animated as before, but no less severe. I watched a desperate woman, crawling, tears dripping on the asphalt, another woman walking beside her with her hand on her. I listened to them. They were looking for her son's body parts for a Muslim burial.

It was the most exhausted I had ever felt, even more than after an eight-hour surgery trying to fix a broken spinal column in Seattle. I hung my hand over Mazen's far shoulder, my arm across his back like we were the best of friends. His silence worried me. In his shallow twenties, no prior war experience before coming to Yemen, I knew he was vulnerable. A bad day like this could last forever in a young person's heart. I knew from experience. But he had been in the country for a year longer than me. He was Yemeni, and they had an eerie resilience, or so it seemed. I smiled at him and asked, "Are you okay, buddy?"

"Tired. Bone tired," he mumbled, his eyes down, directing his footsteps.

I looked up and saw in the olive tree's branches, pieces of clothing, twisted metal, and children's remains, being pecked at mercilessly by black crows. Two Egyptian vultures had joined them in the ghoulish picnic, the rock-throwing officer long gone.

Blood infused into my cheeks. I let go of my end of the trauma bag, grabbed a brick off the sidewalk and threw it into the tree canopy with all my might, shouting, "Get out of here ... you dirty sons of bitches!"

The broken brick bounced off a branch, returning to earth and shattering the rear window of a parked car. I slowly walked to my bike, the car alarm blasting behind me. People had been killed in Sa'dah for less vandalism to an automobile. I didn't give a crap.

We took off on Haydan's mountain road. Mazen and I were both quiet. I turned on my headlamp as the sun settled beyond the mountains' high ridges. I think the sun set early that night, too ashamed of the day he had given us to stay up longer. With the power grid down, the stars were more visible than on other nights, crawling up the eastern sky as the twilight slipped further over the west. The evening air was still warm, blowing across my face.

Above Haydan's buildings, ribbons of gray smoke snaked through the air like a parade of ghostly souls drawn upward into the emerging stars. There were new stars on this night, the lost souls of children. This was the second toughest day of my life. The first, when I lost my dad.

We approached the clinic's compound. I looked up to the hills above our citrus groves to the buildings that had escaped Saudi's three-year barrage. Their windows illuminated by oil lamps. Ancestors built the dwellings in the traditional style, five story vertical homes. The Yemeni were the world's first skyscraper builders. Jabbar and Ghada lived there. Suddenly my thoughts returned to them. *Why the hell were they in Sa'dah?*

CHAPTER EIGHT

I awakened to the morning's sun seeping through the lids of my closed eyes. All the tears had evaporated overnight, leaving my eyes stuck tight by salt. My tent's walls were quiet. No flapping in the dawn's mountain breeze. A feeling of peace.

I placed my arm over my eyes to block the vagrant light, but something was in my way. Something in my bed, and it was warm. I popped one eye open, recognizing the interior of Sheila's room, the portrait of her parents at her bedside. I had been in that room only once before, when I helped her move a chest of drawers.

I rolled over and her curly golden hair swept against my face. It was like a wild strawberry patch, but being unruly, her hair was more straw than berry on that morning. It tickled. She was motionless except for her soft, slow merlot-scented breaths. In and out, her chest expanded and relaxed beneath the blanket, her sleeping face swaddled by a soft grin. *Oh, God, have mercy. What just happened?*

I rotated onto my back, both eyes wide open, my brain slowly spiraling upward toward perspicacity. I flushed my mind to rinse out the last images of the previous night. My head hurt, the light painful to my eyes. I blinked hard and saw images like those in an old picture album of black- and-whites with the wind flipping its pages. Pieces flashed by without order. An image of Sheila and me on the couch talking, kissing, then naked in her bed. Mazen speaking to me at the gate, tears in his eyes. Then images of the children on the street bleeding and dismembered, followed by more images of kissing Sheila. Her taking off her lab coat, me unbuttoning her blouse. Convoluted. Disjointed. My heart was in pain—and ecstasy. I suppressed the bad images in favor of the rapturous. I lay quietly, watching Sheila sleep.

Sheila snored and stirred. I remained almost catatonic, barely breathing, hoping not to wake her. I didn't want to deal with the obvious, not at that moment. I needed to decipher the meaning. Who had Sheila made love to? Me or Michel? Was it for pity's sake? The moment I had dreamt about for a year was upon me but was mired in muddlement.

She rolled over onto her back, eyes still closed, breaths of deep sleep, her smile growing bigger. I slowly let my own breath out, as a sigh. Fear overcame me. It was the dread I would mess this up. I had to put space between us. How would I handle it if she awoke in shame or regret, seeing it as a bad choice she made while drunk?

I slipped one leg from beneath the sheets and placed it on the floor, then slid the rest of my body out, snakelike. Sheila turned over again, her eyes still closed, her breaths serene. I paused, sitting on the edge, waiting for her to either fully awaken or return to her snooze. When she went quiet, I continued maneuvering off the bed, pausing with each of her stirs.

My clothes were scattered across the floor. Grabbing each item, I headed to the door. I stood just inside her room, my bundle of clothes under one arm, shoes under the other, my fingers on the door handle. I paused again. She was stirring. I waited. She mumbled, eyes still closed. She calmed once more but continued to smile in her sleep, like she was swimming in a good dream.

I opened the door. It creaked like a mouse. I tiptoed into the hall, closing the door behind me with a click. The path back to my tent was through the commons. I could hear noises, water boiling, and dishes tinkling in the sink. Ahmed clearing his throat and coughing. He was making breakfast. I dressed in the hallway, only finding one sock, putting it into my pocket. I peered through the cracked door where Ahmed was busy at the kitchen, his back toward me—a skinny man in trousers, a long tee shirt, and white turban wrapped around his head. I lingered there. What would he think of us? American reprobates?

I waited until Ahmed left the commons. I trudged in, taking a seat at a booth. In a minute, Ahmed reappeared, several potatoes in his hands. When I caught his eye, he jumped, dropping a couple of the small spuds on the floor.

Bending over to pick up the potatoes, I could see each of his vertebra in his lean back arched toward me, his shirt falling over his head. I suspected that he didn't eat a bite of the leftovers, which he took home, but gave them to his daughters. He stood and looked up at me, "Good morning, Doctor Bryan. You were here?"

"Uh … yeah. I was watching you cook."

Ahmed gave me an odd glance and returned to the stove. "I didn't hear you come in," he said with a side glance as he sliced and fried the potatoes.

After a moment more of cooking, I followed the aroma to the stove. I thanked him, dished up a plateful of scrambled eggs and fried potatoes, then returned to my booth. My eyes kept glancing at the door to Sheila's quarters, and I caught myself eating faster until hiccups ensued. Sips of water wouldn't calm them down.

As I was chewing, sipping more water to alleviate the hiccups, Ahmed looked over at me. "That was terrible, the bombing in Sa'dah."

"Oh, Ahmed," I said with food in my mouth, egg crumbs falling into my lap. "It was horrible. The worst thing I've ever seen … and I've seen a lot."

"Why? Why the children?" He stood staring at me, waiting for an answer.

"If you're asking why the children were bombed, I haven't a clue."

"Ask your president," he said while pointing at me with a fork. "Tell me what he says." He jerked his head upward, clicking his tongue.

"My president? He wouldn't answer me. I doubt if he knows why."

"Of course, he does!" he said nodding his head.

"Ahmed, what have you heard?"

He leaned his back into the stove, arms crossed, rusty spatula in hand, and looked sternly at me. "It was an American bomb dropped by planes made in America. Very precise, always hitting the intended target. Guided by tasers. But why? Why the little children? Are they terrorists? What have we done to America to make you hate us? Those children have done nothing to you!" He smacked his lips like he was kissing the air or spitting at me.

"Lasers. I think you mean guided by lasers."

"Yes. Lasers. But why?"

My breakfast plate was now empty—my emotional plate, overflowing. Too much to process for one morning, plus, we had a hellish day waiting for us in the clinic. I sighed and rubbed my face with both hands, wanting to never have to pull them away again. Glancing at Sheila's door, I turned back to Ahmed and said, "I really want to discuss this with you, but I need to get to the clinic. It'll be busy, since we weren't here yesterday."

He didn't answer me, just stared. His brows were like two shaggy caterpillars bumping heads. A row of lines gripped his forehead, drawing it into a scowl. Though he was poor and illiterate, his gray beard and tall, thin frame made him distinguished, so much so, if you put him in a suit, a little meat on his bones, he could pass as the president of Yemen. But this morning he commanded only the kitchen. He returned to his stove energized by anger, moving briskly like a Russian acrobat, sliding, tossing the pepper and saltshakers from his left hand to his right. He let the topic of the bombing go, though I could see the discussion continuing in his mind behind his glaring eyes.

About that time, Sheila burst through the door, and I felt my heart skip a beat. Although she had showered and was now dressed in clean scrubs and new white lab coat, she still looked hung over and discombobulated. Her conjunctivas so red, the blue of her eyes had turned periwinkle. Her hair hung around her head like wet coils of golden straw—but still magnificent.

She beamed and said, "Good morning," glancing at Ahmed and me.

Ahmed and I both mumbled the same. His voice seemed bitter, I assumed from the topic we were just discussing. I seemed befuddled because I was.

Sheila walked toward the kitchen area. She reached into her lab coat's pocket and pulled out my sock rolled in a ball, then dropped it in my lap as she passed. She smiled at me.

What does that mean? My heart was about to burst with excitement. *Are we now a couple or was this just a meaningless hookup to her?*

I looked at her with a timid grin. I took the sock and put it in my pocket with its pair. Then I did the most cowardly thing. I got up and strolled to my tent before she had time to return to my booth with her food. I didn't want to discuss what happened between us. If it had been merely mercy sex, or worse, surrogate sex—me replacing Michel—I wanted no part of that. The suspended state between not knowing and knowing was better than knowing what I didn't want to know. I didn't take the time to shower because I was in a hurry but mostly because I wanted the scent of Sheila to linger on my skin.

Arriving at the clinic, I found Mazen already preparing for the onslaught. He was moving fast, earbuds in his ears, tune on his lips, back to normal. The clock on the wall read 7:45 A.M. I was late.

"Good morning, Bryan. Did you sleep okay?" he asked, pulling the white buds from his ears. He was looking up while crouched, putting away sheets for our exam tables.

"Nope. Too much on my mind. And you?"

He stood and stretched. "The same. Fell asleep, then my landlord's noisy rooster woke me up at 3 A.M. with too many dreadful images in my head to sleep again. Alam was on my mind all night. I was worried about you too."

"Me?" I asked with raised eyebrows, then quickly added, "Let me give you a hand."

Mazen handed me a bottle of alcohol, and I wiped down our equipment.

"You weren't so well when I saw you last night," Mazen said with a soft smile.

Shaking my head, I responded, "Mazen, this isn't my first rodeo."

"Rodeo?"

"What I mean is this is not my first war. I'll be fine."

"I noticed the truck is here, so Sheila must have come home last night," he observed.

"Hmm … uh, oh, she did? Good. I'll need her in the clinic," I mumbled.

Mazen added, "By the way, I looked in the garden and counted 115 in line already. That might be a record."

I closed my eyes and let out a loud sigh. "Let's get going."

Mazen and I usually worked together like a team, him going out to the garden and escorting patients back, swirling past me, starting IVs, giving vaccinations, and keeping waiting patients calm—always a step ahead. On that morning, as I was going from patient to patient, I was feeling more like a hung-over mommy bird, with befuddled feathers, going from chick to chick to drop a worm into its screaming mouth.

Mazen, more alert, walked fast, scurrying around carts in the halls, even chased out a stray goat that wandered into the clinic—without missing a step. But Mazen hadn't gone home the previous night to consume enough alcohol to fill a fish tank and then have a tryst with a colleague.

I worked in the south end of the clinic, Sheila the north. In the center was the *markaz* [hub]. It was in the space around the *markaz* that Sheila and I often interacted. But not that morning. Too busy.

Sheila and I shared only a few words the entire day and they were strictly clinical. I tried not to think about her. As soon as my mind was off the patient right in front of me, thoughts of Alam, Ghada, and Jabbar would quickly fill the space.

Later in the morning, an argument broke out between Mazen and a group of men. It started outside, but the sound of it carried through the doorway and into the hallway. I was too far away to decipher the Arabic, but the men's voices were harsh and loud.

Later, Mazen told me, "Some men were asking if you were an American. They were angry about the Saudis' bombing the children. I told them, ''*Akl alqaraf.*'"

"Eat shit? Is that what that means?" I asked with a sneer.

Mazen, with a serious look, answered, "It's an Arabic saying. You can't talk with a mouth full of shit, can you?"

The next time Mazen brought patients back from the garden, he added, while waving his finger in the air, "I clarified to those shit-eaters out in the garden that you were furious too and that you and Dr. Emory worked hard to save as many of the children's lives as you could."

"Shit-eaters?" I laughed so hardily I had to bend from the waist. It was the first time I had laughed in days.

"It's another Arabic term, *'aklat alqaraf,* which literally means someone who habitually eats shit. Like eating shit is their profession. I need to teach you some slang Arabic, Boss. But it is nice to hear you laugh again." He flashed a quick smile.

When I regained my composure, I said, "As I told you before, stop calling me 'Boss.' But I am pissed. I did work hard to save the children's lives ... as did you."

When things in the clinic slowed down enough to have a deeper conversation, I asked Mazen, "Have you heard anything new about Jabbar and Ghada?" My eyes became moist just with the question.

"Yeah. They're back home—" A sharp pain grew in my chest as I waited for him to continue. "An uncle and two cousins of Alam retrieved his remains. They'll have a Muslim burial today at the cemetery."

I bit my lip to hold back the tears. "I'm going for sure."

"Talk to me first," Mazen said quickly.

Hours later, when I was done with my last patient, I sat down in an exam room where Mazen was working. "So, why did you want to talk to me before I go to the funeral?"

He was wiping down the exam table and looked up while rubbing a cloth in clockwise circles on the black vinyl mattress. He poured alcohol onto the cloth and continued with counterclockwise circles, all while remaining silent.

"Speak to me, bro! When is the funeral?" I asked, pinching my nose to subdue the alcohol smell.

He stopped wiping and sat on the exam table he had just cleaned. "Bryan, the funeral was this afternoon ... you missed it."

I stood up, waving my hands in the air. "What? Why the hell didn't you tell me?"

"Bryan, you were busy with patients. I ran up to the cemetery and represented the clinic. Muslim funerals are quick, thirty minutes, at least in this place where they're so frequent. Back home in Sweden they last hours. Music, poetry, statements from every friend and family member. A real mess. I like the short ones better—."

"Yeah, they're short. Don't forget, I've been to many. But damnit, Mazen! I really wanted to be there for Jabbar." I started out of the room. "I'm going up to Jabbar's house now."

He jumped up, "No, Boss, don't do it!"

I turned around and regarded him through the exam room's door. "Excuse me?"

"It's a bad idea, just trust me."

"Jabbar is my best friend! He's hurting. I need to see him."

Shaking his head, looking me squarely in the eye, Mazen said, "Not tonight. Too much raw emotion in Jabbar's house. Give him time ... you know, maybe a few days. I'm going to visit them tonight. I'll share the entire hospital's condolences. I'll let them know that you're thinking about them."

"But Mazen," I objected, "I can't abandon him at his moment of grief. Why do you get to go and I shouldn't?"

"Trust me, Doctor Bryan!" Pounding his chest, he added, "I'm Yemeni. I know what the hell I'm talking about. They feel furious at all Americans and Saudi nationals right now. It's not the right time. Your life could be in danger. Not from Jabbar ... from his relatives. There's no law here and justice is brief. A local man killed an MSF doctor three years ago just because his daughter—a patient in the clinic—died."

"They're blaming us because we are Americans? That's just bullshit!" I shouted back.

"Bullshit it is, but it's the reality we live in here. I bet if Islamic terrorists blew up a school bus in a small town in Texas, killing sixty-five kids, and the only Arab people in that town were two doctors who ran a clinic, I bet their lives would be in danger. It wouldn't matter if they opposed terrorism or even if they weren't Muslims. Some good ole American boy would shoot them, and most people in that town would be glad."

I spoke softly looking down at my hands. "I feel pissed about the whole shit show! The war. The bombing. Losing little Alam. The poverty." Then I screamed, "Then the starvation. Proud people fighting in the dirt for a scrap like dogs! The never-ending cholera. The American involvement. The whole cluster-fucked up mess! I even feel the rage of 9/11 welling up from somewhere deep within me. The whole damn world is fucked up! Wars everywhere! Everyone has gone bat-shit crazy!"

Sheila, who was finishing up her last patient, stuck her head out of an exam room to see what the ruckus was about.

I smiled at her, "Just venting. Everything's okay."

I left the clinic. I marched to the commons, where I cooked a slice of goat meat in the kitchen and made myself a sandwich. The goat had been hit by a car in front of the clinic and Ahmed had claimed it for us and his family. Fresh meat was precious in this land.

A few minutes later, Mazen had finished cleaning the clinic and dropped by on his way to Jabbar's house. "Good night, Bryan," he shouted inside the door of the commons.

My back was to the door, so I stood from my booth, spun around, and waved, pointing at my mouth full of food. He waved and left.

I didn't want to be left alone at the hospital with Sheila. Things would be uncomfortable for sure. I wasn't ready to talk about our night. What if she told me it was a big mistake? That was my greatest fear. She was the one woman I was prepared to let inside my world, but still, I was scared she wouldn't like what she would find there. If she rejected me now, I would never recover.

I rode my dirt bike into the high ridges to burn off adrenaline and grief and clear my head. I paused as I passed Jabbar's street, his house four houses down. The lights were all on and people were standing outside. I continued out of town and up the mountain. I rode hard for two hours. I returned to my tent at midnight, and turned in.

"Oh, dear God, please make last night meaningful to Sheila but have mercy on me if it wasn't." A sincere prayer before dozing off.

The next thing I knew I was suddenly awakened from a deep sleep by Sheila's whispered voice outside my tent, "Bryan … Hey, Bryan."

I sat up. "Yeah?"

I opened the tent flap, put my headlamp on and stuck my head out. I shifted my light downward so as not to blind her.

Sheila stooped beside me. My chest felt tight. "Do we have an emergent patient?"

She didn't answer right away. Oh, God, I hoped it wasn't about our relationship.

"What is it? I asked."

"I got a call on the sat phone from Sana'a," she answered. They're worried about us. They learned there's going to be a protest here tomorrow."

"In Haydan?"

"No … uh, I mean, yes, here at our clinic. They're afraid it could get violent."

Sheila was standing in her black housecoat. I sat up and turned my light off. I could see her silhouette against the night sky, studded with a billion diamonds on that night, twinkling in white, gold, and green. Her hair was soft, framing her face like a medieval angel's nimbus. I wanted to caress it, as if somehow, I now had that right.

I rubbed my eyes. "Sheila, how does the Sana'a office know about the protest? I mean, we're here on the ground and we know nothing about it."

She rubbed her forearms with her hands like she was wiping away a chill, or a worry, "They just know, I don't know how, but trust me, they do. They're sending out six guards. They'll be here tomorrow morning, coming by chopper. I think they're mercenaries. Ex-Egyptian military people, Dorothy said. They provide security at the Sana'a office."

I nodded my head to show I was listening but kept my gaze focused on the ground.

"She added, "They'll stay for a week and we're to hunker down."

I looked up at her. "A week?"

She nodded.

"Hunker down? What does that mean?" I asked.

Shaking her head she said, "Close the clinic I guess."

"No, we can't do that. The security detail can screen patients and then let them into the clinic. That's the way we ran our civilian outreach clinic in Taliban country."

"I agree," Sheila said. "They're bringing a bomb-sniffing German shepherd. Maybe we could parade patients by the dog on the way in."

"This is so disheartening. They should direct their anger at the Saudis eight kilometers away," I said, pointing toward the east.

Sheila shrugged.

After Sheila slipped back inside the commons, I lay awake for another hour until I drifted to sleep at 2 A.M.

CHAPTER NINE

In the morning, I awoke in my usual fashion, showered, and was in the commons eating two hard-boiled eggs when Ahmed came in wearing just his sleeveless T-shirt and a blue plaid *futa* skirt, which I fondly called his "Yemeni kilt."

"Sorry, I'm late," he said with a sudden head nod. "I walked around the village to see what I could learn about the protest. The protestors invited Al Jazeera to film it. I don't think it'll be violent, but I brought my knife," he said pulling up the tail of his shirt, showing me his *janbiya* (traditional Yemeni curved dagger) in the front of his belt.

I smiled. "I never pictured you as the warrior type."

He gave me a stare.

"Oh, we're getting six armed guards from Sana'a," I added. "I think they're Egyptian," I continued with my mouth full.

"What's wrong with Yemeni guards?" Ahmed asked with a nod.

"The Yemenis have so many allegiances, IRC says it is hard to trust them."

"But I say piss on IRC!" He spat on the floor. "Hire Houthis. They're tough."

"Ahmed … aren't the Houthis the ones trying to kill us?"

"Only if you are here to take our land or our children," he replied.

"I'm not," I said in an unequivocal tone. "Not that Yemen isn't a real treasure, but she belongs to her people."

The conversation ended and I finished my egg and walked to the clinic.

Everything seemed calm and crowds were lining up as usual. As Mazen was placing people in straight, orderly rows, a big chopper came over the horizon. As it approached our garden, its down draft threw sand and dust in all directions, throwing Mazen's neat queues of patients into disarray. The flying papers, trash, dirt, and people was a perfect metaphor for the chaos the security detail would bring us for the following days.

The protestors arrived as predicted at about the same time the mercenaries had finished setting up. The hecklers—mostly men, a few boys, and two girls—arrived on the back of a large flat wagon pulled by a well-used John Deere tractor. I don't know how the beat-up, soot-puffing piece of shit made it up our steep mountain road, but it certainly wasn't local. Somewhere, they got their hands on an old battery-operated megaphone.

I watched from a hole in the front perimeter wall. Two people carried homemade American flags, burning them outside our gate. I needed to get back to my patients, but, foregoing lunch, I watched for a while every move the protestors made and listened to every word they shouted.

Two moms were in line with their children. They argued with the protesters with great zeal. One of the women grabbed the burning American flag and pulled it out of the protestor's hand. He in turn kicked her to the ground.

"Damn!" I pushed my way through the gate and took my first step of a sprint to help, but one of the security men got there first. It was better if he handled it.

As the security officer, a dark man in desert camo, picked her up, he accidently stood on her scarf, pulling it off her head. Then I recognized her as Maysum, a woman Sheila and I had performed a cesarean on to save her life. The little girl with her was Wafiq, the baby we had delivered.

I could make out a few of the Arabic words in their exchange, though I was some distance away. The two women were telling the protesters we were helping them. The protesters kept saying, "They are just dirty Americans, don't trust them. They've come here to force our children to be Christians."

Like Mazen the previous day, and maybe because of his example, Maysum called the protestors *'aklat alqaraf* [shit eaters], which made me laugh.

The security guards set up a table, with Ahmed's help, a dozen yards outside the perimeter in an area of spotty grass and dirt. There they registered patients, only allowing them to approach the gate after being cleared by the mangy German shepherd.

The afternoon was busy as usual, and the security detail kept interrupting us as if helping them to set up wasn't enough. Their leader, an older Egyptian man named Mohammed, potbellied and with a well-defined widow's peak, came into the clinic several times to talk to either Sheila or me. A well-muscled bruiser in a medal-adorned security uniform, he resembled a third-world dictator.

The security team brought their own quarters, which were khaki canvas tents, but we had to help them find a place to set up and to create their own toilets. The effort was worth it because it kept them out of our hair.

The protest got lively. But Sheila said several times, "No one will harm us. We give them such good care." Maybe too innocent, but I loved that about her.

In the afternoon, the protesters chanted in English the official slogan of the Houthis, "Allah is Great. Death to America, Death to Israel, Curse on the Jews, Victory to Islam." I tried not to take it personally, but it was hard not to.

That evening, as we cleaned and repacked the cabinets with dressings and IV supplies, I told Mazen, "I'm going to Jabbar's house after work."

He shook his head. "It's still too early, Dr. Bryan. There's rage in the village, but tempers settle quickly here. Give it more time. Just a few days."

I moved closer and squared up my shoulders to his. "Mazen, I must go! I can't desert my best friend at a time he needs me the most. My absence from him is killing me. Don't you understand?"

Stepping backwards, Mazen said, "When I was at the funeral yesterday... well, Mona told me they found pieces of Alam's remains. Four children were missing. All had been sitting at the explosion's epicenter. The families divided up the remains, pulling them from the overhanging tree limbs, those parts left by the crows and buzzards. This relative put the body parts—a finger, a femur, intestines, and an eye—into the little blue backpack bearing the name Alam. They had a service at the mosque. They wrapped the backpack in an Islamic burial cloth and interred it in the Haydan graveyard."

I leaned toward Mazen. "Why are you telling me this?"

He shook his head and stared at me wide-eyed. "Because I knew you couldn't be there, and I wanted to be there for you. Don't you understand? I could go visit them tonight and fill you in in the morning—every detail."

"You won't need to. I'm going tonight myself," I said. "It's personal."

Again, he shook his head. "Let me go first, check out the situation, and then I'll return. You're not Yemeni! You don't understand the rage like I do. One relative said at the funeral that he wanted to 'burn the clinic and kill both Americans.' We should wait until this cousin has returned to Harad."

It was dinnertime, so I walked to the commons. It shouldn't have surprised me, but Sheila was there, leaning back in a chair, reading one of the donated coverless novels. She didn't notice me at first, eating her spaghetti with lamb and curry. I always thought that the Indian spices on Italian noodles with Middle Eastern meat— while very cosmopolitan—made no culinary sense, but she loved it.

I considered turning around and heading to my tent. But I knew that I couldn't avoid Sheila forever. I stood frozen in my shoes. I swallowed hard.

"Hi, Sheila."

She looked up, big smile on her face, "Oh, hi. Didn't hear you come in."

I walked to the cupboard, looking over my shoulder at Sheila, but saying nothing. I pulled out a Mountain House freeze-dried beef stroganoff dinner. Mountain House had donated a case to workers in the refugee camps. I had fifteen meals to spread out over a year plus another twenty military MREs, always carrying one in my motorbike's panniers for emergency use. I was craving stroganoff that evening, a touch of homesickness, so I put the water on to boil.

I turned and leaned against the stove. Looking directly at Sheila, I asked, "Hard day?"

She snickered, "Not too bad. Busy, but staying busy helped me to ignore the protestors."

I let out a soft sigh while pouring my boiling water into the Mountain House bag, not troubling to get a bowl. The hot water made the plastic bag go limp, its mouth gapping open in a giant yawn. I sniffed the top of the bag, eyes closed, and took in the familiar aroma of meat, mushrooms, and sour cream with a big smile on my face.

I walked to Sheila's booth and took a seat across from her. "This is what I ate on the *Protagonist*, Mountain House freeze-dried meals. Reminds me of sailing."

"The *Protagonist*?" she asked.

"Named it for my dad. He was our family's hero. Mom could have been, but her nerves got the best of her."

"When was that? I mean, how long ago did your father die?"

"I think I told you, 9/11. The year 2001. Dad died in the south tower. He was a medic."

"Oh, no! If you told me, I forgot. I'm so sorry … really." She reached over and placed her hand on mine. I shrugged my shoulders and continued eating, looking into my Mountain House bag, but my attention was on her warm touch.

Withdrawing her hand, she focused on eating and reading for a minute. The absence of her hand was like a missing front tooth—impossible to ignore.

Staring at her hands, she said softly, "Bryan, about the other night—"

Pretending not to hear her, I interjected, "Hey, I'm going to see Jabbar tonight, as soon as Mazen gets back. He's doing reconnaissance … about the situation."

She put down her book and gawked at me. "Maybe I should go with you."

"Maybe not," I said. "I mean, I'm good friends with Jabbar, and I owe him a visit. I want my call to be personal. I'm afraid if you came—him not knowing you that well—he'd see it as an official visit, us representing the clinic and IRC. Besides, Mazen thinks it could be dangerous."

"Well, they're friends of mine too. I've taken care of Mona and Ghada. Mona came to see me when you were fishing with Jabbar. She was worried that she might have a sexually transmitted disease. Men fool around, you know," she grinned. "Mona didn't have an STD. She had a yeast infection."

Sheila picked up her book, but then put it back down. "You and Jabbar didn't fool around on this fishing trip, did you?" A mischievous smile flowered upon her face.

"Uh, what? No! Gosh no," I mumbled.

Leaning back in her seat, her book face down in her lap, she asked, "Are there whores in Al Luhayyah?"

"There are whores everywhere … even in Nebraska," I smirked.

My God, did I just say that?

Sheila rolled her paprika lips inside her mouth like she was going to eat them. She laid her book on the table and leaned toward me. I sat looking at her with a stupid grin. Her eyes danced across the room and back to me. She wrapped one curl around her finger, over and over, then asked, "What are you implying … Bryan?"

"Uh, well … I wasn't talking about you." *Lord, help me here.* "I mean I wasn't talking about us." I scratched my nose and fidgeted in my seat, looking down at my slumped Mountain House bag as if it would come to my aid, but it appeared to be sheltering in place.

She glared at me, which I could feel more than see.

I ran my hand through my hair. "Sheila, all I was saying was, uh, there are whores in every town. This had nothing to do with what happened between us. Sheila…" I looked directly at her. "Our night together … it was the highlight of my entire friggin' life."

Her frown melted into a warm smile, and she leaned in toward me.

"Mine too," she said in a soft whisper.

My heart began to beat faster. I felt flushed. My mouth was too dry to let the words I wanted to say glide out.

Looking at Sheila and seeing her smile hold its place, her blue eyes engaged, I had to look away. I stammered, "I'm … uh … mmm … I mean I'm glad she didn't. I mean, I'm glad Mona didn't have a sexually transmitted disease. That would've surprised me. I mean, Jabbar seems like a faithful husband, to two wives at least." I giggled nervously and glanced up at her.

Sheila began shaking her head. Her eyes rolled up, and she fixed her gaze on the ceiling.

I added, "He … uh, Jabbar, that is, he's a good father too. I can't imagine the heartbreak he must have right now. They must be in pain. Life seems so cheap here."

Sheila put her forehead into her hand, her face completely out of view, and let out a loud groan. She shook her head again and then looked at me. "You're pathetic! Sometimes, you make me want to scream!"

I was stunned. What had I missed? I hadn't had a meaningful relationship with a woman since losing Dad. I was disoriented.

Shaking her head yet again, she said, "Okay, what are you going to say to them, to Jabbar and his family, Romeo?"

"Uh, maybe nothing. Maybe that we're sorry and that we care a lot about them."

"What are we sorry for?" she asked with a raised eyebrow.

"That's the hard part. I guess I can say, as an American, and as a previous Army medic, that I'm sorry for the U.S. backing the Saudis in this bloodthirsty war."

"I wouldn't use the word *bloodthirsty*," she said.

"I won't. I'll try to use as much Arabic as I can. I don't have a clue what the Arabic word is for *bloodthirsty*. I know *blood* and *thirst* in Arabic, but I'm afraid if I try to blend them into an Arabic portmanteau, they'll take it literally. I just want him to know that I care."

"A port what?" she asked.

"Oh, a portmanteau is a blended word."

"Must be a New York word," she said, winking. Then she stood and said, "Gotta go. Good night," and headed off to her quarters.

That didn't go well.

What the hell was wrong with me? Why had I allowed her romantic words to drift away without a response?

"You fucking moron!" I whispered to myself. "A romantic imbecile."

I finished my meal and went to my tent. Walking across the compound, looking at the ground, I heard voices and looked up. I saw Mazen talking to Mohammed, the security force commander. Mazen headed toward me, eyes downcast.

"Well?" I asked. "Are we going?"

"I think we can. The three cousins, including the one threatening the clinic, went home." He looked over his shoulder at Mohammed, who was walking away. "I told Jabbar you wanted to come over for tea. Bring a funeral gift. That's traditional. A food item, candy, or fruit would work. You have pineapples in the pantry, don't you?"

"Yeah, two. I've been savoring the moment I could slice them up and eat them with goat cottage cheese. But I will donate one for a good cause. Dorothy brought them to us after an IRC meeting in the Philippines. Just don't tell Sheila."

"Bring both," he said with confidence.

Mazen and I left the compound at seven P.M. The guard questioned me, refusing to allow me to leave until I insisted. He wanted to send an armed man with me, but I told him, "There's no way in hell."

"If they want to kill you, I can't stop them," he said running his finger across his throat like a slice.

CHAPTER SEVEN

Mazen and I clambered back to our little green Shangri-La, leaving Sheila in the dark valley below. I never liked her driving alone in the dark across a menacing landscape defined by war. This day had been so dreadful that I felt more unease than usual.

After parking my bike, I walked out into the street, squatted, and looked down the dark road toward Sa'dah. I don't know what I was looking for, as Sheila wouldn't be home for hours. Maybe not until the light of morning. Thinking of her driving home in the morning's light gave me some solace—though that would mean her spending the night in Michel's arms.

Mazen dragged the trauma bag into the clinic and walked out the gate, joining me in the street. He was renting a room in a house on the hill on the west side of the village. Being Yemeni, he preferred living among the populace. As we said our goodnights, we embraced. He walked away, eyes downcast, hands in his pockets. Atypical. As his boss in the clinic, I owed him words.

"You're a good man Mazen, an outstanding nurse. Thanks for your help today," I yelled.

Slipping into the dim edges of the twilight, he paused and turned, his face illuminated only by a rising crescent moon. "It was my duty, as a Yemeni," he said. "I Wish I could have done more." Then he started walking again, head down, his ghostly figure vanishing into the night.

I closed and locked the compound's gate, put my bike's key in the tent, and grabbed my metal drinking cup. I walked down to the clinic and hung up my stethoscope. Too tired to sleep, I headed to the commons. Suddenly, I heard the rapid tapping of footsteps, shoes against the cobble, coming down the street, reemerging from the shadows. Mazen was running toward me, his eyes big, shaking his head as he ran. My pulse began to beat in my temples. My God, now what? I reopened the gate and let him run through it, stopping right in front of me, bent at the waist, hands on his knees, out of breath.

"What's wrong!" I asked, leaning over to be closer to his words for when he had enough breath to speak.

Mazen straightened up, grimacing. "Bryan, I ran into someone I know in the village. They told me why Jabbar and Ghada were in Sa'dah today. Their son, Alam, was on the bus."

"No!" I screamed, dropping my cup, and grabbing my face. "God no!" I felt like I was falling down a bottomless well; the world growing more distant, the sounds muted.

Mazen continued, "They think he was blown to bits. They haven't found his remains yet and—."

"Oh, my God! Shut up, Mazen! I don't want to hear it!" I shrieked. I grabbed the hair on both sides of my head and collapsed to a squatting position, tears pouring down my face. "No! God damnit! Not Alam." I picked up a fistful of dirt and flung it into the air.

I wrapped my arms around myself and rocked back and forth until I fell over face-down on the ground, crying into the dirt. Mazen stooped beside me, his hand on my back. I raised my head and fired rapid questions at him, not giving space for answers. "Why would Alam be on that bus? Why was he in Sa'dah? How do they know he died? I mean … if they haven't found his remains? Where's Jabbar now? I need to go to him."

Mazen muttered, "I don't know, I don't know … uh, Jabbar and Ghada didn't come home. They're staying with relatives in Sa'dah. They're going to collect body parts at sunrise. For some reason, they think his remains are in the trees."

I fell over on my side, my arms now gripping my abdomen, which was in spasm. I bawled like a child. It took ten minutes before my mouth could form words again, and the first were, "But I just feel so sad, so damn sad. Jabbar is my best friend in the whole world

... like a brother. Alam like a nephew."

Mazen, watched me cry, his hand on my back. After several minutes of silence he whispered, "You're a true Yemeni now. You've borne our pain."

We parted ways for the second time. I wiped the lingering tears from my swollen eyes with the sleave of my shirt, grabbed my cup from the dirt, and stumbled into the commons.

I was depleted, mumbling Alam's name each time I grew a breath—every inhalation inciting more tears. Rather than making a cup of tea, I grabbed a beer bottle from the frig. I had not eaten since breakfast, even vomited up that meal later in the morning. *Should I jump on my bike and head back to Sa'dah? Could I find Jabbar and Ghada at this late hour of the night?*

Ahmed often made snacks for us to eat and put them in the refrigerator. That night it was a bowl of dried dates, olives, hummus, and pita bread. But I was so sad that I could have eaten cockroaches and not cared. I wanted something in my stomach to soothe the ache.

I sat at a booth, stared at the wall, and ate my meal methodically. No haste, but I just wanted to finish and get out of the room before Sheila arrived, if she was coming home. She had to walk through the commons to get to her quarters. I didn't want her to see my red eyes. I didn't want to talk about the day and certainly not about Jabbar or Alam and she better not say anything good about Michel. This was a piss-pitiful day followed by a god-awful night, and I planned on keeping it that way. It would take me months to crawl out of this hole of grief.

I looked at the clock on the wall and was shocked to see it was after midnight. Lost in melancholy. I'd let the two hours since returning from Sa'dah slip by unnoticed. Sleep deprivation was dribbling into the edges of my tired brain, but I knew I couldn't sleep. I felt Jabbar's sorrow, and there was nothing I could do about it. What was he thinking at this moment? What was he feeling? Poor man. Pitiful family.

I went to the sink to wash out my bowl. I caught a glimmer of light tangentially crossing the grimy outside window. Then there was the familiar racket of the Toyota's knocking engine. Sheila. I heard the squeak of the brakes as she paused to unlock the gate. A sound like popping corn ensued as she slowly rolled the truck over our driveway stones onto its parking spot. A minute later Sheila appeared in the doorway.

"I saw the light on," she said. "I'm surprised you're still up."

"Was just about to turn in. Are you okay?" I asked, looking away, hoping she wouldn't notice my bloodshot eyes. But when I did look at her, I could see something lingering in the gentle lines of her mouth, like a subdued frown. Her kinky hair was flat and stuck to the edges of her head, the subtle lines of a surgical mask still imprinted as pink lines in her delicate face. Her eyes looked tired, their whites, ensanguined, probably more than my own. From behind her back, she pulled out a green wine bottle and held it up.

"Well, I've a bottle of fine French wine ... wanna share it with me? Michel was saving it for a special occasion."

"Let me guess," I said. *Gee whiz, could this day get any worse?* "Did Michel ask you to marry him?" I followed my question with a smirk.

She set the bottle down, walked over to the kitchen and grabbed two long stem wine glasses. She was opening drawers around the kitchen, closing them with a slam, then paused, "Where's the damn corkscrew?"

"Top drawer; in the back." *Hmm, how had a proposal put her in such a foul mood?*

She found it, returned to the couch, and opened the bottle. I joined her. She poured the glasses full—to the rims. She held her stemmed glass up like a toast. I stood beside her and lifted mine and touched it to hers, the glasses chiming like dampen bells, the wine sloshing over the edges.

"What's so special?" I asked again.

Shaking her head and looking into her glass she answered, "Certainly, it wasn't a marriage proposal." Her chuckle liberated a tear. She looked at me and continued, "The special occasion was Michel breaking up with me."

The blue in her wet eyes glistened under the florescent light. I set my glass on the coffee table and reached for her. "I'm so sorry," I mumbled as I hugged her.

We stood, me holding her for a minute. Finally, I asked, "It wasn't over Americans being blamed for this tragedy, was it?"

She didn't answer me like I expected but stared into her glass. Wiping the tears from her eyes with her hand, she said, "No I don't think so ... maybe? But he informed me he and Maria have been in a relationship for months."

"Really?" I asked.

"Yep. Really. I knew they were sharing a flat in Sa'dah. He gave her a room a year ago when she first came from Italy. I've stayed there some nights ... you know, Maria in her own bedroom. She's rather cute and skinny," she said with a snicker. "But now he tells me he's been sleeping with her since she moved in. He said it was 'just for fun,' at least in the beginning." She looked directly into my eyes and added, "He told me that most Frenchmen have two lovers, if not three. Anyway ..." she sighed, "she moved into his room and bed two months ago and I guess that's when I became his 'just for fun' romance. He's in love with her now."

"Ouch! Sheila, I'm so sorry. That must be painful. I could tell you loved the man. That was cruel of him telling you today. Did he wait until you worked your ass off in the OR, then dumped you?"

"Sit," she said, pointing at the couch behind us. We sat a couple of feet apart so we could turn and face each other.

"Something like that," Sheila answered. "But it was late when we finished the last case, and he was leaving for his flat. I was expecting him to invite me home. He knew he had to come clean, I suppose, for Maria's sake. Certainly not mine." She sipped her drink, leaned forward, and rested her chin on her fist, a bewildered look covering her face. "But again, he was pissed about the bombing and is blaming the Americans," she said.

I said nothing, just held her hand and looked intently at her.

"Here's the thing you don't know, Bryan."

"Yeah?" I asked, focusing my eyes on her lips, awaiting her words.

"I really didn't like Michel that much. He was my knight on a white horse when I first got here and knew no one. I was scared to death coming to Yemen at twenty-seven, practicing everything from public health to trauma medicine alone." She looked up at me with a grin. "I had never been outside of America before."

"Really?" I asked, surprised about everything she'd said.

"Yeah. I was growing tired of Michel anyway. I just didn't have the heart to break up with him. From the way he talked when we were together, I thought he was in love with me. Then he drops me," snapping her fingers, "just like that. I feel like a fool."

"Well—," I started to say.

"I shouldn't have been so naïve," she interrupted. "What did I expect?" Then she shook her head, her flattened hair bouncing in the air, and she growled, "Grrrrrrrr!"

We sat quietly for a moment, her looking down into her lap, me sitting beside her holding her hand, making a study of her face. I had never finished counting her freckles, had I?

"But Sheila," I asked. If you were wanting to break up with him … what's with all the tears?"

"It has been a long hard day and the way he dumped me was the icing on the cake. I think the tears are more for the kids than Michel."

Through sniffles, she added, "Speaking of the kids, some villagers found a piece of the bomb with 'Lockheed Martin' stamped on the side. Michel's worried about us. Everyone in Sa'dah is pissed at America and we—you and me, buster—are the only Americans in the district. He's concerned that people will take their grief out on us."

A chill went up my spine. I looked in my glass. I spun the magenta wine around the crystal bowl of the goblet then chugged it. "Michel's right you know … they could."

"They would not want to hurt us," Sheila said. "We're the only medical care in the village. They know we have a good intent."

"Sheila," I said. Then poured myself another glassful of wine,

"Uh, Dr. Emory, with all due respect, I think now *you* are being naïve. Maybe not in Haydan, but there are villains in the Dammaj valley who wouldn't think twice about killing us, even if you delivered ten of their babies. It's political, not personal. Didn't you ever see *The Godfather*?"

"*The Godfather*?" she asked with a squint.

I didn't answer.

Sheila stared at me, either flummoxed or just thinking. Then she spoke, "Maybe my parents taught me to see the good in people because it is all personal."

"How were you taught," I asked, sipping my new glass of wine, and sitting back on the couch. "Tell me about your upbringing."

"Now? At one in the morning?" she asked, glancing at her watch.

I nodded so hard it must have looked comical. "Sure. Why not? I want to hear everything."

"Well, I grew up near Lincoln, Nebraska," she said. "A small farming community. My mother was a teacher, dad a Baptist minister. His greatest hope was for me to marry a good man and serve him well ... and stay quiet. I think he wanted me to just finish high school and then marry a preacher like him and his dad."

"How'd you end up in medical school?" I asked.

A big smile erupted over her face. Following my example, she spun the remaining liquid around her glass and then chugged it. Then she filled it again.

She turned to face me on the couch, leaning back on its arm, legs crossed. "Things changed when my grandmother, Grandmother Emory, came to live with us. Despite her son's low view of women, she had high expectations for me. She helped me dissect a toad for a science fair project, using her kitchen knife," she said, then giggled, placing her fingers over her mouth as though to keep the wine in. "She was the impetus for me going to medical school."

After finishing the bottle of wine then a beer each, I stood to leave. I was weaving a bit—having to steady myself, my fingers on the couch's arm. She stood too. Then asked, "What's wrong? I can see something's bothering you tonight, more than just our dreadful day. Is there something you haven't told me?"

I looked down at the floor and took a deep breath. Pointing at the couch behind her I said, "Have a seat."

We both lowered ourselves back on the couch. Once seated, when I looked up at her, the room started to spin. I said softly, "I had other bad news tonight."

She sat up straight and wide eyed, "What bad news? How could there be more?"

I bent over, resting my forearms on my thighs, and mumbled, "I found out why Jabbar and Ghada were outside the door of the MSF Hospital today."

She put her hand up to her mouth as if she anticipated what I was going to say. "Oh, my lord, why?"

Tears came to my eyes once more. Looking up at her, I sputtered. "Because their son, Alam, my dear little Alam, was killed on the school bus, his precious body blown into the olive trees."

"Oh, dear Jesus no!" She leaned over and put her arms around me, pulling her head into my shoulder. "Oh Bryan, I'm so sorry. I know how much you loved that boy. Your heart must be broken."

We held each other as tightly as we could. Shaking as we both were sobbing. We were crying for more than just Alam, for the whole horrific day. I wanted to be held forever. I wanted to lose myself in her scent and never emerge. I inhaled deeply to take it all in, then looked down into her bloodstained eyes as they slowly closed, pushing out the remaining tears, which tumbled down her cheeks.

My mouth touched her hair to taste the strawberries. Then she tilted her face up, toward my mouth. *Is this really happening?* My heart was pounding inside my chest, and I knew she could feel it. I touched my lips against her forehead. It left a salty taste on the tip of my tongue. I slid my lips down to her eye, tasting her tears to absorb some of her exhaustion and pain, uniting it with my own.

Sheila stretched upward, bringing her lips closer to mine. They touched, her wet mouth against my own. I could taste her warm wine-infused breath as our lips merged. With all the sorrow my heart could bear, and alcohol diluting my senses, exhaustion my spirit, we succumbed to desire. How could such a horrible day end in such bliss?

CHAPTER TEN

From our compound, we sauntered up the main street, which ran between the orchards and past the old mill that had sat motionless for weeks. I walked beside Mazen, carrying a pineapple under each arm.

Jabbar claimed that Yemen had invented the grist mill, at least the version of a large runner stone turning on a bedstone and propelled by animals. The Greeks attached the stones to the wind, the Europeans to water. Who was I to argue? With their granite-clad mountains, the Yemenis make use of the huge boulders and abundant stones in roads, walls, bridges, and towering buildings. There is a saying, according to Jabbar, "Yemeni stones brought bread to the world." For sure, if it wasn't for the war, the colorful granite and marble would still be Yemen's major export, ornamenting kitchens, baths, and ballrooms of some of the finest places on earth.

You could hear the tinkling of the water channeling through the old troughs beside our path. In one place you could feel it vibrating in your feet, running beneath the ground, in ancient channels of limestone blocks. The water sounded inviting—it was cool and as clear as liquid quartz when the open troughs exposed it. I could understand why locals stopped to drink it with a cupped hand.

The gravel road to Jabbar's house stretched straight and flat along the oasis' floor and then meandered, unrolling up the hill and into the mountains, turning and twisting like a snake with a freshly severed head. The orange trees were just pushing out their early blossoms and their scent penetrated the air. Soft buzzing sounds emanated from their limbs as bees and hummingbirds had been drawn to the citrus aroma. But the years of war had beaten the village into a relic of its former self. Beneath the glorious trees and crops, the litter of suffering—bombing debris and garbage—was strung out in all directions.

While I was taking in the scents of orange blossoms and the buzz of bees, Mazen was looking over his shoulders to his left and right then back again. He wiped perspiration beads off his brow with the sleeve of his white button-up shirt, and the evening air wasn't that hot.

"Are you okay?" I asked.

He answered me as his eyes shifted and watched, "Just trying to be observant. Observant and circumspect."

"Mazen, what do *you* have to fear? You're Yemeni. They have no reason to hate you."

He kept raising his rosy cheeks into a squint, rubbing his nose, mopping his brow with his fingers, and looking around. He led me up alleys and back to the principal thoroughfare. Being in the imminence of his fear, I felt it too. I looked to my left, my right, and back again. It felt like I was on night patrol in the army, armed now with only pineapples. Without me beside him, I suspect, Mazen would have been walking with his typical swagger, ear buds in his ears, a dance step thrown into his gait, and a grin.

The streets were full of amblers that night, but they didn't make eye contact with us, like we were ghosts.

"Mazen, is it just me or are all the villagers giving us the cold shoulder?"

He looked at me puzzled, a frown gripping his brow.

I added, "You know, a snub. I think the Arabic word is *aizdir.*"

Nodding, he said, "Sure, but I wouldn't use the term *us.*"

I turned and walked in front of him—backwards—so that we could face one another, and I grumbled, "Many of these people, I know by name, having cared for them in the clinic."

Mazen shrugged his shoulders. "It's not that they have a quarrel with you, but they fear for your life, like I do. If someone wanted to harm you, it would be an outsider, like the protestors. They just don't want to be collaterals."

I turned back around to walk at his side. The radiance the orange blossoms had brought to my mood was gone, replaced by worry.

We passed irrigated fields with stone boundary walls, behind which a mishmash of grains—barley, wheat, or millet—waved in the light evening breeze like a stage full of ballet dancers. In still others were small trees or bushes of khat or coffee. Between them the tinkling of the water continued in the trenches beneath and around us.

We came to the foothills where the tall adobe and stone buildings sprouted from the rocky bluffs. The oldest buildings were carved directly into the stone, most a natural beige, some whitewashed with plaster.

They had built the houses on tight footprints, giving them tall and lean physiques, crowned with small open courts where residents would sit on carved chairs of olive wood and drink weak tea, chew khat leaves, or hang out their washed clothes to dry beneath a cloudless Yemeni sky.

As we turned up Jabbar's street, his house came into view. It was the fourth house into the cluster of buildings, adobe tan with whitewashed accents around the windows and along thick lines between its four floors.

I explained to Mazen, as if he didn't know, "Jabbar's house was owned by Ghada's patriarch, and the family offered it to them as a transitory residence after the war came to Al Hudaydah. You could measure the house in generations of inhabitants. It was a work of ancient art."

We met a woman wearing a black burqa hurrying down the steep street. It was almost impossible to see who was inside those all-encompassing black cocoons. But I saw her eyes. I knew it was Mona. In Yemen, a man doesn't stare at or even speak to a woman in public. But I did. "Mona?"

The woman paused and spoke to us in Arabic. "Jabbar is waiting for you inside."

We came to the wooden door, a rectangle carving that could don a museum's noble walls. It was made of olive wood and contained a scene in the middle top panel of people in grain fields with old scythes. Other carvings on the stiles of the door depicted people on tall ladders, stretching from the sill to the top, picking fruit—a testament to this land's history as a place of bounty. The door had a big crack right down its middle all the way through to the inside.

It is no coincidence that the Romans called Yemen *Arabia Felix* [fertile Arabia]. Throughout its history, it was also known as the "Happy Land" or simply in the Arab world as the "Southland," from which the name The Yemen [literally "the right," meaning to the right of Mecca if facing from North Africa] is derived. It was not a happy or plentiful land in recent decades. There were too many mouths to feed. Too many fields had turned into bomb craters. Jabbar's door would sell for ten thousand dollars at Christie's, but here you couldn't trade it for a loaf of bread—or they would have by now. The wood was worn so slick and hard, it looked like a cheap plastic imitation. But it was authentic.

The mighty door hung on archaic forged hinges, a heavy rust-peppered iron knocker in the center. I tapped the metal ring to its base. I heard the metallic click of the latch, and then the door swung inward and the sweet face of Jabbar's daughter, Maritza, appeared in the opening. About five feet tall, with long flowing hair that couldn't be any blacker, wrapped in a scarf, she had stunning brown eyes with a hint of green. I had never seen a child who used so much animation in her face and hands when she spoke, like a pint-sized mime, but with words—plenty of them. She was a delight to talk to, at better times than this.

She said in her rather good English, "Come in."

As she led us up the stairs, I complimented her. "Maritza, your English is coming along, but I detect a British accent."

She looked over her shoulder at me. "We have a teacher who lived in Australia for ten years. Alice Springs, I think. She teaches us English."

The stairs shifted to wood on the second floor. They wound around the building's inside wall, up to the fourth floor, or *mafraj*, the equivalent of the American living room.

Their *mafraj*, like most, took up the entire top floor. Large wood-trimmed windows encircled the room on all sides, like a forest service's fire lookout tower. From that vantage point you could see far out into the landscape and up steep, rocky, deforested mountains above us. To the east, laying out over twenty acres, were rows of white rectangles lit up like Chinese lanterns in the dusk—the refugees' tents, where dreams came to die, swept away by the hopeless winds of war.

The view was impressive. There was one more roofless level above us—a courtyard with a partial grapevine covering, the rest embracing the full extent of the elements, whether it was the sweltering sun, rain, or snow. It was often used to dry clothes and as a makeshift *mafraj* on sunny but not-so-hot days.

I had been on the top floor only once, six weeks previously. I'd had tea with Jabbar and a jubilant Alam on that day. As Jabbar and I planned our fishing trip, the boy was throwing paper airplanes off the roof, and they would sail across the entire village. I showed him how to make one that flew like a dart, another that did loop-the-loops. Now I caught a glimpse of one of the paper planes still in the top of a palm tree. Alam had told me he was going to climb the tree and get it. Five weeks later, Alam himself had ended up in the top of a tree, in shards.

Small square pillows and low-sitting couches enclosed Jabbar's *mafraj* in the traditional Yemeni style, underpinned by a wood parquet floor. Jabbar's couches were foam covered with burgundy velvet with matching embroidered pillows. In the middle of the room sat two round brass tables. On one wall was Allah's name written in Islamic calligraphical gold letters inside a red wooden frame. On another wall was a family portrait taken when Alam was a toddler. An assortment of funeral gifts, fruits, candies, flowers, and trinkets were piled high near the door. I placed the two pineapples there.

Mazen and I took a seat. With a big-eyed look, Maritza said, "You wait here," and left the room.

We waited in silence, our hands folded in our laps, without a hint of conversation between us until we heard a slipping sound coming from below, sandals sliding across the rock steps—lubricated by a fine sand—then tapping on the wooden ones. Tap, tap, tap, each tap getting louder. We assumed it was Jabbar, but it was Maritza walking gingerly, carrying a silver tray with two cups and a teapot.

She stood in front of us. "Tea?"

I could smell cardamom's rich bouquet. It was part of the air here and as important as oxygen. Their lamb stew had it, as did their coffee, breads, and desserts.

Mazen and I both nodded with enthusiasm.

Maritza explained the recipe as she poured.

"Traditional Yemeni tea, or shai, has cardamom, cinnamon, nutmeg, and ginger. We make it in whole goat's milk, sugar, and water. Sometimes we can't find some of the spices and must make it without them. This tea has them all." She added, nonchalantly, "Some relatives brought cinnamon and nutmeg as funeral gifts ... for my brother." Her face then abruptly looked sad, and her eyes glistened under the overhead light, a single bulb on a wire.

She wiped her eyes with her sleeve and finished pouring our cups. Her composure regained, she added, "I had tea once at a hotel in Sana'a at my cousin's wedding. It was British tea. Disgusting." She winced and gave an ugly frown. "Only black tea in water. Of course, I added sugar, lots of it. But still appalling." She gave a quick smile, tossed her hair back over her shoulder, and left us alone again.

I studied the portrait of the family inside the French-provincial gold-leaf frame. Little Alam was standing beside his parents, who were sitting. He was wearing shorts but with an oversized sports jacket and sweater and was holding a little red firetruck. Now the photo hung above the bounty of that boy's funeral gifts. This was Yemen, where a parent's worst nightmares became ordinary.

As we continued to wait, Mazen and I sat like mannequins in a furniture-store display, still and silent. Soon we heard footsteps again. We were sure it was Jabbar—deeper, heavier steps— ascending the stairs. The door opened, but it wasn't him. A man dressed in a white thoob and wearing a traditional white turban entered. He had short gray hair, a full beard, and big round eyes like a tarsier. I didn't recognize his serious face at first but then realized it was Abdul, Ghada's brother from Huth, north of Sana'a. I had gone with Jabbar to deliver fish to him and his family after our trip.

Abdul had a strand of amber misbaḥahs, or ninety-nine prayer beads representing the names for God, in his right hand, and he was rotating them through his fingers like a tickertape machine. His lips were moving as though he was reciting those adjectival names, names like Merciful, The Giver of Peace, and The Great King. Watching him, I remembered he was the family's most religious man. He never smiled and didn't on this night. His stare was as sharp as a well-honed knife.

Mazen and I respectfully stood. For some reason I did a quick head bow, not a Yemeni custom. Mazen gave me a befuddled glance.

"I'm Jabbar's brother-in-law, Abdul," the man said as he sat on the couch in front of us.

I smiled. "Yes, we've met before. I'm Bryan. We brought you and your family fish three weeks ago. This is my friend Mazen."

Mazen spoke to him in rapid-fire Arabic, most of which I understood.

"Have a seat," said Abdul, as he pointed to the cushion behind us. He leaned toward me and spoke through his khat-stained teeth, his breath tobacco-tinged. "Why are you here?" He froze his face with raised brows and a stare.

I was dumbstruck. Abdul's piercing eyes bounced back and forth between mine and Mazen's as we both paused in search for words.

I said, in my best Arabic, "We are here because we're sorry for Jabbar."

Mazen translated it into a clearer Yemeni dialect.

Abdul leaned back on his cushion and started speaking his best English. "What can you say? How … do you fix this sorrow? Are you coming to represent America?"

"Uh, no. I'm coming for myself and for our clinic to say how sorry we are for Alam … uh, Alam's death."

"So, you're sorry. Only the guilty say that. Correct? Are you also saying you're guilty?"

Anger and exasperation washed through me like cold blood through my veins. I wiped my face with my hand and swallowed hard.

"No, I'm not responsible for this horrible bombing. The Saudis are."

Abdul leaned further in my direction, still rotating his beads through his hand, not missing one, even without looking. "The people found the casing. The bomb is from America. Maybe your father made it … perhaps?" he said with a smirk and leaned back on the couch. "You trained the pilots to fly American jets. Aren't Americans responsible for this, this … *fajiea*." He looked at Mazen as if he needed him to translate the last word.

Mazen mumbled in my ear, "Calamity."

Abdul nodded, "Yes, calamity."

I leaned toward him and answered in the simplest of terms. "I'm not guilty! I don't support America aiding the Saudis in this war. I am saddened by the terrible deaths of the children and the bombings. No, my father didn't make the damn bomb. He's dead. He was also murdered by the Saudis."

I saw a look of surprise overtake Abdul's face. But before he could speak, the door sprang opened and Jabbar entered.

My old friend looked tired. Dark bags rested on his sun-kissed cheeks. His shoulders were rounded beneath a black thoob. He wore a white lacy skullcap called a taqiyah on his head. His weary eyes were downcast, his line of sight hardly making it above the furniture. Letting my impulse guide me, I stood up and walked over to him. I hugged him. He kissed my cheek, I his, his eyes still distant. Tears bathed my own. "I'm so sorry, brother," I mumbled in his ear.

Jabbar pointed toward the cushions behind where Mazen was then standing, across from Abdul. I took a seat and Mazen followed.

As we were sitting, Abdul stood and walked toward the door. He kissed Jabbar on the cheek before exiting the room but said nothing else to Mazen or to me.

Jabbar took the still-warm seat his brother-in-law had just vacated. In a moment, Maritza returned with a cup and set it on the brass table in front of her father. She poured tea from our pitcher. She picked up our empty cups, standing up quickly, throwing her long hair out of her face, and asked, "You want more?"

"No, thank you," I said. "But, Maritza, I would love a glass of water."

She nodded.

As I waited for Jabbar to speak, my nerves dried my throat out even more. I was leaning in his direction, eager to catch the first words to drop from his grimacing mouth.

After a few minutes, Jabbar still hadn't spoken. I asked him, "How're you doing?"

A forced smile spread across his face. "Thanks to God, he has been merciful to us."

"Jabbar, my heart is sad about Alam. He was a good boy and would have made a great man."

I saw the tears build up in Jabbar's downward-drifting eyes. He looked to the floor to hide them. As his upper lip finally stiffened, he looked at me and spoke in English, turning to Mazen for help when he needed translation.

"My heart … it is sore tonight. Yes, Alam was a good boy," he said shaking his head. "The best." He paused again, I assumed to gather his thoughts and quash his emotions. Taking a deep breath, a twinkle came back to his eyes. "Do you know why we named him Alam?"

"No," I said.

"It means, 'the world.' Alam was our world, our family's two-thousand-year-old life rested on his shoulders, the only bearer of our linage. Do you understand?" Jabbar asked. "Our personal world has, uh—" He looked at Mazen and said, "*Yanhar lildaakhil.*"

"Imploded," Mazen said with a nod.

"Imploded?" asked Jabbar. "Just one English word says that?"

"Right," answered Mazen.

Jabbar sipped his tea, lifting the cup with his shaking right hand, his left steadying the saucer beneath it. He turned to look out the window. All three of us were soon staring out into the evening, looking for what was drawing Jabbar's attention.

The sun had set since we had entered his house, but still a faint orange glow suffused the mountaintops as if God had dipped them in gold. Was that one of the names of God on Abdul's beads? The Great Gilder? Even nasty wars don't spoil beautiful sunsets, only the souls of those who would have admired them.

I whispered across the room, "Could things become so dreadful in a place that even the sun forsakes it, setting without fanfare? Forgetting to rise the next day?"

No one responded. I didn't interrupt Jabbar's retreat from conversation with more irrelevant words. I gave him his space. Then, after ten minutes I spoke again. "Alam loved his wrestling. That was so much fun." I chuckled.

Jabbar didn't respond. Didn't even move. Like he had become the lone marble statue in a world of flesh. As Jabbar sat for several minutes, Mazen whispered to me, "It's time for us to go."

I said to Jabbar, "I brought you pineapples. They came from the Philippines."

As Jabbar remained nonresponsive to our presence, I reached over the brass table and patted him on his knee. He held his contorted posture, turned away from me, and continued looking out the window, the sunset now drained of light.

I stood. "Jabbar, my brother, we'll go now. But I want to visit again soon. What can we do for you and your family?"

Light casting down from the single overhead bulb elongated his facial features, deepening its shadows and accentuating his melancholic mood. Tears brimmed his eyes as he looked straight ahead, projecting his sorrow through the window and into that night's void. When he didn't respond, Mazen and I just looked at one another. Mazen stood and we left the *mafraj* and began to descend the stairs.

Mazen and I shared few words as we stumbled through the rubble of the streets on our way home. Before arriving at the house where he had a room, I finally spoke. "I'm not satisfied with the visit. I wanted to draw Jabbar out, for him to share his feelings with me. I wanted to console him. He knows how I lost my dad and I thought that would make it easier for him to talk."

"Be careful. Take it slow. Everyone here has lost someone," said Mazen. "There's a seven-day memorial at the graveside. That will be next Tuesday. If the anti-American atmosphere is subdued by then, you should attend. And, Bryan, I'm sorry about your dad. I watched the 9/11 disaster on TV. I was only four, but I still remember it and how everyone in the house was sad. Everyone in the damn world was sad, well, almost everyone." He put his hand on my shoulder and gave it a squeeze.

As I turned to leave, I noticed a chestnut-feathered rooster sitting on the balcony wall. Upon seeing me, it stood in a strut, as if it were showing respect or insisting on mine. I reached out to pet its head just as Mazen mumbled, "I wouldn't do that."

The rooster struck me, drawing blood from my finger.

"Damn! What did he do that for?" I stuck the bloody finger in my mouth.

"I told you not to pet him. He's not a kitten. I know Yemeni roosters like I do the people. You need to learn to listen to me."

"Mazen," I asked. "Was tonight so bad?"

"Could've been," he said. "That Abdul is a bit scary. Glad Jabbar came in when he did."

I flashed Mazen a grin and said, "*Tusbihun ealaa khayr* [May you wake up to good news]."

He smiled and responded in English, "I hope to God."

I ventured on through the village on my own. The streets were still busy though it was after ten P.M. My palms were sweaty, my steps methodical. I was now unprotected, not having even pineapples to throw at them. *Where were the people screaming for my death earlier in the day? Had they gone home?*

When I arrived at our back gate, the guard met me. His black uniform rendered him invisible in the dark, and I wouldn't have seen him if it were not for the orangish glow on his cigarette's tip. He stopped me from coming into the compound by putting his hand against my chest.

"Mohammed wants to talk to you."

Then he called him over his radio, while continuing to hold his palm against my chest. I felt my hands curling into fists as I leaned hard into his outstretched hand.

In a moment, Mohammed bounded across the compound like a bull, nostrils flaring. He was still in his uniform pants but had removed his shirt and wore the kind of undershirt we use to call in the Bronx a "wife beater." His suspenders hung off his shoulders and dangled to his sides. The honorable colonel with the presence of a bum. What the hell had happened?

As Mohammed drew closer, I could see that the whites of his eyes were bloodshot and could smell alcohol on his breath. There was a half-smoked cigarette between his tar-blackened fingers. Two hours previously, he'd been sitting in the commons in full uniform, drinking tea, and flirting with Sheila. He had seemed so professional with his pressed shirt and aiguillette around his shoulder. But that persona had been diluted in cheap whiskey.

Mohammed walked up to me, pushing his soldier to the side, and stepped into my personal space. He took one last draw from his cigarette and blew smoke up into my eyes from his five-foot-seven stature. I waved the smoke away with the back of my hand, barely missing the end of his nose. Words stumbled from his inebriated mouth. "Why … er what … the hell do you, do you think you were doing, son? I brought my men here to keep you safe and then you go wa … waltzing right into the village alone? Are you crazy? Do you want your throat cut and your body thrown down a well?"

"Hmm. Maybe I could find my watch … uh, it's in the well," I said with a stare.

He contorted his face, flipped his cigarette into the weeds, and grunted, "What the hell are you talking about?"

"I lost my watch when we were digging the well."

"Do … do you think this is funny? If you do, I'll take my men back to Sana'a tomorrow. I'm not risking my men's lives if you don't give a shit!"

That night seemed like a damn waste, yet there was a message in it. I needed to be patient with Jabbar and listen to the words of caution. Maybe I was being too cavalier. Of course, Mazen and Mohammed were right, and the days ahead would quickly prove it.

CHAPTER ELEVEN

I opened the door to the commons, and there was Sheila, sitting at a booth, her socked feet up on the adjacent bench, immersed in her novel, her favorite green ceramic cup on the table, surrounded by rings where she had rested her cup between sips. I came to an abrupt halt. *Will this day never end?*

I could have backed out the door, brushed my teeth, and climbed into my sleeping bag. She would have never noticed me, and I could have put off our conversation for a better day. However, I took a deep breath, rubbed my face, and stepped within the scope of her visual field, heading for the kitchen area.

"Did the mosquitoes drive you inside?" I asked, peering into the refrigerator. "They were biting as I walked through the village."

She grinned and glanced at me, so I knew she'd heard me, but she didn't speak.

I walked toward her. She sat up, put her book over her heart, and grinned big. "Wow, what a story." She laid her book on the table and removed her feet from the bench, which I took as an invitation. I sat. I couldn't take my eyes off her. She had never looked more beautiful. I couldn't even muster a blink. She reciprocated with a half-smile and a stare. "Hey, how did your visit with Jabbar go?"

I shrugged my shoulders, "It's hard to say. He is grieving terribly. Almost catatonic. He didn't have much to say, so I'll need to visit him again. He had a brother-in-law at his house, an Abdul from Huth, who was a little creepy."

"Poor man … poor family," she said. "But it was a great day in the clinic, wasn't it? Despite the protesters outside. They're doing it just for show, you know." She rolled her eyes.

"Mohammed is worried. He was mad I went into the village alone. After tonight, I'm starting to think he's right. Mazen's on the same page as Mohammed, Haydan is more dangerous than we think."

"He's also the reason I'm inside tonight. Mohammed and his men," she said, sitting up. "Those guys"—she pointed toward the door— "have taken over the entire garden. They made me feel uncomfortable the way they look at me ... and with their innuendos."

"I'm not surprised. Looks like they got their hands on some booze. In a drunken state, they're more threatening to a gorgeous woman than even the protestors were."

Jerking her head back, she said, "I've never heard you compliment me before, at least not when sober."

"Apparently, I'm not safe when I drink either, am I?" I asked.

"I told you it was a special night for me," she quickly added.

I was speechless. Her peering blue eyes made my heart want to explode.

She reached over and put her warm hand on my forearm. "Bryan, it was a good night. Magical."

I looked up at her glowing face, then to her delicate hand on my forearm, her silver medical school class ring on her finger reminding me who she was. How hard she had worked to get here. How brave she was for coming to a war zone, alone. And to this incredible woman, a night with me was magical? It didn't make sense.

On the surface, I was beaming, and I couldn't contain it. My cheeks were red hot. My tongue—tied. I took a deep breath and gently let it out to slow my heart. I stared at her, studying her face, and resumed my count of her freckles. Then, words began flowing from my subconscious and out of my mouth like a subterranean stream surfacing.

"Sheila, I've cared about you in so many ways. A colleague I look up to. A sister I want to protect. And a strong woman I want to be romantically involved with. I never meant for our relationship just to be a hookup, just to alleviate our pain from a bad day. Since losing Dad, loss terrifies me. I've never let a woman get close to me since losing him. I'm afraid I will fall in love and then lose her. But it's too late. I'm in love with you, have been for a while, and I'm terrified I will mess this up."

She shook her head, "Have you not heard a word I've said?"

Continuing to stare at me, a pout forming around her mouth, she said, "Bryan, dear, we all make mistakes. I dated a man for over a year, a man I didn't even like. You've lost nothing. Yeah, you are impulsive, but that's one of the things I love about you."

"You do?" I asked with wide eyes.

"Most men bury their souls deep within their catacombs and they are unknowable," she said. "Even Freud couldn't find them with a torch. But I knew you better on our first day than I would have known Michel in a lifetime. You let people inside your heart more than you realize."

I took another deep breath, trying to calm my pulse, which was determined to run away. "Sheila, I've been in love with you since I saw you step from that old Land Rover in Sana'a."

"I felt the same way," she said. "After meeting you, I regretted starting that relationship with Michel. Yeah, you're impulsive at times, but, Bryan, your compassion for our patients, your judgement, and persistence make you a damn good doctor too, the best I've ever worked with."

Without moving the forearm on which she had rested her hand, I sat up. "You've been in love with me?"

She nodded. "Ever since you walked out of that airport, looking like the surf had just washed you up on a beach."

I savored the moment in silence, our eyes fixed on one another. Then I added, "That was kind of you to say, about me being a good doctor, but you mean PA," I added.

"Who gives a shit here?" she said. "I don't measure people by what school they attended but by the care they give."

"I'm flattered," I said.

With trepidation, I asked, "Sheila, where does this leave us?"

"Bryan, I feel bewildered. We have been on an emotional rollercoaster. It would make sense to let the dust settle. I don't want to have a false start with you, then lose you either." She paused to gather her words. "I've thought of nothing but this for the past three days. Bryan, we both came here because of our love of the Yemenis, especially the children. I've imagined what it would look like if you and I were in a romantic relationship. How would us working together in the clinic change? What would happen to our passion for the people if it was directed toward one another?"

"Yeah?" I mumbled, staring at her, listening to every word.

"Here is what I came up with," she said. "Let's just focus on our patients for the next five months I have here. We can still be friends, the best of friends, even better than before, but holding off on the romantic involvement for now. If it's true love, it will only grow deeper. Can we do that?"

Choked up, tears in my eyes, I nodded.

"Then, if you are still interested in me," Sheila added, "let's start a romantic relationship. I want to write you every day from Nebraska. I want you to write me back, letting our souls grow together. Then, in just six more months, you'll come home, and we will take our relationship wherever it wants to go."

I inhaled to recapture enough air to propel some meager words. I felt the radiance of the warmth of her body sitting across from me. It took all my strength not to try to kiss her.

I reached over and rubbed the back of her hand with my finger. "Here's my dream for us," I said. "When Yemen is done for both of us, I want to make you coffee every morning, eat ice cream in bed with you, watch sad movies with you, remove dryer lint with you. You know, life. The mundane with you would become the exotic! I want to comfort you when you hurt and dance with you when you're elated, slow dance when you're feeling romantic. I would sell my boat in a heartbeat if it would make our lives better, or sail around the world again with you beside me at the helm. But I don't want to make any mistakes now that could ruin this. Could I wait a year for you? Of course. I would put my entire friggin' life in suspension for you, even if I had to wait on you until I was an old man."

"Dryer lint?" she asked through a laugh.

I blushed.

"How romantic!" She burst out laughing, making the sound of a rooting pig.

The way she laughed started me to snicker. I mumbled, "I guess a poet I will never be."

As our laughter dispersed, quiet returning, Sheila looked down at the white tabletop, dipped the tip of her finger in the wet coffee-cup rings like they were inkwells and wrote my name, *Bryan Rogers*.

With a million thoughts swirling in my head, I knew this was the best deal I could get. I wrote on the back of her hand with my finger dipped in her imaginary inkwells. In Arabic script, which she would not understand, I wrote out, "You are the greatest love of my life."

Leaning close, looking directly into her enlarged pupils, I saw my own reflection. I looked pitifully smitten.

She looked up at the clock on the wall and sighed. "It's after midnight. We'll have another long day tomorrow."

"One favor, please," I said as I sat up on my bench. "Before we start this grand platonic experiment, can I just hold you for a moment? Nothing more, just a couple of minutes before we try to put the love genie back in the bottle?"

She nodded, then got up to join me on my side of the table. She leaned into me, burying her head into my chest, her ear over my heart. I held her tight, just loose enough so she could breathe. Her long golden locks against my face, I inhaled the strawberries, then gently kissed them. I stroked her hair and closed my eyes to absorb the moment. I wanted to sew that instant into my heart with an enduring thread.

I had asked for a couple of minutes, but with neither of us willing to give up the embrace, it continued for twenty, until an inebriated guard stumbled into the room, looking for more alcohol.

"Damnit!" I mumbled.

I walked toward the guard, grabbed him by his shirt, and pulled him to the door. "Tell Mohammed that the kitchen is off limits. It's our private space."

I turned to find Sheila standing at the door to her quarters.

"Goodnight, Bryan. I'll see you in the clinic."

CHAPTER TWELVE

Within the next week, our inebriated tin soldiers left us and returned to Sana'a. I observed the seven-day post-death graveside memorial with Jabbar and his family. It was in a patch of dry dirt outside the village. There were rows of tombs, rectangles of standing weathered limestones, side by side, inscribed with names and dates in black paint.

Some chiseled stones with encroaching lichens, whose sharp edges had rounded like blocks of ice under the hot sun, dated back hundreds of years. The worn letters were barely legible, as if reading in Arabic calligraphy wasn't hard enough. And there were granite and marble stones polished to exhibit their magnificent colors, but they were too hard to engrave. These small, sad rectangle pillars had now become the new stones of Yemen.

A crowd of villagers attended, along with many outsiders who were relatives of the victims or who came simply offering support. The gravediggers had performed their craft in the hard ground the previous week, leaving three small piles of disturbed dirt, a permanent rest made for the Haydan children killed in the bombing. Wilted flowers, mostly orange blooms, adorned the graves—there were little bouquets of flowering spurge drooping in drought and thus well suited to the mood. Even the plastic recycled flowers that some guests brought look withered and sun-bleached. Sadness was painted on the gloomy faces encircling the graves. Few tears fell—after a week, the attendees were all cried out. But a dry wailing carried through the crowd, like a rainless thunderstorm.

Five strange men dressed in Western jackets and ties like they were on official business were hanging around the mourning families. Perhaps Houthis? I kept my distance.

Jabbar was looking better than before, his facial angst a bit subdued as he greeted people on the edge of the burial ground, where the patch of bare dirt turned to sparse, dry grass. He had shaved and wore a pressed white shirt. He kissed me on the cheek and thanked me for coming. I smelled khat on his breath, like musty coffee grounds, and realized I'd never smelled it on him before. He spoke no words to me other than the greeting. Not one. But many people were contending for his attention, and his wavering focus didn't annoy me.

"Can I visit you again?" I whispered into his ear as I was leaving.

He nodded.

With the guards gone, Sheila returned to the garden patio between the clinic building and the outer security wall to eat her dinner and relax after work. I left her alone. After all day in the clinic together, she needed her space and I wanted to avoid the temptation of taking our relationship further.

Four blood dragon trees stood in the garden with their bold circular foliage, like giant umbrellas of tangled limbs and leaves at the top of tall, limbless trunks. People had uprooted the trees from Yemen's Socotra islands to this highland area for their shade and hoped their legends would offer them protection. The strange trees thrived in this highland, which was much cooler than their native habitat. In more recent years, their greatest threat was from starving refugees scrounging for firewood. They were spared the woodcutter's axe because they bleed bright red sap when cut, and the Yemenis have both empathy and superstition.

Beneath the trees were blue tables set in an array with matching chairs of woven wicker. Sheila would take her dinner, tea, book, and sit there for hours enjoying the warm but tolerable Yemeni late-summer evening serenaded by cicadas in their harmonistic soprano.

After the protestors were gone, I followed a routine of biking into the mountains. I made wild goat trails my private motocross track. After burning off my stress and passions, I came back to the clinic and would sit down in the commons to eat, with a book in hand. Sheila turned in early, usually in bed by the time I returned.

The afflicted still lined up each morning. Trying to get ahead of the curve was a hopeless gesture. But each of them expressed gratitude as they left. The protesters were now just a memory.

At night, I lay awake, counting on the coming dawn, so I could see Sheila in more than just my dreams. I constantly had to quell the images of her naked body against mine, a memory relic of my greatest night. Like there is no way to unsee tragedy once seen, there is no way to unfeel passion once felt. Lying in my bag, clasped hands behind my head, I knew that she was just feet away. There, inside her room, within the old stone clinic salvaged from ugly debris, the beauty within the beast. I thought I could hear her breathe, but it was just the lovely song of the nightingale. Each short night was like months without her. I longed, someday soon, to write her real poetry and send it to her in a merlot wine bottle carried by the tides, but somehow the bottle would have to navigate the Platte River—upstream.

On the following Tuesday evening, I was going to take my Yamaha for a spin. From the clinic, I pulled out behind a filthy black Mercedes sedan, its rear window opaque from the dust. I had seen Mercedeses in our area before, worn cars driven in from Saudi Arabia; ruffians drove them through dry wadis at night with their headlights out, to sell on the black market. This one had five or six men inside the grubby windows, and two armed men on motorcycles escorting them.

Men carrying arms, usually AK-47s, were not that unusual, especially in Sa'dah. The shifty sedan turned into Jabbar's street. As I passed the turn, I looked up the lane and saw them stopping at Jabbar's house. I continued going straight ahead, losing them from my sight but carrying the concerns about the men with me.

It had been three weeks since the school bus bombing, September was rolling in, offering the same unbearable heat of August, but with cooler nights, at least in the mountains. It was time to visit Jabbar, not to talk but to listen. My mom said to me once, "The occupation of the sufferer's friend is to heed their thorny words." All I wanted to do was to harvest his grief and help him process it.

I dropped by Jabbar's house after work one evening the following week. It played out similarly to the previous visit, with Maritza escorting me up to the mafraj and seating me on the couch.

"Do you want tea?"

"Yes," I said, "you have wonderful tea."

Jabbar entered the room in fifteen minutes. We kissed each other on the cheek. I noticed he had a misbaḥah prayer bead loop in his right hand. That was a first.

Jabbar took a seat beside me. I turned to look directly at him. "How are you and the family doing?"

"God has been merciful to us all in these hard days," he responded with a stern tone.

"How sore is your heart tonight?" I asked.

He frowned, then his eyes danced across the room and back to me, "What do you think, Bryan? Of course, my heart hurts and it will until Allah takes me to paradise."

Then he said nothing as he massaged his misbaḥah beads through his fingers and continued to stare at me. There was a blush to his leathery cheeks.

"Jabbar, I understand. When I was a little older than Alam, Saudi terrorists killed my father by violence. I know what loss is like. But I don't know your hurt. I mean, I can't imagine what it's like to lose a child."

Jabbar gritted his teeth, "Allah, he'll be faithful and revenge my son's death because he died a martyr! Alam is in paradise now … and for that I'm glad." Jabbar looked over my shoulder and out the window. After a few minutes passed, he turned back to me, "Did you vindicate your father's death?"

"In a way, yeah, I did. The Saudi murderers killed my dad on 9/11. A few years later, I went to Afghanistan where that incident was planned … as a medic."

Jabbar's mouth gaped open. "He was? I knew he had died, but on 9/11? I saw that on TV."

"Yes. You know I'm from New York. My dad was a medic who went into the World Trade Center's south tower to save lives, but the building collapsed around him. I thought I told you that before."

"Only that your father had died in a burning building, not that it was the tower on 9/11," Jabbar said.

"Like with Alam," I added, "we never found his body to bury, only his watch and a couple of bones."

Jabbar shook his head, and a deep furrow pulled his russet eyes closer together. He looked down at the floor and spoke. "We found Alam … just not all of him."

Tears flooded Jabbar's eyes. He stood, walked to the windows, unlatched them, and pushed the wooden frames wide open. The wind that evening seemed desperate to get inside, pouring through the opened frame the moment they opened. He stood there looking out the window for about five minutes saying nothing. Periodically, gusts blew in and around his body, causing the door to slam closed and the curtains to dance like partying ghosts in the silent room. I didn't know what Jabbar was thinking, but I just wanted him to have space to gather his raw thoughts, corralling them into words.

Sitting down next to me again, he said, "This is all connected, you know. The Saudi terrorists killed your father. Then your country stepped up its war against Muslims as retaliation, including this war." He poked his finger into his thigh. "So, America built the bombs, gave them to the Saudis, showed them where to drop them … and … and dropped them on my Alam, blowing him to pieces. And for what? To revenge your dad?" he shook his head violently squinting his eyes almost closed. "Was Alam a terrorist?"

"Of course not! No, Alam was a good boy who I loved like a son. No, I don't have a clue as to why they killed him. The BBC says it was an accident."

Jabbar stood up and shouted. "You didn't love him the way I did, and it was no accident! The pilots direct those American bombs with lasers, they could hit a mouse's ass if they wanted to. Don't give me that *hra'* [bullshit]!"

"Jabbar, I don't know why the bomb hit the bus! I don't know why this terrible war continues. When I dream, I now dream in Arabic, you know, the characters in those dreams, all Yemeni. I love this place despite its ruin. I want to do my best to help you and to save lives that disease would otherwise take. Do you understand? You're my family! My only family."

Tears flooded my eyes. "I'm so sorry this happened. I would rather the bomb had hit me than Alam. I would give my life for your son."

Jabbar left the room. I waited. I could hear his voice echoing up the stairwell.

Soon he reappeared and said, "I'm sorry, I needed to leave because I was feeling furious at you."

At me?

"Oh. Maybe it is time for me to go," I said. "We can talk more later. You're still my friend … and my brother."

Jabbar was looking down. I stood beside him and stuck out my hand to shake his. He took my hand, and I pulled him tighter to my side. I said into his ear, "Jabbar, if the American government was behind this bombing, I'm very sorry. Americans, just like Yemenis, they're good people. They have good souls. They love children and would never want to see them hurt. Please forgive them for this, as I had to forgive the Saudi people and the Muslims for al-Qaeda killing my dad, even those who had nothing to do with it."

He nodded but remained quiet. I walked to the stairs and descended. He followed me. We stepped out his front door.

"Oh Jabbar, I saw people at your house in a black Mercedes?"

"Were you snooping on me?"

"No, I was riding by on my motorcycle and saw them."

"They're with Hezbollah," he said.

"Hezbollah?" I jerked my head back.

"Yes, they have a martyr's fund and gave us money."

"That's why they were here?" I asked.

I had an ill sense of ease with that information, and I pondered it during my entire walk back to the clinic's compound.

CHAPTER THIRTEEN

One week later, on a typically busy clinic day, Mazen brought the next patient in from the garden. It was Jabbar.

Mazen put him in an exam room. I was standing in the hall talking to a mother and her two children, instructing them on how to use rehydration packets. Cholera was back in town. As Mazen and Jabbar walked by, my eyes followed them while my mouth and its words were focused on the young mother. Once Jabbar was in a room, I turned back to the mother and asked her to repeat the instructions. She got it close enough, and I sent them on their way.

I grabbed Mazen's arm the next time he passed and asked, "Hey, why is Jabbar here?"

Shrugging his shoulders, he said, "I'm not sure. He says it's personal and not medical."

I hastily entered Jabbar's room. "Hey, friend, what brings you in today? Are you okay?"

Sitting on the exam table, his hands were folded across his lap, a half-smile on his face. He was more dressed up than usual, wearing a tattered olive-green sports coat over a white shirt, not his typical farming clothes.

His half-smile grew into a wide grin as he said, "Doctor Bryan, I need your help. My brother-in-law, Abdul, in Huth found me a Toyota. I want you to look at it with me. You know a lot about motorbikes and trucks. If I buy it, we could drive back the next day. Is this possible?"

I sat on the bed beside him, "Wait a minute. You're buying a truck? I thought you said once that only the very rich had trucks?"

He nodded. "I'm not rich, but I do have the money for the truck. It'll help me sell our crops across the entire valley. Prices go higher the farther you get from the oasis."

"How did you get the money?"

"Uh, a *ratib taqaeud* [pension]," he answered.

"Pension? Pension from what?"

"From Alam. From Alam's death."

I was stunned.

"Let me think about this for a minute," I said rubbing my head. "You know, I'd love to, however, it would mean me leaving the clinic at a busy time. What day do you need to go?"

"The truck will be at my brother-in-law's house next Wednesday. Then we would return on Thursday."

"Hmm. I'll have to be gone from the clinic for two days. I'll talk to Dr. Emory about it and get back to you tomorrow. Is that okay?"

"Sure," he said, jumping off the bed and starting for the door like he was in a rush.

"Jabbar?" I asked.

"Yes?"

"Anything else?"

"Nope."

"Hey, who gave you this pension? Surely not the Houthis— they're broke."

He answered, "I told you a couple of weeks ago that Hezbollah is giving us martyr's money." Then he shook his head and quickly exited.

When I spoke to Sheila later that day, she said, "Yeah, it'll be hard without you here, but the trip will be a good chance for you to reconnect with Jabbar, and I know that's important to you."

The following Wednesday, I met Jabbar at noon, me on my bike with my overnight supplies in the bike's panniers. I had been able to see several patients in the clinic that morning before leaving. I handed Jabbar my extra helmet.

"Why should I wear this?" he protested.

"For your safety!" I said emphatically, taking it out of his hand and slamming it down on his head.

"Maybe in America your life is worth saving," he said from beneath the helmet, which was on sideways, covering his right eye. He pushed the front of it up so he could see me better. "But here, we feel a fatal crash could be Allah's gift ... our ticket out of this bad dream."

"But Jabbar, all riders on my bike wear helmets. I devoted ten years doing brain surgery. Many of my patients were crash victims who would have been out having fun with friends rather than on our operating table if they just had worn a damn helmet."

He came with a red duffle, like the gym bag we carried in middle school with a flat cardboard bottom, arching up to two round loops at the top and a long brass zipper from end to end. He put his right arm through the black loop handle, carrying the bag like a backpack, and climbed onto the seat, his helmet still around his noggin.

I twisted around and secured the chin strap, which he had left dangling, as if I were his father. "There you go," I said. "Looks like you're ready for the Formula One circuit." Then I knocked on the front of his helmet with my knuckles. He didn't seem to be amused.

The roadway from Haydan to Huth was full of massive potholes—bomb craters, I was sure. Some were so big that the locals had built makeshift bridges across them from one side to the other. Military-wheeled vehicles and tanks, burned black and donning enormous shell holes with rusty edges, sat on the road's shoulders, pushed there to make room for the flowing traffic. On one shoulder was a crashed drone, Houthi, I assumed—Iranian import, of course—almost the size of a Cessna. As we passed the wreckages, I could tell that all removable recyclable parts had been stripped off, most likely exchanged for grain.

Between Sa'dah and Huth, settlements in mountainous areas were tall and lean and those along the valley floor, squat. In places, the Saudis had flattened only one building—in others, the entire village was a wasteland. For this trip, we would stay well within Houthi-controlled areas—unlike our fishing trip, which had taken us close to Saudi-backed government enclaves, making me nervous. On this trip, the highway culture—weaving, driving fast, and disregard for the law—was our greatest threat. Most of the other drivers—like Jabbar in his attitude to wearing a helmet—didn't really care if they lived or died and didn't seem to care whom they took to paradise with them.

Huth is a stunning town on a plain about one hundred kilometers northwest of Sana'a. Khaki adobe flat-roofed structures blanketed the city from the desert's rocky terrain on its east to the serrated cliffs on its southwest. Because it was on a plain, most of its buildings were only one and two stories, but on the southwest side near the bluff, a few rose to the more typical five or six stories.

Huth was lacking in color, blending into the dry-brown countryside except for the central mosque's large dome, which protruded from the otherwise desolate terrain. It looked like a giant pearl, mimicking the shape of the nearby domed mountain, Jabal Sadar, but in white rather than desert-brown. Huth resided clearly in Yemen's eastern desert, nothing between it and Saudi's Empty Quarter but sand, scorpions, and snakes.

As we pulled up to Jabbar's brother-in-law's street, I recognized his rather tall adobe wall topped with broken bottles acting as razor wire. A fortress. Inside the walls of the compound were an array of adobe buildings spreading out over two acres. An old rusty tractor sat in the back of the property along with a couple of wheelless wagons.

There were three flat-topped dwellings. Abdul's was the largest one, a two-story. The other two were one-story structures. A couple of old storage buildings sat along the wall, the roof caved in on one. It appeared to have been a working farm for generations, but

I couldn't imagine how they'd grown anything there because it was so dry. Maybe they had irrigated the land from a well or from the springs around Jabal Sadar. I counted three old olive trees and a few patches of brown grass, otherwise nothing but dirt.

In front of Abdul's house sat what I assumed was Jabbar's new truck, under an aqua-green pinstriped cover. As soon as I pulled up and turned my bike off, I saw Jabbar's attention migrate to the truck. He slowly removed his helmet and laid it on the bike's seat as I hooked mine to the handlebars. He began licking his lips like he was going to eat whatever was under the pinstripes. He sat his duffle down on the dusty ground and slowly walked toward the truck, a spring in his step. This was the happiest I had seen him in the two months since Alam's death. The sight brought a smile to my face.

I helped Jabbar remove the cover, revealing a clean vehicle underneath. The odometer read 120,000 kilometers, which I was certain couldn't be correct. It looked to me like a white 2004 or 2005 Toyota Tacoma with an extended cab. Fourteen years old, yet the truck was spotless, ready for the showroom, making me a little skeptical. These trucks were choice vehicles for soldiers and terrorists alike and got a lot of abuse.

Crawling around beneath the chassis for a look, the underside was as immaculate as the top. No fluid leaks. With scrapes, bullet holes, and a secret compartment under the fender— what stories that old truck could tell.

While I was going over the Toyota, Jabbar was sitting behind the steering wheel acting like he was driving it. The only thing missing was him making motor sounds with his lips. It was nice to see him acting like a kid.

Abdul came out his door with a stranger in tow. They marched toward us, kicking up small dust clouds from their heels.

"Welcome," said Abdul, stern-faced.

"Welcome to you too," both Jabbar and I responded in the typical Arabic greeting.

"Doctor Bryan," Abdul said, "I'm so glad you could bring my brother-in-law today. The road is too dangerous for the owners to drive the truck to Haydan."

"Where are the owners?" I asked.

Abdul hesitated. "Uh, well, they are businessmen in Sana'a who recover and refurbish used cars and trucks. They're good at it."

Did recover mean steal?

The stocky man behind him stepped forward. He sported a goatee and clothes that looked like they were from Walmart—shorts, which I had never seen a Yemeni man wear before, and a blue Nike T-shirt. He reached out his hand and smiled, saying in almost perfect American English, "Hello, I'm Rahman, but most English-speakers just call me Ray."

"Have we met?" I asked, tilting my head.

"No, not before today," he said.

I squinted. "You look very familiar, but I think it's because you resemble the Saudi reporter killed in Istanbul, but with more hair."

Nodding with a smile, he said, "Jamal Khashoggi? I worked with him on projects and knew him personally. To say I look like him, I take as a compliment," he said beaming.

"Okay, you're scaring me. You sound and look very American," I said.

Ray responded, "I'll also take that as a compliment. I got my doctorate from Georgetown and lived in the D.C. area for almost a decade. That's where I met Khashoggi, God bless his kind soul," he placed his hand over his heart. "My two kids were born in the States."

I looked past Ray and noted the scowl on Abdul's face and a blunt stare, and as always, his misbaḥah beads ratcheting through his fingers like a chain through a gear.

Nodding toward Abdul, I asked Ray, "Are you part of Jabbar's family?"

"I'm Abdul's cousin from Sana'a, but I live here for now."

"What brought you to Huth?" I asked.

"Well, it's a long story." He chuckled. "I was a professor at Sana'a University for four years. I taught history and political science. And while I'm Shia by family tradition, I received pressure from the Houthis when they took Sana'a. They thought I was teaching like I was a government sympathizer … which I'm certainly not. So, they had people in my classroom observing me. They staked out my house and followed my kids home from school. Creepy." He looked down and shook his head as if he'd just conjured up a bad memory. "So, we moved here to benefit from my cousin Abdul's hospitality."

We went inside the big house once we could pull Jabbar away from his new truck. I heard women and children in the main part of the house but didn't see them as we walked directly up stone stairs to a large room on the second floor. There we washed up in a basin with water from a pitcher poured by a young boy.

We sat on carpets. Several women, two introduced as wives of Abdul, arrived to attend to us. They served us a fabulous meal—a leg of lamb, with a tomato, cardamon, and onion sauce over rice. This was an enormous feast in a country steeped in famine.

"I thought Americans were about to go extinct in the Houthi-held territories, but I'm glad you're here," said Ray, who was sitting between Abdul and me. Jabbar and two other cousins were on the far side of the spread.

Abdul seemed to be listening closely to every word exchanged between Ray and me. Sitting on the other side of Ray, Abdul was leaning so far in my direction—his ear pointed at our mouths—that I thought he was going to fall over.

We continued eating, and then Ray leaned over and whispered in my ear, "I would like to talk to you in private before tonight is over."

Then, turning to the entire group, Ray said, "This war is in a stalemate. There's no end in sight."

Abdul grunted. With rice clinging to his beard, he exclaimed, "That's not true!" He spoke with such force I felt the spray of his spit from the other side of Ray and a kernel of rice landed on my shirt.

"We Houthis will kick the Saudis out of Yemen soon," he added, holding his finger in the air as if he were trying, like I do on my sailboat with a wet finger, to judge the direction of the wind.

The argument between Abdul and Ray disintegrated into rapid-fire Arabic and in such a low whisper it was hard for me to follow. It was a volley of rolling eyes, smirks, and more spit. For a moment, I was afraid fists were going to fly. But they eventually calmed into a cordial conversation.

Soon, more polite discussions took over the dinner table. By the time the remains of the feast lay before us, mostly bones and date pits, it was clear that Jabbar was buying the truck, so he didn't need to ride back with me. I wasn't sure where I was sleeping and always preferred my tent. I said to Jabbar, "Hey, I may go back tonight because Sheila needs my help in the morning. Sounds like you've made up your mind about the Toyota."

Ray hastily interjected, "My wife, Raziya—you can call her Rosie—well, she is expecting you to stay with us tonight. I was looking forward to discussing more things with you." His back toward the others, he winked.

"Well, I guess I could, but I need to get back as soon as I can. I suppose if I leave very early in the morning, I could get to the clinic by lunch tomorrow." I continued the debate internally.

Coffee was served as the conversation settled down to discussing Jabbar and his farming plans. Then we said goodnight. I followed Ray toward his house, a smaller single-story dwelling about a hundred feet from Abdul's front door.

Rosie served us each a cold Yemeni beer, which was a real treat. I found her to be a very sweet woman and sensed strength in her, in the way she looked at me, squared-up tall and bold in asking me questions about my life. She was a stocky woman, broad hips but not heavy. No one was heavy in a place where food was scarce.

She mentioned—almost in passing—that she had earned a degree in civil engineering from Howard University. She showed me the potential of the Yemeni woman, without the culturally imposed social restrictions. While her skin was a tone lighter than her husband's, her long flowing hair—like most of the Yemeni women—could not have been any blacker. Beside her dangling gold earrings in her pierced lobes, she had a piercing on her left nostril. I had seen rings in traditional women's noses, but Rosie had a single diamond stud. I quickly noticed a habitual mannerism with her, that she tilted her head to her right and pulled it back when she was surprised, as if to say, "Say what?" or "What the hell?"

The beer tasted good. I hadn't had one since the night of the school bus bombing. Sheila and I had consumed much of our inventory that night, and the security guards had finished off the rest a week later.

Ray and I sat cross-legged—facing one another—on the cool tiled floor of their front room. Leaning back on a chair, Ray sipped his beer and then studied the brown pint bottle's label in silence. Meanwhile, I studied him and the room, waiting for this secretive conversation to begin. The walls were whitewashed, lime stucco, sparsely covered with photos and a small tapestry. I'd had to duck through the doorways of the small house whose ceiling was quite low, maybe seven feet tops, with spiders commanding each of the corners, their webs dotted with mosquitoes.

His beer bottle's blue and green label was coming lose, and Ray flipped the edge back and forth with this fingernail making a sound that I found irritating at that late hour. I studied the family photos on the wall. One was of Rosie and Ray standing in front of the U.S. Capitol Building.

I was getting ready to ask him what he needed to talk about when, finally, he held his brown bottle in front of his face and grinned. "It's hard to imagine that this beer was brewed in government-controlled Aden, yet we drink it here in Houthi territory." He took a sip and stared at me. "You would think if they could find a way to sell beer across a war front, they could find a way to stop killing each other's children." A frown supplanted his grin.

I shook my head vigorously. "How do they pull it off, you know, selling their beer here?"

Ray took another sip, shrugged his shoulders, and leaned his head back against the chair. Looking up at the ceiling, he asked, "Bryan, what do you know of this war?"

I squinted at him and repeated, "What do I know of this war?"

He nodded.

Ray asked me to stay the night just so we could talk about this damn war?

"Uh, well, I mean it's just another civil war between Shiite and Sunni factions, isn't it?"

Ray took another sip of his beer. A soft smile returned to his goateed face as he swallowed, belched, and then winked at me. "Well, it is, yet it's also far more complicated than that. To tell the full story would be like trying to unravel a thousand-year-old Islamic carpet, thread by thread … then put it back together, blindfolded. But I will summarize.

"You'll find some Shiites on both sides and some Sunnis and a mixture of terrorist groups that work for and against both sides. But, yeah, for convenience's sake, you could define it as war where a Shiite tribe, the Houthis, centered in Sa'dah, are fighting the remnants of a Sunni government that collapsed around 2011. But then, the Iranians, who are of course Shiite, saw an opportunity to meddle by empowering a fellow Shiite group that just happens to live next door to their old rivals, Sunni Saudi Arabia. This provoked the Saudis to create a large coalition of Sunni countries, along with America and France, to attack the Houthis. They promised to restore the original Sunni government within six weeks, and that was over six years ago."

About that time, Rosie walked into the room with their two children—a bushy-haired boy and a girl with long dark hair tied with a green ribbon—both with eyes black as peat.

"Bryan," said Rosie, "I want you to meet our children before I put them to bed. This is Fadel, he's ten. And this is Zoelle, twelve."

The boy reached out his hand with confidence. I took it, and as we were shaking, he said in good English, "So glad to meet you."

"The girl then, in a manner highly unusual for a Yemeni, especially a girl, reached out her hand and, with equal confidence, said, "I'm Zoelle, but my English-speaking friends call me Zoey."

Their father was beaming as he opened his big hairy arms. Both rushed into that protective ring of strength, Zoey's head on one of his broad shoulders, Fadel's on the other. He kissed them on the tops of their heads, and suddenly they were gone, swept away by Rosie and her hardbound copy of *Harry Potter*, which she had promised to read to them.

Ray had a glimmer in his eyes, still staring at the door through which his family had just exited. He sipped his beer and then turned to look at me with a smirk. "What were we talking about?"

"The war," I said nodding my head.

"Of course. What else is there to talk about?" He chuckled.

Ray pointed his beer bottle at me. "I think you mentioned during dinner you were in the American Army, correct?"

"Yup," I said as I laid myself on the floor, hands behind my head as a pillow.

"Were you deployed to a conflict zone?"

I nodded. "Afghanistan."

"Did the Army teach you about Islamic sects?" he asked.

"Not much. But I studied Islam on my own. After the hijackers killed my father in the World Trade Center, I wanted to understand it better."

Ray frowned and his broad shoulders dropped. "Oh, my God, I'm so sorry about that. What a tragedy." His face twisted into a hard grimace. "Your dad, he actually died in the 9/11 disaster?"

"Yup." I didn't want to say more.

He paused, looking down at the floor as if to reorder his thoughts. He continued after a minute. "Well, this major division within Islam took place in the seventh century. It was then that the Shia believed the proper heir to Mohammed's rule was his cousin and son-in-law Ali. The Sunnis didn't accept that. These Shiites believe Mohammed handed down authority through a chain of imams—sort of like the Pope in the Catholic Church. Around these two traditions, there were hostilities between them from the start ... yet many long years of peace. However, today there are other cultural issues and powers that capitalize on those divisions."

With a grimace working its way back to his face, he added, "This war is even tied up in the 9/11 attack and America's response, but I won't wade into those waters at midnight, maybe another time."

I yawned and nodded.

Ray reached out, touched my arm, and looked into my eyes. "But Bryan, you do realize no one fights a war over theology. Not even Catholics and Protestants. Men fight wars over power, sex, and money. So, this proxy war between Shia Iran and Sunni Saudi, well, it's really about money, power, and sex. Power is addictive. Some men would burn down the world to own the ashes. People wrap these real motivations in theological, business, or patriotic language narratives as a cover. America does the same thing, with its 'war on terror' or 'fighting for freedom.' But these religious wars are like turds dipped in candy sprinkles."

Too bad I had just taken my last sip of my Seera and was still supine because my laughter made me choke on the beer. After wiping the liquid off my face with my hand, I said, "That sounds a little simplistic, but the image is vivid."

"I'm Shiite" he said placing his hand on his chest, "and my wife"—he winked—"and for heaven's sake don't mention this to Abdul—she's Sunni. As a matter of fact, her father was part of the Sunni government prior to the Shiite rebellion. He was a minister of agriculture. The Houthi bastards hung him ... making Rosie and her mother watch."

"That's horrible." I frowned.

Ray continued. "Her mother still sends us food about once a month. Even that leg of lamb"—he pointed toward Abdul's house—

"came from her. If Abdul knew he was eating lamb supplied by a Sunni, he would have had indigestion all night." He chuckled.

I leaned toward him. "But Ray, the nineteen hijackers on 9/11 clarified that they were on a religious jihad. Their religion wasn't just candy sprinkles. It was their real motivation, wasn't it? Doesn't Islam use violence to spread its faith?"

Ray laughed. "What reward did the hijackers expect? Huh, Bryan? My friend, they were told God would reward them with seventy-two virgins. All Islamic martyrs expect the same prize. And for what? I don't think their purpose was to have a Pampered Chef party."

Then he belly-laughed and slapped me on my shoe. "Sex! The Koran promises seventy-two virgins as eternal wives to every man who enters paradise, and martyrs enter paradise directly."

I nodded. "So the Muslims who killed my father did it for sex?"

"You Christians have done the same. Take the crusades. To recruit well-trained knights to fight for the church, the Pope declared the army's mission a 'Holy Pilgrimage,' and they guaranteed the participants Heaven. No, they didn't assure them seventy-two virgins. However, by default they had a 'get-out-of-hell-free' card allowing them to plunder, kill, and rape without consequences, even young virgins, girls … or boys. I suspect that was the true motivation for many of them."

"But that was a long time ago," I interjected. "Surely you're oversimplifying it."

"It was yesterday, Bryan." He sat up straight wearing a big smile.

"Huh?" I stared at him with squinted eyes.

"Don't even get me started about the Greeks and Persians. This whole damn dispute began in 492 BC when Persia invaded Greece. Greece became the Romans and then the Christian West while Persia converted to Islam but remained Persia, and in many respects that old conflict continues today. But, yes, it's that simple. Sure, there were major political factors for 9/11 that I haven't mentioned, but the mules of hate, those who carried out the atrocity, were focusing on the virgins and some axe to grind with the West."

It was getting late, and my head was spinning. Rosie returned to show me where I was sleeping, Ray followed me into the guest room, sat on the bed, and we shared a nightcap, alcohol in goat's milk. Ray had a very serious look on his face, like we weren't done with the story yet.

"You know, on a more personal level," Ray said, "I'm a little concerned about Jabbar."

"Jabbar?" I whispered.

"Of course, he's angry about them killing his son and, well, he should be. But my cousin Abdul is not a positive influence. Abdul is a devout man. Fanatical. His father was a local imam and Islamic teacher. Abdul has had contacts with shady characters over the years, including extremists. He set up this whole transaction with the so-called Hezbollah, to give Jabbar the cash for his son's martyrdom. Abdul said these men are from Lebanon, but they speak Arabic with a Saudi dialect. Abdul has never traveled and wouldn't know the difference. Maybe he doesn't care, but I don't think Jabbar is aware."

Rubbing my tired eyes, I asked, "If they're not with Hezbollah, then who are they?"

"I don't know. But some terrorist organizations have clustered around those who have anger toward their common enemies, such as those who have killed a family member. Victims' families are low-hanging fruit to these groups, good for grooming to take revenge. The mules of hate."

"Jabbar? Taking revenge? I can't imagine it. He's such a sweet man."

"I don't know Jabbar like you do. He married into our family just a few years ago. We didn't meet him until his move to Haydan. He seems like a nice man." He paused to finish his drink, which left a white mustache across his upper lip, then stood. "Do you remember what the people who knew the 9/11 hijackers said?"

I shook my head. Every time I heard the term "9/11," I felt a pain in my stomach.

Ray said, "I was just starting my studies at Georgetown in 2001 when that happened. I can still remember people on TV describing the terrorists as quiet, kind, and causing no trouble, until they made a massive mess." He walked halfway out the door, paused, and turned around. "If you leave before I awake, I hope you know I'm your friend. I'll keep my ear to the ground and let you know if I hear anything." I gave him my sat phone number. His cell phone could likely call out this close to Sana'a, but my cell service in Haydan was spotty, but he could always reach me by satellite.

I lay in the hard bed, black and red wool blanket pulled up to my chin. After fighting to stay awake to hear Ray out, now I had too much on my mind to sleep. I listened to a dog howling in the distance and heard loud irate voices floating through my window from somewhere out in the night.

I had lost my naivety after 9/11. Unlike Sheila who was innocent and credulous, I didn't trust anyone, not even this Ray.

CHAPTER FOURTEEN

I heard someone humming in Ray and Rosie's kitchen. Strolling into the little room, sleepy-eyed but hungry, I smelled breakfast. Rosie, wearing a red apron tied around her waist with a big bow in the back, was cooking over a single butagaz burner with the focus of an artist on a potter's wheel. She was slicing and throwing goat cheese, eggs, tomatoes, and orange slices into a work of art in the skillet. The aroma was penetrating every nook and cranny of the small kitchen as were her musical notes.

"Wow, is that for me?" I asked.

"Yes, Bryan," she said without taking her eyes off the omelet, "you're our guest of honor."

"Oh, I'm sorry if Ray didn't tell you, but I must leave now."

Rosie spun around. "But, Bryan, I have a marvelous breakfast for you, and I was just getting ready to set it on the table … and now you're telling me you're leaving? Food is not so easy to come by here, you know." She pointed the oily spatula at me. "Besides the food, we brought our cappuccino maker from Sana'a. We grind and use local beans. This is a Marriott breakfast in a place where some people eat dirt."

"I'm sorry I didn't tell you, but Dr. Emory needs me in the clinic, and I promised her I would be back by noon."

With her dark olive eyes piercing out from her squinted lids, she said, "I'll make you a sandwich from the eggs and goat cheese and roll it up in pita bread so you can take it with you."

"That sounds fabulous. And somehow I'll chug that coffee before I take off," I said, flashing her a grin.

She whirled back around and continued cooking and humming.

A few minutes later, Rosie was waving as I left the compound, eating my sandwich as I navigated the bike to the street with one hand. Ray soon joined her, still in his pajamas, mug of coffee in his hand, the other throwing me a wave.

I left Huth with dawn's break. There was a red hue injecting into the sleepy sky over my right shoulder from beyond the desert's eastern horizon. A dust storm was blowing in from Saudi Arabia's Rub' al Khali. The new sun was setting it on fire with its early illumination. I bound my keffiyeh around my face to cover my nose and mouth, as the edges of the dust storm were already advancing around me like a chocolate fog. Alone, I opened the throttle through the lawless roads, hoping to outrun the dust cloud and be at the clinic before noon.

I ran by a roadblock at full speed, cutting through a piece of the desert, bypassing a group of men with dented cars parked perpendicular across the road. *Bandits?* In my mirror, my eye caught the Houthi flag on one car's antenna, which had words proclaiming death to America and the Jews. Oddly, those hateful words told me that it was a Houthi check point, and was safer than bandits, who would have chased me down and killed me for any valuables.

I made my way along dusty roads, through the flat plains and into the hill country approaching Sa'dah. There the streets were congested, as always. I drove beneath the twisted old olive trees whose limbs had held Alam's entrails just as his soul had ascended. Now, the bombing was just a burnt mark on the pavement and piles of stones and contorted metal from the store.

Turning onto the mountain road, I arrived back at Haydan at 11:15 A.M. The storm had not reached our oasis yet, and the air was as clear as crystal on the mountain.

When I came through the clinic door, it melted my heart to see Sheila's face beaming. When she hugged me, I felt the warmth of her body penetrate my dirty clothes. The aura of her fragrance surrounded me. Releasing the hug required a focused restraint, my grimy hands slowly dropping from her sides.

"I had to leave the clinic for an emergency cesarean section and now I'm two hours behind," she reported. "I'm so glad you're here." She wrinkled her nose at me and turned back to her patients.

As the aroma of her strawberry hair faded from my senses, I went out to grab a crumpled but clean shirt from my duffle inside my tent. On the way back, I looked through the gate and into the garden and noticed a large crowd of people in line to enter the clinic. I groaned, hiding them from my eyes with my hand, as if that would make them go away.

Mazen shifted into high speed, putting two patients in the same room, filling the entire clinic with double the typical occupancy. It was a fruitful day, and we had seen over a hundred patients once again by the time five P.M. rolled around.

I watched from the compound as Jabbar arrived later that evening with his shimmering white Toyota pickup to parade proudly past our gate at a snail's pace. The truck had gathered a lot of dust on the way home, and the only clear place on his dirty windshield were the two fan-shaped patterns in the film left by his wipers. Through that clearing I could see his glowing face.

I jogged past the orchard and mill, up the hill to his house. By the time I arrived, he was showing off the truck to his jealous neighbors.

"I'm glad you're back," I shouted, breathlessly. "I was sure last night that you were buying the truck and hoped you hadn't changed your mind this morning."

"I noticed your bike was gone when I woke up," he said. "Yeah, I had agreed to buy the truck before going to bed. But I wanted you to take me on a test drive today and you weren't there."

"I'm sorry, Jabbar. We can do it now," I said with a grin.

"I think I just did a test drive from Huth." Frowning, he added, "I did smell oil a few times."

"I'll take a look at it tomorrow when there's more light."

I glanced up at the sky, which was growing browner by the minute. The dust storm I had outrun appeared to have followed Jabbar home from Huth like a stray dog.

Jabbar was a kid again with his new truck. He washed it several times a week and was soon driving down the Sa'dah road with the bed loaded with crops to sell. Our relationship seemed to be getting back to normal, though he was more subdued than before. He was getting his traveling market off the ground, visiting several villages within a one-hundred-kilometer radius, Huth his most profitable.

Life at the clinic was also returning to normal, even a bit easier as cholera had taken a respite. Sheila and I were becoming closer, she drawing my heart like Jupiter draws her moons. It was her refreshing innocence about life, seeing the good in everything.

With November, the air shifted into a cooler mood. While the sun was hot during midday, early mornings and evenings were pleasant. I started joining Sheila in the garden rather than going alone to the commons for my dinner. I treasured each minute of our time together, knowing that soon we would be separated by half the earth. We each enjoyed the other's company more than any novel from the book box. I discovered more about her life, her loves, her losses. She was able to pull feelings out of my protective heart, especially the griefs left unattended for years.

But I felt her slipping away, like one of my sail lines through my wet hands. In four months, she would be gone from Yemen. How could I live without her? I couldn't. The country would turn for the worse.

Early one morning, the rising sun lit up my tent like a hot-air balloon lifting off in the small hours of Albuquerque's morn. Mountain wafts were causing my rain fly to flop, sending wrinkled waves across the big IRC letters imprinted on top. The sunlight was flickering, more than just the tent's nylon casting shadows. The sun itself seeming to twinkle as a nearby star.

I pulled my phone from beneath my pillow to check the time. It read in big digital numbers 2:20 A.M. *How can this be? It's daylight.*

I sat up in my sleeping bag. *Was the moon this brilliant, this orange? This vacillating? Is this a dream?* Before my brain had formed that thought, I heard glass shatter—it was loud—right beside the tent. I unzipped the tent's semicircular door in a hurry and looked outside. Translucent orange flames were engulfing the entire clinic, black billowing smoke rolling upward and melting into the ebony of the night.

"Oh, my God!" I screamed as I bolted from my tent, wearing only boxers, tripping on the zippered edge of the tent's door, and falling on my face. I jumped up. "Oh, God, no!"

Sprays of sparks were flying high into the nocturnal sky, one wave after the other, like fireflies escaping in swarms.

I sprinted toward the clinic, shrieking, "Sheila! Sheila!" The commons window right beside me exploded outward, and a massive ball of orange flames rolled out the window and up over the metal roof, casting a wave of unbearable heat over me.

"God, help me! Oh, my God, help me!"

I reached for the door. The radiant heat was unbearable, yet I clutched the metal knob. The skin of my fingers sizzled like meat on a hot grill, but I turned the knob, pushed the door open, and was met by a suffocating inferno.

"Sheila! Sheila! Oh, my God, Sheila!"

The firestorm filled the structure, and black smoke was pouring out of every broken window. I knew I couldn't enter the building and survive. For Sheila to be alive, she would've fled through the front door and into the garden.

I ran around the building's encompassing flames and pushed through the wrought-iron gate into that front garden screaming, "Sheila! Sheila!"

In response I heard only flames cracking in the air and glass breaking in windows.

"Someone, help me!" I screamed in English and Arabic, hoping to get the attention of someone in this village that never fully slept. But no one came.

I spun around and ran toward the water spigot, stumbling in the dark, hitting the ground hard, bloodying my nose. I jumped up and ran, grabbing the hose Ahmed used to water the trees and turned it on. It still worked, and I sprayed the water on the clinic's door, trying to cool it to the point I could open it and go inside. I continued screaming Sheila's name.

I sprayed the water on the door and reached for the knob. It burned my already-scalded hand. "Damnit!" I pointed the hose at the door again and then kicked it. It loosened and I kicked it again. The burnt door popped open. I stepped into the fire, my arms in front of my face.

From within the darkness behind me, a hand grabbed my left shoulder. I twisted around. "Sheila?"

It was Ahmed, who lived just across the street. He stood wearing his futah, a T-shirt, no shoes, and a dismayed look. He reached for the hose. I handed it to him, hoping to make a run into the building.

As soon as I entered the door, the heat engulfed me. The flames singed my hair and smoke filled my lungs setting them on fire. I coughed hard, giving no opportunity for fresh air to reenter my airway. Dropping to my hands and knees did not help. I felt dizzy, but knew I was the only one who could save Sheila. I crawled in the dirt and ashes, trying to enter again, but Ahmed yanked me from the doorway.

"No!" he screamed, as he dragged me away from the door.

I stood and took a swing at him. "Leave me alone, damnit!"

He kicked me to the ground, sprayed me with water, and returned to spray water on the building.

I lay on the ground in a full panic. I was drowning in smoke and suffocating within the fading hope. Copious tears began pouring down my face. I tried to wipe them away with a blackened hand. I stood.

"Sheila! Sheila!" I ran toward the door again, but Ahmed tackled me and held me firm to the ground.

Over the next half hour, other men arrived to help combat the fire, but it was hopeless. The entire structure collapsed and fell as the flames engulfed the roof and supporting timbers. The metal roof warped and melted from the intense heat. Electrical sparks flew as wiring burned. There was an explosion, and a blue fire rolled up through the orange as the kitchen's butagaz tank blew.

Grabbing everyone I could see, I asked, "Have you seen Sheila?" The crowd continued to grow, and I looked at each surly face in the dark. "Has anyone seen Dr. Emory?"

A hand grabbed my flailing arm. It was Mazen with panic sewn deeply into his face. "Bryan, Dr. Emory must be inside. I'm sorry, but the truck is here … uh, Ahmed saw her go to her quarters. She's nowhere outside. I'm so sorry … bro … but there's no way she could have endured the fire." He was simply stating the obvious, what my mind could not even begin to comprehend.

I now understood the man at the school bus bombing who was punching the air, fighting the imaginary bees of sorrow. I swung my arms through the smoking air, punching, crying, and screaming with what was left of my voice, "Oh, no. Oh, no! Why, my God, why?"

I crumpled to the earth, my legs like ropes of silk, my face hard on the muddy ground, awash by water from the hose, thickened with the fire's ashes. I wanted the ground to swallow me whole, to rescue me from this horrible, fucked up world. I gritted my teeth until I thought they would break. I cinched fistfuls of dirt and then pounded those fists against my chest and rubbed the dirt across my face and my opened mouth.

"God, no! It can't be. Please, God, no!"

I lay in the mud, thrashing and fighting against the moment's certainty. I screamed as loud as my remnants of vocal cords would allow. "God, no! God damnit! No, no, no! Please, God, please, God."

I fell over as dead, my face lying in the mud, mumbling, "Sheila, how I love you. You can't die! I'll save you!"

I felt the heat from the fire on my back, almost soothing, yet tormenting. I raised my head and tried to get up on my knees, but Mazen kneeling beside me pushed me back down.

I looked at him. "Let me up, damnit!"

Mazen's tormented face aglow by the fire's light, dirty tears streaming down and dripping off his chin, shook his head and whispered, "Lay still, bro ... She's gone. Nothing we can do now."

We embraced and both sobbed uncontrollably. It was a boundless anguish concentrated within a finite moment. Not even when I found out about my father dying in the south tower had I felt this much agony.

It wasn't long before the slothful sun emerged from behind the hills, as if it had been hiding in shame, casting a diagonal light through the smoky shadows upon our calamitous ruin and onto the villagers' sullen faces, groups of dozens who had come in support, or at least out of curiosity. Maybe someone came to see if their evil attack was successful. That person, I wanted tied and bound for hell.

I was hoping that somewhere in that crowd Sheila's face would finally appear. That somehow, we had overlooked her. Maybe she had not heard me call her name a thousand times before the dawn. I hoped she had gone back to Michel and was with him, even in his bed, in his loving arms. But disappointment hung in the air like a foul syrup. Sadness penetrated the entire village. Everyone knew Dr. Emory. Everyone loved her, me more than all the rest combined. The God-awful insanity of it all. My heart was broken into a million tiny pieces, the fragments scattered across the empty cosmos. I stared into my blackened hands, bare, save large confluent blisters covering the palms, otherwise completely empty.

My Sheila was forever, gone.

CHAPTER FIFTEEN

Arooster was crowing in the hills above the Haydan oasis, embracing another new day, the second day after the fire. But this day was unwelcome. The previous day—just a blur. I was emerging from shock into a more imperfect world, a fool's paradise.

We sprayed water on smoldering cinders between bouts of sobbing, searching, yelling, and brief moments of sleep. The morning call to prayer reverberated between the half dozen minarets scattered around Haydan, then echoed off the mountains' hard faces. From those prayer towers—standing like rockets of stone—blasted voices from electronic speakers insisting, "God is great and there is no God but God." A pathetic assertion on this morning.

Heat waves spread outward from the smoldering pit. What had been our clinic was now just fragments. It had spent its ninth life. It would be no more. Hundreds if not thousands would die from its absence.

I wanted to look for Sheila's remains, but after twenty-four hours the still-burning flames and immense heat thwarted me. I sat in the dirt facing the ruins just outside the corona of unbearable heat, my elbows resting on my knees in front of me, my face pointing down between my legs to the earth. I inched forward with every drop of a degree. It was a hard soil packed by the steps of ten thousand souls who had sought care at the old hospital over the decades.

I blew my nose, filled with the vestige of spent tears and suspended soot. The mucus flew to the hard ground as chunks of black gel. I could not restrain my head from shaking back and forth. Mazen brought me water. Later, someone brought me two hard-boiled eggs and a bottle of tea. I drank the tea to soften my crusty throat, but I could not think about eating.

Mazen asked me, "Have you spoken to Sana'a yet?"

I shook my head. Calling Sana'a had not crossed my mind. The need to phone Sheila's parents took precedence.

Around me, somehow, the world continued, people walking by, going about their business as if anything still mattered. *How dare they?* Inside me, everything had ended. The apocalypse had arrived. If I had the arm of Atlas, I would have slung invitations across the Milky Way, petitioning any rocky body to come and crash into earth, giving us yet another great extinction. To at the very least eradicate the human species. We had failed to hit the mark, to find a way to live in peace. A hopeless species.

I rarely looked up, but when I did, I noticed the walkers going quiet as they passed our clinic, their gaze pulled down into their steps except for occasional quick glances at our disaster and subtle signs of commiseration.

The sat phone had been destroyed with the building, but I still had my cell phone if the tower was functioning. I didn't know the IRC headquarters phone number by heart, but Mazen said he had it at his apartment. He went back to retrieve it.

With Mazen gone, despondency overwhelmed me with an asphyxiating presence. When I did manage a breath, the awful smell in the air was reminiscent of the school bus bombing—burned wood, plastic, and hair. Sheila's wool blanket? The golden locks of her lovely mane?

My screams of agony mellowed into sincere prayers. "God, please don't let this be true. Wake me up from this nightmare to Sheila's morning smile. Make it just another dream. I'll love her better this time."

I stared into the smoking ashes with bated breath, waiting for the chance to find Sheila's remains—if there were any. Each hour the temperature dropped a degree or two. A foot closer to her space.

What caused this? A bomb? An accidental fire? An attack? Before the light of the fire had awakened me that previous morning, I'd heard nothing. No footsteps. No explosion. No falling bomb's whistle, a sound I'd become familiar with in Afghanistan.

Mazen returned with the phone number. I went to my tent and pulled my cell phone from where I had dropped it, just outside the door, when I saw the fire. Ashes covered it like an early winter's dusting of snow. Wiping off the screen, I dialed the number. Long tones sprang from my phone's speaker, and then the operator answered in Arabic. I spoke in English because I didn't have the energy to conjugate Arabic verbs to create comprehensible sentences.

"I need to speak with Dorothy. This is Bryan … uh, Bryan Rogers in Haydan."

"I'm sorry, but she's in a meeting. Can I take a message?"

"No, you cannot take a damn message! I must speak with her immediately! This is an emergency. The Haydan clinic has burned down."

I heard, "Oh, no" in a whispered breath, then music. Chopin.

I waited on the phone for five minutes.

Finally, I heard Dorothy's calm voice, "Oh, my, Bryan. What happened? Is everyone okay?"

"Hell, no, everyone's not okay! Sheila is gone. She's missing. She must be in the rubble. Dorothy … I'm sure she's dead!" It was the first time I had used that word for Sheila.

"Are you serious? Oh, no. This is horrible! Was it a Saudi bomb?"

"We don't know. It went up in flames."

"When? This morning?"

"No, night before last, but no one heard jets or bombs. What the hell's wrong with this place?" I began sobbing again. "Who would do this? Why so much slaughter, suffering, and hate in this fucking world?"

"Bryan, why did you wait so long to call?"

"I don't know. I don't remember yesterday."

"I'll be out with Mohammed and our security detail as quickly as we can. Touch nothing, as the UN will need to do a careful forensic investigation. It'll take us two hours to get everything together and a pilot."

For the next, almost three hours, I sat in the dirt and watched the smoke and steam rise from the burned stones, melted plastic, and twisted steel. Mazen would sit with me, leave, and return. When they have a choice, men in Yemen cry in private. But I had no choice. My tears came as public as my face, my name, or my clothes. I was the local circus freak show. *Come watch the distraught American sitting in the dirt. Has he become like one of us?* Those were the imagined thoughts I put into the minds of the children who came, stood, and gawked in their dirty clothes and bare feet.

Could Sheila still be alive in the clinic's debris? The heat was intense. It was more likely someone could survive walking on the sun.

Hours later, I heard the distant rhythm of chopper blades. Moments later, I saw a clumsy Mi-17, a Soviet-made helicopter, coming over the mountains. It soon landed in what was the clinic's garden, blowing dust and ash in all directions, whipping up the still-smoldering flames and blinding me for a moment.

I walked in the helicopter's direction only to see Ahmed there already. Dorothy and the security team climbed out the sliding door, heads bent to duck the wind from the blades. Two men stayed back and unloaded bulky duffle bags, lining them up in rows on the sand like beached walruses.

Dorothy gave me a big hug, and I cried once more.

She yelled in my ear over the loud spinning blades, "We have an investigation team from the UN coming later in trucks. I wanted to make sure you're okay and assess things myself. I must fly back with the chopper to work on this from the office. Once we retrieve Sheila's body, we'll take it back to Sana'a by truck to get a positive identification using DNA, and then we'll fly it back to Nebraska."

Through my sniffles, I asked, "Can I be the one to call her folks when we have the ID?"

"Sure, Bryan. The DNA sample is simply a legal formality. I have her parents' number."

I could have called them then, but I put it off until I saw her with my own eyes.

The UN team arrived in four hours along with a Houthi representative. I was sure the reason was that the Houthis didn't want to be blamed for something they didn't do. I watched the UN team methodically go over the site. They sprayed it with more water to cool it down further. They looked for evidence around the perimeter wall, then worked on the pit's cooler edges, with a videographer recording everything. They had test strips checking for accelerants, an arson's chemical fingerprint. One of the men shouted, "Benzene!" This meant the fire was intentional, which we had already assumed.

As things cooled, I made my way to Sheila's quarters. It was just a muddy black mess—burned stones in piles, ashes, and twisted metal roofing. Everything was wet and sticky. I worked with two men to pull the corrugated metal roofing back, bracing myself for the sight of her body under each sheet that we handled. Sheila's bed was just a twisted stack of burnt metal in the corner, like an abstract sculpture. My thoughts fell back to that wonderful morning, waking up in that bed with Sheila beside me. It was the best morning of my life—never to be eclipsed. Was that the reason I was born into this murky world, for that one night? Then it was worth it. But that bed wasn't recognizable anymore. I stared at the surrounding ashes, thinking that Sheila was somewhere there. Maybe a single bone had survived?

Then my gaze moved to the wall as workers lifted another panel of roofing. Just beneath the panel below her window was an elongated black figure looking like something I'd seen in photos from Pompei. A body burned and disfigured, almost shapeless. Sheila. My God, it had to be. She was apparently trying to crawl out her window when she collapsed and died. Oh, what horrors she must have faced at the end, all alone. Was she screaming? Why didn't I hear her?

I walked through the burnt rubble to that figure. I stirred the ashes with my finger and saw the charred bone of her skull. Tears began dripping from the tip of my nose onto the black slag like a faucet. I wanted to pick her up, embrace and protect her. Too damn late.

One of the investigators, wearing a reflective vest over a blue jumpsuit, his long auburn hair tied in a manbun, returned from dragging away the roofing panel. Placing his hand on my shoulder, he said in an Eastern European accent, "You need to back away. This is a crime scene." Gently, he added, "I promise we will be respectful and take good care of her."

I took a couple of steps back and watched their every move. Photos, samples, and then more photos were taken, before they put her remains into a black plastic bag and zipped it up. I screamed, "Let her breathe!" The guy in the jumpsuit indulged me by unzipping the bag a couple of inches.

I sat on the edge of the ashes for the next few hours as the team scoured the ruins. Sometime during my despondent vigil, two more trucks arrived. I looked up and saw the lumpy duffels in a row again, the gear all repacked. Between two of the beached walruses now back in queue, looking out of place, lay the body bag.

I stood and walked toward the trucks and stooped beside Sheila. I studied the bag she was in. I reached out softly with my hand and touched the inanimate material. It was warm, the black plastic heated by the late-day's sun. It felt like her. I laid down beside her, my long body parallel to hers. I could feel the shape of where her head tapered to her shoulders. I put my arm around her warm soul. The stiff plastic crackled with the weight of my hand. I whispered, "My love, I'm so sorry. I'm sorry I didn't hear you, that I didn't come. Please forgive me and know that I love you ... more than you could ever imagine."

A hand suddenly grabbed my shoulder, and I looked up. Through the world blurred by my tears, I saw the kind man in the blue jumpsuit.

"I'm sorry, but it's time for us to go," he said in a whisper.

I wiped the tears from my eyes and smeared them across the impermeable bag with my fingers. I wrote in Arabic script, using my tears for ink, just as I had with coffee cup rings in the commons a few weeks earlier, "Sheila, the love of my life." Clear ink upon black, invisible, except for the glistening in the tangential sun. I sat up and looked around me. All the walruses had been loaded into the trucks, save the one bag beside me. I stood, and the men respectfully lifted Sheila and loaded her into the covered bed.

I had not seen Mazen in the crowd, but he walked over and laid a bouquet of orange blossoms on the bag. I stood beside him, tears pouring down our faces. We embraced.

The truck started its diesel engine with a rumble, and a cloud of black sooty smoke poured from its stack. I kissed my fingers, patted the bag with them, and said, "Goodbye, Sheila, my love. I'll join you in Sana'a." The trucks pulled away and out of the gate of our compound. If not for Mazen holding me upright, I would have collapsed to the ground.

Rows of well-wishers stood on each side of Haydan's narrow street, hands over their hearts, tears over their eyes. The people said goodbye to a great doctor. She would be missed. Now, without Sheila, every child in the village faced a greater peril. If the arsonist was in the line of people, I hoped to God that he realized what an awful thing he had done. And that he would die a slow and miserable death from a disease Sheila could have easily treated.

We had enough circumstantial evidence that the body was hers, including a gold necklace engraved with her parents' names, which she always wore. I remembered it dangling across my face the night we made love. What a foolish plan we had made. If we had only known how short our time was, we would have allowed our passion to flourish. While noble, it was stupid of us.

I called her parents. I was surprised they knew who I was, Sheila's colleague, and love interest. I could also tell from her mother's cheerful voice that she was expecting good news—maybe Sheila was on her way home or I was calling to ask for her hand in marriage, if that was something Nebraskan boyfriends still did. But then, about the time her father joined the call, my tears broke through. Viscous from dehydration, they dripped from my chin like crystalline drops of oil. Her parents knew it couldn't be good news.

As I told them, they had the same question my heart still carried. "Why in God's name?" asked her mother, barely able to talk. "Oh, dear Jesus, no, no, no!"

"Was it a bombing?" her dad asked without emotion.

"How did she die?" her mother asked, her voice showered in tears. "Did she suffer?"

"It wasn't from a bomb dropped from the air. We didn't hear planes, and the investigators didn't find evidence of a blast. There was, however, petrol inside the clinic, a sign the fire was intentional. But who? Why? I don't know. No damn clue."

I slowly hung up the phone when her mother was crying so loudly that we could no longer talk. Her father—sadly—self-controlled.

Dorothy told me she had received a call from Sana'a that IRGC-QF, a terrorist group with ties to the Iranian Revolutionary Guard, posted online that they handled the "attack on the American imperialist clinic in Haydan in retribution for bombing the children."

I sat in my tent, sobbing uncontrollably. Somehow, I found my head lying on Mazen's lap. Mazen, the man-child, acted as the consoling mother to me, wiping the tears off my face with his keffiyeh. He bore the brunt of my sharp words. "I don't want to live anymore. I hate this fucking world! I just want to go home and die. I'll never love anyone like I did her. I'm so tired of pain!"

He left me late with three pita bread circles, cucumbers slices, tomatoes, and a water bottle. I ate most of it and went to bed but was too full of sorrow to sleep.

I thought of a poem I'd read at Dad's funeral that was given to me by an aunt. The words had passed right through me then, as I was only sixteen and numb to the world. The words finally caught up to me on this hollow night, at least those I could remember. Nothing could have framed the mood better than the last stanza of a W. H. Auden poem.

The stars are not wanted now; put out every one,
Pack up the moon and dismantle the sun,
Pour away the ocean and sweep up the wood;
For nothing now can ever come to any good.

The next morning, Mazen returned early with the shameful sun peeking over the hills as if waiting to see if it was safe to come out. The same sun that was supposed to bring us new, refreshing days and hope, had failed miserably. I was sitting beside my tent, arms around my knees, staring up into the mountains, heaviness in my presence.

"You look like shit! Did you eat?" asked Mazen.

"Yeah, I ate the things you left me. Thanks for that. But I didn't sleep. I climbed out of my tent only because I had to pee."

"Yemen has no time for self-pity ... none. You're now one of us!"

"But Mazen, they hate me. Why am I even here?" I mumbled with my raspy voice.

"That's right, damnit, they do," he shouted. "And they love you. They hate America too, but you know, not one would pass on becoming an American citizen."

I replied, "I just feel so damn sad, like the leaves of my life have been collated into the pages of a never-ending tale of horror, leaving me wishing I had never been born."

"Join the rest of us! Everyone in this goddamn country has lost someone they love ... every fucking soul!" he shouted. Then, in a softer tone, he added, "Don't do anything stupid before I get back ... you hear me?"

I nodded.

CHAPTER SIXTEEN

Dorothy, in her graciousness, allowed me to accompany Sheila's remains to Lincoln. It was a tortuous flight in many ways. The course took us to Geneva, Ramstein Air Base, Dover and finally Nebraska. My grief exhaustion kept me awake for the 48-hour journey with my lost sleep finally catching me somewhere over West Virginia's fog-filled valleys. Arriving at Lincoln Municipal Airport, the flag-draped coffin was received by the Denton Funeral Home's director, a nice man with a baritone voice emitting from a breath mint–suffused mouth. He wore a shiny sapphire-blue three-piece suit. Silk, I assume. I'd thought funeral directors always wore black.

I rode with him to the funeral home where I met Sheila's parents. I studied them getting out of their Ford Fiesta, me standing beside the casket in the chapel. They walked—four feet apart—up the steps of the funeral home, no words exchanged. No hand holding, not even a touch between them. They entered the vestibule from outside. I sobbed. I walked toward them, us three standing, bathed in this odd array of colors coming from plastic imitation stained-glass windows across the front wall of that space. On the floor, the prism of colors was overcome by the aquamarine of the worn carpet.

Sheila's dad was tall and lean, sporting a white head of thick hair, no tears, no emotions—as if his face was poured bronze. Her mother reminded me so much of Sheila—blond hair mixed with gray in tightly wound curls she had tied in a bun. I had hoped to have seen Sheila at that age. I could have loved her so much better than her father loved her mother. The woman stared at me with her pale turquoise eyes. Those were Sheila's eyes. Sheila's gaze. I had to look away. I couldn't bear it.

I should have planned on staying a few days for the funeral. But her family didn't know me. I would be this strange man, babbling like a fool, all through the service. That, and the fact that since losing Dad, funerals gave me great anxiety, I scheduled a quick turnaround—my flight to New York was in only three hours.

I arrived at JFK at nine P.M. and was picked up by my sister Angie. It was so nice to see her sweet smile and take full advantage of her listening ear. She took me to her Soho apartment where she lived with Joel. I'd missed her as I did all my family. She was so easy to talk to. I wouldn't trade an hour with her for twelve on the therapist's couch. Her love for me was unconditional. I talked with her for hours about Sheila and about my concerns about Jabbar.

The next morning, my two brothers joined us for coffee and bagels, which we had picked up on our way to JFK. Hank had a new job, in webpage design. Wayne was thinking about going back to school, just couldn't decide on a career. We had all become messed up in our own ways after losing Dad. They were older than me and had lost him at a crucial time, when they were just getting ready to leave the nest. They had seemed directionless since.

Wayne asked, "Aren't you going to see Mom?"

"No. It would be hard for her."

He knew what I was talking about. Mom had a nervous breakdown after 9/11. She was fragile. Medications sandbagged the intrusive anxiety—barely.

Arriving back in Yemen, I felt like a tumultuous wind of confusion had sucked up my world, leaving only hopelessness. I believed my life would not have any more good days. Lingering clouds suspending the clinic's future didn't help. Dorothy had ordered me back to Sana'a for my safety. I told her I couldn't do it. I would wait in Haydan until we had a plan. She said she would let me know what the arrangement was as soon as they figured it out, but her incoming call never came. I didn't blame her for ghosting me, as I was sure she was busy and had no news. I figured it would be almost impossible to find a recruit for Sheila's position, especially after the clinic fire was on the major news outlets across the globe. I was also sure that our clinic's presence in such a dangerous place was under scrutiny by IRC, the UN, and the Houthis' caretaker regime in Sana'a. Everyone had a stake. But those who needed the clinic the most—Haydan's residents and me—had no voice.

For the first few nights, I camped in my tent at the compound. The perimeter wall was mostly intact. The burned building's smell was nauseating, although not that different from the usual smoke smell that perpetually hung in the valley. But this new stench carried with it a sting.

Mazen took a temporary leave to stay with relatives in Sana'a. He told me his mother had called from Stockholm and said, "I'm worried about you. Try to put as much distance as you can between you and the American."

Ahmed came around now and then. He acted like he was going to clean up the site but never started. A daunting task and no guarantee of pay.

To my surprise, the inhabitants of Haydan came—all of them. It must have been planned as there was a steady stream of people, two or three families at a time. They brought funeral gifts for Sheila, although there was no funeral in Haydan for her. These gifts, mostly food items from a starving population and a few crafts, created a huge heap. I had no shelter for the treasures besides my humble tent, and it did rain once. But their greatest gifts to me were their words. Deep sorrows were expressed, accented by ample tears. "We loved her," I heard over and over. They told stories of how Sheila had saved their child or themselves.

Time and time again, they voiced to me that whoever burned the clinic was not from Haydan. One man said that about the time the fire broke out, someone saw a man on a motorcycle with a jerry can racing out of the village and down the mountain road. They were sure he was paid by the Iranians. Even the protestors, several weeks before, were strangers to Haydan, likely paid by the same group.

The one face that did not show was Jabbar's. But Mona visited, bringing me oranges from their orchard.

I looked for Jabbar at his house several times. Mona said he was staying in Huth, selling their fruits and grains in the area. It baffled me that he never came by to see me after the fire. With his strange absence, I started to wonder if Jabbar knew who did it.

Three weeks after returning from Nebraska, I decided to ride my bike to Huth, to Abdul's compound, to find Jabbar and see Ray and Rosie. The waiting alone, with nothing to do, was about to drive me mad. I was still on IRC's payroll. They made sure I was supplied with food, Ahmed cooking at his house across the street and bringing me one meal per day. Dorothy, thinking ahead, had brought a duffle of MREs when she flew in by chopper the day after the fire.

Early the next morning, I put enough things into my bike's storage compartment that I could spend the night if I chose to. I got a call from Dorothy just before I pulled out.

"Bryan, you know we're looking for Sheila's replacement and for the funding to rebuild the clinic." A guarded smile swept my face.

"Well, any leads?" I mumbled.

"Not yet. We've submitted a proposal to New York," she said. "Time will tell where this goes. IRC has a lot of projects right now and a limited budget."

As I arrived in Huth, I saw Abdul walking on the street, a block from his house. I stopped and removed my helmet to speak to him.

"Jabbar was here, but he went home. You must have passed him," he said with a frown.

"No, I didn't see him. I would recognize that truck for sure."

Then Abdul said something odd. "I'm sorry about the fire at your clinic and the doctor's death. However, Americans shouldn't be here."

"If Sheila and I weren't here," I said, "who else would have cared for Haydan's families? How many children would have died if we hadn't been there?"

He twirled his amber prayer beads between his fingers and looked sternly at me, a khat wad between his brown teeth. "Think of all the children who would be alive if you Americans were not helping the Saudis slaughter them!"

Then, out of nowhere, words came flying out of my mouth. "Abdul ... uh, speaking of slaughter, I bet you know who burned down our clinic. Do you?"

Abdul's fisted arms grew tight to his side, like he was a gymnast pushing himself up on parallel bars. "Why would you ask me a question like this?" He gnashed his teeth so hard the khat juice leaked between them, onto his lip, and ran down his chin. He wiped it off with the back of his hand.

"Do you?" I asked.

"No ... I don't know who burned down your clinic! Many people would rejoice with it. Asking questions like that could get you killed."

I started putting my helmet back on. "Is Ray home?"

"Yes, Rahman is home. His Muslim name is Rahman."

CHAPTER SEVENTEEN

Riding my bike to the compound, I turned into the open gate. I pulled up in front of Ray's house, removed my helmet, and set it on the seat. I walked to the door and knocked. Rosie would have typically answered the door, but when it sprang open, Ray's friendly face appeared. On this slightly cooler day, he wasn't wearing his plaid shorts but looked just as American in his Levi jeans and white button-up long-sleeve shirt. He gave me a big hug and kissed me on the cheek.

"Bryan, I'm so glad you're here! I'm sorry about your clinic and your colleague who died. Jabbar told me about that. It's just horrible."

"He did?" I asked.

"Yes, he seemed angry that someone had done that."

"Good to know," I said. "Since I haven't heard a peep out of him."

"Hmm … that's odd." He paused to think before adding, "I was afraid I would never see you again. What's happening with the clinic?" Then he motioned for me to follow him inside. We entered the greeting room of the house, the equivalent of a Western living room. It was a small space with simple furniture.

I felt a knot forming in my throat and quickly spoke through it. "Well, no one knows yet, and I just talked to our headquarters in Sana'a before leaving this morning. They're working on funding and a replacement for Sheila, but I have guarded hope."

I turned away from Ray so he wouldn't notice if I became teary. The sorrow within my heart could send tears seeping from my eyes at the mention of Sheila's name.

He motioned for me to take a seat on their couch, and he sat beside me.

Rosie stuck her head in the doorway. "Hi, I didn't know you were here. I'll make tea."

"What about coffee?" I yelled, my hand cupped around my mouth as she disappeared into the kitchen.

"Sorry, we're out!" came her reply echoing down the hall.

Ray said, "I want to hear all about the clinic fire. It must be devastating losing your colleague."

"Yup, pretty bad."

Ray quickly changed the topic. "I have more information, new developments that pertain to Jabbar. Things that worry me. Then I want to hear about the clinic—every detail."

Rosie brought us our tea in a shiny red ceramic pot. Traditional. It was a Yemeni Shai Adeni (tea from Aden) and, like tea in other parts of the Middle East, made in milk rather than water. Goat's milk, of course.

Ray looked worried, jittery eyes bobbing here and there. He took his first sip, black tea leaves suspended in a clear glass of hot sugary milk. He sat his glass on a round wooden table, and a ribbon of steam curled up from it, disappearing into the taut air between us. He slipped on his tortoise-shell reading glasses as if he wanted to scrutinize my most subtle facial expressions. He leaned toward me, elbows resting on his thighs, his big hairy-knuckled hands suspended between his knees.

"I'm worried about Jabbar," he said, wiping his brow with his fingers. "He's spending a lot of time here with Abdul. He's growing a beard, which—as you know—can mean a deeper devotion to Islam. You could expect it after losing a child, but it's sometimes a sign of radicalization."

I choked on my sip of tea as a chortle ensued. I asked, "You mean, like being recruited to a terrorist group? I just can't imagine that."

"Yeah, or maybe a radical ideology. Not all religious fanatics are terrorists, you know."

"Of course not," I said. "Jabbar has limited our time together since Alam's death. Sad, for sure … but it's hard for me to think of him as someone who would allow his anger to get the best of him."

"Trauma can change people," Ray said, sitting up straight.

"For sure. My mother's life all but ended with it. I'm faring only a little better. We are called 'psychological collaterals' … that's what Mom's therapist says. But what other evidence do you have of his transformation?"

"I'm bothered about visitors in a black Mercedes. It's the same men who brought Jabbar the money to buy the truck."

"Yeah, they were in Haydan. I saw them. Jabbar told me they were with Hezbollah and that the money was a reward for Alam's martyrdom."

"As I said last time, these men speak with a Saudi dialect. I'm not buying the Hezbollah story. They're Saudis."

Shaking my head I said, "I'm totally confused. Why would Saudi nationals be talking to Jabbar, a Houthi? Aren't the Saudis trying to eradicate the Houthis? The Saudis are the ones who bombed the bus that killed Alam, you know. This just doesn't make any damn sense."

Ray chuckled, uncrossed his legs, and leaned toward me. "In the Arab world, there is a saying that explains this: 'I will fight my brother, but if my neighbor attacks us, my brother and I will fight our neighbor. If someone from across town attacks us three, my brother, neighbor, and I will join forces to fight them. If someone from another village attacks ours, then my brother, my neighbor, the person from across town, and I will join forces to fight them. If someone attacks our country, my brother, my neighbor, the person across town, the person from the other village, and I will join forces to fight them.' In other words, the enemy of my enemy is my friend. Alliances here shift in a moment, depending on the threat."

He winked, then sipped his tea again before asking an odd question. "Are you familiar with Wahhabism?"

"Wahhabism? Uh, yeah?" I answered.

"You hesitated, so I'll review it with you. Wahhabism is a movement named after an Islamic scholar from the eighteenth century named Muhammad ibn Abd al-Wahhab. He formed a close bond with the House of Saud, Saudi Arabia's founding fathers. It is a very conservative form of Islam. While it was originally Sunni, it falls into Shia Islam as well. Both al-Qaeda, a Sunni group, and ISIL, a Shiite group, have their roots in Wahhabism. It's like what Christian fundamentalism—especially one of the armed Christian militias from Idaho I read about—is to Christianity. I'm sure in those groups you'll find Baptists, Mormons, Catholics, Presbyterians, and who knows what, but with a shared goal of fighting their common enemy—'the liberals or secularists.' No difference."

He sipped his tea and continued. "Muhammad ibn Abd al-Wahhab taught that Islam should be only Mohammed's purest teachings. He believed elevating Islamic leaders—turning their tombs into shrines—was the work of the devil, distracting from Mohammed's glory. The Muslims who practiced those rituals should repent or be killed. He also taught that Muslims must resist any outside corrupting influence. These ideas are the bedrock for hatred for the West's influence. I'm sorry to say it, Bryan, but it was the root of the World Trade Center attack because these radicals didn't like America's meddling in their culture. For example, America putting their 'infidel' troops on Saudi soil during Desert Storm. Saudi soil is considered holy because it was the home of our prophet. That's why your dad was killed. So, ISIL—a Shiite movement—shares the same goals as al-Qaeda, resisting outside influences, but also establishing a Muslim kingdom or caliphate."

"Okay, the last time I was here," I said, "you told me that all wars were based on power, money, and sex, but now you seem to be agreeing that it really is religion."

Ray smiled. "What I said was true. The real reason for war is not religion, but people using religious doctrines to justify war for more carnal reasons. For most of these people, their religion is only airbrushed."

"Airbrushed?"

"You know, sprayed on, like a bad tan. Only for appearance's sake and no depth. I'm concerned the men in the black Mercedes are Wahhabis, political with a religious coating, not Hezbollah. Maybe even al-Qaeda. Al-Qaeda is alive and well in Saudi Arabia and Yemen, and while the Houthis are fighting against al-Qaeda, they'll work with them to fight an outside enemy like the Americans."

I shook my head, "But what would they want with Jabbar? Just to win his sympathy? What can this common Yemeni, a fishing boat captain turned mountain farmer, do for them? You're not saying that Jabbar started the clinic fire, are you? Lord, I hope not." I waited for his answer.

Ray shook his head, "No, no, no ... never. I mean, Jabbar was staying here the night of the fire, so I know he wasn't personally involved. He's your friend and would never think of hurting you. When he talks about you, he still calls you his 'American brother.' He admires you. But I'm worried about them recruiting Jabbar for something far bigger. That's how al-Qaeda operates. Like I said, harvesting the low-hanging fruits. Those with a grievance. The guys at the top do the planning and financing and recruit the little angry people to be the mules and do the dirty work as martyrs. They bait and control them with emotional religious words like *duty* and *jihad*, but it is all about power and money." He chuckled. "And, of course, sex."

Rosie returned to the room and collected our empty glasses. I thanked her, as did Ray. I was sure Rosie was smart enough to have her own opinions about what we were talking about.

"I've read ... and I could be wrong," I said, "that Mohammed encouraged violence and led an army to attack Mecca, and that was the start of Islam. In contrast, Jesus was a peacemaker who shunned violence. Is that not true?"

Ray grinned like he had heard this argument before. "Yes. Jesus was a pacifist, whereas Mohammed did believe there was a limited place for violence. But Mohammed didn't personally lead the army back into Mecca. He followed the general Abu Ubaidah ibn al-

Jarrah. Yes, there were several military leaders who seized lands and forced the populace to convert to Islam or die.

"But, Bryan, I say this as a historian, not a Muslim: Christianity has caused more deaths than Islam by far. Now, it is hard to argue because many secular wars had either Muslim or Christian banners. Even now, the Saudis are bombing these poor people"—he pointed toward his door— "because of their religion. America is killing the Yemenis too because of so-called 'Islamic terrorism.' So, it's like yet another Crusade, a religious war. Both Islam and Christianity have killed millions in their name." Then he sat up and asked, "Which is worse, a religion that condones violence in some circumstances and kills millions or one that rejects all violence and still kills millions? I think both are culpable. People with airbrushed religion also airbrush their histories."

I had nothing left to say but plenty to ponder.

Ray leaned toward me again. "Bryan, what the hell happened at your clinic? Tell me about your colleague."

"I don't know what to say, just that someone poured gasoline in the clinic and set it on fire. My colleague, Dr. Emory was asleep in her quarters and"—I paused to stifle tears and gave a big sigh— "uh, she died in the fire. IRGC-QF has claimed responsibility."

Ray looked down at the floor and shook his head. "Terrible. Yes, IRGC-QF, the Iranian Revolutionary Guard of Yemen, has done a lot of mischief during this war, and I wouldn't put it past them." He sat up. A soft grin formed around his lips even as his brow continued to hold a scowl. "Did you know this Dr. Emory well? You must have."

Before I could stop them, the tears began to flow. I could barely get the words out between the stifled sobs. "Yeah, you could say that." Looking directly into Ray's eyes, I said, "Ray, Sheila, well … she was the love of my life." Then the sobbing took over. I began shaking so hard I thought I would fall off the chair. I felt Ray's hand on my shoulder as I hunched over. He didn't say anything else but just sat with me, with an occasional whispered, "I'm so sorry."

It wasn't long before I felt another hand on me. Rosie had come in from the kitchen, and Ray must have whispered to her what

I was crying about. Or maybe she just knew through intuition. She stooped down beside me and put her arm over my shoulders in a side hug. I looked up and saw tears running down her face. This woman who had seen such atrocities, having witnessed the hanging of her own father, had the empathy to weep with me. They say, "Hurt people hurt people." But my mother always said, "Hurt people feel other people's hurts better."

The next morning, as I prepared to leave for Haydan, Ray came out to my bike to talk to me, a cup of tea in each hand. Handing one to me, he said in a whisper, "Bryan, I'll watch Abdul, Jabbar, and these visitors. I have a way." He timidly nodded toward Abdul's house.

He continued. "I can slither out of my house and crouch down beneath Abdul's window in the dark and hear everything they say. I may be old, but my hearing is still good." He winked. "Just my knees don't work like they used to." He paused, then added, "You need to monitor Jabbar. Work on your rapport with him, not to spy but try to curb his anger. You have an excellent position, having lost your father in a bombing. Jabbar can relate to that. More recently than that, you lost your colleague and your love."

I had to look away.

"That was horrible, just horrible." He looked down at the ground and shook his head. "How're you doing, I mean on the inside?"

Rosie walked outside about that time. "Bryan, you aren't leaving, are you?" Then her classic right head tilt. "I have a nutritious breakfast and am planning cooking a *Fahsa* [lamb stew] for lunch."

Bobbing my own head, I said, "I guess I bailed out on you last time, didn't I? I would enjoy your company this time and your opinions, and I have nothing waiting for me in Haydan."

The three of us walked back inside. I hung out with them for the rest of the day. It wasn't homecooked meals so much that drew me as their nurturing conversation.

CHAPTER EIGHTEEN

Two weeks later, asleep in my tent in Haydan, I was abruptly awakened by my cell phone lighting up, soon followed by Elton John's *Goodbye Yellow Brick Road*. I had assigned that ringtone to Dorothy for obvious reasons. I grabbed my phone, which was just outside my sleeping bag and then dropped it. I lost it in the dark until it lit up again and the same ringtone ensued. The time read in irritating yellow numbers *6:05 A.M.*

"Hey, Dorothy," I whispered in a groggy voice. I sat up, pushing my fingers against my eyeballs to massage them awake.

"Hi, Bryan, how are you?"

"Fine," I answered. "Was still asleep. What's up?"

"Sorry to call so early," she said in a voice too cheery for that time of day. "I'm catching a UN plane this morning for Geneva. I wanted to give you an update. We still don't have an approval for rebuilding the clinic or volunteers to come out. People aren't lining up for Sheila's slot. So, we're talking to MSF about loaning you to them in Sa'dah until your contract is up. They might come to Haydan to set up a clinic. I just don't like you living in limbo without a purpose. Why don't you come to Sana'a until we sort this out? It's a little safer here, you know. By the time I get back, in three weeks, we should know your future."

"You want me to desert Haydan?" I asked. "Why can't I just open a clinic while we're waiting? The people still need me. Mazen is returning next week from Sana'a, and Ahmed is still here. Of course, I would love to have a new physician here, but kids are still getting sick, and Sa'dah is too far away for them."

"Do you have supplies salvaged from the fire?"

"Not even a Band-Aid."

"So, we would need to resupply you. But here's the other thing. I spoke with our headquarters in New York. The medical director for IRC said a PA should not be working alone. He didn't want you seeing patients until we get a physician on-site."

Now fully awake, I said, "Just a minute!"

I crawled outside the tent and stood, so I could speak with more energy. The three-quarters creamy moon was just slipping behind cloud-clad mountains. "Give me a break! Even in the States, PAs work in remote locations without a physician on-site all the time. Dorothy, people are desperate. Fifty thousand Yemeni children have died from hunger alone in this damn war, and I can help them. They don't have to die."

"Dr. Morales, our medical director, goes by the book," Dorothy responded emphatically.

"What damn book? There's no book that prevents PAs from working alone."

She didn't answer.

"Dorothy, if I sent you an order for supplies, could we set something up here while we wait? Just until you get back? You could pretend ignorance … you know, something off the friggin' radar! Don't even mention it to Dr. Morales. I don't want his heart to burn."

She hesitated. I could hear her breaths against the phone's speaker.

"Dorothy?"

"Okay, Bryan. Call the office when it opens at eight and talk to Aiesha. I'll leave a message that you're calling in an order for supplies, and I won't mention this to anyone. I'll do this for Haydan's children. But if we're caught, I'll deny involvement with this scheme and call you a liar … and pretend I don't even know you." She chuckled.

"It'll be a tall order. I only have my stethoscope. Mazen has a few things that were in the trauma bag in his apartment."

"I'll tell Aiesha to do her best. She's a gem with procurement in a dysfunctional country. We'll send it over by truck. Oh, and Bryan, I'm sending you a new sat phone. I've been trying to reach you for several days. This morning, I must have caught Haydan's cell tower during the rare time it's operational. I'm glad I spoke to you before I left."

"Thanks, Dorothy. Have a safe trip. You're a gem too."

I climbed back into my sleeping bag and buried my face deep within, pulling the drawstring tight, leaving just a hole for my nose. With no reason to get out of bed, I pulled up Dad's playlist on my phone. I felt closest to him when hearing his favorite music. It gave me the feeling I was sitting in his lap, my head beneath his stubbly chin, listening to his rescue stories. That's when I had fallen in love with the art of medicine. With his music filling the empty spaces inside my head, I drifted off to sleep.

Soon I was jolted awake by nothing more than a thought— my desire to move on this new clinic idea. It was 8 A.M., and I tried to call Aiesha. She didn't pick up. I waited five minutes and tried again. She answered.

"Hello, International Rescue Committee, may I help you?"

"Hi, this is Bryan in Haydan. Dorothy told me to call you with an order for supplies I'll need to reopen the clinic."

"Uh, I didn't think we are reopening that clinic."

"Dorothy said she would call you with instructions," I said confidently.

"Let me listen to my messages. I just got here. The road was closed again. Sana'a's streets always have a new prank each morning. This morning it was a camel with its hoof caught in a drain. They butchered the poor thing right in the middle of the street … blood everywhere. Mobs fighting for the meat like dogs after scraps. At least it wasn't human blood this time."

After a moment, she came back to me, interrupting my visual of the butchering of the camel, and said, "Yeah, I listened to Dorothy's message. So, what do you need?"

I gave her a long list that included IV fluids, IV setups, minor surgery equipment, vaccinations, syringes, needles, medications, boxes of rehydration packets, and cast-making material.

"Aiesha, I'll also need a couple of tents."

"We have refugee tents that would work."

"Perfect!" I said, leaving the conversation on a high note.

I spent the morning rummaging through the clinic's fragments, looking for salvageable supplies. The still-wet ashes had a foul odor—like mold. But the ashes were also sticky, clinging to my shoes with each step taken.

Next to one footprint, in Sheila's quarters, was a rectangle shape in the cinders. Out of curiosity, I kicked it over with my boot, thinking it was a piece of tile. It was a photo of her parents. As I picked it up, the burned and broken pieces of glass fell from it. The photo was almost perfect except for singed edges. Easing myself down, I sat on the wires and rusty springs from her bed.

I felt alone in the universe. I had no friends now that Jabbar was aloof. Mazen was gone. Even my big brothers rarely spoke to me—or anyone—after losing Dad. I missed Angie. As soon as I got my new sat phone, I would give her a call. I was lonesome even while mobbed by people right outside my tent's door, giving condolences or begging for my help.

My closed lids floated on thin tears leaking out from their feathered edges. It was only a minute until a voice penetrated my solitude. It was Ahmed, stooping beside me, standing sandal-footed in the ashes.

"Are you okay, Doctor Bryan?"

I wiped the tears off my face with my soot-covered sleeve. "I'm just sad."

"Sadness is the air that we breathe here in Yemen. Suffering, the food we eat. Pain, just the water we drink."

He sat on the bed beside me for a while, neither of us saying a word.

Mazen returned to the village the next day. It was nice to have him back. It would be another week until our supplies arrived, but we started seeing patients immediately, knowing that when Dorothy got back, our Haydan work might come to an end. Without provisions, I mostly served as a traffic cop, directing patients to the MSF Hospital, an hour down the mountain. We transported two such patients in our truck that week. One of those patients put me on a path of direct conflict with Michel.

The day this patient came to us, Ahmed and I were cleaning an area in our garden, making a place where we could set up the tents when they came. I heard someone screaming from the street. Several people were carrying a man on a bed, a typical bed of cords strung between a wooden frame. The sheet over him was covered in blood. He was shrieking and fighting, trying to jump off while holding his obviously deformed right leg. As they paused to turn into our gate, the bed flipped on its side and he fell to the street, his screams penetrating the clouds. Ahmed and I ran over to help carry him the rest of the way to the truck and laid him in its bed. He was hemorrhaging. I quickly used the bloody sheet as a torniquet around his right thigh while I assessed his injuries.

As I was cutting away the man's clothes, an older man with the group squatted beside us and explained in Arabic, "Abdul, my son-in-law, was on a ladder fixing a leak on our house. The ladder broke and he fell."

"How high up was he," I asked as I continued to feel deep into the wound around his femur, trying to pinch off the bleeding artery with my fingers.

The old man pointed and looked straight up. Ahmed and my eyes followed his to the heavens as he mumbled, "*Almustawaa alraabie* [fourth level]."

I removed the tourniquet once I had a grip of muscle around the bleeding artery. Abdul had suffered a compound fracture of his right femur, with closed tibia and fibula fractures on the same side. His head was bruised around his right temple. He was certainly alert, still moaning and screaming, answering my questions appropriately—when he could catch his breath—a good sign his brain was intact.

When Mazen showed up, I turned the bleeding artery over to him, and he squeezed it in his hand. Ahmed got behind the wheel and waited on my signal before pulling out. I worked on repositioning Abdul's S-shaped lower leg until I felt a good pulse return to his foot. Then I tried to immobilize the leg in that position, holding it firm with both hands.

Ahmed started the truck, and we sped down the mountainside to the MSF Hospital. We brought Abdul in on a gurney and turned him over to the acute care doctor, who was Dr. McHenry from Scotland, working with Maria, the Sicilian nurse and Michel's new love.

Both Maria and Dr. McHenry told us we had done an outstanding job. Then Mazen, Ahmed, and I returned to the mountain. We had saved the man from bleeding to death. MSF had a general surgeon who had skills in orthopedics. We had left Abdul in good hands.

A few days later, my cell phone rang. I didn't recognize the number.

"Hello."

"Bryan?" said a man's voice.

"Yes."

"This is Dr. Michel Moreau at MSF. I had to call IRC in Sana'a to get your damn number," he said in English laced with his French accent. "This is not acceptable! The patient you brought to our hospital the other day was an *accident ferroviaire* [train wreck]. If you don't even know first aid, why the hell are you in Yemen?"

I sucked in a deep breath, "What the hell are you talking about?"

"You brought us this man with unstable fractures in his leg. He had a penetrating femur fracture causing him to bleed. It was a mess. It's a miracle that he didn't bleed to death," he said with a loud sigh.

"Why are you telling me this? The man was in good shape when I left him with Maria and Dr. McHenry in your acute room. I checked the bleeding just before I left, and we had controlled it. Of course, I knew about his fractures. What are you saying I did wrong? I don't get it."

"You don't know what you're doing, so you shouldn't be up there alone playing doctor."

I took in another deep breath and shouted, "Okay, what would you have done with just a stethoscope?"

No answer.

After a minute, he said, "Don't ever dump a half-dead patient on our doorstep again! And when I called the IRC office, I made it clear that I don't want you here in my hospital, and we're not coming back to Haydan to babysit you!"

Then the line went dead.

It took me a day to recover from that interaction. I had a sleepless night, hearing cars starting and motorcycles blaring, wandering voices echoing throughout the village and all through the dark hours. I lay in my sleeping bag thinking, *What do these people do all night? Why are they out at 2 A.M.? There's no 7-Eleven here. No midnight bowling. No Denny's.* I had only a few interactions with Michel during my fifteen months in Yemen. The most notable one was the day of the school bus bombing when he refused to let me stay and help in the OR. Then my mind would revert to the default question haunting me: *Why does Michel hate me so much? Does this end my remaining hopes for Yemen?*

Three days later, our supply truck arrived. It had been five weeks since the fire, and I had remained idle, surrounded by suffering with nothing to offer except my knowledge. Mazen and I worked quickly to get the clinic up and running within twenty-four hours. Soon, I'd have a functioning clinic in this stunning green oasis, our little Emerald City. Maybe I alone could make Sheila's dream come true. This lovely town absent the ills of a miserable war would be the most beautiful place on earth, the Arabs' Shangri-La. But after talking to Michel, I had a bad feeling that our clinic would be more like a summer's squall in Yemen, evaporating before hitting the ground.

The next morning, Mazen came running to my tent, his eyes big and bulging. "Bryan, have you looked outside the wall? Looks like the word has gotten out."

I swallowed my hard-boiled duck egg, a gift from a villager, almost whole. Standing up, I wiped my hands on my jeans. I followed Mazen to the wall and looked through the gate. A hundred people were waiting and new ones arriving. I exhaled. "Lord, how can I do this?"

Mazen put his hand on my shoulder and said, "We've got this, Boss."

I looked at him and glared. "What the hell does that even mean? We got what? I think you've been watching too much American TV."

Mazen laughed and took off jogging toward the clinic.

It was a long day, at least eighteen hours caring for patients. Many cases were straightforward—vaccinations, skin infections, respiratory or GI infections, and superficial foreign-body removals. We had four children who had cholera and were quite dehydrated. Those cases took time to set up with IVs and oral rehydration packets.

I retired to my tent late, thoroughly exhausted but satisfied by the hard day's work. I was awakened at 3 A.M. by loud shouting. Stepping outside, I saw four men carrying a young woman on a wooden post bed, with three little girls in tow. She was in distress and pregnant—very pregnant.

"She's been in labor for three days," the young husband told me, his face overwhelmed with worry. "The midwife has given up, saying she will die. She can't die! I cannot raise our children without Safiya. Please help us! I'm a poor man, but I can work for you."

I quickly examined her and saw the midwife was right, she was going to die. The baby appeared to be in a shoulder presentation, one arm in the canal, fingers at the os. My worst nightmare. I could not reposition the baby as the uterus was clamped down hard. The mom was exhausted, barely arousable. The only way to avoid death was a cesarean section to save at least her, if not the baby. I called the MSF Hospital to tell them I was bringing her down.

The nurse on the radio responded, "I need to run this by our night doc. We're busy tonight."

"Busy? This is a life-and-death emergency," I said.

In a moment, the nurse was back on the radio. "Nope. We can't take her. I'm sorry, but we had a bombing earlier tonight in the valley and our OR is full. We can't interrupt those surgeries for a cesarean." Then she added, "Sadly, Yemeni women die in childbirth every day."

I looked at the young pregnant woman, her anxious husband, and the three little girls to whom she was mommy. I had to try.

I had been in surgery over a thousand times with my previous job. I had first assisted Sheila with many cesarean sections over the previous year. Protecting the bladder had been my assigned task, but I had watched Sheila's every move. My concern wasn't so much with my skills. Compared to removing a tumor in the hypothalamus, a cesarean is simple. But the lack of a decent operating room or supporting staff gave me concern. Just one unexpected complication would spell disaster. *How could I get the baby's arm out of the canal?* Safiya could bleed to death with one mis-stroke of the scalpel or, even if things went perfectly, die days later from an infection.

I started an IV and explained to the husband that we could just let her die or I could attempt to operate to remove the baby. I did not mention the baby would likely not survive, or at least loose the arm trapped in the birth canal.

He was clear. "Please, doctor, do everything you can to save Safiya."

I ran across the street and woke up Ahmed. I asked him to go into the village to get Mazen while I returned to my patient. As my eyes fell upon her, I whispered in English, "Lord, what I would give for an obstetrician about now."

I moved Safiya to the tent and started setting up supplies. Mazen and Ahmed soon joined me. I was working by headlamp alone and quickly realized that it would not be enough. We needed more light to have a chance. I mumbled, "God help me, I need some light."

Ahmed took off and in fifteen minutes returned with the headlamp from my bike wired to a battery. "This will be better," he said. He hooked the light to the top of the tent, a big improvement.

We had ketamine, which Mazen had used many times, as a general anesthetic. He watched the patient's airway and breathing with an intubation tube and Ambu bag ready.

When I asked Ahmed for his help with the surgery, a grin as big as a boomerang sprang across his face. "I've butchered sheep and goats." I didn't find the comment reassuring.

I helped Ahmed scrub and put on his gloves. Then I instructed him how to hold the bladder and another retractor. I had to pause twice to take his gloved hands in mine and reposition them, but otherwise he did a rather remarkable job for an uneducated mountain farmer.

To my good fortune, the cesarean went smoothly. I used a transverse incision approach. Closing in four layers, two on the uterus, I sutured up the mom without a hitch just as the slothful sun was rising. I did not have to amputate the baby's arm, like I feared. Ahmed took care of the baby—yes, the baby did survive—while Mazen and I finished up with Safiya. She stayed with us for the day, and then her family carried her home. She lived just two doors down from Jabbar. I checked on her each morning before the clinic opened, and she recovered well without complications. Thank God!

I was hesitant about bringing a precious new life—another mouth to feed— into a place of suffering and death. However, this life may have been the very one to bring peace to this place.

A hundred patients or more arrived each morning, and Mazen and I were thrilled. However, the situation was not sustainable. We were exhausted. After clinic one afternoon, Mazen and I sat down over dinner to discuss how to pace ourselves. Just as we started to pick which day of the week to close, my cell phone rang with Dorothy's ringtone.

"Hi, Bryan. How's the new clinic going?" she asked.

"Really well. Mazen and I were just discussing how to take at least one day off per week, so we don't burn out."

"Hmm," was her only response. I sensed what she was about to say. Then she added, "Well, your problem has been solved ... unfortunately."

My heart sank.

"Bryan, I'm so sorry but I have orders to shut you down. There are no applicants for Sheila's position. And the board has decided to close the Haydan clinic—"

"No! Dorothy we can't close!" I said as I quickly jumped to my feet. Mazen watched me with anxious eyes.

"Yes, Bryan. We have no choice."

"Dorothy, then I resign, and I'll stay here with Mazen and take care of Haydan's sick."

"Bryan ... oh, Bryan. I wish so much that you could. But this is complicated. You're working in Haydan with special permission from the Houthi government, given to the IRC. They would not allow you to stay as an independent American. You may not realize it, but they are protecting you right now, and without their—"

"Protecting me?" I said in a tone dyed with gloom. "What the hell? Where were they when Sheila was being murdered? I bet the arsonist was a Houthi."

"Bryan, it would have been much worse without the Houthis. But now, we'll give you the option of going home or coming to Sana'a to finish out the last nine months of your contract."

With my hand over the phone's receiver, I whispered to Mazen, "They're closing us down!"

He shook his head.

"Mazen too?" I asked her.

"Uh, no. He could go home, but the MSF Hospital in Sa'dah has offered him a position."

"But not me?" I asked.

"Uh ... well, Dr. Moreau said they don't work with PAs."

I just shook my head. "I'll probably leave Yemen," I said, "but I'll give it some thought."

Silence filled the air between us. I could hear Dorothy's slow breaths. She cleared her throat like she was about to speak, and I quickly interrupted. "Say, Dorothy, on a completely different matter, do you know anyone at the American Embassy?"

"The American Embassy?" she asked with surprise. "Uh ... sure. Hunter Philips is a friend of my husband. He's the minister-counselor, or second in command at the embassy after Ambassador Kelly. Why do you ask?"

"I have a tip about terrorist activity. I need to inform the embassy before I leave the country."

"Terrorist activity? Really? Do you think you know who set fire to the clinic?" Dorothy asked.

"No, it's not about the fire. It's about a future attack. Perhaps something even bigger. I hope to know more before I leave."

"Keep me posted but be careful. I'll look up Mr. Philips's private number and get back to you."

I walked outside our dining tent and looked at the last remains of the setting sun, which, like Mazen, had sneaked away before I got off the phone. I felt sad. Mom used to quote a verse from the Bible, "A hope deferred makes the heart sick." I went to bed that night with a heart steeped in sickness.

CHAPTER NINETEEN

The last day of the clinic, over eighty patients came, about the same as usual. Some knew about our pending closure. Others didn't.

"Don't you like our country?" They would ask.

"I love your country. I love the Yemenis," I would answer.

I grew weary of the word *takhlina*, which means "abandoning us."

A lot of goodbye tears were shed. Then, as the day was ending, people congregated along the road. They didn't want anything from me. No words were exchanged. They just stood and stared at what was but could be no more. The arsonist had won.

I considered packing up all my possessions and saying goodbye to Haydan that night, but I had unfinished business. I needed another visit with Jabbar. I wanted to see Ray and Rosie again. I needed to talk to this Hunter guy at the embassy. Only then could I make my decision about staying in Sana'a for nine more months or leaving on the next IRC charter.

The next day, Mazen and I were having tea by a fire in the clinic garden. The trees had been spared from the fire; a few leaves singed. I had become one of the subsistence garbage burners—the ones I'd detested so much when I first arrived. We had invited Ahmed, but he hadn't shown up. Mazen and I were reminiscing about our year together. He was a good man, the best nurse I had ever worked with. I would miss him dearly. I told him I wanted to visit Jabbar again. I'd biked over to his house earlier that week but he hadn't been home and Mona didn't know when to expect him. "*Ay yawm* [any day]," had been her repeated response.

I was contemplating if I should tell Mazen about Ray's concerns. But Ray had warned me not to tell anyone. However, in the silence of good feelings around the little fire, the coolness of the evening gripping our shoulders, I asked, "Mazen, how well do you know Jabbar?"

His face took on a perplexed look, and he sat up. "Why do you ask?"

"Well, there's something his cousin Ray is worried about—"

Just as those words departed my mouth, I saw Jabbar in his white truck pass behind Mazen on the main road.

"Oh, as I was saying … Well, Ray was worried about Jabbar after he lost Alam. But speaking of the devil, Jabbar just drove by. Looks like he's home."

"Why do you call him the 'devil'?" asked Mazen. "What's he up to?"

"No reason. Nothing. Why, did you hear something?" I asked.

"No, not really," said Mazen.

"It's just an American saying—you know, 'speaking of the devil.' I want to visit him tonight. I'll give him time to eat and settle down. Do you want to come?"

Shaking his head, Mazen said, "Can't. I promised my landlord I would help him butcher two goats tonight. His niece is getting married, and they're having the wedding feast tomorrow. My landlord has arthritis so bad he can't hold a knife."

My walk to Jabbar's house took me past orchards with bare trees standing in rows like hunched old men in a season depriving them of blooms or fruit. Jabbar had parked his truck in its usual place, off the street and next to their house's east wall under its pale-green pinstriped cover.

I knocked on the door of his house. Nothing. I knocked again. I heard tapping on the wooden stairs coming down from the top floor. The door swung open, the iron hinges screeching. There stood Jabbar, looking tired and frazzled. His hair was sticking straight up like he had been cuddling with a Van de Graaff generator before I arrived. But I figured he was sleeping.

He said in a dry tone, "Hello."

"Good evening," I said. "Can I come in?"

"Sure."

I followed him up the stairs. He paused by the kitchen level and yelled in Arabic, "Unfortunately, we have a guest. Mona, make us tea, but don't use our good tea."

Strange. Did he mean for me to hear that?

We climbed up to the mafraj and took our seats on the couch. Jabbar tilted away from me and crossed his legs. Before I could say anything, he asked, "Aren't you leaving Haydan soon?"

"How'd you know?"

"Everyone knows," he said.

"I am. Probably in a few days," I said soberly. "I have some unfinished business."

With a blank stare, he said, "I think that's a good thing. We really don't need foreigners in Haydan."

This is the man who calls me his "American brother"?

"How can you say that?" I asked, leaning toward him. "Do you honestly feel that way? Who's going to take care of your family's health? For one, you would be dead if it weren't for Sheila and me helping you when you had pneumonia. What Yemeni doctor is coming? There are still IRC social workers in the camps. They're from India. Should they leave too?"

He raised his voice, "I'll take care of my own family, with Allah's help."

I paused for a minute. "Jabbar, you were my best friend in Yemen, maybe the world. What happened?"

He sat back on the couch and fidgeted. He rubbed his hair with his hand. He soon stood and walked to the big window and opened it. The cool evening breezes roared into the room, peppered by sounds and voices coming from the streets, donkeys braying, children crying, and people talking and arguing. Jabbar looked out the window for a minute and returned to the couch. About that time,

Mona came in carrying two glasses of hot tea. I spoke to her, but she did not acknowledge me.

"What were you saying?" Jabbar asked.

"I said you were my best friend. What the hell happened?"

Sitting upright on the couch—stiffly, as though posing for a portrait—he said, "We were never that close. You don't even speak Arabic, and you're not a man of faith."

"*Laghti alearabiat laysat sayiyatan* [my Arabic isn't bad]," I said quickly and clearly.

Jabbar chuckled so much his just-sipped tea came out his nose. He bent over to catch it in his hand. Oddly, he took that nasal tea in his palm and used it to wipe down his unruly hair. Then we both laughed like middle schoolers until I almost fell out of my chair. The cold stiff air between us warmed.

"Jabbar, I'd like to take another trip to Al Luhayyah before I leave Yemen," I said. "What do you think?"

"I don't know," he said scratching his damp head. "I have to sell our crops."

"What's in season in November?" I asked.

"I still have a few oranges and millet to sell," he said, glancing up at me. "Then winter wheat."

"For how much?" I asked.

"I don't know … uh, how much what? How much money?"

"Yeah."

"I don't know. I would guess about ten thousand rial."

I did the math in my head.

"So, about forty bucks, U.S.?" I asked.

"That sounds about right."

"Okay, I'll pay you one hundred bucks, American, to take the week off and come fishing with me in Al Luhayyah."

He sat and stared at me as though in a trance.

"Jabbar?" I asked.

Suddenly, he became animated again. "It would be immoral and, more than that, sad for someone to pay another person to be their friend."

"So, you'll come with me without getting paid?"

"Nope. I can't."

"Jabbar!" I said, scratching my head and looking out his window. It was dark, save the lighted tents in rows on the hill. Turning back to look at him, I said, "Okay, Jabbar. Would you sell me your entire harvest for one hundred American dollars?"

"I guess I would be a fool not to," Jabbar said. "Really, you would buy my entire crop?"

"Yep." Then he added, "Uh, okay, I'll go fishing, but I must leave my truck here."

"Fine," I said. We'll leave in two days, on my bike. There hasn't been a Saudi bombing raid on the coast in weeks. It's a good time to go, don't you think?"

"As good as any, but in Yemen they say, 'Death always comes when least expected.'"

CHAPTER TWENTY

Two days later, we loaded up our gear on my bike. Jabbar loaned the family truck to his brother-in-law, Tamir, so he could deliver his family's crops to Jabbar's customers. Jabbar wore his duffle as a backpack. We had two long bamboo fishing poles tied to the bike's frame, giving us the look of jousters riding double on a mechanical horse across the beleaguered massifs.

The mountain highway to the west was worse than our last trip to the sea. The Saudis had been busy. We stopped twice to rest and drink water. Dust kept filling my throat, so I had to wrap my keffiyeh around my face for protection.

As each day passed, I observed Jabbar emerging from his shell. But it was oddly sporadic—the old Jabbar sandwiched between moods of the serious, distant one. We sat by campfires at night on the beach. Driftwood from Eritrea and the rest of the horn of Africa was a reliable fuel source. A cold wind blew off the water, and the giddy waves were lapping at the shore like wrinkles blown across silk. Coming to rest on rusty sand, the waves were chased back into the darkness by troops of ghost crabs with long slits for pupils topping their stalked eyes. The briny air reminded me of the Long Island beaches I had visited as a boy where I built marvelous sandcastles, only to watch—in horror—as the tide came in and washed them all away, a metaphor of my life.

The Red Sea's wind was like ice. I had never been cold in Yemen before those evenings—I mean New York, Nor'easter, cold. Not even in the dead of winter when light snow fell among our craggy peaks and covered the IRC lettering on my domed tent's fly.

On our second day, we borrowed a fishing boat from the same guy we had on our previous trip. He was Jabbar's friend's relative, nearly a dwarf. The guy they called *Kasir* [Shorty] would have had to look up to Danny DeVito, but he was as tough as a badger, offsetting his humble statue. Once out on the water, Jabbar laughed, his good mood conjured by the deep. He smoked a cigarette. I smoked one with him. We went as far out as we could, until we saw the line of marching lights that were Saudi patrol boats buttressing their wall of suffering, so impenetrable.

Hours later, we returned by the stars, which Jabbar could read like a GPS. Soon, Al Luhayyah's illumination emerged from the ebony waters like a string of clear Christmas lights twinkling and dancing in the interface between the dry inland air and the moist imminence of the sea. A single green-lighted buoy drew us the final way, onto the beach where the other old, tired wooden boats sat, listing, sleeping in the sand.

To my surprise, Kasir returned on the second night carrying a paper bag with the brown neck of a bottle sticking out of it. It turned out to be a 750 ml bottle of Jack Daniels. I was sure it was from the black market, smuggled to the coast from Israel. He left the drink with us, returning an hour later when our fish was ready to eat. We kept the contraband in its bag. Because Jabbar's pious mood was known to swing, I waited until he drank first to avoid offense. We sipped it from the bottle straight up and talked as we watched the lighted boats coming and going from the harbor. Our conversation dipped into those rich regions of our souls just like they had those nights in the clinic when we first met, this time without the pneumonia death angel encamped nearby.

Sipping Tennessee whiskey from a bag, passing it back and forth, I blotted out all my sad thoughts and those washed-out sandcastles full of lost dreams. *Does life get better than this?* A small postage-stamp-sized space carved out within mayhem's endless spread, in which two friends could share a moment. It was a brief reprise in which the old Jabbar, spirit-like, sifted out through the cracks of his stoic armor to be with me. To laugh again. I had missed him.

But then I said something that ruined that peaceful moment.

"Jabbar, I miss having Alam with us. He was such a joy on our last trip. I can't imagine this now, but If I ever have a son, I'll name him Alam in your son's honor." I smiled. "Sheila, if it's a girl."

As soon as those words tumbled off the end of my tongue, I started to cry. It wasn't the alcohol. It was serenity's inebriation, sitting in the wet sand by the Red Sea, hungry sand fleas biting at my ankles. A pale crescent moon was playing peekaboo with the thin serious clouds moving in from the west, veiling heaven's lesser lights. When you are living in a war zone, you forget what real peace is like.

Jabbar put his hand on my shoulder. It was odd that I was the one crying, not him. I suspected he had done his crying in private areas. In bedrooms, dark halls, or solo trips in his truck—the secret places where men of the world weep in solace, boxed in by shame. A tormented gender. I had been spared only because a profound tsunami of grief had overcome me at an impressionable age. My eyes forever drowned.

I would give the five-day trip high marks except for the catch. Jabbar reeled in one beautiful sailfish, otherwise we were skunked. I had seen sailfish only in pictures. It was a specimen of fine marine art with brilliant purples, yellows, and blues as if dressed that morning by Leonid Afremov in oils with a palette knife and brush. It was a shame that we destroyed it. I was weary of ruin. The fish was delicious though, grilled on long sticks over the campfire on the beach. It had to be eaten that night, so we ate until we were full and shared the rest with beggars who had smelled it cooking. Kasir, shorter than the fish by a foot, showed up and somehow ate half. Payment, I assume, for the use of the boat and the liquor.

Jabbar returned to his distant self as the trip wrapped up. I knew that I was on a mission. If I could spare the country another terrorist act, it was worth the effort. It would also mean sparing Jabbar's life, as likely a terrorist act by him would be a suicide mission. If not, the Americans or Saudis would make sure to turn it into one via a drone.

The campfire's glow was reflecting off Jabbar's face, leaving deep shadows of his features, causing him to appear as if his face had been drawn in pencil. I broke that silent moment, our prelude to sleep, by asking, "Jabbar, are you still interested in returning to the sea as a captain? I mean, when this damn war is over?"

He yawned; his eyes closed. "Yeah. I'm entering commercial sea captain school in Cyprus in December."

"Are you serious?" I sat up, my mouth open wide. "I thought it was just a dream, years in the future." I shook my head. "It must be expensive."

He rolled over and looked at me, his head propped up on his arm. "Yes, it is. It'll cost forty thousand U.S. dollars for six months."

"Jabbar, how will you pay for this?"

"I have sponsors."

"Someone in your family or those strangers in the Mercedes?"

"Well, yes. Hezbollah has funds to help martyrs' families. They'll pay for my school. That's not so unusual. Didn't you tell me your school was paid for because you were the son of a martyr."

"That's true, Columbia gave scholarships to 9/11 families. But I don't consider my father a martyr."

Then the conversation collapsed, Jabbar's dark eyes wandering from me, being pulled back into the lapping waves of his inner sea. He sipped from the bottle, the alcohol fueling the bloodshot of his eyes. Then he lay down again, covering himself with his blanket.

I lay back on the sand. Next to me, soon snoring away, was my pal, yet a possible brutal murderer in the making. His assigned task might be as simple as killing me, finishing what the clinic arsonist started. I was the only American he had contact with. But how would he kill me? The perfect weapon was two feet from his right hand. The sailfish's spear was sticking in the sand. While I slept, he could ram it through my heart. I didn't care anymore—if it would put an end to his terrorism. Maybe my death would send me to another place, call it Heaven or another dimension.

But whom could I trust? I even wondered if Ray was setting me up—Jabbar just a decoy, while Ray did something sinister. I'd never heard the so-called terrorists making plans. Maybe Ray had just made that up. Ray was unequivocal in his opinion that I not involve the authorities, especially the Americans. He could have been running and hiding from something. Damn, so confusing.

The next day, we were back on my bike, heading home to Haydan. We stopped on a cold mountain pass to piss and drink water. Sitting on a rock over the mountain's western slope, we could look down at the Red Sea plain, seven thousand feet below. The old sun was glistening off its surface far out toward the African continent, the waves giving the sea a frosted-glass look from that distance. We sat in silence on limestone boulders, passing the water bottle back and forth.

"Jabbar, how are you really doing, on the inside? Do you still feel angry?"

"I'll always be sad. I've died to this world. My spirit is with Alam already. Am I angry? Of course. All good fathers would be angry about their son's murder. Why do you keep bringing this up?" He took a swig of water and spat it out on the crusty ground.

"Are you going to act on your anger?" I asked in a cautious tone. "I mean, are you going to retaliate? You know, *euquba* [retribution]?"

Jabbar's crow's feet appeared beside his eyes. He stood up and dusted off the seat of his pants and spat again. "*Euquba*? Yes, those responsible deserve *eiqab Allah* [Allah's punishment]. But I will leave that in Allah's hands. But Allah tells us that his justice is *aleayn bialeayn* [an eye for an eye]." He glared at me. "Who told you I was retaliating? Was it Rahman? I just want to do good. Why is that so hard for you to understand?" he said loudly.

"Jabbar, we often convince ourselves we are doing good when we're really contributing to a larger evil."

He continued staring at me, eyes narrowing into slits.

I added, "I'm afraid your boat is listing, my brother, too much *mara* [bile or bitterness] in its hold. Soon it will wreck on the rocks."

Jabbar walked toward the bike. I stood and joined him, putting my helmet on and checking his. Soon we were rolling down the road.

I couldn't hear the jets overhead because of the Yamaha's 250 cc engine whine, but my eye caught chemtrails streaking across the sky. I felt a vise grip my stomach. It wasn't long before I saw the rise of smoke columns right in our path.

The village of Harad came into view, marked by the remnants of Saudi bombers written in the clouds. Broken concrete walls and entangled rebar were still smoking on the ground. Battle fatigued, I wanted to keep heading home. But Jabbar was seeing the same destruction. Failure to turn toward Harad would have shocked him. I turned north and drove straight into the eye of the chaos.

Harad had borne more than its share of the Saudis' wrath. I don't know what the strategy was from the Saudi perspective. It had no military purpose. Was it saving jet fuel by bombing villages nearest the border?

This bombing was "clean." One small two-story house was destroyed. A grandfather, mother, and two children were dead. Four other children had a few scratches. I took the first aid kit from my bike and quickly exhausted its inventory. The scratched kids were severely malnourished, their knobby knees and elbows protuberant on long, thin limbs. Their sparse hair, scaly skin, bloated stomachs, and flaccid dispositions told me that little life was left in them. I took out my one MRE, which I carried in my emergency supplies, heated it up, and watched them eat. Kids without laughter seemed a curiosity. I suspected that some of the kids wished they were the ones being washed in the field beside us, a hope that the next bomb was inscribed with their name and found them in their sleep. Certainly, their parents wished that for themselves.

Within the hour, we were back on the road. As we were leaving, the families were wrapping the victims in the white kafan, or burial shroud. I saw men in the cemetery digging graves. Routine. Sadly, mundane. There was a linen shortage for kafans in this land. New ones were being fashioned from old burlap sacks—intended for chic coffee beans, not little bodies.

Despite the bombing, the trip had otherwise been successful. Jabbar and I were on better terms—but I had gained nothing. I didn't feel I had thwarted anything. I still didn't have enough information to contact Mr. Hunter at the embassy. If Jabbar did something stupid, would they blame me? The Homeland Security motto is "See something, say something." What if I knew something, but said nothing? I had always been angry at the 9/11 hijackers' friends, who later said they suspected something. Why in the hell didn't they speak up? It could have saved my dad, my mom, not to mention three thousand innocents. But if I put my dear friend into the embassy's firestorm, would it push him further into al-Qaeda's hateful arms? Would they send CIA operatives to kidnap Jabbar and waterboard him in a warehouse in Aden's back streets? That would push him over the edge into more hate unless the CIA killed him when they were done.

Back in Haydan, I dropped Jabbar off at his house. I gave him a one-hundred-dollar bill. "Okay, Jabbar, what did I just buy?"

"Uh, I had two bushels of oranges ready to go and then about four sacks of millet and one sack of wheat from my fall harvest." Then he stared at me. "Bryan, are you taking all this with you to Sana'a? You'll have to take it in the old clinic truck."

Shaking my head, I said, "No, Jabbar, I want you to drive up to the refugee camp." I pointed to the rows of tents on the side of the hill. "I want you to drop two oranges and two liters of wheat or millet at every tent until you run out."

I turned to go and then stopped. Looking over my shoulder, I added, "I want to see you again before I leave Haydan."

He nodded with a half-smile. "You can help me with the delivery of your goods to the refugees in the morning. And Bryan, you're a good man."

My face blushed with a smile. "Yeah, I'll help you tomorrow. And Jabbar ... you are a good man too. Please, for God's sake ... stay one."

Jabbar stood and stared as I drove off. In my little round rearview mirror, I watched his solemn face shrink with the distance. What I would have given to know his thoughts.

Then I rode my bike to the old clinic ruins and went to bed. Worry visited me throughout the night, leaking into my mind through the porous moments of respite. I plugged in my earphones and started Dad's playlist, to fill the empty spaces with his presence. But Dad's ghost wouldn't summon. I felt alone. Deserted by fate. Finally, sometime during the small hours of the morning, I dozed.

I awakened while it was still dark and slid—snakelike—out the door of my tent so I could look up at the morning sky, watching for the sun to make its way over the mountains. In the quiet of that moment, I knew I couldn't leave Yemen with unfinished business in my way.

CHAPTER TWENTY-ONE

I waited until Dorothy was in her office, and I called.

"Hi, well, I've made up my mind," I said in an upbeat tone. "I'll take the non-clinical job in Sana'a, if it's still on the table."

"Really? I'm surprised. What made you decide to stay?" she asked.

"I don't like doing non-clinical work, but I'm just not ready to leave Yemen. Not yet. But I need an apartment in Sana'a."

"We can handle that," Dorothy offered. "With the war, it's a renter's market."

I worked with Jabbar the next morning delivering his harvest to the refugees. He was his better self, the nice Dr. Jekyll having replaced the cold and pious Mr. Hyde.

I called Ray to see if I could meet with him on my way to Sana'a. On the phone, he said, "I wish I could invite you to spend the night, but I can't. I don't want you to come to Abdul's compound. It's too dangerous. My cousin is becoming more paranoid about us. He suggests it's time I look for a new home. I'll meet you in a café in Huth. I wish I had a damn car—I would drive to Haydan."

"Ray, I went fishing with Jabbar," I said.

"Really? How did that go?"

"Great. It seems we are on better terms."

"Did you ask him about the plot?" Ray asked.

"Not directly, but I asked him if he would do something bad in revenge for Alam's death, and he didn't really answer."

"I'm looking forward to seeing you. There have been new developments here," Ray added.

After packing everything I owned on this earth onto my bike, I gave the tent to Ahmed in exchange for his promise to take good care of it. The tall, lean man with arms that stretched to his knees, wrapped those long arms around me and cried.

Mazen gave me a strong embrace and kissed my cheeks. He informed me he was going home to Stockholm. His father's Parkinson's Disease was the deciding factor, and he didn't care to work for Michel again, as he had before Sheila came. "It's a shame too," he said. "All the other doctors at the MSF Hospital are great people without, as we say in Sweden, a *gudskomplex* [God complex]."

The war had worn the road to Huth like an old coat. It was full of holes. The December cold winds forced me to zip my jacket up to my Adam's apple, my keffiyeh wrapped around my neck and over my chin beneath my face shield. I stopped at the hospital in Sa'dah on a whim. The route took me near it. I thought there was a slim chance I could change Michel's mind about letting me work there, despite his *gudskomplex*. I should have known better.

The heavy doors with the chicken-wired windows were unguarded on that morning, so I walked into the acute room. I saw Michel right away. He was sitting on the bed of a patient—an old grisled man with a tube in his nose—talking to him. The patient's family members were strewn around on the floor—the man's son, I presumed; a daughter-in-law; and a few children. Lord knows where the old man's wife was, probably dead.

Michel glanced at me as he sipped something from a cup. Though I disliked him on a personal level, I had to acknowledge that Michel was a good doctor. I would've trusted my family's life to his care. His passion was obvious from the endless hours he spent in the clinic and the empathy he showed his patients.

While I waited, images came to me of that terrible day of the school bus bombing in that room. I saw Sheila, her shoulder-length curls bouncing as she walked from patient to patient in her bloodied lab coat. She was an angel. What a loss. What a damn loss. If I had known how little time we had left, I would have pursued her with all the passion my tired heart could muster. Sometimes rules had to be discarded. It was her idea to keep our relationship platonic, so that we could focus on our patients and not each other. I shouldn't have listened to her, although she was right. As the Yemenis liked to say, "It's okay to set the donkeys free when the wagon is going sideways in a wadi's flood." Sheila and I were in the middle of a war where everything was going sideways, and our love should have been set free.

To my left, I heard a throat clearing. Michel started to speak, staring right at me with his dark eyes. "Bryan, if you are wondering why I wanted to see you—"

I held up my hands. "Wait! I didn't know you wanted to see me. I heard that you turned down IRC's offer to loan me here. I'm on my way to Sana'a to do non-clinical work, and I stopped here on a courtesy visit."

"Good," he said. "That you're working in a non-clinical job in Sana'a."

"Why is that good?"

"Bryan, you're not a doctor. It's better if you work in an office where there are no patients."

I felt my throat tighten, my breaths cycling faster.

I asked, "So, the hospital is fully staffed, and you don't have the use for a clinician like me?"

Michel rubbed his head and pulled down on his ponytail as if to straighten it. "We are always short of doctors. We just don't have a need for someone like you."

I scrunched up my face with a confused look as I stared at him. "Michel, help me to understand what your problem is with a PA. I've been seeing over eighty patients per day in Haydan and giving them excellent care. I just don't get it."

He wrinkled his nose. "We are *Médecins* Sans Frontières, *Doctors* without Borders, certainly not doctor's *associates* without borders."

Stay calm, Bryan. "What in my skill set is not useful here?"

Michel sipped from his cup. "We're a doctor-centric organization and always will be."

"So, it's political," I said. "It's not about your patients' best interests."

"Bryan, what you did here after the school bus bombing was unacceptable. Barbarous! Putting an IO needle into a child's skull?" He laughed. "You're in way over your head." His amused expression morphed into a scowl.

"And how's that little girl today? Mazen ran into her grandpa, and he said she's doing well." I raised my eyebrows, awaiting an answer.

"Omaira is doing... *Elle va fantastique!* I saw her two weeks ago. But it's no thanks to you. It's a miracle you didn't kill her. You could've pierced her brain with that needle or have hit an artery. You don't know neuroanatomy like a doctor."

"But you had left her to die!" I yelled, then bit my lip to seal in angrier words. My eyes scanned the room. Everyone was looking at us. I saw Maria sitting with a patient across the room, giving us an angry glare.

I took a deep breath, letting it out slowly through my nose, and then I continued in a quieter voice. "Michel, do you not remember me telling you I spent almost a decade doing neurosurgery? You really don't think I know neuroanatomy? Do you have a clue how many times my hands have been wrapped around someone's brain—in situ?"

He just stared at me and sipped his coffee, which I could smell on his breath a moment later when he leaned toward me and spoke again. "No, we don't need you here. Sheila wasn't a good supervisor for you. She had too much to learn herself. She hadn't finished a residency."

My face contorted into a death stare. I said in a low tone, "I've worked with a lot of great doctors, and she was a damn good one, residency or not. She had good judgment."

"Good doctor? Not so much," Michel said with a sneer. Then he lifted his cup of coffee in the air like he was making a toast. "But she was a damn good lover, wasn't she?" He winked.

The crude comment caught me completely off guard. My jaw dropped. My fists became like sledgehammers hanging at my side. *Do I tear the place apart or get the hell out?*

Through gritted teeth, I said, "Dr. Moreau, you are a physician. You are the director of the hospital. Sheila told me you are a legend in France for your heroics. And, speaking of Sheila, you had one of the most magnificent women in the world as your girlfriend for a year and still … Why are you so damn insecure? I don't get it."

Michel did a quick about-face and walked toward the door to the wards.

I had plenty to say, but I would have punched the man in the face if I'd stayed one minute too long. I pivoted and marched toward the exit, nostrils flared, drool dripping from my mouth, the sledgehammers swinging at my sides but slowing uncoiling. I walked out the door, my anger bridled. *And my sister Angie says I'm impulsive?*

During my ride from there to Huth, I ruminated over Michel's words. If he had been pure evil, I would've had a case for hating his guts. The truth was that he was an asshole but not the devil.

Ray and I met in a small corner coffee shop in the center of Huth, about a mile from Abdul's compound. By the time I found the place in the labyrinthine streets of the ancient city, Ray was sitting inside reading a crumpled newspaper. Four small tables filled the space—two chairs to a table. The chairs were hard on the backs, carved olive wood. But the caned seats were well-worn and conformed to the buttocks, offering comfort and the opportunity for long conversations. The café's doors let the congregating flies out and stray cats in—unhindered. It was a grubby place, but the best one could expect near a war zone where customers constantly trudged in from dirty, bombed-out streets with blood still on their sleeves.

An aproned waiter with a bushy handlebar mustache, like those worn by bare-fisted boxers of the Victorian age, was rushing back and forth between tables and a small TV on which a soccer match was being shown. Ray said he had given him our orders already. The man soon returned with two cappuccinos in his hands and a scrawny black cat under his arm, which he tossed out the door on his way back to the counter. I looked for hair in my cup but didn't see any. I did, however, see the remains of red lipstick around its rim.

Early winter's chilly wind blew across us each time a customer opened the wooden door, sending our paper napkins and Ray's newspaper onto the grimy floor. I watched as the cat reentered the shop with each new customer, only to be escorted back out by the patient waiter. I sat, muted by thought, as Ray tapped his finger on the tabletop and stared out the window, his lips pursed, eyes squinting as if he didn't know where to begin. I was about to start the conversation when I noticed his face become more composed.

Ray leaned toward me, looked over each of his shoulders, and whispered, "I have new information, but let's be careful. Abdul has ears and eyes under every rock in Huth. I wouldn't let a donkey or camel overhear me." He sat up and looked out the window. Then, louder, he said, "So, are you leaving Yemen soon?"

"I was. However, yesterday I changed my mind. I'm moving to Sana'a to finish my contract."

His face beamed. He stood up, raising his coffee in the air, "*Alhamdulillah!* [praise to Allah] I'm so delighted!" Then he sat and returned to his quieter voice. "It is easier and safer to travel to Sana'a than Haydan." Reaching over and placing his hand on my arm, he continued. "I can see you more often. I can't stop this mission without your help. What changed your mind?"

"Well, while I had a great trip with Jabbar, I have unfinished business with him. I can't leave this situation the way it is. I'm afraid that he's going to get killed—or worse—get someone else killed. So, I'm on my way to Sana'a to work in the IRC office."

"So, you're giving up on the Haydan clinic?"

"Yeah, you can say that. IRC wouldn't let me continue by myself. They offered me to the MSF Hospital in Sa'dah, but they didn't want me because I'm not a physician."

Ray was shaking his head. "This makes no—pardon my French—fucking sense to me. We are desperate here in Yemen for people with your talent."

"It's political. I have two strikes against me. I'm American, which means I have a target on my back. And I'm a PA and not a physician."

"Bullshit, Bryan! Our allergy doctor when I was at Georgetown was a PA. She was excellent. She took care of Zoey's asthma and my dermographism." As he said "dermographism," he stroked the inside of his forearm with his fingernail and soon a red welt came up as a line, as if he had written on his arm with a red marker. "Since being off my fexofenadine, it has returned. So, my point is, hell yeah, there's a need for you here."

He leaned toward me again and spoke in a voice so low I could barely hear it above the traffic noise outside. "Bryan, Jabbar was here two weeks ago. He came in an empty truck. Nothing to sell. The next day, the strangers in the black Mercedes were here. I snuck around to the outside window where I could hear them. I stooped in the shadow and listened for an hour. I heard almost every word. I'm now even more convinced these men are al-Qaeda on the Arabian Peninsula, or AQAP operatives. You may remember that it was an al-Qaeda cell that bombed the USS *Cole* in Aden in 2000." Tapping his forehead with his palm, he quickly added, "What am I saying? You were too young to remember."

"Yeah, I know about the Cole incident. However, I didn't give it much thought until after 9/11," I said.

"Anyway," he said, "these strange men, the way they speak gives them away. They're not with Hezbollah. They're too sophisticated for ISIL. The *Cole* bombing, as bad as it was, was only a practice run for 9/11. The CIA killed several of the perpetrators with drone strikes. Some escaped, melting into these mountains, and are still at large. Who knows, maybe they are driving a black Mercedes now." He looked up like he was studying the ceiling. "My point, Bryan, is that this is big."

"Jeez-o-pete, Ray. Do you really think our Jabbar has got himself mixed up in something like this? I just can't imagine it."

Ray took another sip of coffee, and we sat in silence for a minute. Looking at me, he continued, "I still don't know if Jabbar understands who he's dealing with. They're dangerous. They have international ambitions. They're perilous."

In an even quieter voice, he added, "The word they mentioned several times was '*almuhima*' [the mission]."

"My Arabic vocabulary is limited. Is there an innocent way to use such a word?"

"There's not," said Ray, shaking his head. "You wouldn't use *almuhima* when talking about a business transaction, such as selling your harvest. It had to be something more important."

"But what mission are they talking about?" I asked.

Ray sat up straight and rolled his eyes, exasperated. "That's the problem. They're holding their secrets close to their chests. The group's leader appeared to be a man they call Salim. He told the group to only communicate in person. No e-mails, no phone calls, nothing that's traceable. Now why would he say that?"

"You must have an idea what mission they're talking about," I said. "Do you think it could be directed at me? I mean, if I'm the last American in the valley, I wouldn't put it past them to recruit my best friend to kill me."

"I don't think you're a target. They could have killed you easily before now. I think it is something much bigger. It could be sabotaging a government facility. It could be a suicide bombing, even outside Yemen, on American or Saudi soil."

At that moment, we heard a terrifying scream, "Noooooooooo!"

Ray and I both ducked. I turned around to see our waiter standing in front of the tv, his elbows out, his fists full of his hair. Chelsea had just scored.

Turning back around, I added, "As I was about to say, Jabbar is furious at both America and Saudi."

I leaned over to look out the café window at the busy streets. My thoughts scattered to the ferocious winds of war, what was and what could be. Jabbar an international terrorist? My dear and humble friend, a cold-blooded murderer?

To break the awkward silence, Ray asked, "Did you want more coffee?"

I smiled at him. "I would."

As I spoke, Ray reached into the inside pocket of his sports jacket. He took out a long, slender cigar. The brown leaves wrapped into a perfectly round cylinder, tapered on each end.

"Would you like a nice hand-rolled Havana? This was going to be my going-away gift, but now you are staying a few more months ... well, you should have it anyway."

I reached for it, then paused. "No, not really. I've never developed a taste for them. I will smoke one to celebrate something special. But I have no such hope for this day."

Ray put it in my shirt pocket and winked. "Save this and smoke it when this whole ordeal is over."

Then his expression changed and took on a worried look.

"What's bothering you?" I asked.

"I overheard Abdul talking to Jabbar about going to commercial sea captain's school. I was puzzled, and Jabbar was talking too softly for me to hear his side of the conversation."

"Oh, yeah, that's what I wanted to tell you. He's going to school in Cyprus for six months. He told me this on our fishing trip. Apparently, someone is paying for it because Alam was killed."

"Sea captain's school?" Ray mumbled. "That concerns me. If these men are sponsoring him, why? They would see it as an investment, expecting a return. There are several strategic harbors where you could run a ship aground and cause trouble. Maybe in the Strait of Hormuz or the Suez Canal. You could crash a big cargo ship into a U.S. Navy ship. That's how they did it with the USS *Cole*. They used a sea captain for that suicide mission, and they would not hesitate to do it again. Imagine doing that with a big cargo ship? Bryan, you must stop him!" Ray brought his fist down on our table, rattling the coffee cups.

"What should I do?" I asked. "I won't be around him once I'm in Sana'a. Should I go to the U.S. Embassy and talk to someone? Do we have enough evidence?"

"No, no, no! Hell no!" He frowned and slapped the table. Other patrons turned and looked in our direction. "If you tell your government, they'll eliminate Jabbar with a drone strike. That's what worries me."

"Then what do I do?" I asked, shaking my head.

Leaning across the table, he returned to his quieter voice. "I think it's best if we handle this within the family."

Ray then leaned so far across the table that his shirt's buttons were clicking as they brushed the table's edge. He whispered. "Another thing ... I got caught."

"Caught doing what?" I asked. Our foreheads were now almost touching.

He whispered, "Listening. I stood up. My knees can only take so much stooping. Abdul came to the window. 'Who's out there?' he yelled. I had no choice but to answer, 'It's me, Rahman. I'm out for a walk.' Then Abdul came outside and confronted me, 'Are you spying on us?'"

"What did you say?" I asked.

Ray's skin had gone pale. "I gave him a lame story about taking a stroll and meandering by their window by accident. I didn't realize how visible I was. But then I turned the tables on him and asked, 'Why are you so paranoid? Are you hiding something?' Then as a distraction, I asked him a ridiculous question, 'Are you working for the Yemeni government forces?'"

"Did it work?" I asked.

"No ... well, yeah. The question threw him off guard, and he became very angry at me for asking him, a strong Houthi supporter, such a dumb question. But, no, it didn't work because he's kicking me out."

"Really?"

"Yeah, really," Ray snapped back.

"Where are you going?" I asked.

Ray shrugged and looked down at his hands folded on the table. "I don't know. We still have our apartment in Sana'a, but that's not safe either. We are talking about moving in with my mother-in-law. She has a large home in the mountains right outside Sana'a. She also has her own bodyguards, but they would be no match for the Houthis if they wanted to take us. It's a mess. A damn mess. No good choices."

Ray's last words to me on that day were, "Bryan, I've got your cell and sat phone numbers. Let's keep in touch. God willing, I'll see you in Sana'a next time.

CHAPTER TWENTY-TWO

In the center of Sana'a, IRC found me a small apartment with a balcony just three blocks from their office. It was on the fifth floor in a brown stucco building with white trim around the windows and edges, in the same traditional style as Jabbar's home in the highlands.

Sana'a is one of the oldest cities in the world, dating back over millennia. If one were to have excavated the dirt beneath my building, god knows what would've been found. A few buildings had foundations that predated the Parthenon. The city itself, while a contested prize in this tit-for-tat war, had a sense of normalcy. Ignoring the bomb craters and burnt buildings, you would think you were in any typical big city in the developing world. There were people in a broad spectrum of costumes—turbans, newsboy hats, burkas, jeans, and robes—moving in all directions buying and selling what was available, which wasn't much. It was also not uncommon to see long rifles, mostly AK 47s and plenty of janbiyas in men's belts.

Ray called three months after I had settled into Sana'a. "Bryan, we must talk. There are developments. Jabbar is in Cyprus now—."

"Yeah," I mumbled into the phone. "I knew that. I mean, he told me he was going in December and now it's March. Hey, I thought you were moving to Sana'a."

Ray continued in his serious tone. "Abdul hasn't brought it up again, and we have no place to go. But listen. I'm worried. The men in the Mercedes returned. 1 was listening from outside their window, trying to be more discreet. Once again, they spoke about *almuhima* [the mission] several times, without being precise. They said Jabbar will be finishing school in June and his schooling is connected to the mission. I'm afraid we are running out of time. Be prepared to help me deal with Jabbar as soon as he's back in Yemen."

After a few weeks of contemplation, I made a firm decision to visit Hunter Philips, Dorothy's contact at the U.S. embassy, to at least establish a rapport.

The embassy in Sana'a is a windowless fortress—a bleached-white building behind a matching perimeter wall, both structures with concrete chevrons in rows marching across the upper sections. There were security guards scattered around the plaza. I had to show my passport three times to approach the front door. U.S. Marines provided another layer of protection inside.

I passed through a metal detector, got patted down by a security officer, and then was taken to a lobby where about twenty people were waiting, some seated, some in line at a window. An American flag was on display. On the wall were a portrait of our president and a photo of an endless wheatfield; staggered rows of red combines blowing golden grain into fat trucks through long augers. A brass plate at the bottom of the frame read, "Kansas Wheatfield." *American cruelty to a hungry country or just insensitivity?*

A Yemeni woman was sitting behind a thick-glassed window stapling sheets of paper. I took the number 57 from a ring of plastic numbers. Above the window a digital monitor read, "Now Serving Number 44." A Yemeni family—man, woman, and two children—were standing at her window. A few more people were standing around clutching their numbers as if they were tickets to paradise. One man looked American. I was tempted to speak to him but didn't because he had trouble written all over him—tattered clothes, befuddled expression—and I couldn't handle a new problem in my life.

After a while, it was my turn, and the lady behind the glass spoke, her voice emitting from a speaker. "Can I help you?"

I leaned over and spoke into a microphone that protruded from beneath the window on a stick. "Uh, I have an appointment with Mr. Hunter Philips."

"What's your name?" she asked, her face so devoid of animation I found myself reaching into my pocket for a quarter to put into a slot as if she were a mechanical fortune-teller in a box on Coney Island.

Leaning over to the mic, I answered, "Uh, Bryan ... Bryan Rogers."

"Give me your passport" came the voice from lips that barely moved.

"Okay," I said reluctantly, as I had just put it away. I dropped the little blue book into the stainless-steel metal drawer, and she retracted it into her little wonderland behind the glass.

"Have a seat," she said, motioning toward my chair with her eyes. In thirty minutes, she called me back through a secured double door. I was escorted to a plush corner office with no windows. Painted scenes of Yemen's better days adorned the outside walls, giving the feeling of windows, but behind the paintings I was sure was thick concrete. The two inside walls were decorated with Mr. Philips's traveling treasures—I assumed—exotic masks, a spear, and several interesting paintings of places not related to the U.S. or Yemen, such as the Grand Bazaar in Istanbul and Jordan's Petra.

A handsome, middle-aged blond man soon strolled through the door. He looked like a washed-up Beach Boy who was still tanned and fit. You could see the shape of Ray-Bans stenciled on his face and temples in untanned skin. He closed the glass door behind him.

He took a seat and reached his hand over the big wooden desk to shake mine. His smile pointed at me, but there was no direct eye contact as he mumbled, "You're late."

"I arrived over an hour ago," I said.

"Well, you can't just waltz into an American embassy ... not in Yemen."

Glancing down at a folder in his hand, he said, "Welcome, Mr. Rogers." He snickered, "I've never met 'Mr. Rogers' before. You look nothing like your name's sake."

"It's Bryan. Call me Bryan," I said in a monotone.

"So, Dorothy sent you over from IRC. What can I do for you?" He leaned back in his reclining desk chair, hands interlocked behind his head.

"I'm an American citizen, and I'm worried about a terrorist attack."

"Dorothy told me it was your clinic that was burned. That was dreadful. Did you know the doctor who died in the fire?"

My mouth gaped open, then the words carefully slipped out. "Yeah ... you could say that."

"Do you know something about who did it? We'd love to bring them to justice." Oddly, the painted smile remained on his face.

I leaned forward. "Me too. No, I know nothing. Not a clue. But there's a possible new attack, even bigger. A terrorist cell may have recruited the father of a child killed in the school bus bombing in Sa'dah last August. I have reason to believe they might take action against a ship."

"You mean the alleged school bus bombing?" he said, the smile still hanging there.

I fell back in my chair and sighed. "Excuse me? No, not alleged. It happened."

He sat up in his chair and picked a pen off his desk and started to play with it, clicking it out and back in. Then he gave me a serious, dry look. "Well, we don't know for sure. Our intelligence report stated people on the ground possibly staged it. You know, they haul in an old school bus from the junkyard and plant bomb casings around it so they can blame the Saudis and the U.S. The intelligence has found no evidence of children being hurt."

My mouth hung open, then the words rushed out. "Hell, no, it wasn't staged!" My face became infused with fiery blood from deep within. "I'm shocked you would believe such bullshit! I was on the ground within minutes after the bomb hit the bus. My own damn eyes saw the bomb site, and I took care of the injured children. I saw plenty of dead ones too. They weren't made up in moulage—it was real blood, real gore. I felt it. I smelled it. Hell, I even tasted it. My colleague, Dr. Emory, was there when the bomb hit. She was less than fifty yards away. No disrespect, but don't give me that crap about what your intelligence knows or doesn't know. I was there."

Leaning away from me again, he said, "I see you're emotionally invested in the narrative, so I won't argue the point. But I trust our intelligence. These terrorists are clever. I wouldn't put it past them to blow up their own children and plant them as bomb victims."

"Absurd! Argue what point? There's no point." I let out a long breath of air, took in a new breath, and held it. Then I blurted out, "I think we are done here! A complete waste of my time."

"Settle down," he said. The asshole leaned across his desk, twirling the pen in his fingers like a miniature baton, and smirked. "So, as I was saying, I'm busy. What can I do for you?"

"As I mentioned, a father of a victim of the school bus bombing was a fishing boat captain and is now at commercial captain school. I have a tip that he's up to something sinister ... you know, in retribution for the killing of his son. He's very bitter. I hope you can interrupt him before he does anything stupid. He's a dear friend."

"Friend, you say?" He snickered.

"Yeah."

"And you only have a hunch?"

"I've tried to find out more. He became a different man after he lost his son and isn't so forthcoming as he used to be. I came here only because I've exhausted my ideas for finding out more."

"So, no concrete information?"

"No." Then I thought for a moment. "Well, yes."

He leaned forward in his desk chair.

"Well, I have another good friend, Yemeni, who is this friend's cousin. He overheard his cousin plotting with some other men about a big mission. He thinks these other men are with AQAP, you know, al-Qaeda in the Arabian Peninsula."

"Yes, I know who AQAP is. Give me this friend's name, his cousin's name, and these men's names and their information. I'll send word to our intelligence officer. He's a sharp dude. If there's something going on, I'm sure they're already onto it. If there is such a plan, they will interrupt it, most likely with Hellfire missiles launched from a drone right up their little brown mother-fucking asses."

Shaking my head, I said loudly, "No. No, that's not what I'm looking for! I mean, you could arrest him and take him to a deprograming center. I know they have those in Saudi."

With a laugh, he said, "It's a cruel world, Bryan."

"So I've heard," I mumbled.

"Well, it doesn't work like that. You don't get to order our actions like you do French fries at a McDonald's. Do you think Guantanamo Bay is a rehab facility like the Betty Ford Center? Well, it's not. If we find something on this guy, we'll take him and his friends out. We will pulverize them before they even have a chance at doing anything sinister."

My mind explored the possible outcomes. My friend could get killed by special forces, or he could kill a shipload of American sailors, or tourists? Was there an endgame that wasn't a total disaster? *How can I leave Yemen with Jabbar still scheming? Ray's idea of keeping it in the family wasn't working.* It was larger than any one family.

"Bryan, did you hear me?" he asked, tapping his pen on his desk.

"Yes," I said. "Every word."

He stared into his computer screen for a moment and typed like he was sending e-mails. Was he taking me seriously or not? I didn't know how to read this man. Then he looked back at me. "You know, after someone like you has gone through a tragedy, like someone setting fire to your clinic and you losing a colleague, it tends to make them paranoid. Which I understand."

I sat quietly as I continued to think, my fist against my mouth.

"What's this terrorist dude's name and where does he live?" he asked.

I bit down on my fist.

"Hello, Mr. Rogers?" He began tapping his pen on the desk to the rhythm of the old "Shave and a Haircut" tune.

"Damn," I whispered. "Yes, I heard you! Uh, Jabbar. Jabbar El Haddad is my friend's name, the one being recruited."

"Where does he live?"

"He's in Cyprus now … Like I said, he's in training to become a commercial sea captain. But he's from Haydan."

Philips jotted down the information, then looked up. "And the other guys' names?"

"Uh, I have no idea who the men are with AQAP as I've never met them."

"So, it is just hearsay?" He kept the pen poised over the paper.

"More than that. I mean I've seen them, just never met them."

"Okay, and this cousin?"

"Can't say."

"So, he's a ghost too?"

"I didn't say that! Yes, he's real, but I promised him that I wouldn't give out his name—he's a, you know, confidential source."

"Hmm, so you feel more loyalty to AQAP than your own damn country?"

"No! Hell, no. But if I give you this cousin's name, he'll stop talking to me and then I won't know what's going on."

"Hmm," he mumbled. "They may want you to wear a wire."

A wire when I talk to Ray? Is he shitting me?

The room was quiet for a couple of minutes, as Philips appeared to be thinking. Finally, he asked, "Bryan, have you gone through any mental health counseling since the clinic fire?"

"Noooo." I said, shaking my head.

Does he think I'm nuts?

"We could help arrange that," he said with a smile.

I didn't answer. I just let out another long breath, looking down and away from him.

Then he abruptly stood up and reached out his hand to shake mine.

"Well, Mr. Rogers, thanks for dropping by. We get many tips about terrorist plots, and the vast majority, thank god, are baseless. But we'll check this out, and if there is anything to it, we will take care of it." Then he asked, "Do you play golf?"

"What?" I asked.

"Do you play golf?" he repeated.

"No. There's a golf course here, in Sana'a?" I asked.

A big rubbery smile burst across his tanned face. "Hell, yeah. A damn good one. They have sand traps from hell—old bomb craters—but otherwise it's not bad. I thought maybe you would want to join me sometime."

"Not really," I said. "Will you keep me informed on what you find out about my tip?"

"Nope," he said with poise.

"Nope?" I repeated.

"The CIA doesn't give updates to anyone outside their organization. If they need your help, they'll ask for it. If you have any more information, well, you know my number. Same number if you want to play golf." He winked.

I left the office with my head down, studying my steps, the world around me a blur. His last silly words to me as I was going out his door were, "Give my regards to Mr. McFeely!" Then he belly-laughed.

On the way home, I walked through Sana'a's narrow, tangled streets. If it's possible to go snow-blind from being surrounded by white, in Sana'a you could go taupe-blind. The tall buildings were all taupe, some with white accents, but the rest with some shade of taupe. The streets and the surrounding mountains were the same color. Taupe, taupe, taupe. If it weren't for the gray-blue sky that covered that day's ceiling like riveted steel, I would have gone mad. Flocks of black kites, looking for insects or lizards, were overhead in swarms, a thin sight of normalcy. I thought how birds must have been looking down on humans as morons, always destroying our world for nothing.

Back at my humble apartment, I grabbed a water bottle for my parched throat and sank into the thick foam couch. Ray had been right. My visit to the embassy had been a complete waste of time and had put him and Jabbar in danger.

I felt so disheartened and lost that I thought about leaving Yemen again—immediately. I had done my part to help the Yemeni people and to warn the Americans about a potential terrorist act. My hands were clean. I said something because I saw something. That's all they asked, wasn't it?

I wanted to jump a fishing boat that night and have them drop me off in Eilat. The airport was closed again. I figured maybe the black-market Jack Daniels runners could take me north. If there wasn't an active warfront between my apartment and the sea, I would have skipped out of the country that night. In Eilat I could get my boat and head east or south. *Who cares?*

I packed my duffle.

CHAPTER TWENTY-THREE

I awakened the next morning to roosters crowing. Was I back in Haydan?

Opening my eyes, I saw only the bare robin egg blue stucco walls of my Sana'a bedroom. I had a framed family photo—of Mom, Dad, my two brothers, and my sister Angie—beside my bed. Inside the same frame was a black-and-white photo of Sheila I'd cut out of an IRC newsletter.

I pivoted in my stiff bed—it had a mattress made of goat hair that was as hard as cement—giving me nightmares that I was covered with bedsores. I awoke and ran my hand along my buttocks and back, finding intact skin. I closed my eyes for a few more winks. Before long, I smelled the haunting aroma of burning paper and plastic, which provoked images of the clinic fire.

Besides the smoke of burning garbage for warmth and cooking, Sana'a had a faint sewage smell drifting through its streets. A city burdened with an overtaxed sewage system of four million people crammed into a small space during a civil war had to have a stench. Breakfast meals, ful medames (fava beans, cumin, garlic, onion, and parsley) being cooked in our building, brought more pleasant odors seeping in between the foul ones.

I closed the window. The winds of Sana'a, a city perched at an even higher altitude than Denver, can run cold even in May. It looked bright outside—the high sun meant it had to be late in the morning. It was Friday, my day off.

I walked to the bathroom and stumbled over my packed duffle on the floor. I stood over the squat toilet and peed. It came out like dark tea. Was I dehydrated? I looked in the cracked mirror above the sink. My sclera had a cornsilk tint. *Damn!* I had hepatitis.

I laid down on my bed and counted the months since I'd sucked blood from that child's chest. It had been nine months — much longer than the incubation period for hepatitis B. It was the same nine months since I'd had sex. It was four months since I'd been with patients, including the cesarean section, which was inside the incubation period. Of course, it could have been food-borne, but I didn't eat out. I hoped that, like most cases of hepatitis, it would be self-limiting.

I unpacked my duffle. I'd gone to bed the previous night hell-bent on getting out of the country but now was having second thoughts. While I had done all I could, I still felt discontent. *Could Ray stop Jabbar without me? Could the embassy?* Lord, I hoped so.

By June, life had settled back to a routine. I was going to work every day in the office. I didn't seek medical attention, being too distracted by other things, and assumed the hepatitis would resolve on its own. I had not heard from the embassy or Ray, but I felt the tension building. I had tried calling Ray but couldn't reach him as I was sure his cell tower in Huth was down.

Then one early July evening, I was sitting on my balcony, when my phone rang. It was him.

"Hey, Ray. I've been thinking about you, hoping to see your face in Sana'a. So glad you called! Where the heck are you?"

"Hi, Bryan. We're still in Huth. How're you?"

"I'm fine and how's the family?"

"We're doing, as you Americans say, peachy, thanks to God's help," he said. He cleared his throat, then continued, "Bryan, we need to talk. Things are heating up. There have been developments. The men in the black Mercedes have been back, and it sounds like the mission is imminent. I listened to them. They were talking about the mission. They used a new term that's even more disconcerting — '*aqsaa eadad min aldahaya*.' Do you know this term?"

I reviewed my mental Arabic dictionary. The phrase *aqsaa* means the "maximum," and *daha* is the root to the word "victim," but the full meaning eluded me.

"No, I don't think I do."

Ray sighed. "It means 'getting the maximum casualties.'"

A chill went up my spine.

"Jabbar finished school and is now out at sea on his apprenticeship. I think Abdul said he was acting as an oil tanker's captain, going from Iran's Kharg Island to Yingkou, China. He's being supervised by an experienced commercial sea captain. After that, he'll return home for a visit in August, and then he'll be co-captaining a ship in September, his first real assignment."

"You overheard all of this?" I asked.

"I did, until my knees gave out," Ray said. "I was skeptical that Jabbar had a job lined up so quickly. I think those same men who financed his training found him the job and they'll be back to Abdul's house in August. It'll be their last planning session. I'll keep an eye out for Jabbar. I know that if he shows up, the meeting will be imminent. Bryan, do you understand what this means? This is show time. We have enough light on this mission now to know its real. But I'm completely confident that you will stop Jabbar, and all will be saved."

"Ray," I said in a soft voice. "I also have things to tell you."

There was silence on the other end of the phone. "Ray?"

"I'm here, go ahead, tell me."

"I met with a Hunter Philips at the U.S. Embassy—"

"What the hell, Bryan!" Ray said in a loud, angry whisper. "I told you that was a bad idea ... an unbelievably bad idea! Now look at what you've done. These people in your government don't know what the hell they're doing. It's a, how do you say it, a bull in a china shop. They'll kill somebody, like Jabbar and his entire family. They may also kill me and Rosie... and my kids."

I put my hand to my brow and sighed. "Ray?"

Silence.

"Ray?"

"What!"

"Why would they kill you?"

"Why weren't you patient until I could figure this mess out? I don't want a terrorist act any more than you do. Jabbar can't die, he's my cousin. I don't want the Americans or Saudis to have an excuse to step up this war, and that's exactly what will happen if Jabbar pulls something off. But if U.S. intelligence is any damn good, they'll track down Abdul and then fire missiles into his compound, blowing us all to hell. They don't consider the collaterals, just if they kill the fucking 'terrorists.'" Then he mumbled, "Damn it."

Shaking my head, I said, "Ray, I'm so sorry, but I wasn't sure what else I could do. I couldn't leave Yemen with this hanging in the air. I had to say something. We weren't getting anywhere on our own with Jabbar. Ray, you've got to understand, this is much bigger than me. Much bigger than us. I feel like the single piece of china in a shop full of bulls."

I could hear the man breathing, but the words were damned up. Finally, Ray spoke, "Do you know the adage, 'The millstones of the gods grind slowly?'"

"The millstones of the gods? No, I don't think so."

"It has been around since the Greeks. Some argued that if the gods' vengeance for evil was too slow, the perpetrators would not associate the punishment with their crime. Therefore, mortals had to take revenge for the gods. But the wise men reminded them that the millstones of gods' punishments turn slowly, so they should be patient and let the gods grind the criminals in their own time. We must be patient."

"Don't worry. I don't think this Philips guy took me seriously."

"How do you know that?"

"When we finished, he asked me to play golf, like he wasn't listening."

"If Mr. Philips does nothing—which I pray to God you are right about—then you have one more chance with Jabbar—when he comes home in August. I'll contact you, and you must get your ass to Huth as soon as possible and meet with him. I would do it, but I barely know the guy. You, on the other hand, are his best friend in the world. He respects you. If anyone can dissuade him, it's you."

After hanging up the phone, I glanced at the clock on the wall and realized it was still morning in New York. It was time to give Angie a call. I stepped out onto the balcony and pointed my antenna toward the stars, which were hardly visible through the light and smog pollution of Sana'a's early evening.

After I filled Angie in on my story, she responded, "I understand your fear. Your predicament is serious. How do you always find yourself in such complex situations? Is ordinary life, the kind your brothers and I live, too boring for you?"

I told her about Hunter Philips. She responded, "His attitude doesn't surprise me. I don't know what it means either. Did he just drop the ball or are they working on this in secret? You may never know."

"Then what do you suggest I do?"

"Maybe it's time to pay this embassy guy another visit," she said. "You know, to get clarity."

"Well, I thought about that," I said. "But here's another problem. My good Yemeni friend Ray is an inside man and Jabbar's relative. He's very smart—he was a university professor. However, he's livid that I went to the embassy. Ray thought we could handle this alone."

"I'm not sure I understand. If he's trying to stop this, why didn't he welcome the embassy's help?"

I paced back and forth on my narrow balcony, while answering. "He says that he's afraid they'll do something reckless, like shoot a missile into Jabbar's or his own house."

"Why would they shoot a missile into his house?"

"It's complicated," I said.

"You're telling me. But be careful, Bryan. Watch your back around this Ray character. If it were me, I think I would trust the embassy more than this Ray guy. Maybe he's the one who burned your clinic."

"No. Not him. Never!" I said with conviction.

"I love you, bro," she said as we hung up.

I watched the weeks slowly roll by. Yemen's summer cumulus clouds steadily dissipated, leaving blue patches by late August. The encroaching drier fall air would soon blow in from Africa, riding on the great reed warblers' steady wings. My anxiety continued to build as the day of the confrontation with Jabbar was almost upon me. Any moment I was expecting Ray to call, and I be on my way to Huth. For that reason, I kept my motorbike's tank full.

As if I didn't have enough to worry about, my yellow eyes became even more yellow. My pee, browner. I was starting to feel worse and wasn't sure if it was the hepatitis. I didn't have a doctor to see or the time to see one. Fortunately, my day-to-day tasks with IRC helped distract me from my anxieties.

But one Thursday afternoon, Dorothy strolled into my office, softly closed the door behind her, and parked half her butt on the corner of my desk.

"Bryan," she said, "I have something I need to talk to you about." I sensed anguish behind her superficial smile.

"Sure." I said, as I spun my chair around to look at her.

"You asked for the information about Hunter Philips at the embassy a few months ago," she said. "You said something about a terrorist threat."

"Yeah, that's true."

"So, where's that situation now?"

"Oh, well, we're keeping an eye on this individual, and I talked to Mr. Philips. He said the embassy will investigate it."

Dorothy sat fully on my desk, legs dangling, and stared at me like she was expecting more details.

I added, "The individual lost his only son in the school bus bombing and is distraught, and we think he's being recruited by a terrorist group to take revenge."

"Oh, shit. What a bloody mess. I'm glad it's in the embassy's hands. You're not still involved … are you?"

"If you're worried about my safety, I'm keeping a distance from the situation and letting my friend Ray handle it."

"No, that wasn't my concern. I want you to be safe, but my concern is you getting IRC involved with all of this. If IRC got involved with U.S. intelligence, it would create huge problems for us in the Arab world. It could hamper our work and our reputation for being independent and neutral."

"Gee whiz. This gets more complicated by the hour." I shook my head. I thought about it for a moment. "Here's the solution, I'll resign now. I'm doing so little for IRC and my contract ends in three weeks anyway. I'll stay in the country until we figure this mess out." I stood and started clearing my desk.

Dorothy stood up and grabbed my arm. "Bryan, I didn't mean to imply you had to quit. You're welcome to stay with IRC if you're not involved with this other situation."

I patted her hand on my arm and then continued packing up my personal items, a coffee mug, a pen and notebook. I walked toward the door, giving Dorothy a hug on the way. She was speechless and wore a stunned look on her face.

It may have been my overwhelming curiosity or hearing Angie's worried voice in my head, but I called Hunter Philips as soon as I got to my apartment. The U.S. Embassy seemed my only true ally in Yemen.

"Mr. Philips, I'm just following up on the conversation we had in April."

"I'm sorry, but I have a lot of conversations. What's this about?" he asked.

I answered sharply. "It was about a lead on a possible terrorist mission."

"I don't think you talked to *me*, as I would've remembered that."

I sighed loud enough for him to hear over the phone and said, "I did talk to you, in person, in your office."

"I'm sorry, but I don't remember meeting you. What can I do for you today?"

"Never mind! I'm leaving Yemen soon and just wanted to say goodbye."

"Going back to Nebraska?" he asked in a cheerful tone.

Nebraska? Where the hell did that come from? I've never said anything about Nebraska. Was he somehow mixing me up with Sheila?

"New York," I said, and then just to mess with him, I added, "Oh yeah, Mr. McFeely sends his regards. Have a good day."

I sat on my balcony and stared into space. If U.S. intelligence were to take out Jabbar and Abdul with a drone strike, maybe that would be the best thing that could happen. While full of regrets, I was to the point of feeling I couldn't save Ray, Jabbar, or their families. Hell, I wasn't sure I could save myself. If I couldn't persuade Jabbar to stop the mission, I'm sure they would want me out of the way.

With my heart still unsettled, I repacked my bag and my passport was always in my pocket. All my U.S. dollars were rolled up and hidden in a drawer.

The first week of September, I got a call from Ray.

"Jabbar's back! He's in Haydan but will be in Huth in two days. I suspect the men will soon follow. Be prepared to get Jabbar when I call. We may even have to kidnap him. Whatever the hell it takes to stop this."

I hadn't been feeling well for months, my eyes still yellow, and as if prompted by his tense words, I suddenly felt severe abdominal cramps and explosive diarrhea. I stuck the phone in my cargo pocket and ran to the squatting toilet. Not quite making it, I got shit on my ankles, just missing my pants and phone. While cleaning up, I yelled into the phone, "Just a minute, Ray!"

When I returned to the call, he said, "That's all I wanted to tell you. I'll keep listening, and you stay near your phone."

The diarrhea convinced me that it was time to see a local doctor, at least for blood tests. Dorothy had given me the name of her British-trained Yemeni internist after seeing my yellow eyes. It was time to visit him. All hell was about to break loose, and this would be my last chance. Maybe I needed to be on an antiviral, but there was little chance it would be available except on the black market and those would be worthless Chinese imitations.

The next night, I got a call at 2 A.M., the worst call of my life. It came in on my sat phone. It was Rosie sobbing and screaming something to me. While her English was as good as Ray's, I couldn't make out a single word.

"What? What? Rosie, settle down. I can't understand you!" I shouted into the phone.

I heard her take a deep breath and then leak out between sobs, "Ray's dead! They shot him! In the head, they shot him! The bastards killed him!"

CHAPTER TWENTY-FOUR

O h, my God, no! Who did this?" I shouted into the sat phone. "They killed him! He's here, in my arms. He's dead! I'm covered with blood. My dear Ray ... such a good man! Oh, God, why?"

"Rosie, I'm coming, but who did this? American Seals? How can he be dead?" I dashed around my room, putting on my pants and shirt, my heart beating in my throat.

"Bryan, oh my God! Abdul did it! That son of a bitch ... that son of a bitch! Abdul shot him." She sobbed louder. "Abdul said he thought he was a burglar looking in his window. He's lying! The bastard is lying! Bryan, help me!" The last three words came out as a high-pitched shriek.

"Rosie, are you and the kids safe? Where are you?"

"I'm in my goddamn house! They dragged his body here ... and just left it. There's blood everywhere. Allah! Allah!"

I could hear the kids screaming in the background.

"Get out of the house. Run into the village and hide. I will find you!" I shouted.

"Bryan, I'm not leaving Ray!"

"Then, lock your doors and stay inside." I fastened my belt and began slipping on the nearest pair of shoes. "Do you have a weapon?"

"Weapon? ... uh, no, just Ray's janbiya. Bryan, help me!" She sounded like she was starting to hyperventilate.

"Get it, the janbiya. I'm on my way. Make sure the gate is unlocked. It'll take two hours. Stay safe. Don't let anyone in your house but me. Abdul will quickly figure out that he can't let you or the kids survive to tell what happened. He'll be coming for you soon. I'll try and get there first."

Now dressed, I snatched my packed bag and cash. I felt for my passport in my pants' cargo pocket—it was still there. The only weapon I had was my Leatherman knife with a three-inch blade. I grabbed an eight-inch butcher knife out of the kitchen and put it in my belt. I jumped on my bike, and with the headlamp cutting a path of light through the deep night's pitch, I began the ride north toward Huth.

As fast as possible, I maneuvered through Sana'a's gnarly maze of streets, which at 3 A.M. were empty save a few stray dogs, workers restocking the markets, and a couple of drunks. I evaded them all like I was playing a video game set in a war zone, zigzagging to the left and right over the rubble, between broken down cars, around potholes and a dead donkey. At one corner, a police officer in a khaki uniform was sitting on a crate drinking from a mug, both hands caressing the cup. When I approached him, at a recklessly fast pace, he set down his mug and stood up to yell at me. In my mirror I saw him lift his rifle to his chin and then heard two loud cracks. The asshole had fired at me.

I turned the corner to dodge the bullets. After putting two more blocks between me and the trigger-happy officer, I got back on the main road.

The buildings were flying past me as I was doing over ninety miles per hour. In this part of town, the city shrank in height, with two- and three-story houses. I climbed the big hill that led northeast. There, large homes with grand views dotted the mountainside. Yemen's Beverly Hills. Every city has them, mansions in a land of poverty, the trophies of ill-gotten gains. Kabul was the worst. Rosie's mother lived somewhere in that plush Yemeni neighborhood. It could be a safehouse for Rosie and the kids.

Soon I was on the dark road with the throttle wide open, outrunning my own head lamp's illumination. My mind focused on the crumbling road before me—only visible as my front tire rode over it. The asphalt dwindled into a dirt and gravel path in places leading through the mountains to Huth. I shot through the quiet villages of Al Hayfah, Raydah, and Khamin like I was on a crotch rocket, my hand never touching the brake or the clutch.

Despite the terrible roads, my dirt bike made good time, arriving at the outskirts of Huth in sixty-five minutes. The town was just coming to life, as I traversed its dark and tortuous streets.

My best plan was to go straight to Rosie's house and check on Ray, hoping he wasn't dead. Maybe Abdul had only wounded him. *Magical thinking?* I would have asked Rosie to call the medics, but Huth had none. If she called them in Sana'a, maybe medics would arrive in twenty-four hours—if we were lucky. It was the same with the police.

Arriving at Abdul's compound, I kicked the closed gate, and it swung open with a rusty squeak. I took a deep breath. I killed my engine and propelled my bike with my feet, standing and leaning over the handlebars, tiptoes pumping against the dirt, through the gate, and coasting to Rosie's door. It was quiet, with only one light on at Abdul's house. I saw the beam of a flashlight pass Rosie's curtains from the inside.

Was this an ambush? Were Ray and Rosie in cahoots with Abdul? Would Ray walk out, gun in hand?

I kept my helmet on, not knowing what I was about to face. As soon as I got to Rosie's door, I noticed blood on her beige limestone threshold and all over the iron doorknob. I tapped the door with the pads of my fingers, then waited but heard nothing. I knocked again, using my knuckles but softly. I saw the curtains move in the window beside the door, as if someone had looked outside. The door latch rattled and then opened. Rosie was standing in a bathrobe, blood all over her hands, her face, her robe. I hugged her and walked in.

"How'd you get here so fast?" she asked through a raspy voice.

"Doesn't matter, I'm here."

Fadel and Zoey, also covered in blood, lay beside their father's body. Zoey's eyes looked swollen shut. I kneeled beside my dead friend. The entry wound was between his eyes, exit wound on the top of his head. Yes, he was dead—must have died instantly. If he had lived, his brain would've been damaged beyond repair. A good man. What a damn waste! I felt my tears coming, but I didn't have time for them—not now.

I let out a long, hard sigh. My personal griefs were like crowded beads on a short string. The futility of it all. So much sorrow, and for what? This murderous chaos was leading nowhere.

Kneeling beside the body of my friend, I reached into my pocket and pulled out my cell phone. It was 4:30 A.M. Morning prayers were not too far off. *What should I do?*

I stood and looked at Rosie sitting on the couch, leaning over Ray's body, her puffy eyes red, her tangled hair stuck to her wet face.

"Rosie, you must get out of this compound! Do you have a place to go?"

She took in a quick breath. "We still have our flat in Sana'a," she said in a whisper.

"They'll look there first," I said. "What about your mother's house? Ray said your mother had bodyguards ... right?"

Wiping her hair away from her eyes, she said, "Yes, my mother lives near Sana'a, in the mountains above the city. We could go there. But how?"

"Do you drive?"

"I can drive, but we don't have a car."

"Perfect, but is there a car you can use? Something we can put Ray in."

Rosie squinted like she was thinking but said nothing.

"I saw an old truck parked in the compound. Is that Abdul's?" I asked pointing toward the door.

"Yes," she answered with a nod.

Using my cell phone screen for light, I went outside and opened the truck door, which squeaked much louder than I'd hoped. I looked over at Abdul's house and didn't see any movement or lights. I studied the steering column for a way to take it apart so I could bypass the ignition switch. However, the screws to the column required a special star-bit screwdriver and I didn't have such a tip on my Leatherman tool.

I glanced at my cell phone. 4:45. The Fajr, or first prayer of the day, would start around 5:07. While Abdul or the men would not participate, unless it was beside their beds, the call from the minaret would likely wake them.

I ran softly on my toes back to Rosie's house.

"What's wrong?" Rosie asked as I slipped in the door.

"There's no keys in the truck and I can't get the steering column apart to hotwire it, and we're out of time."

Rosie left the house, disappearing into the dark, and after a minute returned.

"Bryan, there are keys in the ignition of the black Mercedes!"

"Great! Quietly move the kids into the back seat," I whispered. "I'll get Ray ready for us to carry him. Come back and help me if you can. Where's that janbiya?"

"It's on the chair … over there," she said pointing. "Oh, my god, I can't believe Ray is gone. I can't live without him!" Tears erupted from her eyes once more.

Rosie left with the kids. I heard the Mercedes door open. I was praying there was no car alarm …

Silence.

Thank God!

I tossed my kitchen knife on the floor and grabbed Ray's janbiya and its sheath and stuck them under my belt. I bent down and took Ray's arms, which were straight at his side, rotated, hands in fists, wrists flexed. A decerebrate posture, a testament to a severe brain injury prior to his demise.

I tried bending his arms at the elbow so I could fold them on his chest. I would carry him from his head end, my arms under his shoulders and holding on to his wrists. Rosie could manage his legs—or so I hoped. He was too big for me to carry alone unless I dragged him, which would make too much noise.

As I was bending Ray's arms, which were stiffening, I noticed long red wheals on the soft side of his left forearm. Abdul and his men must have scratched him up when they dragged him home. But then I saw a pattern in the scratches. I remembered him telling me he suffered from urticaria and dermographism, the ability to write on your skin by pressure alone—like an old Magic Slate tablet. As I stooped beside Ray's body and waited for Rosie, I heard the back door of the Mercedes shut with a loud thud. I studied my friend Ray's remains. Had he written on his forearms with his fingernail?

I turned his arm to see if I could read it. It wasn't Arabic. I didn't recognize a single letter. Then I turned his forearm to see it as he would have seen it. Looking at it from that angle made it clear. Yes, it was English. The letters were materializing. "PYTHEAS-ANFO-NYC."

What the hell does that mean?

I quickly made several photos of the lettering with my phone as the image was already fading, his dark skin reabsorbing the raised wheals even in his post-mortem state.

Rosie reentered the house. "The kids are in the car."

I slipped my phone into my pocket. I picked him up, my arms around his chest. Rosie carried him from between his legs. He had soiled his pants and there was a stench. The blood was now dried and was caking in his hair and smeared over his face.

Rosie made it halfway to the car and then had to drop his legs. She moaned between deep breaths. I dragged him and whispered for her to open the trunk and help me roll him in. Ray was heavy, over two hundred pounds. I was exhausted from the physical effort and the prolonged adrenaline surge. I walked to the driver's door and opened it for Rosie. She got in, but just as I was about to close the car door, another light came on inside Abdul's house. I froze.

The back door to the house opened, and a figure came outside. None of us batted an eyelash, no one breathing. Even the kids knew to stay quiet. Sweat dripped from my armpits. The night air was as quiet as unbroken glass, a single dog howling somewhere in the distance. I saw a blast of light. *A muzzle flash?* Then it became clear it was a match strike and a cigarette being lit. Rosie and I looked at each other. She let out a soft sigh.

Putting my lips to her blood-covered ear, I whispered, "Go fast and don't look back. I hope to see you again, but please stay safe. I'm so sorry about Ray. He really was a good man."

She quietly nodded and closed the door. I sprinted to my bike, pausing by the old pickup and slicing the front tire with the janbiya. It was sharp and made easy work of the old rubber. To my dismay, the air whistled as it escaped the tire into the night air.

I continued running softly on the dirt and jumped on my bike. I had my kick-start poised, waiting for Rosie to start the Mercedes. As soon as she turned the ignition, I saw the glowing cigarette behind Abdul's house move, as if the smoker's head had turned toward us. I put my foot on the pedal and threw my weight on it. The bike started. I folded the foot peg in with my toe and spun the gas throttle wide open. I beat Rosie to the gate, pushing it wide open with my hand and when I turned the throttle, I inadvertently threw dirt in my wake on the car's windshield. I turned right, she left.

Where am I going?

My intuition seemed to know. I was heading northeast on the road to Alharf, where I turned northwest toward Sa'dah, the bike wide open on the beat-up road, my teeth clenched to avoid chipping them over the bumps. I felt so alone, like a solo sailor on an endless sea.

My thoughts were churning. *Ray isn't one of them. He was a legitimate friend. My only Yemeni confidant.*

I had the photos of Ray's scribbles. When the bullet penetrated his frontal lobe, his ability to think, organize language, and move his hand to write would have ended. He must have scribbled the message on his arm before they shot him. They must have had a verbal altercation first. He must have known his death was imminent. He knew the words he was scribbling would be read on his corpse. What courage!

I tried to recreate the words in my head. *ANFO* was one. The only thing that came to my mind was the name for a fertilizer bomb made with ammonium nitrate and fuel oil. I knew it well from college chemistry. *Pytheas?* I knew little about the name from ancient Greek history. Was Jabbar going to drive a truck full of ANFO into a building? Why the sea captain's school? A ship perhaps? A ship with ANFO heading for New York? My God ... a ship named *Pytheas?* Maybe not a ship but a code name for something else? I wished I had access to the internet.

Soon the bright morning was lighting up the rubble on the outskirts of Sa'dah. I knew where I was, and it was as if my body had been driving my bike at full speed without my brain's engagement. Distracted by puzzle solving and grief, I had missed my west turn to Hayden.

While contemplating my turn back toward the Hayden road, I passed the MSF hospital, and to my disbelieving eyes there stood Michel outside, leaning against the wall smoking a cigarette, a surgical mask dangling over his bloody scrub shirt. It was surreal. As I passed him and slowed to turn the corner, his eyes rose and met mine. He knew my bike. He recognized me as I passed. I could tell from how his gaze followed me. He tossed me a nod. He looked tattered—probably recovering from an early-morning or late-night emergent surgery. Whatever it was, I could've been there to have shared his burden.

Maybe it was the panic of the crisis I was in the middle of, but my savage reptilian brain was surfacing for air. Doing a sudden U-turn in the street to head back to the Hayden road, I gunned it, causing a rear-wheel side slip in the dust. My bike blazed the road back to the MSF hospital in a full sprint, me crouched down on my fuel tank to reduce the drag, then slamming my brakes and sliding to the curb. With my bike still running, I jumped off and walked over to my nemesis.

"Michel," I mumbled.

With a puzzled look, he pulled the cigarette from between his lips. "Bryan?"

To his total shock—and mine—I punched him in the face. A year of pent-up rage poured down my arm and into my knuckles as if I had no control. His head went back so hard, it was like it was attached to his body by a spring instead of a neck. His cigarette ricocheted off my forearm and then into the weeds. He fell backwards, coming to arrest against the hospital wall, then slid down to a sitting position. I stood above him, feet apart, hands fisted, jaw clenched, prepared for him to come after me. But he didn't.

His eyes were rounded like saucers, his mouth still open with a look of horror. His nose began gushing crimson blood. He quickly pinched it. "What the hell was that for?" he screamed.

Still in my boxer's pose—awaiting his punch back—I mumbled, "That's for Sheila. She was a damn good person, much better than you'll ever be." Then I felt the resurgence of my prefrontal cortex. "Uh … but you're a damn good doctor and I'm sorry for the punch. Gotta go."

I turned and ran for my bike, not fearing retaliation but suddenly remembering the urgency of reaching Jabbar in Haydan before he left for Huth. Giving Michel one last awkward grin, I jumped on my bike, my punching hand throbbing. *What the hell's wrong with me?*

Continuing south, toward the Hayden road, I passed the site of the school bus bombing—unnoticed on my way in. Someone had cut down the magnificent old olive trees. A row of huge round stumps stood in their place like pillar bases from an ancient Greek ruin. A slaughter of trees, if not for firewood then as an arboreal execution for failing to protect their children.

My turn to Haydan quickly came up, and when I hit the brake lever to slow down for the turn, I felt intense pain in my right hand. "Damnit!" Boxer's fracture—well deserved. There appeared no obvious deformity, so I assumed the fracture was incomplete and stable.

I reduced my speed as I met a stream of pedestrians coming down the mountain oasis to Sa'dah. Too far to walk in a single day. Some, I'm sure, were going there to shop and sell. Others looked ill, a couple were being carried on beds, on their way to visit the hospital. I could've cared for them in Haydan. Pure absurdity! I hoped that Michel would recover enough from my assault to help them when they arrived.

After climbing the last steep hill, the road leveled off into our oasis. The trees were greener than I remembered. The burned-out ruin that was once our clinic was blacker than I recalled. A stray dog was digging in its rubble.

I drove through the village and turned up Jabbar's street. He had parked his truck in its usual spot.

I jumped off my bike but left it running and pointing away. I banged on the door with my left fist's soft flesh, my right still throbbing. The door rattled within its frame. I banged on it again, harder. What was I going to say? So much at stake. *God help me.*

I heard the familiar footsteps moving down the stone stairs. The door opened, and there was Jabbar's sleepy face, his dark eyes squinting. I wedged my toe in the crack, forcing the door fully open.

He glanced at my hands, no doubt to see if I had a gun. He saw the janbiya in my belt. I put my hand on its handle as if I were ready to draw it out, but I wouldn't have had a clue how to use such a weapon except for slashing tires.

Through gritted teeth, I said, "Ray's dead! He's been shot! Abdul, your cousin, murdered him!"

Nodding his head calmly, Jabbar said, "Yes, I know. Abdul called me during the night. Ray wasn't a good man." He shook his head. "He wasn't devoted to his religion. He drank alcohol. He was an infidel. Abdul caught him peeping in his window, and he mistook him for a robber. It's Ray's fault."

My mind was racing with so many elements to this crazy story. If I said the wrong thing, I would die. Without saying the right thing, thousands might.

Stepping into his personal space, looking directly into his sleepy eyes, I said, "Jabbar, you were a good man. You were a good father. Look at what you've become. You cannot go through with this mission. You just can't! It'll not be retribution; it'll not be an eye for an eye. It isn't too late to turn back. If you cause deaths of Saudis or Americans, they'll come back and drop their merciless bombs on more children, creating a thousand more mourning fathers who will kill more Saudis and Americans, who will drop more bombs." Then I screamed, "This won't end here!"

Returning to a softer voice, I added. "Jabbar, don't do this! I've told the authorities and they're watching you. They'll come for you, and America's Navy Seals will kill your entire family!" I pounded his chest with my finger.

Jabbar's eyes widened. He grabbed my finger, the one pounding his chest, and pushed it away. While keeping his eyes on me, Jabbar yelled in a hateful voice, "Mona, bring me my walking stick!"

I stepped back. It confused me. I was sure the phrase *easana almashi* was "walking stick." But Jabbar had never used such a stick or cane.

There was a motion inside the door and Mona handed Jabbar a long, towel-covered item. It was an AK-47! I pivoted and ran toward my bike. It took him seconds to get the towel off the gun and then sighted. I heard a pop, followed by the familiar whiz of a 39mm bullet going past my ear. I dove to the ground, rolled, stood again, and continued running. As I approached my bike, I heard two more rounds go off, both hitting my bike's seat as I saw the dust fly. I felt no pain and was hoping I wasn't hit. Had Jabbar ever fired a gun before?

I twisted my bike's throttle, sending dirt and gravel flying toward Jabbar. The gunfire continued. I looked in my mirror and saw him standing outside his door, aiming at me, the front sight block protruding in front of Jabbar's eye, the magazine curving toward me from below the gun. These were not warning shots. *Pop, pop, pop.*

CHAPTER TWENTY-FIVE

I zoomed down Jabbar's street at full speed, hoping I wouldn't hit a pedestrian or one of their animals. I was also hoping that Jabbar's wayward shots into my bike's seat had not caused significant damage. Coming to the Sa'dah road, I turned left, west into the mountains rather than east to Sa'dah. Something dripped from the bike onto my right foot. Gasoline? I felt no new pain, just the sting in my right hand from punching Michel. No blood on me. Jabbar's bullets had all missed.

The road over the mountains was even rougher than that rubble path we sardonically called the Sa'dah Highway. However, I knew the mountain road like my boyhood street. I had spent many hours riding my bike on backroads and across goat trails that networked in the high places. I turned off the road and onto one of those elusive trails where evading a four-wheel vehicle would be easy. After passing the highest crags, the trail led me back to the road on its downward journey toward the Red Sea.

There was nothing for me in Sana'a anymore. Jabbar, Abdul, and the other conspirators all wanted me dead. However, this mountain road uncoiled precariously close to the Saudi border where mischief dwelled under every rock and therefore was no safer. Then it turned south, out of the mountains and down to the coastal village, Al Luhayyah. Beyond that was the contested city, Al Hudaydah. Thanks to two fishing trips, I knew my way to Al Luhayyah well. From its port, I could hitch a contraband-running vessel heading north to Eilat.

With the late-morning sun well above the horizon, my bike's tire was spinning on the parched dirt leaving a dust trail that was as conspicuous as a jet's contrails across the heavens. In my mirror, I saw nothing unusual, certainly not Jabbar's Toyota or Abdul's old pickup with its distinctive repaired front tire. I couldn't imagine what was happening back in Huth. Abdul and his friends most likely would pursue Rosie to Sana'a. I hoped to God she'd find her way to her safehouse first. I was sure Abdul would kill Rosie and her kids, if not her mother too. A bullet to their heads, just like with Ray. It seemed a miracle they didn't kill Rosie and the kids right after Abdul offed Ray.

I suspected that Jabbar, once he got his truck started, had taken the eastern route toward Sa'dah, but I wasn't sure.

On a normal day, I could have traversed the 130 kilometers to Al Luhayyah in two hours. However, as I came down the 7,000-foot-high mountain's western slopes, my bike sputtered. I had smelled gasoline along the way and was constantly glancing between the road, the rear-view mirror, and the fuel gauge. The gauge's black arrow had been dropping much faster than expected and was now on the big "E." Jabbar's errant bullet must have hit the gas tank after passing through the bike's seat. The bike had a larger 16-liter tank, making it an easy target. I could get 350 kilometers when full, but I had only traveled 155 kilometers since leaving Sana'a that morning, and the tank was empty. *Damn!*

I rode on until the dirt road passed over a six-foot culvert made of rusted metal through which ran a dry wadi. I stopped and rolled my bike off the road and into the shady tunnel. I was out of the sun and hidden from sight, if perhaps Jabbar had followed me.

I inspected my bike, and the problem was obvious. The gas tank had a bullet hole through it about halfway up. From that hole, the gas had leaked down the bike's frame and onto the road. The hole didn't worry me so much—I could fix it—but being out of gas was a huge problem.

Inside the culvert, I saw water-worn stones and sun-bleached sticks that the rains had washed down the wadi. In this season, it was bone dry. I picked up a stick that was slightly bigger than the bullet hole and carefully whittled it down into a tapered piece about an inch long. After inserting it into the lower hole, I pounded it tight with a stone. Hole fixed, now I needed fuel.

From my previous trips, I knew there were no petrol stations for another forty kilometers. It was frustrating because I could see Saudi Arabia, the world's largest oil producer, from that mountain top, and all I could think was *Oil, oil everywhere, / Nor a drop for my tank.*

The day had worn me out, frayed my nerves, leaving no space to mourn my friend Ray, and it wasn't over yet. Only two hours of sleep had visited me the previous night before Rosie's call. I was running on pure adrenalin.

As the day cooled, I could have coasted my bike into the land of trouble. That area, according to Jabbar, had had border runners smuggling contraband through Saudi's backdoor for centuries. There I would be within two miles of the border, where bandits and smugglers ran wild. These people frightened even Jabbar. It was a dangerous land that I'd always tried to race through on our fishing trips. Now, an empty fuel tank would trap me right in the middle of it.

I considered my options. If I walked up to someone's door, offered them money for fuel, there was a decent chance they would kill me as soon as they heard my American accent. Maybe put me in a cave or locker and hold me for ransom ... for years. If not that, they would assault me and take the money. I decided the safest thing to do was to slip down, steal the gas, and leave the money—one hundred American dollars, a month's salary for many Yemeni. Then I would get the hell out before they discovered my presence.

I waited for hours. The sun was settling into the milky haze along the horizon where the scorching desert air congealed within the Red Sea's cool aura. The surrounding shadows elongated and merged as if the bronze landscape was melting. A few lights appeared and dotted the barren valley below. The only sounds were from the occasional traffic, a sporadic dog bark, rooster crow, or hawk squawk. The vehicles on the road above my culvert became sparser as the light faded. I left my bike in its well-concealed shelter in search of fuel.

In my emergency supplies, I had a Foley catheter. It served as a tourniquet, chest tube, urinary catheter, or replacement fuel line on my bike. I also had a couple of plastic bags as emergency containers. On this night, I was going to use the catheter to syphon gasoline.

I had a liter water bottle that I carried on the bike. After drinking its contents until my stomach couldn't hold another drop, I could hear the water sloshing when I walked. Then I poured two cups' worth into a plastic bag and left it with the bike. What remained in the bottle I would consume before syphoning the gas.

It was a three-kilometer walk to the first settlement. As I got closer, I came upon a flat-roofed stone cottage in a dry field beside the highway. It was built of large limestone blocks, its windows arched and trimmed in a gray stucco. It was a two-story affair, with the ground floor appearing to be a garage or workshop with the living quarters above it. An outside staircase went to an arched wooden entryway on the upper floor. The door was a beautifully carved work but hard to appreciate in the dim light. There were people inside the house, their shadows passing across the sheer drapes of the lighted windows. Chairs were sliding on a wooden floor above me, followed by men's muffled voices.

The ground floor of the residence had two large metal doors, one painted green and the other blue. An animal shed next to the house was one story and, in the moonlight, I could see it had two metal doors painted with large yellow flowers. All was quiet except for the occasional sound of a car on the highway behind me and the rustling and bleating of sheep inside the shed.

Stumbling around in the dark, tripping over a scythe, I search for a fuel source while trying my best to be quiet. The moonlight revealed a motorbike leaning against the shed. *Perfect!* I felt for the gas cap and unscrewed it, releasing the scent of gasoline. What a relief.

I squatted down on the ground beside the shed, which shadowed the quarter moon's light. I drank the last swig of water in my bottle and shook the remaining drops out. I went by feeling and placed the catheter into the gas tank and sucked on the bottom end. Apparently, the tank was full, as the gas rushed down the catheter and filled my mouth, down into my windpipe. I coughed and spit, which aroused the animals in the shed. They began bleating in unison.

I watched the tube drip gasoline at a fast clip into the bottle. I wanted it full.

Suddenly, I saw bright lights moving and flashing like from a disco ball suspended above me. Then everything went black. Face down, I felt my open mouth stuck in the salty dirt—the world having gone distant.

A pain exploded in the back of my skull. In slow motion, I felt my body rolling over and over. Detached from the living world, I was blind and desperate to know what was happening around me. My vision returned, pixel by pixel. I could see a shadow, someone moving about me. No, there were two figures!

I felt a kick to my ribs. Agony!

I tumbled again, backwards, striking my injured head on the ground. I was still clutching the half-filled bottle of gasoline in my right-hand, contents spilling across my chest.

As I was getting up on my hands and knees, they kicked me again, hard on my buttocks, sending me face down into the dirt. This happened so fast that I couldn't get into a defensive posture. I was at their mercy.

A man landed on me, smelling strongly of body odor. He wrestled my hands above my head, pinning me to the ground, the other man now standing on my hands with his hard boots and full weight. I fought back, kicking at him. Then I grabbed the ear of the man on top of me in my mouth and bit down hard. He screamed. I tasted blood. He punched me in the face.

I heard "*Alsaariq* [robber]" and "*Binzin* [gasoline]" and then cursing.

Were they going to kill me? Maybe throw a match on my gasoline-soaked Henley. Why not? At that moment, I didn't give a damn anymore. All the bullshit had worn me out.

The attackers paused long enough for me to wobble into a sitting position. I looked up at them, two heads in silhouette eclipsing northwest Yemen's partial moon and star-soaked sky. They stood side by side as only dark outlines. I heard snickers and words mumbled between them, too low to understand. One of my eyes was swollen shut, and I had the taste of someone else's blood in my mouth. A lone car passed on the highway, its headlights briefly brushing over us. I saw the rage-filled faces of my assailants flickering in the light like an old silent movie. A tall older man with a white beard and a younger man, short and thin with blood dripping from his ear.

What do I do? If I yelled, who would hear me? If someone heard me, who would they help, me … or their Yemeni brothers?

I decided to play the only card I had—money. But I knew that the moment I spoke, they'd know I wasn't Yemeni. That alone could get me killed.

But if they took the money, it could save my life.

I spoke with a lisp, incomprehensible. A cut on my swollen lip was dripping blood. Now, two men's blood in my mouth, my own and the attacker's. I felt my lip with my finger.

I picked an easy Arabic phrase to say. "I'll pay you for the gasoline."

The two men shared a sinister laugh. The older one demanded to see the money. He stepped closer to me, out of the shed's shadow, the moonlight illuminating his rough and red rhinophymic nose. I reached into my front pants pocket. After Rosie's call, I had grabbed my entire cash reserve, two thousand dollars, a roll of twenty-one hundred-dollar bills, and stuck it in my pocket.

How could I remove the money and offer a generous one-hundred-dollar bill for the gasoline without them seeing or wanting the rest? I couldn't.

As I pulled the large roll of bills from my front pocket, I thought the man's eyes were going to pop right out of his head. He yelled to the younger man in Arabic, "Allah! He's got a wad of money."

Before I pulled one bill from beneath the rubber band, the older man grabbed the entire roll. As I watched him pull the money out of my hand, the younger man walked up beside me and sucker-punched me in the stomach. I couldn't breathe and slowly fell over. They grabbed me by the ankles and dragged me across the rocky ground for what seemed like a hundred yards.

I didn't know where they were taking me, but they had my money, all of it. *Were they throwing me down a well? Off a cliff?*

The second guess was more accurate. They pushed me, and I rolled down a very steep bank, picking up speed with each rotation. I bounced. Each rebound slammed me again into the hardened earth, rocks cutting into my flesh. I felt pain each time I hit the ground from my ribs and possibly other bones that had been broken. I felt like my sick liver had ruptured right inside of me. Then I started to free-fall for at least ten feet and crashed into the earth, which knocked the air out of my lungs. There wasn't a place on my body that didn't hurt.

It occurred to me that if I died right there, Angie would never know what happened to me.

I'm sure my assailants thought I would die that night or the next day under the hot sun. My corpse would then become a nocturnal smorgasbord for the striped hyena, sand cat, or desert fox. Then the mice and ants would take their turns. I would methodically disappear from the face of the earth. I'm sure somewhere in that gully were human bones bleached out by the sun like carved ivory. It was the type of inaccessible space in which desert kooks tucked their secrets. I was afraid my bones would soon be one of those riddles.

The darkness passed over me like the flow of cold black glass. The lesser light of the dwindling moon was soon absorbed into the sea. My body, every part, was yelling out to my brain, "Misery!" Even my hand still hurt from punching Michel's face. That pain, I deserved. My ribs hurt, my back hurt, my head hurt, my face hurt, and my liver hurt.

With the passing of hours, I was giving up hope. Then a pink tinge leaked into the eastern clouds. The twilight brought with it a hint of optimism. Soon, those eastern embankments could no longer contain the morning, and it spilled over and poured into our valley once again. The yellow sun made its full debut above the mountains' tops, illustrating my desert world. *Is this to be my last sight?*

My concussion seemed to be wearing off. Maybe it was the daylight that was making me more cognizant. Confidence infused my soul again, inflating me back to strength. Damn, I was thirsty. I attempted to stand, but the pain in my back forced me down to my knees again.

My eyes traced the deep wadi I was lying in toward the mountain from which it flowed. I recognized it was the same crevice that journeyed through the metal culvert where I had hidden my bike somewhere above.

If I could stand, or at least crawl, I could make it up this steep path, back to the culvert's kind shade and my bag with water still within the panniers. I wasn't sure what I would do next. But I knew I would die there by the day's end if I did nothing. If I climbed up the wadi and found the water bag empty, the culvert would become my grave. At least at the bike I could call Angie with my sat phone and say goodbye.

After another hour of rest, I stood. Then I scrambled, first hand over hand, then partially upright like some human ancestor who'd just descended from the trees. Meter by meter, I climbed the three-kilometer hill in three hours through the dust and sharp rocks. I had to free-climb a couple of sheer rock faces, likely the sites of waterfalls during times of rain. At the top, I charged into the welcoming shade of my familiar culvert and chugged the hot water in the bag. Only a pint.

The hours it had taken to reach my bike had pushed my day into the late afternoon. I sat with my eyes closed, my grimy face against my hands, trying to think of a plan.

I could coast down the mountain on my bike, but the road rose again just past the assailants' settlement, putting me back in harm's way. I could also stop traffic and ask to buy fuel, but I had no money. I regretted that hadn't been my chosen plan rather than trying to steal petrol from people in this shady land. But what was the difference? Any person I'd have stopped could have easily beat the shit out of me for the money just like the sheep farmers did. Or worse, shot me.

When I finished drinking, I put the bag back in the pannier and grabbed my sat phone. The big sky on the mountaintop made a sat phone call easier, more room to troll for a satellite. I stood, pointed the antenna into space, and called Angie. Soon I heard the buzzing sound of a phone ringing.

"Bryan! Are you okay?"

"Hell no!" I responded. "Hey, sis, just listen for a minute and write things down."

"Sure."

"I confronted Jabbar, my friend, about his mission. I tried to talk him out of it. It didn't work. He almost killed me! His accomplices killed my good friend Ray. Ray's dead!"

"Oh, my God, Bryan—" came her cry.

"Angie, I can't talk long, so just listen!"

"I am!" she moaned.

"I'm on the run. I'm alone in this damn mess. I need you more than ever."

"Bryan, I'm here for you. I'll come to Yemen if you want."

"No, I need to get the hell out of this country, but it won't be easy. The airport is down again. I'm presently in Yemen's northwest corner, near the Saudi border. They robbed me last night and beat me up, leaving me for dead. But now I'm back at my bike— "

"Wait! Wait! Who robbed you? Jabbar?"

"Just listen, dammit!" I said growing impatient, unfairly. "I'm not going to Sana'a. I told you the airport is down, and Sana'a is the first place they'll look for me. Jabbar and his men are looking for me there now, I'm sure. Just look at a friggin' map! I'm heading for the coast to find a boat to Israel. Jabbar shot at me and hit my gas tank, causing me to run out of petrol here. I went to buy gas from a local, and they robbed me when they saw my money and left me for dead."

"How are you getting to the coast now without any gas?"

I scratched my head. "Well, I guess I'm going to hitchhike as soon as I get off the damn phone, before it gets dark. But Angie, I'll need your help to stop Jabbar. He's going to attack New York City!"

Silence.

"Angie! Did you hear me?" I asked.

"Yes, of course. I heard you. He's coming here? How do you know this?"

"Ray overheard them before they shot him. Jabbar is going to crash a ship into New York with a fertilizer bomb, they call ANFO. I believe the ship's name is *Pytheas*, p-y-t-h-e-a-s. Write that name down. See what you can find out. Maybe the embassy is working on this here, but go to the damn authorities in New York, just in case. I'll call you when I can."

"I'll see what I can do."

"Just get help, Angie. For the love of God, please help me."

I heard her saying, "I will," as I hung the phone up and put it into a cargo pocket on my pants. My hand felt for my passport in my back pocket and pulled it out. I flipped through the pages to make sure it was intact. It was.

Dusting myself off, I looked in the bike's rearview mirror. I looked like hell, like a fucking jaundiced zombie walking a haunted road to eat brains. *Who was going to give me a ride?* I washed the blood off my face with my remaining water.

I waited by the road. By the sun's position, I knew it must have been about four P.M. Cars were only occasionally passing overhead, about one every ten minutes. Houthi army troops—in a convoy—crossed over, moving east from the Saudi border, the opposite direction I wanted to go. I thought about waving them down, just for water, but it would be a dangerous move. They might have shot me as a spy as soon as they saw my passport.

A compact car was coming west. A red Fiat knockoff from India or China. I stood and waved. It had at least eight people inside. They were not picking up hitchhikers. Two cars whizzed by.

Then I saw a pickup loaded with burlap sacks. A grower of coffee beans heading for the coast perhaps?

I jumped up and flagged them down. They stopped on the shoulder. In the cab was an older gray-haired man wearing a keffiyeh, a woman with a black scarf around her face, and a young boy whose shaved head barely stuck above the dash. The driver turned to look at me. His sagging face looked like a pair of worn-out boots. He took off his aviator sunglasses—duct tape around the right temple piece—and peered at me slit-eyed, as the sun was just behind my left shoulder.

I said to him in Arabic, "Hello, can you help me? I've had a bad motorcycle wreck and I need a ride to Al Luhayyah."

"Al Luhayyah? No, we are going to Al Hudaydah."

"Al Hudaydah? Is it safe?" I asked.

He chuckled. "If you want to be safe, go to Egypt or Norway. It's safe enough. I can take you there, but we are poor people." He curled up his nose and added, "Phew, benzene."

"Yes, I spilled gasoline on my shirt. I would pay you for a ride, but I have no money. If you get me to Al Hudaydah, I promise I'll find money for you. How about one hundred American dollars?"

He looked baffled, turned to the woman, and muttered something. She shook her head and laughed.

"I can't feed my family on promises," he said, leaning out his window. "The pay for transporting this coffee won't even pay for my petrol. This coffee is going to rich people all over the world, Berlin, Paris, and Shanghai, but not a penny left for me!" He furrowed his gray eyebrows and frowned.

"I understand, but I have no money. Robbers took everything," I said shaking my head.

"I'm no fool," he said. Then reaching out his hand, he added, "Give me your passport and I'll give you a ride." He winked. "I think I could pass for you, if I beat my face in with an axe." He snorted.

"No. I'm not giving up my passport," I said, placing my hand over my pants' pocket. "And this" —I pointed to my face— "isn't how I normally look."

The man chuckled so loudly he had to wipe tears from his eyes with the corner of his black and white keffiyeh. His gaze followed my hand down to my pants. "I see that antenna sticking out of your pocket. I'll take your phone."

"Nope, I need my sat phone," I said with a half-grin.

He waved and said in English, "Goodbye," as he stepped on the gas and started moving the truck slowly forward.

But he went only as far as a few meters. *Was it a bluff?*

He called out of his window, "What are you doing here?" now in Arabic.

Over the sound of his loud, muffler-less truck, I yelled, "My name is Bryan, I'm American. I was a doctor at the International Rescue Committee's clinic in Haydan. I had to leave because someone burned the clinic. I was on my way to the coast to catch a boat home. The airport in Sana'a is closed."

He turned the engine off and looked at me from head to toe. Nodding his head toward the rear of his truck, he said, "I have coffee in the back going to America."

I didn't respond except for a shrug.

"So, you're a doctor?" he asked with a jerk of his head.

"Yes," I said with a nod.

He stepped down from the cab and walked up to me, his nose to mine, then said in a whisper, "Here's what you can exchange for a ride to Al Hudaydah. I have a daughter who lives with her husband near here. She's very ill. I'm afraid she's dying. If you can help her, that'll be payment for your ride." In English, he added, "Okay?" He stared at me, awaiting my answer.

"Well, I could try. But I only have a stethoscope, and she may need more help," I said.

If I examine his daughter and can't help her, he might abandon me beside the road ... or kill me in a fit of rage.

He continued staring, and I wondered if he'd heard me. I started to repeat it. "Like I said, I could try —"

"I heard you, I heard you!" he said, now looking down like he was thinking.

I added, "Here's an idea. My motorbike is down in the culvert behind me." I nodded in the direction of the bike. "It's in great shape except for a hole in its gas tank, which I've already repaired. The bike is yours if you give me a ride to Al Hudaydah. I'll look at your daughter for free and help her if I can, but I can't promise anything."

Concern stuck to his sweaty face like his cotton shirt to his sweaty back. He stooped down and looked in the culvert. Then he turned to me, cocked his head, and grinned. "Okay!"

"I'm Bryan. They call me 'Doctor Bryan,' but you can just call me Bryan."

I rolled the bike up from the culvert to the back of the truck. The man helped me lift the bike into the bed and then on the bags of coffee. I climbed onto the bags behind the bike, but he grabbed my wrist and pulled me down. He yelled in the cab's open window, "*Zawjati* [my wife]" and the woman stepped out, then climbed into the back of the truck, like it wasn't her first-time riding there. However, she didn't seem happy about the arrangement and argued with her husband, as she passed by, saying in Arabic, "You want me to freeze up there, don't you? It will be like ice by the time we get to the coast."

"Oh, shut up, woman," he mumbled. "We are to show kindness to our guests. That's what the prophet says."

"Please, let me ride in the back. I would love the fresh air," I added.

"No, you need to ride with me. You look like *alhimar alqaraf* [donkey shit]."

I climbed into the cab, flashing a smile to the little boy in the middle. He stared at me with big gray eyes and a flat demeanor. "Hello," I said in Arabic. No response. I wondered if he was deaf.

"My name is Mohammed, like the prophet," the man said as he climbed back into the driver's seat. He reached across the boy to shake my hand. Nodding at the boy, he added, "This is my son, Saleh."

Smiling at the boy, I asked, "Did you say grandson?"

"No, son." Mohammed winked, "My wife is half my age."

I looked at my reflection, this time in the truck's rearview mirror. Mohammed was right, I did look like donkey shit. A bar of soap, a sink with running water, and a good mirror would work miracles. We pulled back on the road, the boy sitting just behind the gearshift and watching me, every move.

We drove down the mountain. After three kilometers, Mohammed slowed down. Then he turned into the same cluster of buildings where I'd been assaulted the previous night. My heart began to race like it was going to take leave of my chest. I reached for the door handle.

"Where are we going?" I shouted, lifting myself off the seat, my hand still on the door handle, now pushing down.

"My daughter lives here. I need you to look at her. I told you that already!"

How much worse can this day get?

CHAPTER TWENTY-SIX

Mohammed turned the pickup into the two-track dirt driveway. The ruts were worn deep into the tan soil, and a stripe of dry grass ran down the middle like a blond mohawk. I clutched the vinyl seat's front edge with both hands and squeezed until I thought my fingers would dislocate at the knuckles, my boxer's fracture screaming at me. This was going to be bad—maybe worse than the previous night. Was Mohammed bringing me back to this awful place because he saw I was only half murdered and wanted them to finish it?

I held my breath as I considered my choices. *Do I roll out, hit the ground, and run? Do I try to fight them off … all three?* I could do better this time. Starting without a blow to my head would be helpful.

The stone house and shed was a more observable crime scene now in daylight. My rubber catheter was still on the ground, S-shaped and limp like a dead snake. I saw an axe handle lying in the dirt near the tubing. That must have been their skull-crushing weapon. My head was still throbbing.

Mohammed continued inching the truck toward the house. I held my breath. But then the house was right next to us, and we kept rolling.

"Where are we going?" I asked.

"I told you we're going to my daughter's house," he said, exasperated, raising his right hand from the steering wheel. "Why don't you understand?"

The stone house and shed were drifting behind us.

"But why didn't we stop?" I asked, sitting on the edge of my seat and looking behind us.

Mohammed looked at me and asked, "At that house?" He pointed over his shoulder with his thumb. "That house behind us?"

I nodded ferociously.

"Because that's not her house. That's where her father-in-law lives. My daughter's husband's brother lives there too." Pointing his chin at a cluster of buildings in front of us, he added, "My daughter, she lives in that house."

Behind the attackers' farm, the two lanes continued across the field to a group of four stone buildings, three with peaked roofs that appeared to be sheds or barns. The larger, two-story one with a flat roof was presumably the house. All were set amid a landscape of rocks and dry grass.

Relief flushed over me. I let out a slow sigh and felt my tight muscles slowly relax. Yet, this meant his daughter had married into the muggers' family. They could be in his daughter's house waiting. Foreigners like me were a rare sight in this part of Yemen. The muggers had heard my accent and seen my American dollars. Hell, they had taken them. If Mohammed introduced me as an American doctor, and they saw my face covered with bruises and cuts, of course they would know I was the man they'd left for dead. My whole body began to tremble. I just wanted out of this place. I wanted out of this damn country.

Our truck rolled to a slow stop at the little house's door, and I looked out the window of the truck to assess the situation.

The house was dowdy, like the other houses in this area, but with white accents and yellow sunflowers tied to the wooden windowsill. It looked old, the whitewashed wooden trim weathered and dried, wide cracks in the wood's grain. An ancient artisan had carved the front door, like many doors in Yemen, with beautiful vines that evolved into Arabic script. Some cracks were so big that bugs could fly through—maybe even small birds. Natural sand, driven by relentless mountain winds for a hundred years, had polished the door as smooth as glaze.

Mohammed looked at me as he stepped down from the truck. I stepped out and onto the hard baked ground, but he pointed behind me and scowled. "Stay in the truck!"

I climbed back in and pulled the door closed.

He walked toward the building. I noticed he had a limp, like something was wrong with his right hip.

A man about my age stepped out from the weathered door wearing a dirty brown thoob with wide stripes of lighter brown and a black vest, woolen I assumed. He was small and his hair could not have been any curlier. He was sporting the start of what I would call a "fro." His face appeared scrunched, perhaps with worry.

My ears picked up on the bleating of sheep. I looked behind the house and saw the animals scattered across the field. Patches of tall grass moved like a turbulent brunette sea, pushed here and there by the shifting breezes. The low sun was casting a yellow hue over the fields, its horizontal light deepening the shadows and giving everything more texture. What a beautiful place. If only people weren't trying to murder me, I could've made my home here.

Could this man, the one speaking to Mohammed, be the assailant? I didn't think so because he seemed too short, maybe five-foot-five or-six. The mugger had been shorter than me but only by an inch or so.

The man engaged in a quick conversation with Mohammed as they kissed each other on the cheek. Mohammed turned and pointed at me. I cracked open the truck's door again so I could hear the conversation. Saleh in the middle of the truck's seat was making a study of me, his big brown eyes sliding to the top of my head and back down to my shoes.

With my limited Arabic vocabulary, eavesdropping was always difficult. The other man's name was Fakhir. I understood that Mohammed was explaining I was an American doctor. Mohammed said he believed Allah had sent me to them, to help Ghazala, his daughter.

Fakhir looked at me, squinting as he stared. I couldn't hear or understand everything because he spoke half as loud as Mohammed, but I heard him ask his father-in-law twice, "Where did you find this man?" I could see the confused look on his face even from a distance.

Then I heard Fakhir say, "We had a robber last night, but Ameen and Qasim killed him. He spoke English."

"Oh, good," said Mohammed with a grin. "Must have been an American or British spy." Then he oddly glanced at me over his shoulder.

Mohammed motioned for me to come. I stepped down from the truck. I looked at Mohammed's wife. She was sitting on top of the mountain of sacks, her face still carrying a sour look, her black scarf half blown off and her brown hair windswept. I nodded and smiled at her. Then she jerked her body to face away from me, pulling her scarf tightly around her head.

I walked toward the men.

Mohammed introduced me. I shook Fakhir's hand. He pulled me in his direction, and we kissed each other's cheeks. His were salty as I'm sure were mine. I found the little man to be jumpy, his movements quick and uncertain. His words were short and rapid. Maybe it was the worry about his wife that was wearing on him. Maybe he—like me—had seen too much war.

Then he studied me—just like the boy—from the top of my head to my feet and back up again. He looked me in the eyes, no doubt noticing the swollen one. With a smirk, he said, "It appears the doctor needs a doctor."

I smiled and gave a fake laugh, "Ha, ha … maybe I do. I was in a motorcycle accident coming down the mountain this morning."

"Do you think you can help Ghazala?" Fakhir asked, concern having pushed away his smirk.

"What's her story? How did she become ill?" I asked, trying my best to show heartfelt concern.

Fakhir shook his head and looked down at the ground. "I think she was not obedient to her father and mother when she was a child. She disappointed Allah … uh, because of that, she became ill." Then he looked back at me, cockeyed.

"When? How old was she?" I asked.

He shrugged his shoulders. "She was thirteen when she became sick, her skin became like a strawberry, bumpy and red, and she couldn't walk. She recovered from that, thanks to Allah's help, and became stronger. But she was never a healthy woman. She gave me my daughter the year I married her, when she was fifteen. But since then, she has grown weaker. The Imam came to see her and brought a healer with him. The healer said that having our daughter, Jaafar, drew away pieces of Ghazala's life. Daughters are weak and can drain life from the mother. The solution, he said, would be for Ghazala to become pregnant with a boy ... you know, the boy will give the mother strength, and she draws life from him. Do you agree?"

I did one shake of my head and paused. "I need to see her and to examine her. I'm concerned about her heart or her lungs, and pregnancy may not be good for her. But I'll listen to her first."

"To hear her talk?" Fakhir asked, his eye defaulting into their cockeyed position again.

"No, no, to hear her heart," I said. "With my stethoscope," I said, putting my fingers in my ears.

I climbed onto my bike. Mohammed's wife turned, avoiding eye contact. Grabbing my first aid supplies and stethoscope out of the panniers, I jumped back down, my shoes stirring up yellow dust in a cloud when I hit the hard ground. I beat my pant legs with my hand to knock some of the dirt off, residue from my three-kilometer crawl up the wadi.

I followed the two men inside. It was dark but cool. A young girl, who I assumed was Jaafar, brought us water in two frosted plastic glasses. I gulped mine down quickly. Mohammed shook his head and pushed his glass away. I grabbed it and drank it, the entire thing in one swallow—hoping they had a good well.

The furniture was simple, with bright fabrics in reds, greens, and blues that dissipated the surrounding drabness. Beautiful but well-worn wool rugs covered the floor, some threadbare. I assumed they'd made them from their own sheep's wool or had received them as family heirlooms. The walls were decorated with Arabic inscriptions, photos, and one beautiful painting of a common village scene in Yemen. They also had the Houthi motto in red and green Arabic script in a wooden frame: "Allah is Greater, Death to America, Death to Israel, Curse on the Jews, Victory to Islam." It gave me the same feeling—I supposed—of a black man in the American South invited to the home of a white coworker who was flying a Confederate flag.

Fakhir knocked on the bedroom door, then walked in. I overheard him speaking to Ghazala. "There's a man here to see you."

"Man? What man?" I heard the strain in her voice.

"A doctor. An English doctor," he said.

"What's he doing here? I don't want to see him," she said loudly.

"Your father brought him here. He found him upon the mountain. He was in a motorcycle wreck. Mohammed thinks Allah sent him to help you."

Fakhir motioned for Mohammed and me to enter the bedroom.

Inside the small room was a double bed that took up most of the space. A delicate woman, her head propped at 45 degrees on embroidered cushions, rested in the bed. Her dark hair was tangled and appeared thin and brittle, a few loose hairs clinging to her pillow. Her face was pale for a Yemeni, her skin wrinkled, her lips pursed. I would've guessed she was in her late forties by her looks, but I figured she had to be much younger, maybe thirty. Her mouth-breathing seemed labored even though she was reclining—not a good sign. The inappropriateness of a strange man, notably an "infidel," in a married woman's bedroom limited my time to assess her.

"Hello, Ghazala," I said with a smile and my hand over my heart.

She gave a brief smile but stayed silent.

"Uh, my name is Bryan. I'm a doctor from Haydan." Her eyes seemed to brighten when I mentioned Haydan. I asked, "Do you know someone there?"

She smiled and whispered that her cousin lived in Farat and an American doctor, a lady, had delivered her baby at the Haydan clinic when the midwife couldn't."

A grin captured my pummeled face. "That doctor was Sheila, my good friend." My heart swelled. "May I examine you please, Ghazala?" I asked.

She pulled the sheets up to her chin and scooted down into the bed but then nodded.

Still smiling, I gently removed the bedsheet from her neck, leaving the sheet over her face for modesty's sake. From two steps back from the bed and with my head tilted, I noticed that her outermost jugular vein was distended.

I put my right fist, all scraped and swollen from the punch to Michel's face and the brawl the previous night with her in-laws, on the ridge of her breastbone, the "sternal angle." I noticed the vein's engorgement extended to just below the top of my fist. Since my fist was about nine centimeters wide—or more since it was swollen—I estimated her external jugular vein was distended for seven centimeters above where the sternum angled in. Since the sternal angle sits about five centimeters above the right atrium, or the heart's upper chamber, I could say with confidence that her central venous pressure was around twelve centimeters of water, as blood and water measure the same, equaling almost nine millimeters of mercury. Way too high. For her body size, I estimated that it shouldn't have been over nine centimeters of water pressure. This meant she had back pressure in the heart's right atrium, which told me that an infection had damaged the tricuspid valve, precipitating a right-sided heart failure.

I felt for the deeper but larger internal jugular vein. The pulse, much more subtle than that in an artery, was level with the external vein.

I adjusted her head until the light struck her internal jugular vein so I could keep my eyes on the pulse within it. I watched carefully for the different waves of the pulse in the vein and noticed that the first, what we call the "A, Wave," was higher than expected, confirming to me that there was some obstruction between the right atrium and ventricle, likely a stenosis of the tricuspid valve.

I pressed my hands down on the upper right side of her belly. The internal jugular vein's pulse rose two additional centimeters until I released the pressure. I suspected that this finding indicated she had more than just a tricuspid valve problem. I guessed there'd been a left heart failure too, causing an increase in the pressure, or "wedge pressure," of her pulmonary capillaries. From her story, I suspected she'd had complications from a strep infection that had led to rheumatic fever. It would be unusual for only the right major heart valve to be affected. Listening directly to the valves would confirm my suspicion.

"Do you recall when you were sick as a young girl and your skin turned red, did your joints become swollen and painful?" I asked, pausing from my exam to give her answer my full attention.

"Yes, I do. I couldn't walk for several weeks because of the pain. My mother thought I was lazy and beat me for not doing my chores."

I glanced at her father. He rolled his eyes and mumbled, "Allah."

Ghazala continued in a soft whisper, "But I still couldn't walk."

I moved down to her feet. When I pulled back the gray blanket and flowered sheet, I saw she was wearing woolen socks. I removed one. The sock's elastic band caused a deep indentation around her ankle. I pressed her ankle with my finger, and it pitted, my finger leaving a deep impression in her soft tissue for over a minute after I released it.

I came back to her face. Now that my eyes had become accustomed to dimness of the room, I noticed a blue tinge around her lips. She was not getting enough oxygen. I had her sit up so I could run my stethoscope down the back of her nightgown. When I asked her to breathe deeply, I heard fluid at the bottom of her lungs—not a good sign.

"How old are you Ghazala," I asked.

"Twenty-two," she said.

"My lord," I whispered in English.

Fakhir quickly corrected her, "Twenty-three."

"I am?" she asked.

"You had Jaafar when you were fifteen and she is eight now."

I saved the exam that required the most immodesty for last. This part would allow me to fine-tune my diagnosis. I listened to her heart over the areas where you can hear each valve best. I heard an opening "snap" sound and a continuous rumbling murmur along her sternum's left lower side, indicating that blood was passing through her narrow tricuspid valve like a river passing through a rapid. I also heard a low-pitched rumbling at her heart's lowest part, called the "apex," during the time the left ventricle filled. I could feel this larger murmur as a vibration with my hand against her chest, indicating a more serious narrowing, or stenosis, of her mitral valve, which is the most common injury from rheumatic fever. I could also tell, by thumping her chest and listening to the echo, her heart was enlarged, compensating for ineffective valves. This was serious. Life-threatening.

According to custom, I needed to speak to the men outside the bedroom, telling the patient nothing, as if none of it was her business. The two men had remained silent during the entire exam.

I thanked Ghazala for her time, promising her I would give her father and husband my best opinion. I also reassured her that if they followed my advice, she would be okay. Tears came to her eyes, and she began crying, her hand over her mouth as if to muffle the sounds of the sobs.

Once outside the bedroom, the two men surrounded me.

"Well, I know what's wrong with her. Her two major heart valves were seriously damaged by an infection she had as a child." I looked at Fakhir and pointed toward the bedroom door. "If you impregnate Ghazala, with a girl *or* a boy, it doesn't matter ... Allah as my witness"—I placed my hand over my heart—"you will be her murderer."

Fakhir stepped back, shaking his head. "How do you know this?"

"My exam told me. It's very clear," I said.

Mohammed pushed his way between Fakhir and me. "Is Ghazala going to die?"

I looked from one to the other and back again. "There's a hospital in Sana'a that's still doing heart surgery. However, I don't think Ghazala could make their waiting list, not unless she has a lot of money. I don't think they would accept sheep as payment."

They stared at me with sad faces.

"But I do have some good news." Then pointing at the couch, I said, "please sit and I will explain."

The two men slowly lowered themselves to the brightly flowered couch. I stooped in front of them.

"I'm now working at the International Rescue Committee's office in Sana'a. A wealthy family in London had a daughter with the same heart problem. They were so happy with her life being saved by the surgeon, they created a fund to fly refugee families from all over the world to London for the surgery."

"We're not refugees!" Fakhir asserted.

"Yeah ... I know," I said rolling my eyes. "But because of the civil war, the English think all Yemenis are refugees. It won't be a problem. Here's the hope. Without surgery to fix the valves inside her heart, Ghazala will die. She may have only a few months. She is deteriorating so rapidly. I'll give you a woman's name, Dorothy Robinson, at the IRC office in Sana'a. I'll write down her address for you."

After a moment of silence, Mohammed said loudly to Fakhir, "*Ya ghabi* [hey idiot], get the doctor some paper."

Fakhir jumped up, went into the other room, and returned with a pencil and a single piece of paper.

I wrote a note in English. "Dear Dorothy, Ghazala has severe mitral and probably tricuspid heart valve stenosis from rheumatic fever. She only has weeks to live. She is a perfect candidate for the Richardson family's grant."

I said to the men, "They'll fly her to London for the world's best care. Then she can return home and bear you many wonderful children ... but not with that heart, the one she has now."

Mohammed looked at me and asked me an odd question.

"Will they use a pig's heart to fix hers? We can't allow that! A pig inside her would defile her, says the prophet ... unless it is necessary to save a life."

I sighed. "No. I don't think so. I think they would use artificial heart valves, ones that don't come from any animal. But if they do ... certainly, it'll be to save her life."

Fakhir eyes were glistening with tears. "Is there no other way? How do you know the Imam's healer isn't right? That she needs to give birth to a boy."

"Trust me!" I said in an irritated tone. "I know what I'm talking about. Having a baby right now, male or female, will certainly kill her. Go to Sana'a. Tell this Dorothy lady at IRC that I, Bryan Rogers, sent you."

When I stood up to leave, I saw a man sitting on a stool by the door. He must have slipped in while I was with Ghazala, though I hadn't noticed him when I came out the bedroom. I assumed he was Fakhir's brother, one of my attackers. His brown eyes measured me up and down. When he stood and turned toward the door, I saw three scabs in the pattern of my teeth on his ear. He left quickly without speaking to any of us.

My heart began to race. I could still sense his ear's salty taste in my mouth as we struggled on the ground.

"What was he doing here?" I asked Mohammed and Fakhir.

"That's my brother, Qasim," said Fakhir. "He comes and goes whenever he wants. He lives in the house in front of us."

"Mohammed, are you ready to go?" I asked quickly. "Your wife and boy are still in the truck."

Nodding his head, he answered, "Yes, yes, I know. I'll say goodbye to my daughter, and I'll be out. Go to the truck."

I left the house and sat in the truck. After fifteen minutes, Mohammed came out and clambered in. Fakhir followed him to the truck and stood near the driver's door. Mohammed closed his door but continued talking with his son-in-law through the open window. It was like they had forgotten that I spoke Arabic, despite my having spoken it quite competently for the past hour.

Fakhir kept shaking his head. "I don't like his idea. I can't imagine leaving Yemen and going to London. We've never been out of Yemen except for the hajj, and that was by bus. It is fearful to think they will cut Ghazala's heart open. She could die. We need to follow the Imam's advice first. We'll see if we can bare a boy to give her strength."

I cringed. Thankfully Mohammed spoke, "No, you won't! Ghazala is my daughter, and you're taking her to London. The best doctors in the world will treat her. You wait here. When I'm done dropping my coffee off in Al Hudaydah, I'll be back." Then he yelled, "I'll take you and Ghazala to Sana'a as soon as I can. We will load her bed in my truck ... and that settles it!"

It reminded me of something my father had once said to my sister. "Angie, there's no man's love for a woman that can surpass what a father has for his daughter." After meeting Sheila ... and her father, I think I was the exception.

"We should go," I said to Mohammed. "It's getting late." Fixing my eyes on the side door of Qasim's house, I fidgeted in my tattered vinyl truck seat. Sweat beaded across my forehead. I looked down at the little boy, who was silently staring at me, picking his nose—and eating his findings.

Mohammed looked at me as he was returning his aviator glasses to his face, "I know how to drive at night. Settle down." The truck shook. Then he looked in his rearview mirror with a frown and commented, "Now where's *she* going?"

His wife walked past the cab and into the house.

I quickly said, "Uh, well, I must find a place to stay in Hudaydah and I don't want to fumble around in the dark."

"Don't worry ... I'll find you a place!" Mohammed shrieked. Then looking at Ghazala's house, he mumbled, "She must be visiting her daughter."

My worst fears were suddenly realized when the side door to Qasim's house flew open. I was about to shit in my pants. The two assailants came out and were walking toward us in a hurry. *Damn!*

"Mohammed, we must go now!" I said with urgency in my voice.

"No!" he said, pointing toward the approaching men. "The men want to ask me something ... and my wife is visiting her daughter."

The older man came to Mohammed's side window and looked at me. I remembered his crackly voice and his gray beard rubbing against my face as he and Qasim wrestled me to the ground the previous night. The man who thought he had murdered me was now staring at me, smiling. I lost my social bearings, not knowing what the hell was about to happen. If he didn't remember me, I was sure the gasoline smell on my shirt would've triggered such a recollection.

Then the older man spoke in English. "Thank you, doctor, for helping my daughter-in-law. I want to pay you for your troubles."

Pay me?

He reached into his pocket and pulled out a crisp one-hundred-dollar bill—mine, I'm sure. He handed it to me, reaching across Mohammed's lap, then smirked and winked. His gesture stunned me, but I took it.

Mohammed, with a serious look, said, "He is being very generous ... keep it. Our doctors would only charge five American dollars for a visit, or maybe just a piece of mutton."

I nodded, too afraid to speak.

Mohammed started the truck, and the men stepped back.

We took the dirt road out to the highway. I looked back. The three men, Fakhir, his brother Qasim, and his father, were all waving to us like it was the end of a family reunion. Then suddenly Mohammed stomped the brakes and we slid in the gravel just before reaching the highway.

"Why are we stopping?" I said with growing agitation.

Mohammed raised his calloused hands off the steering wheel and gasped, then pointed behind us. "My wife. Allah, I almost left her!"

CHAPTER TWENTY-SEVEN

I looked in my side mirror and saw Mohammed's wife running down the dirt driveway toward us, holding the helm of her dress up out of the dirt, moving like she was in a trial heat for the Olympics. She climbed into the back of the truck huffing and puffing. Mohammed checked his mirror to make sure she was secure and pulled away again.

I held my breath until we pulled out onto the mountain highway. I saw the houses in my side mirror shrinking—fading into the sea of brown grass.

We drove out of the foothills and continued down the coastal plain toward Al Hudaydah—tall dry mountains to the east, the Saudi Arabian border to the west. Yemeni's broad plain and the Red Sea replaced the Saudi settlements on our right after fifty kilometers. We passed through two Houthi checkpoints where they questioned me, searched me, and made me show my passport. A bruised-up American medical worker in a coffee bean truck on a remote Yemeni road was an enigma. It was like the guards were teetering on the edge of arresting me or letting me go. If it hadn't been for Mohammed advocating for me, they might have shot me.

As evening progressed to night, I rolled up my window to ward off the desert's chill. I couldn't imagine how Mohammed's wife was coping up on top. I must have asked him a dozen times if I could trade places with her. He assured me she was fine. I never saw him ask her how she was doing or even say a single word to her.

"Often she prefers to ride in the back," he said. "Malika enjoys the fresh air ... and she doesn't like the smell of my farts."

The little boy, Saleh, who had been sleeping—leaning on my left thigh—suddenly awakened and giggled loudly, then covered his mouth with his hand.

So, he wasn't deaf.

Mohammed looked down at him and back at me. With a big grin, he said, "I eat ful medames with onions every morning. It gives me the farts of rotten fish."

I concurred. They did smell like rotten fish and burned the nostrils like the fish was garnished with rotten wasabi. I had been thinking it was the boy with soiled underpants. But I didn't know if Mohammed was being insensitive to his wife or sympathetic to my needs. Yemenis greeted their guests, kissing them on the cheeks, serving them their best food and tea—unless the "guest" was trying to steal petrol from them. Then they beat them to death and tossed their body in a gully. Not much in between.

Now that I knew he wasn't deaf, I tried to have a conversation with little Saleh in Arabic, but he seemed shy. Once he did start speaking, he seemed to love saying his few English words repeatedly, especially *hello, okay,* and *Stephen Curry.* I handed him my stethoscope, thinking it would capture his curiosity. He studied it, looking in the earpieces and the listening bell. I placed it in his ears and put the diaphragm over his heart. He sat mesmerized for twenty minutes. He then listened to his arm, lungs, and belly. After a while, I looked over and saw he had my stethoscope in his pants— fortunately, they weren't soiled. *What the hell was he doing?* With his shorts pulled out, I saw that he was listening to his genitalia. He kept the stethoscope in that position for the remainder of the trip.

We arrived on the outskirts of the city, which faced the sea— it was the main port for the Houthi-controlled part of Yemen. Its four million residents were under Saudi Arabia's constant siege.

Along the beach, outside the major commercial port, large wooden boats painted yellow, green, and blue sat in the sand, leaning left or right, their captains waiting for the flooding tide and their turn to venture out into the Red Sea to fish. These boats were also used for illicit activities, such as supplying the black market and taking refugees north toward the Suez Canal with the promise of

Greece or Italy as a dropping point. I'd heard on the BBC two weeks earlier of such a boat leaving this very port and capsizing in a storm in the Red Sea, drowning seventy. The passengers were only wishing for a better life for their kids. I hoped one such boat would be able to take me to Israel—without sinking.

Al Hudaydah bore the scars of conflict more than the rest of the country. It had been the target of the largest Saudi and United Arab Emirates bombing campaign of the entire war. They'd called it Operation Golden Victory, intending to extricate the Houthis from this vital seaport and thus starving the rest of the Houthi-held lands into submission. The falling bombs had damaged or destroyed most buildings, yet the Houthis kept control. In a different universe, a different time, the town could have been Yemen's Miami Beach or French Riviera.

"I need to look for a guest house," I said.

"I told you not to worry," Mohammed replied. "I know a guest house that'll take you. The owner lost her husband and two sons during the bombing in 2018. She turned their home into a boarding house so that she would have money for food. There's no pension in Yemen, you know, so if you are widowed, you starve."

We drove through town along the waterfront, then turned a block in from the sea. He pulled his truck in front of a concrete house. We got out. I looked up to see Mohammed's wife sleeping, lying on a burlap sack as if it was a plump mattress, her head wrapped in her scarf in layers.

Mohammed talked to the guest house's owner, an older woman with a wrinkled face like an old dried-out potato. She was dressed in mourning black. Mohammed forgot again that I spoke Arabic and said to her, "You can charge this man more because he's a foreigner. He'll pay in hard currency, American dollars."

"Fine, fine ... but give me a minute as I have to kick other guests out," the woman said with a scowl.

She then gave a quick, forced smile and said to me in English, "It will be forty dollars a night."

If I were Yemeni, I could have found a room for ten bucks. But I wasn't complaining. My only problem was that Mohammed's in-laws had robbed me. I had the one-hundred-dollar bill still in my pocket. But that money would buy me two days. During those days, I hoped to call Angie and get her to send me additional funds.

I'd been careful to clean out my bike's box and had my sat phone, water bottle, Leatherman, passport, the cigar that Ray had given me, Ray's janbiya and my one-hundred-dollar bill. Those were my remaining life's possessions. Apparently, my nice Littman Classic stethoscope was hiding in little Saleh's pants.

My new landlord's name was Gamila, meaning "beautiful." I'm sure she had lived up to the name in her younger years, but a tough life had left its marks in the crinkles of her face. At first glance, I would've said she was seventy, but upon closer inspection of her eyes and energy, I determined she was younger than sixty. Her hair was black as coal but frosted with natural gray curls penetrating her crown. She was heavy, which was a little unusual where food was scarce. Maybe the harbor environs were better supplied.

Gamila didn't wear a burka but had a black sheer-fabric scarf around her neck, which she pulled up over her face when she was outside.

In front of her house were four plastic chairs. "Take a seat," she said. "I must clean your room first."

I sat. The flimsy chair started to lean as one leg was broken so I had to continuously lean in the opposite direction.

Soon, I heard arguing inside the house that was not clear enough for me to understand. After a few minutes, a young man and a woman wearing a full burka and carrying a baby came out of the house. The man mumbled *Ayreh Feek*, the Arabic equivalent of "screw you" as he walked by me. It was obvious I was displacing them, and I felt bad about that. But I was so tired that I didn't have the energy to insist they stay.

They walked to a tiny car parked on the side of the house and left.

Gamila took me to a windowless bedroom on the first floor that wasn't much larger than the bed. It had one old wooden chest of drawers on which sat a well-decorated but worn ceramic pitcher and basin. In the corner was a teak wardrobe with a Japanese family walking past tree limbs bursting with cherry blossoms painted on its door. The room's fractured stucco walls, dreary and water-stained, were decorated by two colorful paintings—one of a Yemeni fisherman and, oddly, one of Queen Elizabeth.

I laid down my possessions and turned back the bed covers. The sheets had big oval stains that looked like old blood. A dirty— poop-stained—pair of men's boxers sat between them. I didn't have the impetus at ten o'clock at night to wash and dry sheets. "Damn!" I muttered.

I had not showered in three days. Gazing into an oval golden mirror on the wall, I saw my face was still caked in dried blood and mud. My eyes were yellower than before, enhanced by the gold tint of the glass.

Rather than trying to navigate the community shower down the hall, I walked to the beach to bathe. There wasn't a towel and Gamila was gone, so I grabbed a tablecloth off a clothesline. I don't think it was linen as it wasn't very absorbent. Maybe polyester. I went back inside and grabbed the dirty pair of boxers and a bar of soap from the kitchen sink.

I unloaded my cargo pockets. It was then I realized that Mohammed's son evidently had stuffed my stethoscope down his pants. "Rats! A whole damn family of swindlers," I mumbled out loud.

I went into the darkened streets and walked two blocks to the beach. In the surf, I scrubbed my body and washed my clothes as well as the vagrant boxers. I dried myself off with the impervious tablecloth and placed it and the boxers on the clothesline, along with my shirt and underwear, and returned to my room. I stripped off the sheets and lay directly on the stained mattress. My cuts and abrasions—cleared of their dried blood—were now stinging from the salt water. I would've given a king's ransom for clean clothes and a toothbrush, not to mention a hot shower in a pleasant hotel. But I had no money for shopping.

Realizing it was three P.M. in New York, I pulled out my sat phone—which still had a fifty percent charge on its battery. I called Angie.

"Bryan, what's up?" she asked in a cheerful voice.

"I'm safe at the port city of Al Hudaydah," I said.

"You must've found a ride."

"I did, on a coffee truck."

"Bryan, listen," she said with excitement. I've worked nonstop on the problem since yesterday and I've made some progress."

"What have you done so far?"

"Well, Joel knew someone at the NYC FBI office, and I called her."

I hated that she'd brought her boyfriend into this mess. "Who is she?" I asked.

"I think her name is Anne. She seemed less engrossed in the story than what I had imagined. She told me I had to keep in perspective that they get about a dozen serious tips per day on terrorist threats to NYC. Trucks with fertilizer bombs, she said, and ships with nuclear warheads, and even armed drones or blimps were in these threats. But they all end up being part of unfounded conspiracy theories. Then she felt obligated to tell me … well, that it's a federal offense to falsely report a threat. You know, crying wolf."

"Angie!" I said. "Didn't you tell her it's your own brother, your brother on the ground in Yemen who has this tip?"

"Of course! I told her the details, Bryan," she said in a brusque tone.

"I'm sorry, but I've been through hell in the last forty-eight hours, and I'm worried. Two days ago, I was trying my best to save my dear friend Jabbar. But now it's too late for that, isn't it? I would even feel relieved if the CIA or whoever the hell would fire a missile up Jabbar's ass, as they threatened at the embassy. I still love the guy, but after they killed my friend Ray and tried to kill me, you know, it's too late for redemption. Hate has taken him and won't let him go."

"I'm sorry, Bryan," she said. "I know how much Jabbar meant to you. But this lady at the FBI, while seeming underwhelmed with it all, did say she would investigate it and get back to me."

"We don't have a lot of time. Jabbar is going out to sea in a couple of weeks and that maiden voyage of his ... well, could be the attack. I want out of this mess. I've done all I can do, and I just want to come home."

"There's more to report," Angie said. "I reached out to a man who's a member of the New York City Yacht Club, where Joel keeps his boat. Gary knows everything about ships and boats. He was in the navy and then commercial shipping for forty years. I called him, and he told me several interesting things. Ships must register with the International Shipping Federation. He looked up the name *Pytheas*. It's a ship for sure, an LR1 tanker ... meaning a long-range tanker type one. They're too large to fit through the Suez Canal but can navigate rivers and smaller ports. They're common, according to Gary. The ownership of the *Pytheas* changed hands just last year. A shipping company based in Jeddah now owns it. They own several tankers, all in the super tanker class except this one, a much smaller ship."

Static was seeping into the conversation's margins, the satellite moving toward the horizon, so I hurried the exchange.

"Angie, that's a great lead. Good work. Here's another thing, I told you the robbers took all my money. There's one hundred bucks in my pocket, and I need clean clothes and a place to stay that doesn't have poop and blood stains on the bed, and I want to bribe my way to Israel. I need you to wire me money somehow. I saw a bank on the way in called, *Yemen Kuwait Bank of Al Hudaydah*. I'll pay you back."

"I'll do it as soon as I get off the phone," she said.

"Great, thanks. I'll talk to you later."

Her voice was fading, but I heard her say, "Oh, Gary also told me, we can track that ship in actual time. They're required to carry a GPS beacon, and the ISF—*static static*—to that site—*static*—a log-on."

I said, "Angie, you're breaking up ... but fantastic! Okay, take care—"

"Yes, Bryan. Poop stains, are you serious—"

I lost the signal.

CHAPTER TWENTY-EIGHT

The next morning, I had little trouble finding passage out of Yemen, which was a great relief. I went to the harbor where the fishermen docked their dhows. There were more than thirty side by side in the sand.

The Yemenis had been building dhows with the same design for at least a thousand years. To the casual onlooker, they looked rustic, like they'd been cobbled together in a hurry. But upon closer inspection, one could see the iron adze's fine marks. Artisans had meticulously shaped logs by chopping off slivers of wood piece by piece on the beach under the scorching sun. They then methodically fitted the massive beams together like a 3-D puzzle. Jabbar had told me the beams slid together easily, lubricated by the sweat that had dripped on the timbers from the shipbuilders' heads and the blood from their spent fingers. The builders then painted the boats in bright colors, running down the hull in stripes as if their boats had rubbed up against a rainbow.

At the first dhow, men were sitting cross-legged, sewing up holes in their fishing nets with long wooden needles held by grimy fingers, smoking stubby cigarettes and laughing. Their gaze fixated on me as I approached.

"Can you take me out of Yemen? I need passage north." I asked the group of net-menders.

The men snickered. One stood up, cigarette dangling while stuck to his lower lip, and pointed up the wharf. "Go and ask at harbor twelve."

At harbor twelve, I asked, "Is there a boat here that takes passengers north?"

One tall, skinny man walked up to me, his face in mine, and asked, "Where are you going?"

"Uh, north," I said.

"Saudi?" he asked, his beady eyes staring into mine.

"No, just north. Farther north."

In Houthi territory, the word Israel can get you killed, unless you have business with the Jews. Commerce erases all political boundaries. It never crossed my mind to say Jordan.

"You need to talk to Ibrahim," he said, nodding toward another group of men on the pier.

I found Ibrahim drinking tea. The tea would drip from his long, brown-stained mustache between each sip. He was sitting on a crate playing backgammon with gnarly looking fishermen who could have been mistaken for pirates. One of them was wearing a black patch over his left eye and had a deep scar falling from the patch down his cheek as if his face had been folded in and then stapled from the inside. But I didn't see any peg legs or hooks for hands among the group.

Ibrahim had a strange sense of humor, guffawing with the slightest comment. When I asked him if he had a boat that could take me north, he replied, "Sure, we have one heading for Iceland ... boarding in ten minutes. First class?" Then the whole group laughed, leaving me standing and staring.

In a more serious tone, I said, "I heard I could get out of Yemen on your boat."

Chuckles spread in both directions around the backgammon table like dominos falling. Ibrahim stood and motioned me to follow him. I did but with cautious steps.

Behind a warehouse, he offered me a cigarette—which I declined—and gave me his answer. "Maybe. It depends. Where are you going?" His unlit cigarette bounced up and down with each syllable.

"Uh, north."

"You told me that already! I have a boat that goes north, but where exactly do you want to go?" he said, pulling his cigarette out of his mouth and stuffing it into his shirt pocket. Then he gave me a vile stare.

"Israel," I whispered.

His rubbery face twisted into a big chuckle. "Israel? We get close enough. Can you pay in euros?"

"Dollars," I said.

"Are you an American?"

I hesitated but then nodded my head.

"Well, we don't have many Americans around here anymore. We have Yemenis trying to get to America, not Americans trying to escape Yemen," he said with a thunderous laugh.

"What would it cost me?"

"Five thousand dollars … U.S." He gave me a serious stare.

"That's too much!" I said. "I can just take the bus to Sana'a, wait for the airport to open, and fly to Israel."

"Aren't you running from the law? If so, they'll catch you in Sana'a and—"

"I'm running from lawlessness," I said hastily. "I don't fear getting caught, but I'm in a hurry."

"Okay, three thousand U.S., half now, half when we get there."

"What about one thousand U.S., seven hundred and fifty now?" I asked.

Ibrahim nodded.

We shook.

"I need to get the money from the bank. When do you leave?"

"You're in luck. We have a boat going out tomorrow morning, in the dark hours. I'll be captaining that boat."

"Can you show me the boat?" I asked.

He took me to an old wooden dock with the number fifteen painted in white on a square board. They had moored a smaller dhow there, tying it to the dock's post. The boat was rough, the beams worn, the bright paint now faded.

"This is a barijah. They're smaller but nimbler than dhows," said Ibrahim. "Yet, it's as seaworthy as a yacht. Barijahs have only a sail and an outboard. However, we've fitted this one with an inboard motor, a diesel truck engine. The driveshaft goes to a propeller. She's fast and can outrun a Saudi war ship."

"Can I go onboard?" I asked.

"Just don't snoop too much or we'll cut your throat." After a long serious pause, a blusterous laugh ensued.

The boat was twenty-five feet long with a single forward-leaning mast. It had a small hold, with only a five-and-a-half-foot head clearance. In that hold, the squat engine sat on pallets looking like it was held together with scrap wire and ropes. Two metal drums served as fuel tanks. A long shaft sloped from the motor to the stern. There was a diesel smell permeating the below deck space along with the odors of dead fish and urine. It was a sty, a place where even a drove of pigs would turn up their pug noses. It appeared to be where the crew slept. Old wool blankets and pillows were strewn around. I wouldn't have felt safe sleeping there, fearing suffocation by carbon monoxide poisoning, not to mention the stench itself.

We went back above deck. Ibrahim said, "Our boat also has a lateen sail. We use wind power whenever we can, as diesel is becoming scarce. We depend a lot on the wind, Allah's gracious breath."

I suspected that if I were not an American, I could have arranged the passage for five thousand Yemeni rials or about two hundred dollars U.S. By avoiding Sana'a, I could dodge Abdul, Jabbar, and their associates. But were Ibrahim and his crew safer? I wasn't sure, but at least they appeared to be funnier.

I returned to my guest house. I looked at my sat phone. There was a text from Angie that read, "Can't send $$. US prohibits it to Houthi cities. Can send through IRC in NYC to Sana'a."

Damn! Suddenly my whole situation became much more complicated. I dropped backwards onto my stained mattress and looked up at the ceiling. What the hell was I going to do? After a second night in the guest house, I would have twenty bucks left. I would need some money for food. It was over two hundred kilometers to Sana'a. If I hitchhiked there, possibly I could hunker down with IRC friends until the airport opened. But I had nothing to barter with for a ride.

Then my mind wandered back to Jabbar and Abdul. I was trying to imagine what they were thinking or doing. I assumed they were in Sana'a looking for me ... to kill me.

I had an epiphany. I was in Al Hudaydah, Jabbar's boyhood home. I remembered him telling me about the city when we first met, when he was battling a serious case of pneumonia. He shared a secret.

When Jabbar sold their house to flee from Saudi's endless bombardment to relatively peaceful Haydan, he took the proceeds— three thousand American dollars—sealed it in a jar tied to a string and suspended it down a well. It was the family's entire savings and was meant to go to Alam. With that thought, I jumped up and sat on the side of the bed. I rubbed my eyes trying to force the memories back to the surface.

Then I recalled him telling me that the well was part of the *minbar*, or wash area, of an ancient mosque where believers perform *wudu*, the cleansing wash before prayers. He told me that the mosque was one of the oldest in Islam, over fourteen hundred years old and very famous. He said the money was safe there because the well—while now outside the main mosque—was on sacred land and the Saudis wouldn't bomb it. A modern *minbar* had been built inside the mosque in the 1950s with running water, and this old well had been taken over by the poor as a common water source. But what was the name of that mosque? I hadn't a clue.

I walked outside. My eye caught Gamila at her clothesline. "Good morning," I said.

"Good morning," she responded in the traditional Arabic greeting. Looking perplexed, she added, "I hung my tablecloth up yesterday, and it's still damp. I don't understand it."

"Hmm. I don't know. Maybe a heavy dew? Hey, I was going to do some sightseeing, and I couldn't remember the name of the famous mosque."

She stared at me. "Mosque? Do you mean the Al-Asha'ir Mosque?"

"Yeah, I think that's right."

"It's famous alright, a World Heritage Site. It was built by one of Mohammed's descendants … but it's more than ten kilometers from here."

"Really? How could I get there?"

"I don't know. I don't have a car."

"Damn," I mumbled to myself.

"Do you ride a bike?" she asked.

"A bike? Sure. I usually ride a motorbike but can ride a bicycle, if that's what you mean."

"There's a bike behind the house that one of the guests left. I think he was killed in a bombing in town. All I know was that the Saudis did a bombing of the city that morning, a lot of people were killed, and he never came back for his clothes or his bike. I was going to sell it. Maybe if you like it, you'll buy it."

"Maybe," I said.

To my surprise, it was a rather nice mountain bike and certainly ridable. But I was feeling a panic building inside of me. I was supposed to meet the smugglers for my trip north before sunrise and had to have the money by then. What were the odds that Jabbar's money was still there? If there, what were the chances of me finding it? Jabbar had fled Al Hudaydah four years earlier, surely someone had already found the money.

It was a long hard ride against the wind, but fortunately the terrain was flat. I found the mosque using Gamila's directions without a problem. The mosque stood out with its pearl-white stucco walls amid a cluster of olive trees. It looked more like a fortress—its bulky minaret more like a lighthouse. The building showed her age with rounded edges and concave stone steps from centuries of wear, like a stick of white butter sitting on a kitchen counter on a sultry August day.

I scouted out the area around the mosque where ten men were sitting on the steps, several smoking a tall silver *mada'a* (Yemenis waterpipe). Ten pairs of eyes were watching my every step. Fortunately, I didn't have to enter the mosque complex, as the old stone well and *minbar* was—like Jabbar said—outside the mosque's wall.

The courtyard around the well was certainly old, paved with massive cut stones, now worn smooth. It was reminiscent of what I had seen in photos around the Pyramids at Giza. Jabbar told me the well even predated the building of the mosque by hundreds of years. The water access was a circle of stone with a wooden cover and the stereotypical bucket on a rope.

A woman, completely covered in black, was pulling up water, and I kept my distance. She gave me the evil eye, casting her eyes so far to the right her sockets could barely contain them. I waited as she slowly retrieved the bucket from the well and poured the water—via a funnel—into a blue plastic jug. I took a couple of steps in her direction to prompt her to finish. Her eyes never left me. I got closer until I was invading her personal space. Finally, she got the cap on her jug and lifted it to her shoulder. She took three steps and dropped her jug down again. I thought because it was too heavy, but it appeared that she just wanted to gawk at me.

"Go away woman," I whispered to myself.

Looking down the well, my eyes quickly found the red and white rocks that held Jabbar's string. On his death bed, when I first met Jabbar, he told me how to retrieve the money so it would go only to Alam's inheritance. He instructed me that if I just pulled on the string, it would pop out of the mortar line. He had buried the string in clay for about ten feet. Then the string was free from there down to the surface of the water, which looked to be about thirty feet.

I made quick work of the clay mortar with my Leatherman knife, and to my heart's delight, I found the nail and its attached string. Half of my concerns were laid to rest.

Meanwhile, the woman was still staring at me, holding her sheer black scarf over her face with her right hand, her left steadying the jug on the ground.

Next, I pulled on the string, but it would not budge. I was afraid if I pulled too hard, it would break. The clay mortar had set like cement. *Damn!*

I had only one choice and that was climbing down to where the string was no longer covered. I hated climbing ropes, ever since gym class in high school. But the well was only three feet in diameter and with a strong nylon rope in the center, on which the water bucker was retrieved. I thought I could walk down the rough stone lining with my feet, my back against the wall behind me, while supporting myself with the rope. Scary, but everything in this damn country was scary.

Methodically, I worked my way down the stones to the place where the clear fishing string came out of the mortar and down to the jar. I could tell the jar was above water and was surprised no one had noticed it.

But maybe they had. Maybe it was empty. There was only one way to find out and that was by pulling up on the string. The jar came unhindered except for bouncing against the stones. It didn't break. Once it was in my hand, I noticed it had been sealed in wax. I could not make out its contents due to a thick layer of algae over the glass. I balanced in that position, one foot on each side of the well, the rope wrapped around my right hand, my back resting against the wall, the jar under my chin. With my left hand, I tried to peel off the wax and then open the jar.

About that time, I looked up to the bright circle of sky above the well and saw two faces peering down at me—a woman and a man. The man shouted, "What are you doing?" The words echoed in the well.

"Nothing," I replied, though it was an absurd answer. Then with more thought I added, "I dropped my water jar down the well!"

I opened the jar, and my delight brought tears. The money was there.

I took the wad of cash and put it into my cargo pocket and wedged the jar under my arm. I started to shimmy my way back up to the waiting faces.

At the top of the well, I realized that the two faces were my water woman and a security guard, a thin man in a dark uniform and a policeman's hat. This would mean trouble. The Yemenis, just like their American counterparts, were awash in baseless conspiracy theories. The Yemenis believe that the Jews and the Americans want to kill them or force-convert their children to either Judaism or Christianity. But they saw America as omnipotent. They blame the scorching—crop-killing sun—on NASA. They thought the Americans sent the locust with microchips inside them, telling them which crops to eat. So, an American in your most famous mosque's well—with a jar in hand—could only be a very bad thing.

With my feet back on the ground, the guard placed his right hand on his pistol and asserted, "You're poisoning us!"

"No, hell, no! Like I said, I was getting water for my jar, and I dropped it. I biked here from Al Hudaydah's beach and was thirsty."

"Who are you? Your Arabic is good but accented."

"I'm Bryan Rogers. I was a doctor at the IRC clinic in Haydan. The airport in Sana'a is closed, and I was trying to find passage on a boat to … uh, Egypt. I had heard about this ancient mosque and wanted to see it, but I was thirsty."

He squinted his eyes. "Are you an American?"

"Yes."

"Then you *were* poisoning us."

"No, no, no! Let me show you. I pulled the well's bucket up to the top and chugged water directly from it, until it ran down my chest."

The two of them watched me with great curiosity, the guard's hand still on his gun.

I added with a big, wet smile, "I was collecting it in a jar because I heard the water from this well was … uh, holy."

It was another long ride back to my guesthouse, the wind having shifted, coming off the Red Sea and once again a headwind. I tried to pedal hard while balancing the jar full of well water above the crossbar and between my thighs. I made it a couple of miles before it fell off and splattered on the road. But I had the money!

When I got back to the guest house, I counted the money on my bed and found there was, just like Jabbar had said, three thousand America dollars—oh, and three dimes. I lay on the bed, my few possessions packed in my daypack, and just stared at the ceiling. I was afraid to sleep for fear of missing my rendezvous, as I was sure they wouldn't wait on me. They had Saudi patrol boats to duck in the dark.

I couldn't see the water, but I could smell it and hear it lapping against our hull. I dozed off sitting on the deck, leaning over the gunwales. I awoke an hour later with sun lighting our small piece of the watery cosmos.

The boat felt tinier once the omnipresent blue sea besieged it. The sea had nothing red, not even the red algae—its namesake. There was no cabin in which to escape the elements except the filthy space below deck, most of it filled with bales of khat. I passed on sleeping there. The boat had an old sail draped over a pole, functioning as a tent. Under it, you had limited protection from the sun and chilly winds at night. I didn't have my sleeping bag, so I covered up at night with an old fishing net. Great for catching fish … useless as a blanket.

Nevertheless, being on the sea infused a thrill back into my solemn heart. I lay in the bow watching the water slide beneath us, the spray dampening my jaded face, on which a hardened grin slowly began to spread. I felt I was drifting a million miles away from all my troubles, across the Moscoviense Sea, on the dark side of the moon.

The briny waters had become my friend during my long trip across the Pacific with Angie two years previously. I had still been a greenhorn then, seasickness keeping me on my back for a week—a swinging hammock no help. However, as I acclimated to the sea, seeing only water in all directions, the Pacific became like a mistress, as I felt her soft roll beneath me. When you are at sea by yourself, the world leaves you the hell alone—your thoughts the only intruders.

Qarasinat (pirates) was the affectionate name I gave the four-man crew, even to their faces, and it drew a chuckle from them each time I used it. They sat playing backgammon, smoking self-rolled tobacco cigarettes, sipping whiskey from a brass flask, fishing with a long bamboo pole, or taking turns steering the boat with its rudder. I kept my distance from them at first, not fully trusting them—nor they me. I was expecting them to rob me and throw me overboard.

Fatigue was my adversary, making me not care if I lived another day or ever went ashore again. But then the thought would come back to me, blowing in on the forlorn wind like a lost albatross, whispering into my ear, "You must stop Jabbar."

Confined to such a small space with nothing to do, I became restless. When I had sailed alone, I was always busy. Besides the chores that required my attention, I had books and the internet to browse. But on this boat, I had nothing. They wouldn't let me touch the tiller—afraid I would divert the boat. I lay around on the deck staring east and west, hoping for a brief sight of land.

The khat below stole my attention away from the doldrum. It was certainly khat in our hold, baled for Israel's contraband market. The sailors would often go below and pull dried leaves from our cargo. Then they would sit dazed, ogling the sea, with brown drool dripping from their stained teeth and down their unshaven chins. They would sit like this for hours. I was always curious where their minds went when it vacated their bodies.

One afternoon, while bored senseless, I went down below and pulled a wad of khat from a bale. I stuck it in my mouth, realizing that if they caught me stealing from their cargo, it would piss them off. Give them one more reason to tie me to an anchor and drop me overboard. In Haydan I'd been surrounded by khat plants but was never tempted by it. But there, I had a clinic to run.

I chewed a little bit of the bitter plant like tobacco, mimicking the men. I then stuffed as many leaves in my mouth as it would hold. I noticed nothing at first, maybe a little tingling on my tongue. In a while, my heart raced. I felt hyper, like when I'd had one pot of coffee too many. Then I felt invincible, as though I could take on all the pirates single-handedly and commandeer their boat. That I could certainly save this world from Jabbar's group of little men with a grudge. It was a joy to feel a confidence I lacked when sober.

I kept chewing, and after the euphoria passed, I was catatonic. I couldn't move beyond batting my eyes, scratching, and staring into the void of the below deck space. I could raise my hand before my eyes, but I couldn't see it. Was I blind or was it too dark? I didn't care. Eventually, my heart slowed, and I drifted off to sleep on the piss-soaked beams beneath the diesel's deadly plume. Fortunately, they started the engine only intermittently, otherwise I would have died.

Four hours later, after the sun had set, I awoke. Two of the pirates were sleeping in the hull beside me. One was face down in a pool of brown drool, his leg across my legs. Too close. I rolled over, got up, and returned to the deck.

We caught sight of land twice. From a distance, the Egyptian desert looked like a brown line floating above the azure sea's horizon. Water birds sat high in the empty white sky with angled wings stretched but motionless in the lifting breezes.

As we were converging on Sinai, rugged mountains that bedecked its southern tip came into view. Closing in on that dry, craggy area from our blanket of blue, I felt like an Apollo astronaut dipping down from black space to the moon's surface. I just wanted to get close enough to swim ashore if I had to.

The mountains on both sides of the Gulf of Aqaba were closing in on us, squeezing the ship traffic into tight lanes going north and south. After ten days at sea, I knew we had to be close to Eilat. That night, on all points of the compass, civilization sparkled like earthbound constellations. Ancient civilizations at that—Israel, Egypt's Sinai, Jordan, and Saudi.

Ibrahim came to me as the western sky still held only a slight remembrance of autumn's war-weary sun. He stooped beside me, looked seriously into my eyes, and said, "In t days, we'll be at the rendezvous point. You'll finish paying me before then."

That evening, I climbed below to grab more khat leaves. I don't know why. The experience had not been enlightening. Long days confined to the small boat were getting to me. You can watch water flow by only so long before succumbing to psychosis.

As soon as I tore a handful of leaves from the stash, I caught the white eyes of one crew member lying in the stern's shadow peering up at me. I froze. Was he watching me or dispersed into his own khat daze?

The man stood and came toward me. "What are you doing?" he shouted at me in Arabic, his brown teeth clenched. "Are you stealing from us?"

"Uh, no," I said, affecting a puzzled look. "What is this?"

Grabbing the leaves out of my hand, he said, "You know what this is … and you're stealing it."

"No … uh, hell no," I said. "I was just going to try it. I've seen other *qarasinat* using it."

"Yes, but this is ours, not yours. You're stealing from us!" he yelled. "This is worth a lot of money in Israel. You're the damn pirate!"

Then he looked over his shoulder and shouted, "Ibrahim! Ibrahim!"

Ibrahim came sliding down the ladder. "What's up?" he asked as he studied me.

The man pointed at me. "I caught him stealing our khat."

Ibrahim appeared to be horrified. "Is this true?" he asked me in hateful English.

How could I have been so stupid?

I responded in Arabic so all would understand, "No, I wasn't stealing anything, just trying it for myself. If I liked it, I was going to buy it from you."

"We do not tolerate thieves on this boat. You need to pay me now for what you've taken ... or swim."

"How much?" I asked, reaching into my pocket.

"Five thousand dollars U.S.," he said confidently, sticking out his palm.

"You're out of your friggin' mind! I don't have five thousand dollars."

"Then you need to get ready to swim. The shore is ten kilometers away. You have your pick, Sinai or Saudi."

Could I make it? I didn't think so. The water was warm ... but I was not that good of a swimmer.

"I'll give you what I have," I said.

"How much is that?" he asked with a jerk of his head.

"I had three thousand dollars, and I've given you seven hundred already. So, twenty-three hundred left."

"Give it to me!" he said, raising his palm again.

I reached into my pocket and grudgingly pulled out a roll of hundreds. Jabbar's hundreds. I gave him the whole roll. I couldn't save the world if I kept making mistakes.

He took the roll and counted it up. Then he turned to the crew member standing behind me and said in Arabic, "Lock him up."

"Wait a minute!" I yelled. "I just paid you for the khat!"

"Yes, you did." He smirked. "Now you'll pay for stealing it. You'll be my prisoner until we arrive in Israel. You're two thousand dollars short, and I don't trust you anymore."

Suddenly, a guy hit me behind my knees with his knees, forcing me down to a sitting position. I saw leg irons attached to the keel. This wasn't the first time they'd had prisoners. He locked one around each ankle. They were old, heavy, and rusty. Hand forged. Perhaps a relic of the slave trade.

I hoped Ibrahim would come back for me in a few hours, but he didn't. The damn pirates left me in leg irons for the next seventy-two hours. Only once they brought me bread. A single piece. Each day I had one water bottle, just enough to keep me alive in the stuffy space below deck. Slaves lived this way for three months—surely, I could make a few days.

I had to pee where I lay. Fortunately, I was on an incline. My pee, the color of the brown timbers, flowed toward the stern. The wood was hard and damp and curved up toward the bow. Every few inches, a wooden rib protruded three or four inches into my bony ones, still sore from the scuffle with the sheepherders. I tried to hold my bowel movements, but after two days I couldn't.

I yelled, "I've gotta shit! Hey, up there, I have to shit!"

No one responded to my despairing pleas. I shit a foot from where I was lying. I rattled my chains day and night, but nothing gave. No one came. I looked over at my stinky poop. It was the color of light clay. No question, I still had hepatitis, now chronic. *Am I in hell?*

The hours passed so slowly I could watch my fingernails grow. Then they started the engine and the space below deck filled with thick diesel exhaust. I was going to die.

"God, please save me! I must live to stop Jabbar."

Through the hull beside me, I had glimpsed a daylight's tiny beam, penetrating the inky air, leaving a round bright spot on my chest. Maybe it was a bullet hole.

Placing my mouth over the hole, I sucked clean air into my lungs. I held the air to absorb each oxygen molecule, hoping to displace the carbon monoxide in my blood, then slowly released it inside the hull. I put my mouth over the hole again and sucked air in once more. Over and over, I repeated this process until they turned the engine off an hour and half later. I was so exhausted I wept. I couldn't understand this kind of heartless cruelty—the slave trade had to be one of the greatest crimes against humanity.

The next day, Ibrahim came below into my dark sewer. "I'm going to let you up. We'll meet our buyers at three in the morning. You need to get cleaned up."

After three days chained to the floor, I could barely stand. With trembling arms and legs, I climbed the ladder through the hatch and into the fresh air and blinding sun. I grabbed a rope and lowered myself into the sea, with barely enough strength to hold on without the torrent sweeping me away, the salty brine flowing around me at six knots. I climbed back up to the deck a little cleaner but now smelling like a seal. Lying flat on the smooth deck, then rolling over on my back, I sucked clean, salty air into my lungs. I fell asleep.

I awoke to someone kicking my sore ribs. I raised my head. It was dark. My neck was stiff and my skin sunburned.

"Get up!" the pirate growled.

I sat up. I saw lights approaching. Slowly, the white and green illuminations came across the still water as if across the surface of a mirror. It was a similar-looking boat but without the bright colors coming up beside us. Five Arabic-speaking men unloaded khat bails from our boat onto theirs. They moved other boxes from their boat to ours. I could tell from the tinkling, bottle against bottle, whiskey was coming on board—destined to burn the throats and numb the souls of the Yemen's hungry and war-weary inhabitants. These new pirates, likely Palestinians, were khat runners.

Just before the boats separated, they handed me off. I said, "Thank you," as if they had been marvelous hosts on a Disney cruise ship. I watched with great curiosity as the Palestinians converted their boat back to a typical fishing vessel, including the nets—and the fish.

As we approached the familiar harbor in Eilat, we encountered a Zodiac boat with a cabin painted in Hebrew letters, which I couldn't read, and "Israeli Border Security" in English stenciled on its side. My new pirate friends and the police knew each other by name. I wasn't sure in twilight's pale light, but I thought I saw money exchange hands. Maybe it was papers. Even if they paid bribes, Israeli security would never have allowed dangerous contraband into the country, weapons that could fall into the hands of the Palestinian Islamic Jihad.

Soon we were drifting toward the Eilat harbor. Once docked, I simply stepped off the boat onto the sandy beach and went on my way.

I walked to the harbor where my boat was in dry dock. One of the harbor workers, a stocky man named Reuben helped me. We started the paperwork and paid up my drydock fees using my credit card number, which he had on file, and then he led me to my boat. The *Protagonist* was inside a white plastic shrink-wrapped cover, making her look like a giant flour burrito. A zippered door led to the cockpit. I unzipped it and went inside. I lay in my old hammock, tears of joy wetting my eyes. I was so tired and so happy to be back to my paramour of the sea.

I checked my boat and fortunately found my old debit card in a galley drawer. The card was three weeks short of its expiration date. Thank God, I wouldn't have to ask Angie for money and explain—once again—that someone had robbed me.

I met with the harbormaster to schedule the launch of the boat. They had seven boats in line ahead of me, which would take the entire day. The earliest they could do it was the following morning. It was a delicate process of lifting the boat with a huge forklift and carrying it to the harbor to dock in the water.

"Where are you going?" asked the harbormaster, sitting at his desk, earphone in his ear, the other end attached to a cell phone.

"Uh, I'll have to find a hotel for the night. Then tomorrow I'm going out in the bay and will moor her for a night before sailing to the canal."

"Well, you hire the mooring from me," he said.

I paid him one hundred dollars for one night mooring.

Down the street from the marina was an outdoor café. The clear air under the warm sun was so refreshing. My stint chained below deck now seemed like just a bad dream. I ordered a Turkish coffee and a plate of awameh (donut holes in syrup) and set up my phone. It had been ten days since I'd spoken to Angie.

She picked up right away. "Bryan, are you in Israel?"

"Yeah."

"Thank God! I'm so glad you're out of Yemen. I can wire you money there if you still need to pay them. I've made progress in areas ... but ran into headwinds in others."

"Speaking of headwinds, I got the money I needed while I was in Yemen, but that's a long story. I gotta find a place to stay tonight. I can use my debit card."

"Five stars!" she said assertively. "You need a five-star hotel tonight. I'll send you more money, if I must. And Bryan," she said in a serious tone, "you didn't bring those dirty boxers to Israel, did you?"

I chuckled, "Yeah, I did. But they're not dirty anymore, and they fit!"

"Bryan—"

"Hey, sis, tell me what you found out."

"That commercial vessel website is a godsend. I'll text you the link. Do you have a computer?"

"Well, I didn't check, but I hope my laptop is still aboard the *Protagonist*."

"Great! If it's not, buy one. You're going to need it. You'll have internet if your satellite dish is working. Right now, they've docked the *Pytheas* at Iran's Chabahar Port. It's their only port outside the Straits of Hormuz, and it's a major oil terminal. However, I just got the ship's departing manifest, and it is due to leave in two days, without any cargo, but with a seven-man crew. The list had Jabbar El Haddad as the co-captain. They posted the pre-arrival documents just this morning."

I felt a burst of acid in the pit of my stomach. *So this nightmare was really happening!*

"Go on," I said.

"The ship is to arrive in Suez, Egypt, in five days. There it'll pick up five hundred and fifty thousand barrels of No. 2 fuel oil. I'm still waiting for them to post their bill of lading, which will tell us its destination. It's odd, but that information—according to Gary, the expert at the Yacht Club—is generally available with the initial manifest. We'll be able to track the ship in actual time through its required GPS beacon, but we may not know their navigation plan.

Once we see the bill of lading, we can guess their route to their destination.

"Bryan, are you there?" Angie asked.

"Yeah."

"What's wrong? Why are you so quiet?" she asked.

"Uh, well, I can't believe this is happening," I answered quietly. "Ray's scratches on his arm meant what I feared. A mission with an oil tanker full of ammonium nitrate and fuel oil to blow up New York City. This is huge. Much bigger than us."

We both fell silent for a few minutes. I could hear Angie breathing, otherwise I would have thought I had lost the signal.

Finally, I spoke. "Wait a minute. You said that ship was too big for the Suez Canal, right? Won't it have to go around the Horn of Africa and the southern cape?"

"That's true," she said. "Gary was confident. The canal can't accommodate such a ship. If a ship got stuck in the canal, it would be a disaster to world markets."

"Then why are they heading to the canal?" I asked. "Makes no friggin' sense."

"I don't know," she answered. "The city of Suez, Egypt, has a large petroleum harbor from its Red Sea oil operation."

"But they'll leave an even bigger oil port in Iran empty. Why?"

"Bryan, I asked Gary the same question. He wasn't too disturbed as he said they based it on oil prices. This ship may have found the best oil deal in Suez. That happens all the time. A two-dollar price difference per barrel, according to Gary, would save a million dollars. Plus, if it were Iranian oil, they couldn't sell it in the U.S. anyway because of the embargo."

"There must be another reason. Angie, what's the capacity of that ship in barrels?"

"That's it," she said with a rising inflection.

"What's it?" I asked.

"What I said, five hundred and fifty thousand barrels!"

"So, the manifest says they will load it to capacity with No. 2 fuel oil?" I asked. "Where do they get the ammonium nitrate? I don't think he's trying to blow up a tanker of just fuel oil, although that would certainly be better ... but still a mess. Have you shared this additional information with the FBI?"

"Bryan, I did. They listened to all the evidence I had to give them. I was still surprised how calm they were. This Anne I spoke to had to remind me—once again—that people have floated fertilizer bombs as weapons almost daily, ever since the World Trade Center bombing in 1993 when they used such a bomb and the Timothy McVeigh incident in Oklahoma—"

"Angie! Didn't you remind her that your brother was on the ground in Yemen?"

"Bryan, like I said before, I told her about you!" Her voice was so loud that the speaker hurt my ear and I jerked the phone away. Then she mumbled, "I didn't want to tell you but ... she had questions about you."

"About me? What kinds of questions?" I asked shaking my head.

"When I told her you were in Afghanistan, she asked if you had PTSD. She said their most common source of terrorist threats are from conspiracy theorists who are suffering from it."

"Angie, we're running out of time!"

"Bryan, don't you get it? I've taken a leave from work. What else do you want from me?"

Her voice broke. "Bryan, I understand the gravity of this situation! I've been looking at a map of Manhattan and the surrounding area and estimating the bomb's potential. An ANFO bomb that size would yield—get this—a million tons of TNT."

"My God!" I whispered. The blood draining out of me.

"Bryan, I looked it up." I could hear her breaths becoming more rapid. "That's about four times the size of the bomb dropped on Nagasaki and just a little smaller than our present nukes. So, no one in New York City or the surrounding area would be safe. I won't be safe. Your mother and brothers won't be safe. I figure at least a million people would die instantly and New York City would not be salvageable … ever again!"

"Damn you, Jabbar!" I whispered.

CHAPTER TWENTY-NINE

Eilat was as stylish as any world-class resort—Israel's Caribbean. Warless, although conflict had visited its past. Egypt's Sinai pushes in from the west, the towering, dry mountains of Jordan looming in the east, and the Red Sea to the south locks Eilat into its own little aquatic world. The Jordanian border transects the city itself, with the resort of Aqaba Ayla on the Jordanian side. Aqaba Ayla was grander, as far as population goes, being Jordan's only access to the sea.

The twin cities themselves reminded me of the border area between San Diego's southside and Tijuana. But the sea in Eilat differed from the waves tumbling on California's broad bikini-clad beaches. There were no tall, thin bodies tethered to hydrodynamic surfboards in Eilat, although occasionally you could observe a game of beach volleyball. The long and narrow Red Sea tamed the salt water into ripples by the time it dissolved into the Israeli flats. Tame enough for paddleboards and kayaks, even those piloted by preschoolers. The wavelets came right up to a narrow beach backed by kiosks and storefronts with glass hotels rising above them.

In the strip of white sand between the salty water and sidewalk, umbrellas were blooming like a giant mechanical flowerbed awakening under the new day's sun. A worker was—hummingbird-like—making her way up the beach visiting each closed flower, leaving it open in her wake. Choirs of seagulls in gray tuxedos, white shirts, yellow socks, stood in the surf, backs to the waves, waiting for the onslaught of humans and their delicious scraps. In September, the beaches were full by afternoon. The autumn weather was more inviting than summer's dog days. I knew, having arrived in late August on the *Protagonist*.

I followed my sister's advice and walked around the touristy area where the largest hotels crowded around the sandy shore. To my surprise, all the hotels were full, even though the beaches were bare on that morning. My confusion waned when I saw a poster that reminded me it was Rosh Hashanah weekend. "Of course!" I mumbled.

Then I walked toward the Jordanian border. Looking east, I whispered to myself, "There's no holiday over there. But, if they allowed me into Jordan, what would happen if I couldn't cross back?"

I stood outside the pedestrian gate into Jordanian Aqaba, looking into that side of the twin city. Large white hotels adorned its shore, each with shiny windows and balconies floating above the beaches like Babylon's legendary hanging gardens. One difference from when I'd been there two years earlier was that I now spoke fluent Arabic. Not perfect, but conversant. As I walked toward the entry point, I saw the ease with which pedestrians were going back and forth. I decided to try it.

In my line, a short olive-skinned Israeli customs official sat at a gray metal desk in his navy-blue uniform. Behind him stood two border police with MAGAV on their lapels in bold capital letters, carrying M-16s. The official was drinking coffee as white smoke curled up from the end of a short plastic-tipped cigarette beside him. I stepped up to the desk, passport in hand.

My uneasiness became a full-blown panic attack when the customs official glared at me. "Where is your entry visa?" he asked in a harsh tone as he flipped aggressively through the little blue book.

I was perspiring even though the sun was just peaking over the Jordanian mountains, its heat still confined to the other side. The day seemed already long, although it was just eight A.M. If I told a lie, it would come back to haunt me. These security people took their jobs seriously.

I smiled big and answered, "Oh, I came here two years ago by my sailing yacht. I left my boat in Eilat's marina and flew to Sana'a where I worked with the IRC. I caught a ride back on a private boat, arriving last night. Your harbor customs official stopped us, and they looked at my passport but didn't stamp it, because I was living in Yemen … and may return."

The stocky man reached down and picked up his cigarette. He took a long, hard draw from it as if its smolder was life-sustaining oxygen. He flipped one of its turds into the already-full ashtray. He continued looking at my passport with eyes so slitted, I thought they were closed. He slowly released the exhaust from his nostrils, two parallel smoke streams waffling up, like a fire-breathing dragon. He looked at me and said, "You stay here." Then he jumped up and walked away.

He strolled around the corner. With armed men still sitting behind his desk, he knew I wasn't going anywhere. I could hear him shouting at someone in Hebrew, a language I knew not at all.

In five minutes, which seemed like five hours, he returned.

"I guess you don't want me to stamp your passport?" he asked while standing beside his desk.

"That's right, if you can avoid it, because I may be going back to Yemen, and they may not let me into the country with an Israeli stamp," I said with a soft smile.

He handed me my passport without making eye contact, and I walked to the entry station on the Jordanian side. I was already regretting this decision. However, my further passage into Jordan was not that difficult. Following Angie's mandate, I soon found a five-star hotel—the Aqaba Kempinski Hotel. It seemed more luxurious than I could imagine.

I took a suite, as no single rooms were available. I felt like I was stepping into the Dolmabahçe Palace in Istanbul. The suite had three large luxurious rooms, a tiled and glass shower that could accommodate a small basketball team, and a kitchenette. It cost me two weeks' salary for a night. The stonework on the floors and bath walls was so predominant, the room could have passed as a quarry—an excavation into the luxurious.

I did a mental inventory and realized it had been thirteen days since I'd had a shower, eleven since a good night's sleep. On the pirate boat, sleeping for three hours was the best I could hope for. I got no sleep at all the nights of my confinement—a single wink when released. I couldn't even remember what a good day felt like.

I strolled down the beachfront sidewalk to a sandwich shop, where I got a falafel and a Carakale beer. I sat down to eat at a picnic table on the sand. A Jordanian mom, dad, and three children, soon sauntered over, laughing at silly jokes told by their dad and eating burgers. They quickly recognized me as Western, not realizing that I understood their Arabic. The dad looked at me with a smile and asked in English, "Do you mind if we share the table?"

I pointed at the bench on the other side of the table and smiled. With a mouthful of food, I said, in English, "Help yourself."

I saw the woman looking at me, and then she whispered to her husband in Arabic, "What's wrong with that man? He looks awful. Why does he have yellow eyes?"

Damn, I had forgotten about my yellow eyes.

Her husband took a big bite of his burger and said, without even looking across the table at me, "He's a hippie, American or Dutch. Drugs cause yellow eyes."

As the afternoon sun lowered over Sinai's rocky landscape, the air turned chilly. After finishing my meal, I sat and stared out to sea, the noisy family by then gone. I ate their leftover fries, competing with seagulls that watched each bite enter my mouth. They'd grab the occasional soggy vinegar-soaked French fry as it fell before it hit the ground. I welcomed them as my only friends. I reviewed my whole situation with them, in whispers. They shared no opinions on my best course.

I darted into a pharmacy. I was so exhausted I was doubtful I could sleep. A generic bottle of doxylamine succinate tablets was on the shelf, advertised as an allergy or sleep aid. After returning to my room, I took a forty-five-minute shower while I watched the BBC on the shower's TV. Yes, the shower had a big screen, and there was a gold phone by the toilet.

One wall was a giant mirror. I stood naked, looking at myself, the woman's comments at the beach still on my mind. I looked like I'd survived a holocaust. Skinny and scratched up. Sunken dark eyes, a shiner around the left one. The leg chains had roughed up my ankles. And encompassing everything was my yellow skin. I worried hepatitis would kill me before I convinced the authorities to stop Jabbar.

After taking two tablets and closing the shades to darken the room, I threw back the crisp Egyptian-cotton sheets on the giant bed and threw four of the five Euro pillows on the floor. The clock reported it was only four P.M. I didn't care. Goodnight world.

As soon as my weary head hit the thick, soft pillow and I began drifting off, my sat phone chimed. I had just plugged it in to recharge. Mumbling to myself, "Angie, now what?" I rolled over and grabbed the phone.

"Hey, sis."

"Bryan?" said a British-accented voice.

I sat up. "Hello. Uh … Dorothy?"

"I'm sorry for disturbing you. But I needed to call you and was so glad I still have your number. That lovely family brought the woman, Ghazala, with the heart problem by." She sounded excessively cheerful. "You're right. They did qualify for the Richardson family grant. They're leaving for London on a medivac flight, uh … oh, tomorrow. That's the good news."

I could hardly wait to hear the bad news.

Dorothy's cheery tone changed to one of exaggerated calm. "Bryan, we had another visitor looking for you, an Arab man who said his name was Rahul. Aiesha assumed he was part of Ghazala's family, as they had just left twenty minutes before. There were three or four men in Ghazala's group, so it was an honest mistake."

"What are you talking about?" I asked.

"What I'm trying to say, Bryan … you see, this bloke Rahul was looking for you and, uh … and when Aiesha asked him if he was part of Ghazala's family, he said he was. So Aiesha called me, and I came out of my office to talk to him. He said he needed to find you urgently, and I assumed it was for sending you a gift for the help. I thought it was odd because the day before, Ghazala's father told us you had taken a boat from Al Hudaydah to, I assume, Israel. Anyway, I said that you were probably in Eilat getting your boat if not sailing by now."

"Yes, Dorothy, I'm in Israel. You told that to a stranger?"

"Then he asked me the name of your boat, and—while I thought it was an odd question—I remembered your boat was called the *Protagonist*. I told him."

"Uh ... oh no. You didn't."

"Yes, Bryan, I did. He asked for your phone number and e-mail address, and I gave him both. After he left, I started to worry. To make things worse, I saw Ghazala's father the next day when he came by to pick up the paperwork for the trip, I told him his relative Rahul had stopped by. He said he doesn't know anyone named Rahul."

"Damn!" I moaned. "Dorothy, what the hell? I told you I was on to a terrorist plot. That plot is more real than ever. Your friend at the embassy was a waste of my time! Those plotters killed my friend Ray. My friend in Haydan, Jabbar, tried to kill me. I've been on the run since. I'm sure they are on their way here now to murder me. But I'm keeping this out of IRC's hair so as not to compromise your precious reputation. They're zealous to murder me dead, dead, dead!" I yelled into the phone. "They'll stop at nothing."

"Oh, my god, Bryan. I never meant to endanger your life," she said with a strained voice, deep breaths into the phone. "I'll call Mr. Hunter as soon as we are done talking."

"Good luck with that. He's useless," I said with a sigh. "I'm sorry, Dorothy, but since being shot at and chased, my nerves are on edge. I know you meant well."

There wasn't anything she could have done to help. After the call, I lay awake for an hour. I felt another layer of paranoia coming over me like a fog, encroaching on every notion, penetrating every crevice of respite. I would have to watch behind each shadow, suspecting all strangers until I could get the hell out of town. If it were just *my* life, that I could bear. But the only thing standing between a million dear people and their violent deaths was me. I had to stay alive until they were safe. Until the government got onboard. Then, hepatitis could devour me … every damn cell.

CHAPTER THIRTY

In my slumbering mind, I visualized Jabbar walking across the big iron ship's teetering deck. I stood up from behind a large rectangular hatch cover, sucked in a deep breath, and went after him. I tried to overtake him before he reached the exposed staircase that led to the bridge. I was too late.

"Damnit!"

The ship rolled so far to starboard, I tripped toward the gunwale rail and had to grab on. I saw the coast of Staten Island on the horizon. My heart was racing, sweat dripping into my eyes and blinding me until I wiped them with my trembling hand. The ship was turning, heading toward the Verrazzano-Narrows Bridge.

I heard Jabbar's footsteps clinking up the metal staircase above me. He turned to look down at me, his angled jaw set like stone. Once the deck was flat again and I could stand, I sprinted to the stairs, grabbed the handrail, and leapt up the steps, catching up to Jabbar just before he arrived at the top. I clutched his long thoob's tail. He turned and kicked me, clenched teeth showing. I would have fallen the twenty feet back to the deck if I hadn't maintained my grip on him. He fell toward me with his eyes bulging from their sockets like a tree frog.

"Stop this ship, Jabbar!" I screamed.

"It's too late, Bryan!" he yelled back.

He gritted his teeth and kicked me again, this time my tug of his thoob pulled him with me. We tumbled down the stairs, with edges like serrated knives, man over man, cut over scrape, scrape over bruise, until we hit the bottom. Jabbar sighed, as the fall had knocked the air out of his lungs.

I stood first and took a wide stance, fists clenched. In my belt was the curved dagger, Ray's ceremonial janbiya. I pulled the knife from its sheath. As I whirled it in my hand, it glimmered in the sun like quicksilver. Jabbar crouched down, put his arm above his head, and turned his face away.

"Turn this damn ship around, Jabbar!" I screamed at the top of my lungs.

He turned back to face me. "It's too late, Bryan. It's time for Alam's retribution. New York will pay!" he screamed. "America will pay!" He stood and pounded his chest with his finger. "I will redeem my son's life because I'm an honorable father!"

Lunging toward Jabbar—the knife penetrated his belly. I yanked it toward his chin, the sharp blade dividing his skin and fat until it struck his xiphoid process and seized. His intestines erupted out of the wound when he tried to inhale. There was a look of terror on his face as he glanced down at his wound and back at me. His thick blood oozed like molten lava. He slumped to the metal deck, and I fell to my knees to stay with him, the knife's handle still in my hand. Blood pooled around us.

I placed my left arm behind his back to hold up his head.

His face grim and pale, eyes still bulging, he said, "Bryan ... I thought you were my friend." Tears ran down his reddened face. "You've betrayed me."

"I'm so sorry," I said, letting the knife slip out of my hand. "I had to save New York ... and the world."

His voice became a whisper as his eyes closed. "But Bryan ... uh, you're too late. The ... the *Pytheas* was just a de ... decoy." He then went limp. Death gently sealed his eyes.

A sudden wave of air pressure passed over me, and my ears popped. I quickly stood and twisted my body, looking to the west. A giant mushroom cloud, black and cyclonic, was swirling and rising above Manhattan. My eyes followed it upward and into the stratosphere to find a debris-infused haze. City life had pixelized into a billion meaningless particles and was raining down into the sea in gray curtains like a late-summer squall.

I stood with my face pointed to that ghastly sky, arms wide open, hands outstretched, and screamed with all my being, "God, no! God, no! Oh, God—" I felt my vocal cords shred.

I began thrashing and fighting against the wind as concrete fragments pelted the top of my head. I looked down at the deck of the ship to protect my eyes from the storm. I covered my face with my hands. A melted ink pen fell from the sky and landed at my feet, followed by a pink unicorn whose white stuffing was falling out and then a bloody finger with a wedding band still attached. I fell backwards off the edge of something and onto my back. My landing was soft. Probably unicorn stuffing.

The cyclone's wind had gone silent. I was blind. My eyes were open, but in a totally dark world. I could feel my heart pounding. I could hear my breaths rattling. *Is this paradise?*

Slowly, I became aware. The room was murky, except for one minor source of light to my right. My sat phone's light was green—fully charged. I was in my hotel room in Jordan. I was lying on the floor atop a mountain of discarded pillows. Drenched in a cold sweat, I reached to the bedside table and turned the clock around. The digital red numbers were piercing through the opaque room air, 3:14 A.M. It was only a nightmare. Just like my entire life, a friggin' nightmare!

I walked to the glass wall that divided my fifth-floor room from its balcony and slid the door open. The musty sea air rushed in. I stepped outside. The streets were wet and shiny like lacquer. A couple of itinerant drops of rain landed on my face. The nocturnal shower had washed the cocoa-colored dust off the palm's green leaves. Rain gave so much grace to the desert. I needed such an act of mercy. I was the walking dead. There was no safe way out of this anymore—no happy ending.

The crescent moon was thwacking its way through the remaining cirrocumulus clouds. The clouds spread out in a million round clumps like celestial cobble spewed across the night sky. My seagull friends were making a racket by the beach, fighting over a red and white KFC box—the colonel in a Western bowtie seeming not to care that a beak-shaped hole penetrated his face.

At the street level, a dark figure stood up and moved. I squinted for better view. He had been stooping behind a car. He abruptly walked into the shadows. *Who could that be at this hour? Dorothy's visitor? My assassin?*

Despite the morning being so crisp and raw, I had slept for eleven hours. I needed to get the *Protagonist* moored before noon. But the two cities straddling the border were sleeping like an elderly couple snuggled together in their parched bed, sand as a mattress, the sea pulled up to their chins like a blanket. It would be hours before the marina was open and my boat ready to sail.

It was still evening in New York. I gave Angie a call. I had spoken to her the previous day, but I needed an update—to calm my nerves.

"Hey, sis?" I said with excitement when I heard her answer.

"Bryan, what's up? What time is it there?"

"It's early here," I said. "Uh, four A.M. I had time to kill. Finally caught up on sleep in a five-star hotel like you told me to, but in Jordan."

"Jordan? The country Jordan? Why are you there?"

"Look at a map, sis. It's down the street from Eilat. It was your idea to get a five-star hotel, and none were available on the Israeli side. But sis, there's a new problem. An Arabic-speaking man went to the IRC office in Sana'a, and my boss told him I was in Eilat."

"So?" she asked.

"Angie, there's no reason for an Arab man to be searching for me."

"Could be Jabbar," she said.

"Angie, if it's Jabbar, it's to find and … kill me, but the man said his name was Rakim … or Rahul, something like that." I felt the panic rising.

"You don't know they're trying to kill you," she said.

"Angie," I said. "My life is in real danger here."

"Bryan, I know that you are alone and in a tough place. But my life is in real danger too, as are those of a million New Yorkers. So keep your shit together. Remember, you are our only eyes and ears until the authorities deal with this. But in the meantime, well, just think about what Dad would do."

"Angie! That's all I think about!"

I waited, and there was only silence on Angie's end. Finally, I asked, "What's new on your front? Please, for the love of God, give me some good news."

"Joel talked to Homeland Security yesterday. He has a friend, Jarred, who works there. Jarred said that since this is an imminent threat, we should talk to the New York and New Jersey Port Authority Police, which is nimbler than the feds. The feds are bogged down in the elections."

"Elections? What elections?" I asked.

"Presidential. A lot at stake."

"I don't get it. What do elections have to do with a terrorist attack?"

"Everything. A sitting president would not want a successful terrorist attack on his watch … yet a foiled one might win him the election. The opposite is true for the Democrats."

"You must be kidding me. God have mercy on us."

"Bryan, just relax a little … but stay vigilant. I'll get the Port Authority Police on this."

At eight A.M., I headed for the border. Jordanian workers were in a queue at the crossing. It took much longer than I expected. My neck was constantly turning, spinning left and right, my squinting eyes probing. Everyone looked suspicious. I paced back and forth in the small space where I stood in the queue. I suspected my killer would wait until I got away from the crowd at the crossing before acting. Would it be a knife? A shot to the head? A vested bomber?

I swore an oath to myself right there. I had to survive long enough to make sure someone stopped Jabbar—at all costs! After that, nothing mattered.

As soon as I cleared Israeli customs, I stuck with the flow of the crowd. However, the people quickly dissipated, melting into the ghostly streets of Eilat's sleepy morning. The aroma of breakfasts cooking penetrated the air.

It was a beautiful day, the rain clouds of early morn having now returned to their celestial burrows, and—contrasted with the buff terrain—the dark indigo sky was stretching from mountains to sea. The air was perfect, temperatures somewhere in the seventies. A gentle breeze intermediately kissed my cheek and moved my hair. I was still five blocks from the marina. My gaze bounced back and forth between the beach and the storefronts. Each person was a suspect, a potential killer. I continually rubbed my face and combed my hair with my fingers, unable to keep my hands still as if I had a neurological tic. I finally made it to the elevation leading up to the harbor footbridge, a lift bridge for pedestrians that led to the marina's west side. That bridge would raise soon, I hoped, for my boat.

It was thrilling to be with the *Protagonist* again, a lost boy coming home. She was beautiful. Coal-black hull and white topside. The Farr 45 was wide with a cockpit space big enough for a large racing crew. Before leaving Seattle, I had enlarged the cooking area by replacing the one-burner racing stove with a three-burner and adding a refrigerator. She had a small cabin with only hammocks for sleeping. That was alright with me. She was still home, and she was fast.

My mooring was in the bay, a kilometer from Eilat's beach but closer to Egypt's Sinai. That location gave me a better perch for watching for perils. Boats and ships in steady streams were heading back and forth from the twin ports of Eilat and Aqaba.

My only way to shore was my dingy, which was a single kayak. I had a firearm—a sawed-off shotgun. It had come with the boat. The previous owner had said he used it to signal friends at sea and to warn off pirates. I chuckled thinking how I'd just spent a week with a gang of them.

I took my "mooring catcher," a grappling hook on a floating rope, and threw it toward a big round ball stenciled with a "37" — my buoy and mooring for the night. Soon after setting the boat on the mooring, I had my satellite dish up and running, snatching signals from space and pumping them directly into my laptop. Angie had texted, via satellite phone, the link to the International Shipping Federation's website. After creating a log-on, I looked at Jabbar's ship's real-time location — still anchored in Iran's Chabahar Port. I set up an alarm that would ring my sat phone's number if the ship moved.

I had to decide whether to sail or fly to Suez. While slower, having the *Protagonist* under me would give me more flexibility to follow the tanker, especially if it suddenly changed course. I also wanted to see what the draw to Suez City was. I wanted to be on the water when Jabbar arrived. I still had a fantasy that over a friendly cup of tea I could simply persuade him to come home to Haydan and forget this madness. But then I would remember he tried to kill me in cold blood. Nothing could stop him now short of his own demise.

Why was the ship going to Suez City, Egypt? Where was it going to load the ammonium nitrate? It took me only minutes to answer both questions. Ammonium nitrate's largest producer in the entire Middle East was in Suez City — the descriptively named Ammonium Nitrate Factory of Suez (SNFS), Egypt. The two components the terrorists needed were in the same port. *How damn convenient!*

I studied the ship's blueprints and engineers' drawings, all of which were in the public domain and online. Most tankers I had seen only had pipes going into their hulls to pump their liquid cargo in or out. But as I read, I learned they built the *Pytheas* to hold either solid or liquid cargo with just minor modifications to switch between the two. The compartment could carry both liquids and solids at once.

There were large cargo hatches and pipes leading to the holds, also called cargo chambers. The ship had five such holding tanks, each with its own loading hatch and pipes. It was the perfect choice for this macabre mission.

The last piece of this dreadful puzzle was finding out who in New York had ordered the No. 2 fuel oil. Someone had to have, in order to get a manifest. The ship would need an approved manifest to get past the Coast Guard.

I found the bill of lading in the archives on the ISF website. It was for No. 2 fuel oil at $0.65/gallon from the Olympia Fuel Oil Depot on College Point in Queens.

"Bingo!" I shouted.

I sat back in my chair. The pieces were all there. I needed to get this information to Angie as soon as possible. The feds would take notice now if they hadn't already. Maybe Mr. Philips wasn't as big an idiot as he'd seemed.

I called Angie and woke her up early.

"Good morning," I said.

"Good morning. What time is it?" she asked.

"I think it's four A.M. New York time."

"What's wrong?"

"Nothing's wrong ... well, everything's wrong, but nothing new," I replied.

"So, why are you calling?" she asked.

"I'm confirming the mission. Jabbar is going to steer the *Pytheas* into New York Harbor with an ammonium nitrate and fuel oil bomb. The entire ship will be the bomb. It's huge."

"We knew that already," she said.

"I know, I know," I said. "But I'm confirming that because I now know where the ammonium nitrate is coming from ... a factory in Suez City."

"Give me a sec to find a pen and paper," Angie said. "I'm still in bed, like a normal person is at four A.M. Some of us try to sleep at night, you know."

Angie was never a morning person, even with so much at stake. The sound of a crash emanated from the phone. "Damn.

Turned the nightstand over. Okay, I'm writing this all down and I'll go to the Port Authority, as I can't seem to grab the fed's attention. As soon as they are in their office, I'll call them. I won't go to work today anyway," she said with a moan. This is too important.

I explained, "Angie, I considered flying straight home from here. But I've picked up the *Protagonist* and am sailing her to Suez, Egypt. The *Pytheas* will head there soon. I want to rendezvous with them there and maybe stop them before they get the ammonium nitrate onboard."

"Why don't you wait for the authorities?"

"Because I'll be on the water near them, and I want to take advantage of a unique opportunity to end this peacefully. I still love Jabbar, even if he is a terrorist."

"Be careful," she mumbled. "Don't forget Jabbar shot at you."

"I never will forget *that*," I said.

"Bryan, I am sure that once the Port Authority Police has taken this over, they just want you to stand down. However, there is a chance that they would want you to be in the area and available by a secure phone or radio to negotiate with Jabbar. But that's the most involvement you will have, I'm sure. I have my notes," she said. "Sail safe. Love you, brother."

Before leaving my mooring that morning, I took an hour to prep the *Protagonist* for her long journey. While still in the marina the previous day, I had topped the water and fuel tanks. I now filled the kitchen and pantry with dates, dried fish, canned foods, and other staples. She was ready. *Was I?*

I left before dawn. I had slept well, despite my apprehension. I meant to keep one eye open for mischief, but I dozed off. I always slept well on the water—unless in leg chains.

I quickly booted up my navigation equipment and set a route around the Sinai to Suez City. Despite the cover the predawn darkness offered me, I was eager for morning. With light, I could orient myself with the landscape and make sure I was safe. I watched the soft glow over the Jordanian desert inflate the morning sky with new life, chasing the restless birds into the sky.

I unhooked from my mooring and turned the boat by motor power to face south. We had a good westerly wind at fifteen knots that I could use the whole way to Suez. I set my sails for close haul for the entire trip. The winds came across my starboard going south and would be port side when I turned north on the other side of the Sinai. If I kept my sails properly trimmed, I could maintain a sailing speed of fifteen to eighteen knots—warp speed for a sailboat—and get to my destination in under twenty-four hours.

With my boat pointing south, I secured the sails. She had a small triangular headsail and a larger downwind sail, both attached to a single mast. I could also use a large spinnaker with a downwind, which wouldn't happen on this leg. Once we were moving, I could manage the sail's trim from the captain's chair. I ran back from the bow, bare feet on a teak foredeck, and jumped into the open cockpit. I heard the water parting and slipping along the side of the black hull like a brook.

The sun continued to rise off my portside, over the barren mountains. If the winds remained favorable, I would find the turn at Sinai's southern tip by sunset. The stream's burble grew louder, and my clean hair was whipping around my face.

The chase had begun!

CHAPTER THIRTY-ONE

Vibrant waters besiege Egypt's Sinai arid peninsula on three sides: by the gulfs of Aqaba and Suez on its southern flanks, and the Mediterranean across its north. The contrast between the dry dead land and the wet teaming waters surrounding it was stunning, like the boundary between life and death itself.

With the red sun peaking down over Jordan's and Saudi's rusty coastal mountains, I could visualize the world around me in color and not just in chartreuse specks on a radar screen. There were more boats than I'd expected in this narrow strip of sea—cargo ships, fishing boats, yachts, cruise ships, barges, and smaller power boats. It was hard for me to monitor them all in case Dorothy's visitor was now in hot pursuit. The sea beneath was rolling in soft two-foot waves, creating with its friend, the wind, perfect sailing conditions.

My sat phone rang. A computer-generated text message popped up, telling me that the *Pytheas* had just left Iran's Chabahar Port. My heart beat cold. My palms turned so sweaty I couldn't grip the metal wheel of the helm without it slipping.

When sailing conditions are perfect, as they were that day, sailing becomes mundane, leaving room for anxious thoughts to meander through a barren mind—towing ponder and worry. *Dorothy gave her curious visitor the name of my boat.*

I rigged a short hanging thwart to sit on over the stern so I could work to change my boat's name. Fortunately, I had a little palm sander in my toolbox. I dropped over the stern's edge and in a mere twenty minutes managed to scratch off the eleven letters that spelled *Protagonist*.

Now I was in the crowded waters around the Egyptian resort of Sharm El Sheikh. Thirty diving boats were anchored near the coast, so I moved into deeper waters. Tiran Island came into view on my southeast, looking like a giant dirt pile sitting in the middle of the grape-colored sea. We must have passed it on the way in when I was in leg irons in the hold, because I didn't see it then and barely remember it two years early when I sailed up to Eilat to dry dock my boat and to catch a plane.

As I made my way around the Ras Mohammed Nature Reserve at the southern tip of Sinai, I encountered more diving boats. There I reset the navigation for the northwestern leg to Suez. The onboard computer kept the rudder in the right position for our coordinates, and once I had the sails trimmed and in their right positions, they needed no further attention, the winds still steadily out of Egypt's Sahara.

I created a mahogany paint using ground-up coffee beans and my fiberglass resin. I painted my new letters with a lather brush from my onboard shaving kit. A salty green river rushed beneath me, and dolphins were breaching on both sides as if curiosity were keeping them engaged. I picked *Ace* as my boat's new name, for the simplicity of the inscription, the ease of masking it off with tape, and my limited supply of "paint." The dolphins seemed to approve as they nodded, arched, and disappeared beneath the waves.

My trip through the Gulf of Suez was uneventful. The traffic going north toward the Suez Canal was a multitude of that leaving Eilat. In the waters not occupied by shipping lanes, there were oil rig clusters on the east and west sides. Soon I came upon a line of ships queuing up for the canal. The Red Sea's Gulf of Suez—my friend for a long night—ended at the tranquil Suez Bay.

Around the bay, ships and boats filled the little harbor, as most of the mooring slips had been taken. On my port side, tankers were loading with Egyptian crude at the industrial complex on Adabya Point. On my starboard sat the large Port Tawfiq Marina, and bordering its east was the canal. In the center of Port Tawfiq was a large white mosque with a tall round dome in the middle, like a head, and two arms—pointy minarets—shooting straight up into the sky on each side of the dome, looking like a referee declaring a touchdown.

Having arrived in Suez, it didn't take me long to realize it would not be the best place to confront Jabbar, even if I could find him. It was over five nautical miles from Port Tawfiq to Adabya as the Egyptian vulture flies. On the Adabya Point's triangle piece of land was a thousand acres covered with countless structures—buildings, tanks, pipes, and containment ponds. The twin ports had about a million residents, so Jabbar would be that needle in the haystack. *What was I thinking that I could stop him here?*

Then it became obvious that if I stayed with my boat, I needed a head start. I would need to take the canal before the *Pytheas* arrived. Otherwise, by the time I reached the Atlantic, the tanker would be well on its way to New York, and I would arrive a couple of days late.

Angie had mentioned that the Port Authority Police said they might need me to negotiate with Jabbar by a secure radio hookup from a position in the area, while maintaining a safe distance. Who knows, once the ship was disarmed, they might even want to fly me by chopper to talk to him—face to face—into surrendering. So I couldn't be late unless they had taken over the whole operation—my sincere hope.

I suspected that within the labyrinthine network of operatives, Jabbar's simple role would be that of a mule of death, guiding the ship into position in New York's harbor and pushing the button while the instigators sat around a luxury suite in Jeddah. I imagined the planners, wearing starched boxers under perfectly pressed thobes and ghutras around their duplicitous heads, watching everything unfold on a big HD screen, sipping cardamom coffee with puckered lips and playing footsie with the Saudi prince. When the disaster had played out to their satisfaction, one of them would pull out his iPad, and with the stroke of his pinky move a great sum of money from Zurich to Sana'a, then with another flip of the same pinky move a bundle from Zurich to Suez. Transaction complete.

I needed to wait until the Port Authority took the baton from me and made Jabbar their problem.

Sitting alone in King Tut's Pub in Port Tawfiq, drinking a cold beer and considering my options, I decided to stay with the *Ace* rather than catching a train to Cairo and flying to New York.

The bar was mostly an outside affair decorated in the tiki style with a palm leaf covering, protecting its patrons from the desert's cruel sun. There I overheard other sailors chatting. One couple who spoke with American accents were part of that group on the other end of the bar. I shouted down to the couple, "Where are you folks from?" The woman answered, "America." The others soon reported Malta, New Zealand, Italy, and France. I nodded and said, "Seattle." The group asked me to join them, and I did. I gave them all the impression that I was just another adventurer, out to circumnavigate the planet solo.

The delightful couple, Jan and Peter, were about my age and from Rhode Island, sailing around the world on their Turkish Gulet, a wooden boat that was like a piece of art. But it had an odd name, *Cellulite*. They tried their darndest to get me to sail with them to New York. I kept finding excuses until they got the message. My unwillingness to go with them seemed to take them aback, and they stopped talking to me or even making eye contact with me around the big table.

Back on my boat, I spent my first evening studying the maps and instructions for the transition through the canal, including the two thousand dollars in fees. Hiring an Egyptian agent was the best way. The first opening for transit was in forty-eight hours.

Monitoring Jabbar's precise location from the International Shipping Federation's website, including where the ship would take on the fuel oil, was very helpful. The next afternoon, I paddled my kayak from where I was moored to the harbor's other side, a grueling ten-mile round trip, propelled by paddling arms that were out of shape. If my job was to be the Port Authority's eyes, I needed more proof of my theory. That the *Pytheas* was going to load with fuel oil and ammonium nitrate in the harbor. As I got close to the oil terminal, I marked it on my handheld GPS, which was part of the equipment left onboard the *Ace*. Navigating close to the ammonium nitrate factory's wharf, I marked it as well. Then I would know without question when it was loading. I could set the alarm on the ISF's website so it would alert me when the ship was near those GPS coordinates. This was how the owners tracked their own ships.

I returned to my boat well after dark and for a half hour I got lost in the maze of channels and docks before finally reaching the *Ace* again.

The next morning, I walked through the marina until I found Jan and Peter's boat, *Cellulite*. I heard their voices coming from the cabin, so I knew they were home. In a minute, Jan came out to the cockpit and I caught her eye.

"Oh, hi. Uh, Bryan, isn't it?"

"Yep. I'm just nine slips down. I am leaving in the morning, catching an early convoy through the canal, and I thought I would say goodbye."

About that time Peter came out of the cabin and looked at me, with a cold stare.

"Beautiful boat," I said.

"Thank you," he responded.

Jan looked at Peter and told him, "Bryan is taking the canal in the morning."

"Really. I would like to hear about it when you're on the other side. We're taking it next week. We are catching a train to Cairo tomorrow to visit the Pyramids and museums for a couple of days. When we get back, we're taking a Jeep tour of the Sinai."

"Hey, come down to my boat for lunch, I said. "I have a bottle of Israeli wine I want to try and some interesting sheep cheese and Italian smoked sausages."

"Sounds delightful," Jan said.

The two of them, athletic and well-tanned, made themselves comfortable on my boat. They looked like they had just stepped off a tennis court—he in white shorts, she in a blue skort, both with short blond hair and a similar demeanor, like Tweedledee and Tweedledum. We talked about life and dreams. To my surprise, both had blue-collar jobs back home—Peter worked at FedEx, Jan at a windmill-blade factory. I was puzzled how they could be sailing the world in a seven-figure boat until Peter explained, "My late father had been a cosmetic surgeon—hence, the name of the boat. I inherited the *Cellulite* from him after he died. Mom had moved on a long time ago and was no longer interested in sailing."

I craned my neck to look up and down the marina's docks in both directions. I said in a whisper, "I have a secret that I can confide only to fellow Americans."

Both seem interested, nodded, and leaned even further in my direction, forearms on their knees, wineglasses sandwiched in their hands.

"I'm a CIA operative." I cleared my throat, not making direct eye contact with them, except for glances. I continued, "I just stumbled across something important … uh, concerning national security. It involves a tanker called the *Pytheas*, which will sail into Suez in three days. When it arrives, I won't be here. I'm on an important mission, and I must be in the Mediterranean in twenty-four hours. However— "I looked directly at them— "if I called you on my sat phone, could you take your dinghy over and snap images of the bow of that tanker? I paddled the route yesterday, and it took six hours. But I see you have a Zodiac with an outboard, and you could do it easily within an hour."

They looked at each other.

"What?" Peter said. "Mission? Are you pulling our legs?"

"I wish I were. This is very serious, and I desperately need your help."

Quickly, their nervous frowns transformed into broad smiles.

"Sure," said Jan with confidence, sitting up straight. "We have a nice Nikon with a telephoto. It sounds exciting."

Exciting? No, a damn nightmare.

"I'm monitoring the tanker's GPS position by satellite and can call you within an hour of the ship's arriving," I said. "Ships like that usually start loading straight away, unless there are other ships in line. But I didn't see ships in queue at either terminal yesterday. I suspect they time their arrival so there is no waiting in the crowded harbor. You will need to take your boat over immediately. If they go to the oil terminal first," I said while pointing at it across the water at the terminal, "they will put a floating boom down around the ship before loading, you know, in case there is an oil spill. You will not be able to get any closer than the boom. I need you to take several photos of the draft marks on the bow as the ship loads with oil. Now the ship might go to the south harbor first," I said while pointing at it, "and then I doubt if they will put a boom down and might start loading right away. But when I call, I will tell you exactly where the ship is, but you need to get over there as soon as you can because the ships load in just an hour or so."

They nodded.

"What are draft marks?" asked Peter.

Seriously? This man is sailing around the world?

"Uh, haven't you seen the lines and numbers on the bows of ships?"

"Yeah. I thought that's what you meant," said Peter. "But I don't know what they're for."

Jan grinned. "We'd love to do it, but we can't get in trouble, can we ... you know, for taking photos?"

"No, there's nothing wrong about taking photos of ships. There are ship-spotter clubs who do this all the time, like other people watch birds. Any other questions?"

They both nodded. We exchanged numbers, and I left it at that.

That afternoon, I met my canal agent. Youssef was tall for an Egyptian, maybe six-foot-three. He spoke good English, having studied law in the UK. As we walked to the Suez Canal Authority office, he told me, "After I finished my law degree at the University of Glasgow, I had to return to Egypt when my mother became ill. Then I couldn't find a job as a lawyer. My uncle, who is a canal agent, recruited me to be an agent because of my command of English and the law. It can be quite lucrative if you play your cards right."

I already knew that it was a tradition for agents to try their best to swindle each boat out of money, so I was on my guard with Youssef.

I figured it would take me ten days to cross the Mediterranean and another twenty on the Atlantic. Likewise, it would take the tanker about thirty days to reach New York via South Africa. I ran the calculation on my laptop. If the winds were perfect, and we both left Suez together, we would arrive in New York two hours and twenty minutes apart, me arriving first. But as all sailors knew, there was no such thing as a perfect trip.

The canal authorities scheduled me to join a northbound canal convoy at five A.M. the next morning. I was getting antsy until Youssef finally boarded my boat just two minutes before the scheduled departure time. He carried a green laminated card that was our passage through the canal. I'd paid him seventeen hundred dollars already, which was to cover a litany of fees and taxes.

Once we were on our way, the orange disc of a sun appeared to levitate over Sinai's barren yellow land. I was at the helm of a boat in a river green like a stream of molten apatite, a narrow strip of ocean within an endless sea of sand. I couldn't imagine what it looked like from a camel's saddle on a caravan coming across the desert. I imagined the heat waves were playing tricks, making our row of ships appear as if they were floating across the dunes on magic carpets.

Youssef sat quietly behind me in the cockpit, sipping coffee from a red plaid thermos and playing with his cell phone. In tight spots, he was required to pilot the boat, but since the Suez has no locks, I kept the helm for the entire passage.

Just an hour into our twelve-hour trip and very little small talk, I heard Youssef clear his voice, the sound growing closer as he leaned toward me. I could feel his presence before I turned to look at him—literally breathing down my neck.

"You know, Mr. Bryan. I have financial hardships," he mumbled. "It cost me a wad of dough to go to school in Glasgow. There are no lawyer jobs in Egypt. I want to move to America and become an immigration lawyer, but my mother is ill … and I just found out that my wife has cancer."

The soft music of a well-tuned Stradivarius started playing inside my head, but I devoted my attention to the narrow highway of water in front of me.

"Sorry, Youssef," I stammered, my back to him. I didn't believe a word. I had read in sailing magazines the stories of Suez Canal transits and they all described the same scene, sob stories followed by a request for *baksheesh* (a tip).

He added, "Most customers are so pleased with my help that they give me a tip in the same amount as the fees."

I turned and said emphatically, "There's no way in hell I'm giving you seventeen hundred dollars for a tip. I bet you inflated that fee price and much of it'll end up in your pocket. Besides, I'm now broke."

Silence fell between us for several minutes. I heard him slurping his coffee. The only other sounds were our diesel engine, the desert winds whistling across the naked mast, and an occasional blast from a ship's horn to tell those ahead they were going too slow.

Finally, Youssef broke the silence. "Mr. Bryan, I understand if you don't have that much money. There are ATMs in Port Said, at the canal's terminus."

After I didn't respond, he added, "What else do you have onboard? Do you have jewelry?"

I spun around to look at him again and said in a sarcastic tone, "No, Youssef! Do you think I'm sailing with a chest of jewels in my hold? Do I look like a friggin' pirate?"

"Well, how about alcohol, guns, tobacco … or perhaps"—he looked both ways as if to make sure we were alone—"pornography?"

Turning back around to face the bow, I pictured my old sawed-off shotgun. As I had approached Suez, knowing they could confiscate it in Egypt, I had taken it and its shells and placed them into a secret compartment in the engine room. If he searched my entire ship, Youssef could never find it.

Mumbling again, I said, "All I have is a stethoscope and medical supplies stored on the boat."

"Why do you have those?"

I glanced at him. "Because I'm a medical provider!"

He sipped his coffee and spit overboard.

"Hmm … so you're a doctor?"

"Yep … something like that."

"I know a reasonable baksheesh that you can give me for my services. My wife, thirty-two years old, has large bumps on her legs for the past two weeks. Her doctor in Port Said says he thinks it's bone cancer and there is nothing he can do for her, that she will die. Would you come to my house and look at her?"

"Sorry to hear that." I thought for a minute, then asked, "How long would it take?"

"Not long. We must report with the canal authorities in Port Said. I live just three blocks from that office."

"Okay, I'll do it," I said with hesitation.

A broad Cheshire grin came across Youssef's lanky face as he gulped his coffee's last swallow and methodically screwed the top back on his thermos. I turned my attention to the ships in front of me.

My processing through the termination office was expedient, thanks to Youssef's help. We left the building outside the marina. I looked over the blue-green waters of the Mediterranean, a sea I had never crossed. I took a deep breath of its air and found myself grinning. I had been dreaming of sailing the Mediterranean since leaving Seattle.

We walked a few blocks from the marina, then turned down a narrow side street lined with tall dusty palms and stubby trees with big, shiny plastic-looking leaves. "Are those trees fake?" I asked.

"No ... they're a type of magnolia," Yousef said.

The air in this crowded port city was thick with oily dirt and car exhaust. The concrete sidewalk beneath was dyed red and stamped into small rectangles to resemble bricks.

We came to a simple two-story concrete building, the top still unfinished with rebar sticking up from its corner pillars. Threadbare rugs were draped over its balcony walls. A lady in a long dress and head wrap was beating one rug with a woven wicker stick. Each strike birthed a small brown cloud that drifted over our heads. We went up a flight of stairs. Cardamon and garlic filled the stairwell as well as the voices of at least a dozen people. Youssef opened a wooden door with the number 206 in Arabic.

"Sharifa! Sharifa!" Youssef yelled, throwing his keys and cell phone into a basket inside the door. "We have a guest."

A woman came from the hallway and through a curtain of wooden beads wearing a long robin-egg blue skirt and black scarf wrapped around her neck. On her hip was a baby. I noticed crescent stains on her dress around her breasts and quickly averted my gaze.

"Hello," she said in English. "Welcome to Egypt. This little man is Baahir."

"Hi Baahir." I said with a big smile.

Youssef and I took seats on a French provincial couch covered in a gold fabric with green flowers. The room was clean and cheery—sparsely furnished with only a wooden coffee table in front of us, another stuffed chair facing the couch, and an aquarium full of goldfish on a white dresser beside a small flat-screen TV. The room had a wood parquet floor whose finish was worn in places. The glass doors to the balcony stood open, but their tall green shutters were closed, blocking out the broiling late-afternoon sun.

Youssef whispered to his wife in Arabic, which I easily understood, "He's an American doctor. He's going to look at the tumors on your legs. He hasn't given me any money yet, but I think when he sees your legs … he will."

"Can I get you a cup of tea?" she asked me in English.

"Sure," I said.

She left with Baahir still on her hip. Soon I heard a baby crying.

"He doesn't like his mother setting him on the floor," said Youssef with a chuckle.

She returned with the baby, handed him to her husband, and disappeared into the kitchen once more. As she walked quickly past me, she left the whiff of sour breast milk in her wake. In a minute, she was back with a tray of teacups, a teapot, and amber sugar cubes in a bowl. I was waiting for them to explain about her legs, but they just sipped their tea in silence.

Finally, after looking at the time on my phone, I took the initiative. "It's getting late, and I need to get back on the water as soon as possible. So, you have a problem with your legs?"

"Show him," said Youssef. He set down his tea, reached over, and pulled up the hem of her dress. Her cheeks reddened.

I could see raised lumps along each leg, scattered between her ankles and her knees. Each one was about the diameter of the bottom of my teacup. I stooped to the floor as if I were a shoe salesman and looked closer. The lumps were firm. When I pressed on one, she responded, "Ouch." The bumps were darker than her normal skin but with a reddish hue and not attached to her tibia.

Sitting back on the couch, I said, "We call this erythema nodosum, which means reddish lumps in Latin. I'm sure that's what it is. I doubt it's caused by cancer."

I looked at Sharifa, her mouth open, eyes squinted by confusion, and asked her, "Are you taking medications?"

"Uh, no."

"Do you have pain in your abdomen or diarrhea?"

Shaking her head, she said, "No."

"Joint pain?"

"No."

"Are you pregnant now?" I asked.

"Allah! No!"

Looking back and forth between her and Youssef, I explained, "Most of the time we never know what causes these bumps, but she needs to have a workup." I paused to think for a minute. "Have you been around anyone with TB?"

Their mouths both popped open and their eyes bugged.

"Yes," she said, nodding her head. "My mother came out when Baahir was born five months ago. She lives in Cairo. She was sick when she was here with a nasty cough. She stayed for a month, and after she returned home, they diagnosed her with TB."

"I'm suspicious that you have TB too and that caused the lumps on your legs. You need to find a better doctor," I said. "It's not cancer."

About that time, my eye caught the big clock on the wall, with its two obelisks as hands and an image of the Pyramids at the center. Five o'clock.

I quickly set my teacup down and stood. "I just realized how late it was. It was so nice to meet the two of you, but I must get back to my boat. It was a temporary slip and I have it rented only until five."

Youssef rolled his eyes and said, "*Malesh* [no worry]. They don't pay that close of attention."

"But I must get on the water before the sun gets any lower."

Youssef walked me back to my boat, and we said our goodbyes. He seemed grateful.

I had left my sat phone in the *Ace*'s cabin. Upon my return, I looked at it. I had a message. It was from Angie: "I tried calling and there was no answer. R U okay? Call me. I have additional information and you need to hear this!"

CHAPTER THIRTY-TWO

I was thrilled to get onto the Mediterranean's crystalline blue waters, the waters in which Western civilization had been conceived and baptized. On these waves, Jason and the Argonauts had learned to sail. The great pharaohs had created trade routes with their long wooden ships and laten sails. The Greeks and the Romans had moved boats loaded with pithoi filled with olive oil and wine. Mark Antony and Cleopatra had consummated their liaison in a tent on a boat en route from Alexandria to Rome—lured into passion by these clear waters' graces illuminated by a harvest moon, and within that passion had merged two of the greatest empires the world has ever known. Their descendants still bathed there.

I had no plans to stop anywhere before New York. In case I ran into trouble at sea, I plotted a course that would take me close to Crete and Malta before reaching Gibraltar. Somehow, I had to make it to the Atlantic in ten days. While my boat could sail faster than that, it was still an ambitious plan of 110 nautical miles per day with uncertain winds.

With the *Ace* cutting through big rolling waves, I set the autopilot and gave Angie a call.

"Bryan, where are you?" she asked almost immediately after I had punched the last digit of her number.

"I'm about thirty miles off the coast of Alexandria."

"So, you made it through the canal without any problems?"

"Yeah, wasn't too bad. You had something new to tell me?"

"I do. I'm finally getting traction," she answered.

"Fantastic!"

"I have someone here who will help us," she said. "I found a great captain with the Port Authority Police Department. The story fascinated him. He thinks it's a bit ridiculous—a whole tanker ship as a bomb—but he was concerned. They have been most worried about a dirty nuclear bomb coming in by boat. But in this case, he thinks they'd just blow a hole in a tanker and fill the harbor with oil. That would be a mess—"

"But, Angie!" I said loudly into the phone. "You know that's not the plan! They're preparing to blow a hole in the damn earth the size of Manhattan!"

"Yes, Bryan. I told him, the ammonium nitrate and the whole nine yards. That's the only part of the story he was skeptical about. He said the International Chemical Society controls the manufacturing and sale of ammonium nitrate. They must account for every pound sold. So, while ANFO bombs sound scary and sexy—his words, not mine—it is virtually impossible to pull off such a stunt."

"Ask him about Beirut. Three tons of ammonium nitrate exploded in August, and it was off the damn radar," I said.

"I'll ask him," she said.

"Well, we'll know for sure in four days," I responded. "I deputized a couple from Rhode Island, and they're still in Suez. They'll take photos of the *Pytheas* loading and send that to me."

"Deputize?" she asked with a rise in her voice. "Bryan, what are you talking about?"

"I told them I was with the CIA," I said.

"You've become a great liar these days. I've never known you to lie before. I hope it doesn't stick after this is over."

"It won't. I hate lying, but I don't know any other way. Hey, did you tell your captain friend about tracking the *Pytheas*?" I asked.

"Yes, of course! I told him all about tracking the *Pytheas* online, but he chuckled and said they've been tracking ships for years. They work with the Coast Guard. Since 9/11 all commercial ships must present their manifest to the Coast Guard ninety-six hours before entering the harbor. He also told me that fourteen hundred ships enter daily, and the Coast Guard boards and inspects around four hundred. So, while Washington is distracted with elections, Captain Clark is working with the Coast Guard."

"I'll be in touch after I hear from my deputies in a few days," I said. "Remind this captain that they must intercept the *Pytheas* far out at sea even if he doesn't believe it has the ANFO, just oil. If they detonate it, even in the Lower Bay, and it is full of ANFO, it will kill many people on shore."

"I'm sure he knows that already, Bryan. Remember, you're just an observer. Leave it to the authorities. I am confident they'll take care of this. I bet your embassy guy is working on this as we speak, just keeping us in the dark."

"Well, remind your captain anyway!" I said. "And make sure he knows that Jabbar is ... or was a good man. His son was killed, and it broke his heart. He's not your typical terrorist."

"I'll tell him. I don't think it will matter, but I'll make sure he knows." Then she added with a sigh, "Bryan, Jabbar tried to kill you. He is on an evil mission to kill a million people. This is not the same Jabbar who was your dear friend. He's a completely different man, a monster, a terrorist, and you need to get that in your head."

"I know. He *is* a monster, a dirty devil." I said, and we ended the call.

I leaned over the gunwale and stared at the water for what seemed like hours. It was getting dark, and the thick, threatening clouds brought night sooner than expected. I held my hand out over the bow and let the cool waters slide between my fingers. I saw dolphins breach behind my boat. I listened to the gulls begging for food ... or warning me to turn back. But I carried on, turning my sails toward Crete, three days away. With my satellite dish on the boat, I was never without the internet.

My online tracker showed me that the *Pytheas* had turned north into the Gulf of Suez. Then I went to bed.

The next morning, I saw the *Pytheas* was approaching Suez Bay. I called my deputies on the ground, or more accurately, on the water.

Jan answered, "hello."

"Hey, Jan, this is Bryan. I wanted you to know that the *Pytheas* will be at the oil terminal in about an hour. Get ready to get the pre-load photos."

Silence.

"Hello, Jan, are you there?" I adjusted the settings on my phone.

"Uh, Bryan, we aren't in Suez right now," came Jan's strained voice.

"Where the hell are you?" I asked.

"Well ... we're still in Cairo."

"Did I misunderstand your plans?" I quickly asked. "I thought you'd be back in Suez yesterday."

"You had it right," she said softly. "But we ... well ... we changed our plans and stayed in Cairo a couple more days. There's so much to see here." Then, suddenly sounding enthusiastic, she added, "This is a once-in-a-lifetime visit."

I didn't want to lose my temper with this delightful couple, whom I barely knew ... but I did.

"Jan, are you kidding me? Don't you understand how important this mission is? That damn tanker is going to blow up New York City, and I needed to know if it filled up with fuel oil ... and now I have no way to find out."

I heard her whispering to someone, Peter, I assumed.

"Jan, are you there?" I shouted, pushing my sweaty hair back with my hand.

"Bryan, we're sorry. I guess we didn't know how important this was to you. We'll leave now and get to Suez. We have tickets for tomorrow's train, but if we hurry, we can make the three o'clock today."

I could've been nice and said, "It's okay, hon. Enjoy your time in Cairo and be sure and ride a camel for me." But there was too much at stake.

"Great," I said. "As soon as you get there, even if it's dark, please get the damn photos."

Peter was listening and added in a methodical but irritated tone, "Doesn't the CIA have drones and satellites? Why would they depend on civilians for something this serious?"

He was on to me.

"We can, but can you do your part or not? It's too late to get such reconnaissance assets dialed in."

"We'll do it," came Jan's quick reply.

What was I thinking asking strangers to do such an important task. After hanging up the phone, I put my head between my knees and let out a loud, "Grrr!" and stomped the deck. The photos would have been just one more piece of the puzzle, the actual proof they were picking up fuel oil and ammonium nitrate.

That night I lay on my back on the teak floor of the cockpit and watched the stars strutting across the ebony sky like conquering kings. No one has really seen the stars until they've seen them at sea, far from any lighted shore. I drifted off into a deep sleep with the sound of water waxing the hull beneath me. The nylon lines slapping the aluminum mast sounded like Trinidadian steel drums.

I awoke in a cold sweat still flat on the hard teak. Nightmares had visited me throughout the night like murderous bandits, attempting to steal the peace I had found. Sheila had been part of that haunting. I also felt fear for Haydan's children, who now had no medical person to look after them. But I was trying to save New York—and by that—saving Yemen.

The full moon had come up sometime during the night and was then setting into the shimmering sea off the port side. Sleep eschewed my yellow eyes for the rest of the predawn. Once alert, I checked my charts and the sail's trim. After a refugee boat came precariously close to me, chasing me with its outboard motor in full throttle, I decided to turn north again, sailing closer to Sicily than I had intended. I felt pity for the refugees, but if they capsized and swam to my boat, it too would meet its watery grave. The cool wind of the early morning sent a chill down my spine, and I pulled my sleeping bag off my hammock to cover me.

After a few hours, the eastern sky was glowing in a thin blood-red line above a lighted cobalt sea. Morning was budding. I made coffee and nursed it for the next hour, holding the cup between my cold hands and watching as the light erupted into that waning nocturnal sky, the warden of the stars. In the distance, was the silhouette of Mount Etna. It's cone, was white with new snow and spewing out puffs of smoke from its crater as if announcing a new Pontiff in Rome. Billows of Etna's breath, inhaling and exhaling, one after the other, each expanding as they floated off toward the crimson east. The new morning in bloom would have been glorious if not for the ill feeling in my gut, from the hepatitis … and nerves about the pending fiasco in New York.

After a few hours, I looked past my stern, into the eastern sea. Etna was gone, even her smoke sliding over the horizon. No land in sight.

Jan and Peter finally sent me a link to the digital photos of the boat. Making up for their tardiness, they had collected 80 images, far more than I needed. It helped seeing with my own eyes the ship in the oil terminal harbor, and then—as predicted—later anchored at the wharf connected to the industrial complex, the same complex where they manufactured ammonium nitrate. It loaded with something there as the draft marks rose from 3.2 meters to 2.5, indicating the ship getting lighter as it pumped out its ballast, and then it sank again to 3.6 meters. One photo caught a giant auger hovering over one of the cargo compartments. They had to be loading something. After the pellets were fully loaded, I predicted, the boat would be sitting deeper in the water than before, and that's exactly what happened. This was the proof I needed to convince the authorities that this was much bigger than just a planned oil spill.

Two days later, on the western horizon, I saw land again—an isolated mountain sticking up in the mist. Gibraltar. The sight left me breathless. Passing to the south of the mighty rock, I thought about the Neanderthals who had lived in a row of caves along the rock's underside for more than a hundred thousand years. DNA had confirmed it was the same clan. I couldn't wrap my mind around that number, thinking that Jason or the Pharaohs had traveled these waters only four thousand years ago, Cleopatra and Anthony only half that time ago. I'd lived in Seattle for less than a decade and then had to move because it had become mundane. What I wouldn't have given for the mundane now. I wished I were a Neanderthal. None of them had attempted to blow up the damn world. They had lived together in peace for ridiculously long periods of time, content eating clams.

Many people consider crossing the Atlantic in a sailboat alone their crowning achievement. But for me it was just the last leg of my journey, a long and isolated twenty-plus days of dread. Luck had been on my side during my entire Mediterranean transit. I had a steady fifteen-knot wind, a northwester. However, once in the Atlantic, things change drastically.

Fortunately, I was early, having reached Gibraltar in nine days. At that pace, I would reach New York City three days before the *Pytheas*. I felt the tension brewing. I paced, walking miles in my ten-foot cockpit like a caged lion. Nervous energy with no place to go. *Damn the Port Authority! Why were they taking so long to end this?* Before that thought had completely cleared my head, I heard the tone of an incoming e-mail on my laptop in the cabin.

I climbed down the steps and looked at the source. "Speaking of the devil," I muttered as I opened the e-mail from Captain Clark of the Port Authority of New York and New Jersey Police Department. Angie had given him my e-mail address, but his communications had always gone through her, until now. But I hadn't heard from anyone in days, resting on Angie's promise that she would call if there were any new developments.

I opened the e-mail.

Dear Mr. Rogers,
The Port Authority of New York and New Jersey has the situation with the incoming tanker under our full observation and we have a plan for disarming it and taking the perpetrators into custody. We appreciate your help in this matter and will make sure there is an

appropriate awards ceremony for you when you are in New York. But for now, we want you to stand down and remain out of the area until we notify you this is over. Thank you for your service to our country.
Captain Jim Clark.

I forwarded the e-mail to Angie as I didn't see that it had been copied to her.

"Wow," I said. This was over? Anticlimactic was an understatement.

I felt the stress draining out of me like dirty water from a bathtub.

Though the winds around Portugal's coast were quarrelsome, with gust and deluge, and the meaner weather put my sailing ability to the test, I felt more peace in my soul than I had in months. My boat, with its wide beam, could handle winds near hurricane force, tipping to the point of dipping sails in the water. While the boat had automatic sail adjusters, electric winches, and an autopilot for the tiller, it took a crew of at least three to sail it to its full potential while a crew of six would be required for racing.

I could let the mainsail out or take down the smaller headsail to make her easier to handle. However, that trim wouldn't capture the maximum power the wind was graciously offering me and that I was accepting. I kept the boat trimmed for the fastest ride, like we were racing. And we had been. But it was hard to stand down. That was my old buddy in that ship, and while I no longer saw him as a good man, something still drew me to New York to be there when this all unfolded.

A thousand nautical miles off Europe's coast, the sea's anger quieted. With slow five-foot rolling waves, the sailing couldn't have been better, the evening more perfect. A translucent three-quarter moon was being launched from Europe into the night's sky as if by a trebuchet while the sun was falling toward America's still distant shores.

Thinking about America reminded me it was time to call Angie. I wanted to thank her for her help and encourage her to go back to work now that this crisis was out of our hands. I went into the dry cabin, picked up my yellow sat phone from its charging cradle, and punched Angie's number.

"Hey, sis, anything new in New York?"

"Bryan, I'm so glad you called! There *is* something new and very strange. That e-mail you got from Captain Clark and forwarded to me, well—"

"Yeah?"

"Bryan, that wasn't from Captain Clark. I called him. He had no idea where it came from."

CHAPTER THIRTY-THREE

say what?" I asked, now standing.

"They are still following the *Pytheas*, and they still want our help. It puzzled him. Then he got back to me late last night and their internal security team had figured it out. The e-mail appears to have originated from within the Port Authority, but he didn't write it. So, it wasn't an outside hack ... it was someone sitting down in front of a computer inside the Port Authority Police, accessing Captain Clark's e-mail account, and sending it."

I dropped the sat phone and it hit the bottom of the cabin. My words, all of them, deserted my mouth. Nothing was making sense anymore. Was someone at the Port Authority in on this?

After my thoughts and words started to coalesce in my brain again, I picked up the sat phone. "Angie, are you still there?"

"Yeah ... where did you go?"

"Uh ... I dropped the phone. Angie, are you freakin' kidding me?"

"No, Bryan ... no joke. Someone inside the headquarters of the New Jersey and New York Port Authority Police sent you that bogus e-mail, but why? Nobody has a clue."

"Angie, we have three weeks before the *Pytheas* enters New York Harbor. Someone out there must know what the hell is going on!" I shrieked. "What's the plan for stopping Jabbar? I, for sure, cannot!"

"Bryan, relax," she said in a soft tone. "You won't have to. They have this. They wanted you on standby, but Captain Clark now says it is unlikely they will need you. They will block Jabbar from entering the ten-mile radius around New York City, and he will either detonate his bomb, open the oil to spill there, or surrender.

They'll have an oil spill containment team nearby. The Coast Guard has ways of stopping ships, and if they can't, they'll call in their friends at the Navy to bomb them. Anyway, Captain Clark said they have everything under control … yet he was as puzzled as we are about why someone would send you that e-mail masquerading as him."

"This is a big fucking deal!" I said. "Why would an organization as big as al-Qaeda go to all this trouble to try and get me out of the picture?"

"I don't know. Captain Clark doesn't seem too worried … he even … oh, never mind."

"Never mind what?" I asked.

"Oh, he asked me if there was a chance that you edited that e-mail to make it look like someone was giving you these false instructions … you know, that you took a legitimate e-mail sent from Captain Clark and changed the wording before sharing it with me."

"Now, why in the hell would I do that? Does he think I'm making up this whole story?"

"Don't take it personally. He's just covering his bases. You just worry about getting home. I'll take care of things in New York. Love you, bro."

We hung up.

Halfway across the Atlantic, now four days early, I came to a dead zone. I called it my Sea of Tranquility, as it was flat as a swimming pool … with no swimmers. The sails rippled now and then in a delicate puff of air but otherwise hung like sheets on an indoor clothesline. I had about twenty gallons of diesel left in my tank, the Suez Canal having drained the rest. I had enough fuel for about ten hours of cruising, or about eighty nautical miles. But I might need my fuel approaching the harbor and I had to save it.

I tried my best to push the anxiety out of my mind. The weight returned to roost on my shoulders, the bar of ice in my gut. With time to burn, sitting still in the middle of the sea, I could pretend I was Christopher Robin. I could lie on my back on my teak deck in my cockpit all day and count clouds, pretending none of this shit was really happening. Did the Port Authority really have my back? Were Hunter Philips and the CIA really working behind the scenes? I wanted to give up. I wanted to just relax and live in the moment, absorb the peace around me, and let nature take its course. But, damn, a million people would die if they screwed this up.

I knew when I became a medic and then a physician associate that there would be days when I held the lives of people in my hands, but a million at once? *Why did God pick me for this? I'm a nobody. I make bad choices all the time. I punched the face of one of France's national heroes. I may have broken his damn nose.*

I went to the website to watch the locater, as the *Pytheas* had to be gaining on me. She was now coming up Africa's west coast and turning toward Brazil, taking the central Atlantic crossing. I was concerned she would get to New York before me unless I found some wind. While a big part of me didn't want to be near New York when the intercept went down, until I knew the police had a hold of this, I felt obligated to be there.

I spoke to Angie at sunrise each morning for updates. The Port Authority people were still following Jabbar's ship but keeping their specific plans a secret. Meanwhile, I was worried about the inside operative. Surely, someone was up to no good. Ray had told me that the bombing of the *Cole* had been a practice run for 9/11, and that act, as horrible as it was, may have been a prelude to this even bigger one. Their motivation now could be payback for the U.S. killing their leader, Ayman al-Zawahiri, in a drone strike in Kabul. Jabbar's personal tragedy, just an opportunity to find a willing mule. My old friend, just a pawn.

On my fifth day in the Sea of Tranquility, Angie called me before sunrise. She whispered, "Captain Clark said the Coast Guard was still tracking the *Pytheas*'s GPS, and it was crossing the north Atlantic via a major shipping lane. But I shouldn't be telling you this. He told me to keep quiet on the phone. I mean, they compromised your e-mails, and who knows if they're listening to this call."

"But, Angie, that's not true!" I yelled. "First of all, it wasn't *my* e-mail they compromised, it was the Port Authority's. Secondly, what they are telling you about the *Pytheas* isn't true. I've been following it since Iran, and I can see it's off Brazil's coast. I find it disconcerting that he said the 'north Atlantic.'"

"I don't know, Bryan. He seems to know what he's talking about. He said Jabbar's name wasn't on the manifest but added it's not uncommon for people to give a false name if they have something to hide."

"Bullshit!" I said. "Are you listening to me? You saw the manifest yourself and Jabbar El Haddad's name was on it as co-captain. Someone inside is working against us."

"Bryan, I trust this guy. He's bright." She paused for a moment and then gently added, "Maybe you *are* becoming paranoid, and I don't blame you given what you've been through."

Despite Angie's best attempts at reassuring me, I was left unassured. There was too much at stake. The sea might have been tranquil, but I was not. A storm was building inside me.

I checked the location of the *Pytheas* again. As my curser hovered over the dot that represented the tanker, the identifier number C1749332 came up. I copied that number.

As an experiment, I relogged into the website with a new account and typed in the name of the *Pytheas*. This time, it identified a dot just south of Iceland—and with a different identification number, Q99725641.

What the hell was going on?

I logged on again with my previous account. The ship I was following was a dot represented by the number, C1749332. Clicking over the dot, it brought up the name *Eirinopoiós*. *What the hell?*

Lying in the cockpit, looking up at the leaden sky, I saw nothing. No birds. Not even a stray cloud to count. The line going up the mast was still, the sails themselves lifeless. "Damnit!" I screamed to no one. The echoing silence was getting to me.

Then I asked that pale blue sky, "What the hell does all this mean?" That was my last thought before falling into a deep sleep.

I awakened sometime in the middle of the night to the halyard's metallic clattering against the mast. The Trinidadians were playing their steel drums again. Wind. It was music I could dance to. The sky was darker than previous nights—a cloud ceiling had moved in. Clouds usually bring wind. I looked toward the horizon. The moon, a big white disk filtered by the haze, was less than an hour from immersion in the sea. I heard a flapping and looked at my sails. Large rolls were moving up and down the Dacron to the rhythm of the soft evening breeze. The airspeed indicator was spinning but not fast. This was the first movement of air I had seen in almost four days. Thank God.

Below deck, I pulled up my laptop and studied the photos Peter and Jan had taken of the *Pytheas* in Suez. Most were of the bow, but one captured the stern. I enlarged that photo. There were two men on a thwart working over the name, just like I had. I saw just *theas*. The six-foot letters P and Y of the name *Pytheas* were gone. Those bastards were changing their ship's name right in port.

I stood up and gulped down a glass of wine to calm my thoughts. The two tankers and I were heading for a frightening and confusing rendezvous in New York—*if* I were to get decent winds to pull me to the coast. I stared out the porthole in thought. If Jabbar's ship was a decoy, why did it stop in Suez? Was that just a deception, and they loaded nothing there? What about the new *Pytheas*? Was it loaded with the deadly mixture?

I rechecked a few hours later, and the new *Pytheas* had posted its manifest and bill of lading online. According to it, the tanker had loaded with five hundred thousand barrels of diesel from the refinery in Mongstad, Norway, and was heading to a fuel depository at Hunter's Point in Queens, just across the East River from Manhattan. I called Angie.

"Hey, are you sailing again?" she asked.

"Yeah, sailing again, not fast, but back under wind power … but listen to this—."

Angie interrupted, "Bryan, you can stand down, this time for real. The Port Police and the Coast Guard have things under control. I think they have even captured the interest of Homeland Security. They can't share with me the details, but Captain—"

"Angie, hell no, I can't stand down! We have an additional problem. The police are following a ship that changed its name to *Pytheas* while the *Pytheas* changed its name to the *Eirinopoiós.*"

"What? You lost me!" her voice exploded from the receiver. "Why are these ships changing their names?"

"To confuse us! Don't you get it?" I said through clenched teeth.

"Well, which one has the bomb?" she asked.

"I don't know, Angie! I'm trying to figure that out. My point is, things aren't under control. Call them. They must follow the *Eirinopoiós* too."

"I'll call Captain Clark in the morning. But, Bryan, don't panic! You've done your part."

"Tell your police chief what I told you. I could call him myself if you want, I just need a good number and time. If the winds pick up like the forecast says they will, I'll be just two hundred miles away by this time tomorrow."

I had sailed on smooth seas throughout the night with a steady ten-knot wind blowing in from the southwest. It provided me a close-haul power position with the boat. In those ideal conditions, I could keep the boat at fifteen knots for the night and morning, making up lost time.

With the new wind and passing weather front, the clouds had blown away. The brilliant stars blanketed the night sky like a celestial gem show. Breathtaking. New York's lights were not visible this far out. However, dots of lights thickened on the horizon the closer we got to the continent, revealing my neighboring ships' positions. Was one the new *Pytheas* or the *Eirinopoiós*?

My sat phone beeped. It was Angie.

"I wanted to call you before I left for a meeting for work," she said quickly. "I told Captain Clark there could be two ships with bombs, or one a decoy."

"What did he say?"

"Frankly, Bryan, well … it made him angry. He told me they had invested plenty of resources following the *Pytheas* and had a plan to stop it far out at sea, which went beyond their proper protocol. Now, he says I've doubled their work with my warning about the *Eirinopoiós*. Then he said, 'I guess you want me to check out all fourteen hundred ships coming into New York Harbor?' I said to him, 'No, sir, just two.' Then he said, 'I'll think about it.' But yesterday he called me back. He said he wanted to talk directly with you. Can you call him?"

I took a deep breath and then shrieked, "Angie, you need to get Mom, your brothers, and Joel and get the hell out of town! Maybe Jersey or Connecticut, but away from the coast."

"No, Bryan," she answered calmly. "I'm not leaving. You want me to abandon all my friends? My city? No, we need to stop this thing, so no one gets hurt. So, are you going to call him?"

"Yes! Send me his damn number. What is a good time to call him?"

"He's in the office by eight," she said.

"I'll call him tomorrow at eight. We're in the same time zone now." I said. Then we ended the call.

My stomach was in knots. "Damn you, Jabbar," I whispered for the umpteenth time.

CHAPTER THIRTY-FOUR

The sea conditions had been perfect. Great winds. An almost cloudless day. There were three-foot waves, very manageable in a big boat. I thought I would have forty-eight hours to rest before things got hairy.

I woke up early and waited two hours until it was eight o'clock and then I dialed Captain Clark's number.

He answered, "Captain Clark."

"Hi, this is Bryan Rogers, you've been talking to my sister Angie."

"Let me put you on hold a minute." There was a thirty second pause and then he picked up again. "Hi, are you in New York?"

"Uh ... No, I'm still at sea. I'm calling on my sat phone."

"Of course. I thought that Angie said you were still a few days out. I wanted to discuss some things directly with you. I'm not sure you are aware of how many assets we now have invested in this lead. We have the Coast Guard, Homeland Security, and the FBI involved. We might end up spending seven figures on this exercise. Fortunately, most leads about attacks against New York end up being nothing. But now, you want us to follow two ships?"

"No, it is still the same ship I've been following from the beginning; however, it has changed its name from *Pytheas* to *Eirinopoiós* and I don't know what the name of your ship was before, but it has now changed its name to *Pytheas.*

"No. That's not possible. Ships don't just change their names at their will. That's against maritime law. You may not know it, but it is a tedious process to register a commercial ship."

"No, I don't know the rules, but I do know what I'm seeing. The same dot that started out as *Pytheas* in Iran two months ago, is now showing up as *Eirinopoiós*, and that worries me."

"We have a lot of resources, great men and women here," he said. "They will figure this out and take appropriate steps."

"And you also have an al-Qaeda operative inside your team," I said.

"Excuse me?" asked the captain.

"Someone sent me a bogus e-mail from your office."

But then he continued without responding to my statement as if he hadn't heard me. "Hey Bryan, I wanted to talk directly with you about some things that I have not discussed with your sister. In our due diligence, the FBI has done a background check on you and I wanted to talk about some of their findings."

I slowly sat down in the cockpit. "On me?"

"Yeah. We do this on all people who are reporting serious attacks."

I heard papers rustling over the phone.

Captain Clark continued, "I see that you dropped out of high school for a semester for mental health reasons? What was that about?"

"That was my fall semester in 2001. My dad had just been killed in 9/11 and my counselor recommended I take that time off. But I caught up later that year."

"Your dad perished in 9/11? I'm sorry to hear that. That was the worst day of my life," he said.

How the hell do you think I FELT about that day?

"I see that you were in Afghanistan."

"Yeah. I was a medic."

"Did you see combat action?"

"Yeah, I did. I watch a lot of friends die, some as I was trying to save them."

"That must have been hard."

"It was." I answered.

"Yeah," the captain continued. "Uh, the other thing, we have talked to the American Embassy in Sana'a. They told us that you had reported the same tip to them there, but they found no evidence of such a plot. However, they did mention that there was some suspicion about you."

"Suspicion?"

"Yeah. Apparently your clinic burned down killing your colleague, but you were left completely unscathed. Sure, the Iranians always take credit for terrorist attacks against their enemies, but it was never proven that they were the arsonists."

I sighed. "What are you implying?"

"How did you escape that fire without being hurt?"

"It happened during the night and I was sleeping outside in a tent."

"Well, I guess you were damn lucky. I mean, to pick that night to go camping."

"I slept in a tent every night! I preferred sleeping outside. What are you insinuating?"

"Due diligence. Before we invest another seven-figure worth of assets in yet another ship searching, I just needed to understand our informant better. This is routine police work, don't take it personal." We finished the call.

Back in the cabin, still thinking about that conversation, I was preparing to cook my last two Israeli eggs, just to lighten my mood. For just a second, the smell of fresh eggs was the only thing on my mind, displacing all my worries. Having just set the frying pan on the stove, a loud thud came from the port side. I heard fiberglass cracking as I was thrown sideways and tumbled to the floor, egg yolk all over me. The boat rolled so far over, I was sure it was capsizing. There was a loud clanging as pots and pans, having jumped the rough-water guardrails around the burners, scattered everywhere.

As the boat up righted, water poured down the steps like a waterfall. I scrambled to the deck, pushing through the torrent to figure out what ship had hit me. I looked over the port side and saw no ship. I looked to the starboard to see a twenty-five-foot wave moving away from me, a fine spray erupting from its crest as if saying "Adios, sucker."

"What the hell? A tsunami? A rogue wave?" I whispered.

I remembered seeing on the nautical map, in fine print, the warning, "Rogue Wave Danger Zone," written over this area where the Hudson River emptied into a network of bays and the bays entered the sea.

When I could finally stand and assess the damage, I saw the sails were intact and still trimmed and functioning well. The helm was in order and the autopilot still controlling the rudder.

Then I noticed two loose brackets sticking up on the cabin's top. The wave had ripped the solar panels completely off the boat. I saw a loose wire hanging over the side, and when I pulled on it, it came up unhindered. No solar panels attached. The satellite dish was gone too.

I scurried down the steps into the cabin. The lights didn't work. I grabbed my emergency waterproof flashlight, which I had clipped to the wall. I surveyed my cabin.

"What a damn mess!"

There were eighteen inches of water sloshing back and forth around my shins. Eggshells, papers, and maps were floating around the cabin like dead fish.

Through the water I could see my submerged sat phone near the floor, still plugged into its charging station, its light off. I grabbed it. It was dead.

My mouth went dry. "Shit!" I moaned.

The engine compartment was a swimming pool. My bilge pump, which was supposed to turn on when water was present, was silent. It had no power. Something had shorted out between my lithium battery bank on the floor in the engine compartment and the cabin circuit. The battery bank, in a watertight casing, was underwater, the casing cracked.

"Why in the hell were the batteries on the floor? Why was I cooking with the cabin hatch wide open?" I scolded myself. The hull was intact, although I heard it crack. The water came through the open hatch. A good sailor thinks through all possibilities. I'd never had water in my boat before, except rainwater.

I let out a chorus of "Shits!" so loud that it gave me laryngitis. I was only just beginning to imagine all the complications this turn of events had handed me. No lights. No sat phone. No laptop or internet. No electronic navigation. All at a crucial time. At the crux of disaster … comes yet another one. I was blind to the world. "Damnit!"

While I had backup analog navigation equipment, an accurate clock, a sextant, and a compass, it had been two years since I had used them. I wasn't sure I recalled how. But I knew my last position on the GPS. I was due east of New York City and seventy nautical miles out. I had to keep going west, at least until I got my power back online.

My priority was drying out my things. I knew I would have to use the manual bilge. It was a long handle attached to a diaphragm pump. The hand-pumping took two hours before I could call the boat dry. At least there was no standing water. I was hoping my battery bank would work again, but it didn't.

I tried to start the engine, thinking that its alternator could recharge the batteries. But it would not start. Was there water in the fuel?

What killed me was realizing I had been on Jabbar's trail for two months and now it was going to end like this. A friggin' rogue wave.

CHAPTER THIRTY-FIVE

I had given it all that I had but had come up short. Angie was right, it was in the police's hands. If they screwed this up by stopping the wrong ship, then they'd have no one to blame but themselves.

But a million dear souls would perish.

Thinking again of those instigators and funders of this whole hateful mess, those in their starched boxers sitting in Jeddah eating dates, now I imagined the one who was swiping his iPad with his sticky finger sending a load of cash from Zurich to someone in New York—the inside man. Thinking of how slow the government was because of an election cycle, I imagined the money man winking and swiping his iPad twice more, sending seven figures of cash from Zurich to both the Republican and Democratic National Committees, then looking at his mates and saying with a smirk, "*Firaq tasd* [divide and conquer]."

I kept my eyes peeled on the compass—west. That was the only navigation I needed. I wouldn't be able to see anything in the approaching dark of night except the lights of ships and boats dotting the seascape like celestial bodies. D-day was still eight hours away. I started to see gulls, as I was approaching the continental U.S., maybe fifty miles in front of me. This would mean Long Island's northeast tip was already north of my position. How far, I hadn't a clue.

I turned the *Ace* in a south-southwest orientation, which put me on track to be in Virginia in two days. I wanted to get as far away from this fucked-up mess as I could. I was done with it! If I couldn't save anyone else, at least I could save myself.

I suddenly remembered that when we had first purchased the boat, Angie had found a 500 ml bottle of fine Scottish whiskey in a velvet bag tucked away in the same hidden compartment as the sawed-off shotgun. We had looked at it and then put it back. I scrambled down below, opened the compartment, and pulled out the bottle, now with three more years of barrel-less aging. After pouring a glass full, I grabbed the cigar Ray had given me and that I had saved for the moment of resolution.

The tightly trimmed sails were skimming through the dense air like an albatross's wing. I lit up my cigar, sipped my whiskey, and watched as the anemic sun was just peeking through a milky layer near the western horizon and then sank softly into the sea without a fight. The tip of the cigar glowed bright red in the wind. Sighs vented from my soul, coming with each deep exhalation. *What will morning bring?* I couldn't even watch it on the news.

I reached for my glass and brought it up to my lips. On the crystal's convex surface, I saw my yellow-eyed reflection. *Oh, my Lord, I'm going to die from liver disease.* It wasn't a good time for alcohol … except for one drink. What I wouldn't have given for a lab. A king's ransom for a HARVONI prescription. If I survived to Virginia, I would have to find a doctor there. What I needed to worry about now was … just myself.

This self-absorption lasted only minutes. "God, please protect my family and New York. This is now in your hands, not mine." I stood and prayed to the sky. I cried tears of frustration and grief. Fear gripped me, as I felt the goose bumps across my spray-soaked arms.

Damn my liver, I finished both the bottle of whiskey and the cigar. Fortunately, the bottle contained only eight ounces, just enough to quiet my nerves for sleep. I dozed in the captain's chair, feet upon the gunwales.

Dread awakened me in the small hours of the new day. After a while, the sun's first light was revealing the world around me. I saw a ship convoy lining up, heading north toward New York's Lower Bay. I was much closer to the big city than I'd thought, the Gulf Stream pushing me north. In that mix of ships could have been the *Eirinopoiós*. But I no longer gave a damn. I didn't want to think about it. Surely, the Port Authority Police had this.

I turned to a more southerly direction to avoid the major commercial channel, the northbound ships passing a mile to my starboard side in a line. Most were cargo, heading for the big shipping terminals in the Upper Bay or North Jersey, or so I assumed. I saw two tankers in the queue. I jogged down below and checked my electrical supply. Still dead. Sat phone, still in a coma. My radar and GPS, still blind. I grabbed my cell phone, turned it on. One signal bar appeared and then faded away, so I stuck it in my pocket. Grabbing my binoculars, I ran back to the helm.

I studied the tankers as they came nearer. The first one had the name *Ayame* painted on its stern. A couple more container ships passed, and then another tanker came into view that looked eerily familiar. I examined it as it moved closer.

Eirinopoiós was painted on the stern as plain as day. She was sitting so low in the water that her terra cotta bottom was just a narrow stripe. Fully loaded.

What were the odds? "Holy shit!" I dropped the binoculars, and they dangled around my neck by their strap. I stood impassively, leaning on the gunwale, my stunned eyes drawn to that ship cutting through the water, passing just two hundred yards away. Surreal. I had chased that damn ship—whose captain was my estranged best friend— around the world from Yemen's dry and dusty hills ... and here we were. Him going north and me south. Two lost comets passing in the night.

"Jabbar!" I shrieked, frightening the three seagulls perched on my cabin into an immediate flight. My thoughts went to Angie, Mom, my brothers, to my million neighbors in New York City. What if this ship had the ANFO? What if the police and the Coast Guard were too busy inspecting its decoy to catch it? Without a radio or sat phone, I was in the dark. I didn't know how many miles I was from New York, but it must have been less than ten. I didn't see a single police or Coast Guard boat in sight. Not a damn soul but me and that ghost ship.

I yanked my wheel, twirling it clockwise. The boat pivoted as if the sea were ice and the keel a metal skate blade, the boom just missing my noggin as the sails readjusted to the prevailing winds. My breeze shifted from starboard beam reach to port close hauled. Dashing to the left and then right, I adjusted my sails to harvest the maximum power from the wind, allowing it to pull me directly toward the *Eirinopoiós*. I could never catch the tanker at its open-sea cruising speed of twenty knots. However, she couldn't have been going over ten in that line. With that speed and my good winds, I could overtake her.

Once I had established my position, I reached into my pocket and took out my phone. Two bars. I noticed I had a message from Angie. Her text said, "Where are you, Bryan? We need you! This is for you." In the text was a play button. I clicked it. I heard an electric guitar's familiar tune. It was Chris Isaak's "Wicked Game," with the opening lyric, "The world was on fire, and no one could save me but you, It's strange what desire will make foolish people do—" and it ended.

Tears came to my eyes, blurring the vision that I urgently needed. "God help me!" I cried. "God, please help me!" My knees gave out, buckling in fear. The spray of the cold sea across my anxious face made it difficult to see even with the tears wiped.

I tried to call Angie's number, rapidly punching the buttons, but there was no answer.

"Angie, this is Bryan. I'm in cell range. I broke my sat phone. What's going on? I'm closing in on the *Eirinopoiós*. Unless I hear from you soon, I'm going to try and board her. Pray for me, sis. Please, please … pray for us."

Putting the phone on vibrate, I stuck it in my pocket. The ring wouldn't pierce the thick sounds that were gathering around me. My boat was cutting like a porpoise through the loud wind and rushing water, giving me her best, twelve knots or more.

I was closing in on the *Eirinopoiós. What will I do if I catch her?* For six months, I had lain awake planning, imagining, and fearing the moment that was now falling upon me like an avalanche. But I had been assured over and over again that I would have no responsibility except to help negotiate with Jabbar, from a distance. Now, here I was. Alone.

The humongous tanker was intimidating, to say the least, when viewed up close, taking up my entire visual field. I could feel the rumble of the tanker's giant screws in my abdomen.

As I passed the ship, I studied it with my binoculars. Somehow, I had to get aboard that moving metal mountain from my low perch. There were two vulnerable spots.

Its giant anchors offered me one opportunity. They hung on each side of the bow. With the ship sitting so low, they were just ten feet above the water, suspended by massive chains that led through the bulwark and onto the deck. The problem would be getting from the water to the anchors. If I made it to an anchor, I would have to climb the chain to the deck.

The other option was a staircase leading down from the deck to a point about fifteen feet above the water. While that offered an easier way to the top, getting to the bottom step would be a big challenge.

Pipes, valves, hatch covers, and box-like objects in rows, some the size of small houses, covered the deck's surface. I knew that only from online photos of the ship—I couldn't see them from my position on the water. The array on the deck would afford me an abundance of places to hide until—until what? *What was I going to do once onboard?*

My greatest hope was to find the ship empty and then assuming that the police were intercepting the armed one. But that would be more magical thinking as it was obvious, from how it sat in the water that it was full of something. If not empty, my hope was to find Jabbar and talk him out of this ghastly act. My worst dread was that I'd find this ship armed and have to kill Jabbar and then anchor the ship and wait for the police.

But there were a hundred other scenarios that could play out, and I could picture none with clarity.

The ship was behind me, on my port side. I kept my speed at maximum, praying the tired winds wouldn't give out or shift. After gathering the sawed-off shotgun and the mooring grappling hook and rope from below, I went topside. I tied loops in the grappling hook's floating rope three feet apart. I hated climbing ropes, even when I was healthy, and figured the loops would help. For some reason, I grabbed Ray's janbiya and hooked it in the front of my belt. Then I studied the physics of my sailboat, its wide beam and limited space on the edge.

How can I do this?

If I sailed far ahead of the ship and then jumped into my kayak, I could wait for the ship to pass. I could intercept it, but in a kayak struggling at three knots I had little chance of keeping up with a massive tanker going ten. I could only navigate perpendicular to the ship's course and try my best to close in. But the wake from the bow would push me back. I would have to fight like crazy in the water and then hurl my grappling hook upward with one chance to catch the anchor.

I rubbed my face and moaned, "Oh, my Lord!"

I worked pragmatically but swiftly, setting up the kayak, hooking my gear on the boat and myself while calculating the course. Any failure would end my life, and the opportunities for such were plentiful. My heart rate and breaths were out of control, and I could no longer subdue them. To be thrown out of my kayak and ground up in the huge propellers like sausage was one outcome I didn't like. Not wearing a lifejacket, I could drown. Wearing one would make me too bulky to be as athletic as I needed to be.

Fear overcame me like I had never known, not in Afghanistan, not in fighting the clinic's fire or any day of my life. But my death would take me from this messed up world. Maybe there I would be released from the sorrows that my heart bore, loosing Dad, Sheila, and the Jabbar I once knew. I tasted blood, my blood. I had gritted my jaw so hard I'd bitten my tongue. Yet, fortitude came to me from a source I couldn't identify. Something that allowed me, despite the terror, to put one foot in front of the other; putting one hand over another as I packed my gear for a suicide mission. Dad's presence was with me, and his words from my boyhood echoing in my mind, "Son, you can do this." I heard Sheila's voice too, her telling me that despite my impetuosity, I had good judgement and Jabbar telling me I was a good man. Those voices I needed in this moment.

I maneuvered the *Ace* near the tanker, attempting to create enough space between us to launch the kayak and position it for the intercept. I knew the crew might be waiting on me with a bullet from an AK-47.

Everything was in place. I was at the *Ace's* stern, the gun over my shoulder, the janbiya in my belt, the grappling hook and rope under a bungee cord on the kayak's deck in front of me, and the paddle in my hands. The big heap of a ship was one hundred yards behind me, giving me just seconds to position the kayak.

I laid the kayak across the sloping transom behind the stern. It was a forty-five-degree angle, three feet of slick fiberglass to the water. I had done this many times, never when the sailboat was at twelve knots. It was difficult to hold the kayak long enough to jump in, but I did. I held on to the stern briefly, then released the kayak and it slid into the rushing water sideways. I braced myself with the paddle over my head to keep from capsizing. Then, all hell was set in motion—water gushing, splashing, my arms flailing in all directions, complete chaos.

The *Ace* sailed off on her own.

The huge tanker was towering over me and closing in rapidly. I paddled with a fever-pitch intensity to the ship's port side. I grabbed the grappling hook and spun it around my head like a lasso, ready to throw. The massive bulbous bow was cutting through the water and, as expected, was forcing me to the side in its five-foot wake. I fought against the waves, paddling with both hands, my right hand also clutching the rope and paddle.

I waited for the perfect moment, the anchor passing overhead, then let go of the paddle with my right hand and tossed the hook straight up. The rope entangled on itself, the loops I had tied being the culprits.

"Damn!"

The hook fell directly down, hitting me in the head. A full panic ensued.

My kayak slammed into the ship's side and then stuck to the hull like a magnet. A force that had missed my calculation was the blunt bow pinning me between it and the sea. I was caught against the ship but slipping slowly down the iron hull toward the propellor end. Water was pouring into my cockpit, and the kayak was quickly becoming swamped.

I pulled in my grappling hook and tossed it again, seven feet above my hands. The hook wedged between the anchor and hull — and held! I clutched the rope with both hands.

My arms jerked up, almost pulled out of their sockets, and I banged into the side of the ship, hard as a concrete wall. Hanging in the air, I felt the water-logged kayak still around my waist. The kayak's bow was tipped down, skimming the surface of the sea. The janbiya was caught just beneath the cockpit combing. Holding on to the rope with my right hand, I dislodged the knife handle from the kayak. The boat fell into the sea and quickly sank.

The hook had secured itself enough that I was dangling with my full weight without it slipping. I climbed, my feet bracing myself against the hull, my arms feeling weak already.

I made it to the anchor and sat on the massive iron blade, long enough to rest my arms and catch my breath. The green sea was rushing beneath my dangling feet in a torrent, curling over in a standing wave from the cut of the bow. The wind blew cold against my wet face, my hands begging to let go and let me fall into the surf.

I secured the gun, hanging from its strap, the knife still in my belt, and began the twenty-foot climb up the chain, arriving at the deck. The hole through the bulwark was small. I couldn't fit through it without pushing the shotgun and janbiya in first.

Making it through to the deck, I sat to catch my breath again and to study the superstructure. With its rows of forward-sloping windows, thirty feet above the stern, I knew I was in plain view of anyone on the navigation bridge. If the crew had been looking ahead, they would've seen me. Hoping they didn't, I jumped behind a square structure that inhabited the deck. I lay there to plan my next move. I could hear my own heart beating as I lay face up, my back on the iron. I kept the shotgun across my chest, my finger on the trigger, my eyes constantly leaping from object to object, looking for a threat. My throat was so parched I couldn't swallow.

A foul smell, like rotting meat, soon overwhelmed me so much I couldn't breathe through my nose, despite being hungry for air.

I looked around for the source and found nothing. I rolled over and crawled, keeping beneath the edge so no one could see me. I peeked around the corner and a small flock of seagulls flew away. Beneath where they had been sitting were a few blue jumpsuits lying on the deck. Then I noticed they were surrounded by a pool of black tar. With horror, I saw that inside the jumpsuits were bodies—four bloated corpses, side by side. They were only five feet away. I could see that someone had cut their throats. The old black blood encasing their chests had solidified. The crew I presumed.

"Filthy birds," I said to the remaining gull.

Would the terrorists kill the crew of a decoy ship?

The bodies had to have been there for at least a week. The blood surrounding them had congealed into asphalt. As I got closer, I scared flies into a swarm. It was the maggots that had drawn the seagull's interest, not the human flesh.

I sat up. Above the bulwark, a gray sawtooth pattern was on the horizon, Manhattan's skyscrapers.

We were closer to the target than I had realized. I had to act! Clearly, no one was intercepting this ship. This was completely on me.

I crawled across the rotting bodies to the next hatch. I moved from raised hatch to raised hatch, behind and around pipes, working my way up the ship toward the superstructure.

Once I was away from the dead crew, fuel oil's familiar aroma overwhelmed my every inhalation. Vivid memories encroached on my hectic mind. My grandma Rogers had used a fuel oil furnace in her house in Connecticut. The entire house smelled of fuel oil, including her long, gray braided hair. I hoped to see her again in paradise by that day's end.

As I passed a round port hatch, I stopped and studied it. When I turned a wingnut, it released, and I slid the hatch open just six inches. I unbuttoned my cargo pocket, reached in, and took out my cell phone. Using it as a flashlight, I looked inside the tank, hoping it was empty. It wasn't.

A white pellet and fuel oil stew filled the holding area up to within inches of the cover. I reached down and scooped up a handful of the slurry. I brought it to my nose and sniffed. No question the liquid part was fuel oil. This ship was locked and loaded to end the world. I had an urge to run to the nearest edge of the deck and dive into the sea, possibly saving my own life.

I didn't see detonator wires, something I could cut like they did in the movies. My heart took leave of my chest as it was beating so hard. I darted for the next box-like structure, then to a huge valve, then another pipe cluster, and to another hatch. I made it to the superstructure. A long metal staircase ran from the foredeck to the navigation bridge.

I climbed the stairs. Now I was in full view of anyone who was watching. If the manifest was correct, with four dead on the foredeck, Jabbar and two others should have been at the helm. But then again, who really knew?

Stepping lightly, I could hear the musical reverberation in the metal staircase, my shoes striking each step. The marine air whipped my hair and clothes. I made it to the windowed door that led onto the bridge. I looked through the glass and saw a thin man with a long beard at the helm, staring straight ahead. *Jabbar?*

He was standing, trance-like, palms raised, staring out the window and to the horizon. I reached for the steel door lever and pushed down. The door popped open. I heard Arabic prayers coming over the intercom.

I stepped inside without disturbing his trance.

"Jabbar," I said in a subdued tone.

No artist could have depicted the look on my old friend's face, except for maybe Edvard Munch, the painter of *The Scream*. Jabbar stumbled backward against the console, which kept him from falling. His hands were free, save a misbaḥah string rotating between his thumb and index finger. No detonator that I could see. I sighed.

"Bryan ... uh, you're here," he said in a whisper, his eyes big as owls'. "How?" He looked toward the sea.

"By kayak," I said in a nonchalant tone, legs spread, fisted hands by my side.

He said nothing as if he were cast in stone, frozen in bewilderment.

I took slow steps in his direction. "Jabbar, don't do this. This tragic act is far beneath you."

Shaking his head, he responded, "Bryan, it's too late. What is done is done. I don't have control anymore. They armed it from Yemen, through the internet." He pointed at the computer screen on the console. "They've set the timer."

I glanced at the screen. The digital clock was at twenty-three minutes.

Through clenched teeth, Jabbar said, "There's nothing you can do. It's over. Come with me my American brother to paradise."

I stared while contemplating my next move. I took another small step in his direction.

Tears began to flow down Jabbar's somber face. "Alam was a good boy. He deserved a long life, the good life Allah had prepared for him. But you Americans took it from him—"

"Jabbar, I had nothing to do with that nightmare, and you know it! Turn this ship around!" I screamed at him, while taking another step.

He stepped backward and shook his fist at me. "Americans made the bomb." Pointing at me, he screamed, "The Americans hate Islam. You are Allah's enemies!"

Feeling his spittle hit my face, I responded, "Jabbar, think of how many innocents you'll kill."

I took one more step.

I pointed at the window behind him. "Those kids in New York had nothing to do with that bomb that fell on Alam's bus. Nothing! Yet, if you steer this ship into that harbor, a million people will die today, including good Muslims, by the thousands."

I took another step toward him, squared my shoulders, and yelled, "You'll kill my entire fucking family!" Tears came to my eyes. I pressed my hands together as though praying. "Please don't do this. What have I done except to come and try my damnedest to save you and your children, the Yemenis I love with all my heart? If you do this, it'll unleash the devil's wrath. Hate begets hate. Multiply hate, as you're doing, and it'll only proliferate tenfold."

We stood and stared at each other, squared off, fists clenched at our sides. Looking into his wet eyes, I saw my own reflection. A madman reflected in the eyes of another madman. He stood only five feet away. Behind him was the New York skyline, growing ever closer.

"You said I was a good father," Jabbar said calmly. "I do this as a noble one, taking retribution for Alam."

"Don't fool yourself, Jabbar! This has nothing to do with Alam." I shook my head. "He would be the first to beg you to stop. You're doing it for hate, the hate you have toward Allah. No, you're not a good father ... not anymore. You're a disgrace to fatherhood, to being a man. You're a disgrace to Islam ... and to all of humanity."

His face became infused with blood, his veins distended. "How dare you say I hate Allah—"

"You do!" I yelled. "Allah created those souls in New York, and you're going to destroy them. Jabbar, turn this damn ship around now! Aim it out to sea," I said pointing through the window at my side. Nodding my head, I continued, "Come with me. We can still escape this."

"No, Bryan. Today is the day of our martyrdom. You will die with me. We will redeem Alam's death and the death of Dr. Emory. We will end this war that ravishes our beautiful mountains. We'll be in paradise soon. No more wars, no more pain."

I spoke in a calm voice. "It is said, 'The millstones of the gods grind slowly but surely.' Leave this in God's hands. He is Yemen's grindstone of vengeance."

"I am the donkey who turns the millstone of God's retribution!" Jabbar shrieked. "I'm the stone of Yemen, the grist of his mill. I will do this, and then the pain will finally be put away."

I snickered, then laughed out loud. "Oh, there'll be more pain, maybe not for you, my friend, but for the rest of the world. You'll create the same losses for ten million people who survive this, by killing the people they loved. Spiritual collaterals, like my mother … like you … like me … with hollowed souls. Irreparably damaged. Then this evil will return to roost in Yemen's beautiful mountains once more, and the hope for her children, like Maritza, lost forever. If America brought hell's fury to Afghanistan's plains after 9/11, surely, they'll do the same to Yemen's ragged peaks after this. America will tear down Yemen's beautiful mountains … grinding them into sand and tossing them into the sea, their revenge for this terrorism."

I took a big step toward Jabbar. He was standing in front of the foremost console beneath the forward-sloping windows. Screens filled the console — radar screens, computer screens, dials, and levers. Beside him was the free-standing helm, a box about the size of a washing machine with a small steering wheel attached like that on a car-race video game. I stepped around the helm to get closer to him, the New York City skyline looming ever taller above his shoulder.

I raised my shotgun and pointed it at his legs.

"Jabbar, turn this damn ship around … now!"

"Bryan, are you going to shoot me?" He laughed. "I don't think you can do it. You're too good ... and it won't make a difference."

"I'm asking you one last time, my friend, turn this damn ship around!"

"Go to hell, Bryan!" he screamed, beating his chest with his fist.

My time had run out. "God forgive me," I whispered and pulled the trigger.

There was a click, but the gun didn't fire.

An image appeared in my mind of me grabbing the gun in the bow compartment of my sailboat after the deluge. The gun had gotten wet. The shells wouldn't fire.

With my gaze still drawn to my gun, Jabbar whipped me across my eye with his string of ivory prayer beads. I was dazed, and then the pain exploded. With rage, I hit him across his temple with the gun barrel. He ran to the back of the bridge, where navigational charts covered large wooden tables. He slung papers and charts in the floor between us. From the table he lifted a box cutter and pointed it at me. I stood back.

"Is that how you murdered your crew? With that?" I asked, nodding at the blade.

"I didn't. The four other martyrs were all Saudis. It was the plan as we grew close to America that they would cut each other's throats. We didn't want anyone backing out before the mission was complete, so they killed each other, after throwing the Indian crew into the sea. Each placed a knife on a brother's throat and when I blew the ship's horn, they all sliced."

As he was talking, I was inching closer.

"Bryan, don't underestimate me." He held the box cutter in front of his face. "I will cut your damn head off."

Drawing my janbiya from my belt, I lunged at him. He stumbled backward, slipping on the charts he had tossed on the floor, and fell, cutting my left forearm deeply with his blade. He landed on his back. I fell on top of him and pinned him to the floor, the janbiya's blade against his belly. I felt warm liquid running down my cut arm and saw it dripping onto Jabbar.

I hissed in his ear, "Turn this ship around Jabbar. I don't know how. I need you to end this. Then we'll die together at sea ... as friends once more."

He grunted as I lay on him, the knife's blade pushing against his skin so hard it penetrated his shirt. I saw he was bleeding.

"Bryan," he whispered. "The ship is on autopilot. It will steer itself to the precise location and explode. If you kill me, there's still no turning back."

I pressed the knife harder against his belly. I knew it was sharp, but not like a razor's edge. It penetrated. I gasped. I could feel the knife sliding through his skin and minuscule fatty layer like I had felt a scalpel in surgery a thousand times before. It continued to slip downward. I saw the panic building in his russet eyes, the terror tightening his face like a mask. I felt the blade's tip, having perforated his intestines, come to rest near his aorta. The pulse was transmitted up the knife and into the brass handle. The knife moved up and down with each beat of Jabbar's heart, well over a hundred beats per minute.

He looked at me with sullen, desperate eyes bathed in gray tears. Our faces an inch apart, I could smell cardamom tea on his breath. I was in shock. I had never killed anyone, certainly not a friend. Never with my bare hands, staring death in the face.

"Jabbar," I said softly. "I can still save you. Please help me stop this madness."

Jabbar's eyes had been closed, but he opened them to narrow slits. He struggled to raise his head up closer to my ear. He whispered, "Bryan, I will not make you a murderer ... I must do this myself."

Then he lowered his head to the floor and murmured, "You can turn off the autopilot ... it's not too late."

Then he put his trembling hands on the janbiya's handle and pulled the blade straight down into his aorta. Red blood erupted from around the wound, running across his belly and onto the floor. His face was pale and flaccid as his eyes closed.

I whispered into his ear, already cool to the touch of my lips. "We'll leave it to God's mills. I pray he will forgive you for what you've done. Go in peace, my lost brother."

I had no time to waste. No moments to grieve for a dear friend, once lost to hate, now to death. I wiped the tears from my eyes so that I could see. I turned to face the helm. The New York and New Jersey coasts were closing in.

Blood was dripping from my left arm. I took off my shirt and tied it above the wound, pulling the knot tight with my teeth. If I passed out from blood loss, I would fail.

The timer on the computer screen read 15:10. I sprinted to the console. To my right was a large knob marked "Autopilot" with "Engage" and "Disengage" settings. I moved it to "Disengage." A brief alarm sounded.

I ran to the monitor and touched the keyboard beneath it. Immediately a log-in box came up asking for an ID number and password. I knew it would be futile to guess. *Damn! I can't disarm the ship.* Time was quickly running out.

I dashed to the helm in the room's center, where I found the chadburn, which controls the ship's speed and direction. I had to slow down to make the turn without running aground. Shifting the chadburn from "Half Ahead" to "Full Astern," I felt a vibration in the ship that reassured me the chadburn itself controlled the power without requiring someone in the engine room.

"Thank God," I muttered.

I turned the wheel in a clockwise direction until it wouldn't turn anymore. The screen in the front console showed the ship now turning north. I could see the horizon moving to my left.

At the front console was a screen for speed. With the engine in reverse, the speed was dropping. Eight knots, six knots, four knots and eventually three. The ship in line behind us, still a mile away, would have to steer around. I rushed back to the chadburn and shifted it to "Stop."

Meanwhile, my left arm was starting to go numb. I cut the shirt off and released the blood back to the wound, but the bleeding had slowed.

The speed dial showed forward motion continuing at a slow three knots, but we were drifting closer to shore.

"No, God, no!" I shouted.

Running back to the front console, I slipped in a puddle of Jabbar's blood and fell face down on the floor. My wound reopened. Regaining my footing, I left a row of crimson tracks, the lugs of my soles and the word "Vibram" stamped in red across the white tile.

I dashed toward a control station that read "Bow Thruster." It had another chadburn and joystick. Per my study of the ship a month earlier, I assumed this controlled a propeller set sideways in the bow for steering the ship when it docked. Pushing the chadburn from "Stop" to "Quarter Power," I felt a vibration in the ship. I pulled the joystick to the right to where it said "Starboard." The big ship moved faster to the starboard side. An alarm went off, followed by a digital voice, "Draft danger! Draft danger!"

The sonar showed that we were about to run aground. I turned the bow thruster to full. It turned faster, but I felt the rough vibration as the bow hit something and the ship started to list toward its starboard side.

"Damnit!" I screamed.

We were slowing to a halt. A new wave of panic flooded over me. I stuffed my hands up into my wet armpits, closed my eyes, and held my breath. This was going to be bad. I peeked under my eyelids to see that we were almost dead in the water, turning at a snail's pace.

I looked around the bridge. On the console I saw a dial labeled "Ballast Tanks." I ran to the console and turned the ballast tank switch to "Out" and the dial on full power. A gauge showed the water level in the ballast tanks, which were only a quarter full, slowly dropping. Soon the land started moving to our port side again, and the course vibration and terrible scraping sound was abating. In a while, open sea was before me, the direction screen showed us pointing due east. I put the bow thruster back into the stop position.

The digital clock now read 7:22 and was continuing to drop. I ran back to the helm. I pushed the chadburn to "Full Ahead." A terrible vibration came up through the hull as the ship was trying to pull free from the last remains of its sandy grave. In a moment, the vibration stopped, and the ship started to pick up speed. Tears of joy flooded my eyes.

I went out the starboard door, the salty wind carrying away my breath within its clutches. I stepped upon a grated metal platform above which I saw antennas and spinning radars. From here I was going to dive the sixty feet into the sea with a slight chance I would survive the dive, only to drown during my swim. I climbed the railing, stepped over it, and, on the outside, looking down into the rushing waters, I let go with my left hand, which caused me to pivot and cast my gaze toward the stern.

Fifteen feet away was a bright orange lifeboat. Two cables of its davit launch system suspended the enclosed capsule, which looked like a stubby submarine. I grabbed the railing and climbed back over it. I raced up a couple of steps to the lifeboat. Climbing through its hatch, tripping as I worked in haste, I closed the door behind me and locked it. Above was a large handle that showed an arrow and the word "Deploy." When I pushed the handle, the mechanism lowered the boat by cable to the sea. I hit the water with a thud and the lifeboat detached from the cables.

The boat had a small gas engine. When I turned the ignition key, the motor turned slowly as if the battery were dying. Looking out the small porthole, I saw nothing but the terra-cotta hull in my visual field. I was still a dead man.

In a panic, I studied the insides of the boat in the dim light of the porthole. The closed fuel valve on the motor caught my eye. Opening the valve, I turned the start switch again.

Putt, putt … putt, putt … putt, putt … silence.

I adjusted the choke and tried again. It rattled and then started, with blue smoke puffing out of the exhaust behind the boat.

Pointing the lifeboat toward land, a good five miles away, I opened the throttle.

I watched the *Eirinopoiós* moving away from me, shrinking in size through the stern porthole, down, down, until the whole ship fit inside the small port window. *Was it fast enough?* I had two minutes before the detonation. With my onboard motor at full throttle, I could add another mile before the blast.

Would I survive? I had my doubts.

Holding on to my seat and my breath, I felt prepared for the worst. There was a seat-belt harness, like in racing cars, and I buckled it around me. There was nothing else I could do. I closed my eyes and waited in murky silence. Then I sensed a horrendous flash through my eyelids, coming in from the craft's porthole windows. I felt the heat on my skin and heard a deafening sound.

A second later, a powerful blow hit my twenty-foot boat, flipping me end over end in chaotic tumbles until my head smashed into the side of the cabin and things went dark.

I felt my conscious mind slowly floating up from a dark chasm. Disoriented in a black, quiet world. *Where am I? Who am I?*

Bits and pieces of memories began to form in my brain like old photo negatives, sketchy outlines around reverse colors. A terrible headache pulled me back into something like consciousness. But I was unable to see my fingers in front of my eyes. I could hear water lapping against the wall beside me. The air was as thick as a steam sauna gone cold. No oxygen.

Did the robbers just knock me out? Am I in Yemen?

Feeling around, I knew I was inside something. My tent?

It was a boat. I was in the lifeboat.

Damn, I had survived!

Suffocating, disoriented, I felt around in the dark for the hatch. I opened it, and cool sea air rushed into the stuffy space. I took a deep breath. The waves were lapping around me. I felt like I was being rocked in a cradle.

Was New York saved?

I saw lights on along the coast. Helicopters in the air. Something was going on, spotlights flashing here and there.

My cell phone vibrated in my pocket. I pulled it out. It was Angie.

"Hello."

"Bryan! My God, it's you?" she screamed. Sobbing ensued.

"Yes. Who did you expect?" I asked.

"Bryan," she said through howls, "I've been calling all day, and no one answered. I was afraid you went up in the blast."

"The blast ... you saw it?"

"Bryan, everyone saw it! Everyone in the Western hemisphere. It was enormous—a ball of fire that pierced into the clouds like a rocket. They saw it on the International Space Station. A shock wave penetrated the entire city, breaking windows."

"Was anyone hurt?" I asked in a soft tone.

"Yeah, Bryan," she said in an even quieter tone. "There were casualties. How many, I don't know. They're still doing search and rescue. But it could have been so much worse."

"People died?"

"Yeah, Bryan. A tidal wave came ashore at Long Beach, killing a family of four who were collecting shells. Several small boats sank, at least six fishermen died. A cargo ship sank, but no one died on it. But they're still assessing things."

"So, I failed."

"Bryan, hell, no, you didn't fail!" she shouted. "You saved New York. You saved the whole fucking world ... it was you, wasn't it? I mean, something diverted the ship away from the city, and the police and the Coast Guard were tied up ten miles off Long Island's coast boarding an empty ship."

"Yeah, I was on board."

"How did you survive?"

"Angie..." My voice faltered as I started to weep. "I had to kill Jabbar. It was the only way. He was my fishing buddy. My confidant. The best friend I ever had. I promised myself that no one would die, but I failed—"

"Where are you?"

"Don't have a clue. I'm in a lifeboat, one from the *Eirinopoiós*, somewhere in the sea. I can see the lights on shore, a few miles away. There are helicopters overhead."

We were both quiet, consumed with sobs, speechless on both ends of the signal.

Finally, getting control of my emotions, I whispered, "Hey, sis, could you do me a favor?"

"Of course."

"Can you ding my phone to find out my location and send that to search and rescue? I wanna come home. I'm so tired. I just want to go to bed."

CHAPTER THIRTY-SIX

Five days later, there was no place on this earth more serene than my sister's fire-escape landing. Six stories up, plants standing in small, round terracotta pots lined up along the outside edge—Angie's attempt at urban farming. There were tomatoes, basil, rosemary, and mint, the remaining plants struggling deep in the throes of autumn's vanishing sun. The pots themselves sat on small bone-china saucers to keep their drips from following gravity down to a complaining neighbor's landing below.

The little bone plates had their own fascinating history, which they brazenly carried in their chips and stains. They came from a set Grandma Rogers had inherited from her grandmother and were brought to America from Germany in a steamer trunk. I had glimpsed the Statue of Liberty through the windows over Jabbar's shoulder when I was confronting him in the engineering bridge. I had a thought about my ancestors sailing into Ellis Island on the second of June 1892 and seeing that view, their first of America and what I thought would be my last.

Because of the wear on them, Angie didn't use the saucers anymore, except to catch the overwatering of her plants. But for their one hundred and thirty-year life, this might have been their noblest function—helping small plants find a foothold inside the most densely populated and concreted city in America.

Was it a plantlet of promise? Was there a promise of a better life anymore, hope for Yemen, hope for the world?

I was sitting on a lime-green vinyl beanbag chair that leaned against the outside wall of the apartment. It was my nest on the fire escape. From this perch, I got a bird's-eye view of East 32nd Street. It was the hurricane's eye, peace amid chaos. I had rescued the chair from a dumpster and convinced Angie to let me keep it even though she thought it was tacky. People around Central Park throw away the most amazing things, often hardly used. The papers once had a story about someone finding a ten-million-dollar Jackson Pollock in such a dumpster, it having finished serving the owners' needs.

Angie had returned to work at the publishing house, and Joel to Congresswoman Estepp's office. I was alone but felt safe despite presuming that I was still on al-Qaeda's shit list. Maybe it was because I had grown up near the city. Maybe because I knew Angie loved and protected me. Mom was a subway ride away, as were my two brothers, Hank and Wayne. I was home.

That morning, a Coast Guard official with a Texas accent had called to tell me they had found the *Ace*. It had run aground on Jones Beach, pushed ashore by the tidal wave from the blast. I was being fined nine hundred and eighty dollars by the Coast Guard for "watercraft abandonment."

"But I was on the tanker that exploded," I explained. "I boarded the tanker from that sailboat to stop them. I had to let the boat go."

Silence.

"Sorry, buddy, but the reason doesn't matter. You'll also need a salvage company to get her off the beach this week. That'll cost you another five grand. Looks like she's had some water in the cabin."

"You don't say." I murmured.

The death count was ten so far. The Claymores, a family of four, had been wading in the late-October surf at Long Beach, looking for shells. They probably heard the boom, maybe saw the flash fifteen miles out and beyond the horizon. But they never expected the twenty-five-foot wave that washed them into the sea. Lizzy, their seven-year-old, saw shells suddenly appearing, her grandmother said on TV, tearfully adding, "My baby ran toward the receding water to pick up the shells, not realizing it was the outwash before the big wave. My daughter Judy and her husband were not far behind. The police found the girls' bodies and their mom. The dad's body still missing, but they are still searching. My God, why? Who did this?" she asked.

It's always the same question, "Why?" But no one wants to listen to the answers when they appear untidy. The cycles of death and sorrow perpetually endure. I wish to God no one had to die.

There were five fishermen, not six as Angie had reported. But one more person died, a lone sailor out enjoying autumn's coastal gales. He was a quarter mile away from the *Eirinopoiós* when she detonated. Didn't have a chance.

The damage had so far been estimated at a little over five million dollars on shore. That's what the reporters said. Most of that was to replace windows shattered by the shock wave. There were fish on the Palisades Parkway, seaweed hanging from trees around Washington Square, and seashells on Bleecker Street, the whole Village reduced to aquarium décor minus the bubbling treasure chest.

Angie described how a thousand car alarms went off in the city after the shock wave passed. No damage except to nerves and ears. It took an hour before they quieted.

Jabbar's ship bomb went down in history as the largest explosion on the planet outside of a nuclear blast. Only a modern high-yield nuke was bigger. The "mother of all bombs" (MOAB), the largest conventional bomb ever made, which the U.S. had threatened to use in Iraq, paled in comparison.

Strangely, no one talked to me about what happened. Not the Port Authority Police, not the FBI, not the Coast Guard, not Homeland Security. I was a ghost to them, someone they wished would disappear. You would think they would have a thousand questions. But so far, nothing. The election was a week away, and everyone was working to get their candidates elected. Nothing else mattered.

Looking down from my perch while sipping coffee from a paper cup, I thrilled to the sounds of ordinary life—children laughing and giggling as they walked to school, making the sounds normal, untraumatized children make. Garbage trucks clanging their cans. Conversations between pedestrians. I thought of what might have been—all these dear people dead. *Why?* One Saudi pilot, one wayward target, one bomb that bred a hateful world. *And for what?* And these same dear people who just barely cheated death get up in the morning, go to the factories that make the bombs, go home at night, and vote for the leaders who used them … without ever once connecting the dots.

Looking back through the window, I saw the image on the screen, a CNN story about the explosion, with the president making comments and New York's Harbor Police and Coast Guard as a backdrop. For five days, this had been the only thing on TV … and political ads.

I opened the window and stepped into Angie's living room so I could hear the president speak.

"It was our administration who stopped these bastards. We were on their trail for months. They turned the ship around when they saw our strength in the harbor. If the Democrats had been in power, New York City would no longer exist. They treat terrorists with mindfulness therapy … we, with bullets. Millions would have died if not for the New Jersey and New York Port Authority Police and Coast Guard. They are American heroes. I've signed an executive order to increase our support for the war on terrorism in Yemen so that this never happens again."

"God help us! What did the Coast Guard and police do except board an empty ship?" I mumbled to the fancy edge-lit smart tv. It didn't answer. Not that smart. Maybe the Port Authority had been more compromised than they'd realized, directing interceptors to board an empty ship.

I couldn't stomach it and muted the tv. I went to the bathroom to pee—brown as tea. Not being recognized as a hero didn't bother me. As a physician associate, I was used to it. I didn't want the damn stardom. I wanted anonymity. I wanted everything to go away.

I came out of the bathroom, grabbed my coffee off the dusty bookshelf, and walked toward the still-open window to the fire-escape landing. But then I saw the talking heads from the Democratic Party. I turned up the volume.

"But it was someone in Democratic Congresswoman Estepp's office in New York that alerted the FBI and the Port Authority Police about the terrorist plot. The Republicans didn't get involved. They were too busy with their campaign. After all, a terrorist act would help them hold the White House. Thank God, the Port Authority Police with the Coast Guard's help, chased these terrorists out to sea, saving New York."

I hit the off button aggressively. "Liars!" I said to the flat display on the wall. "What a bunch of bullshit from both sides! Is this all that we've become? The blue team verses the red team and winning at all costs? Do we live in two different universes of our making, opposite cosmoses? Neither side gave a rat's ass about this plot. Is the world black and white, good guys and bad? If we kill all the bad guys, will the world finally find peace?"

I sat on the landing, holding my coffee cup, fingers still sensitive to its heat since the burning clinic's hot doorknob. The air whistled from the beanbag as my weight compressed it, scaring away the pigeons that had landed on the railing.

In this moment of quiet, when this nightmare seemed to have found its conclusion, I allowed my mind to go back over my previous two years. I needed to process all that Yemen had taken from me and had given me. With my eyes closed, the images came in fragments. Frame by frame, highlights, then details. "Oh, Lord, how I miss that place!" I mumbled out loud. There were no better people on this earth than the Yemenis, despite the few haters.

I heard footsteps reverberating on the metal fire escape. It wasn't the first time someone had descended while I was hanging out with Angie's plants. But this time, it was an angel, semi-transparent and within a white glow.

As she reached my platform, I could see it was Sheila, wearing her knee-length white lab coat. But rather than being covered with Yemeni dust and blood stains, her coat was snow-white, the creases ironed to a pristine crispness. A small black otoscope was in her chest pocket, like always. Her contagious smile spread from dimple to dimple. Her blond corkscrew curls bounced with each step. I stood in her presence … out of respect.

"Sheila," I said, tears quickly overcoming me, "I never told you … how much I love you." Sobs quickly engulfed my presence. When I had tamed my emotions, I continued. "I do love you … and with all my heart. I'm so sorry I didn't save you!" Trembling overwhelmed me to the point I could barely stand.

"You didn't have to tell me you love me," she said. "I could see it in your silly grin." She reached out and stroked my face. "I could feel it in your eyes' embrace. Neither did I tell you, buster, that I love you too, with all my heart. I was waiting for you to sweep me off my feet, back on Nebraskan soil. We were damn fools to have waited."

We embraced. We kissed, her warm paprika lips against my cold chapped ones.

Was this an apparition? I wanted to suspend all reason. I didn't want to make sense of it.

She pulled back and stared into my eyes. "Bryan, I'm so proud of you! You saved the whole friggin' world!"

I pulled her close to me. I enfolded her within my arms, wanting to squeeze the breath out of her. She was soft. She became softer and lighter in my arms the longer I held her—until I could see completely through her body.

"No! Don't go! Please, God, don't take her!" I screamed.

She held her smile but remained silent as she became translucent, dissolving into a mist, then flowing between my fingers and out of my grip.

I felt inundated with sadness. Tears dripped from my chin through the holes in the graded landing. No shabby china saucers to catch them. I loved her. Our romance measured only a few hours, between midnight and the dawn's break. The most magnificent woman I'd ever met. Compassionate, selfless, intelligent, and patient. Lost forever. Maybe I had saved the world ... but it didn't matter anymore, I'd lost Sheila.

"What a waste! What could have been! What a fucking waste!"

EPILOGUE- Letters

It was taking me much longer to recover than I had hoped—from my concussion, my liver disease, and my uncertainty. My malignant doubt. Angie's doctor had checked out my liver and confirmed it was acute hepatitis C, evolving into a chronic form. I was under treatment and on the mend.

It was six weeks after the horrible blast. An icy wind was blowing in from New England. The elections were over. Who had won? I hadn't a clue. Didn't give a damn, just hoping for the lessor of liars.

I took long walks in Central Park. Street vendors for lunch, breakfast, and dinner. I was a shipwrecked soul, washed ashore by a tidal wave of the world's resentments.

Angie was starting to worry about me. One afternoon, I took a long walk out in a chilly rain mixed with icy pellets and wind with no jacket. When I returned, Angie and Joel were eating dinner. Angie said my quietness and withdrawal made her think I was taking the same path Mom had after we lost Dad. I wasn't. I just needed time. Too much to process.

It was helpful to have Angie and Joel around to keep me from my darkest thoughts. And there was Mom too. She was managing okay living on her own and so happy to have me back. She didn't know her son was a hero. I was meeting her for lunch about three times a week.

Across her little yellow kitchen table in her Brooklyn brownstone apartment, her steel-blue eyes strained to see me. She wore her nerves on the surface. Her three drugs kept them from going deeper but left her persona as only a shadow of her former self, disconnected at times from the reality around her. I couldn't tell her what I'd been through. She would have worried, retroactively.

"Did you hear about the big bombing?" she asked one time, bending over her soup, eyes on me, sipping from a big spoon, careful not to spill a drop on her flowered blouse.

"Yes, Mom. I heard it was massive," I answered sipping my soup and gazing out the window.

"Awful," she said and then acted like a chill went up her spine. "It cracked my kitchen window. I thought my building was exploding. I hope they catch that evil person who did this."

Leaning toward her, my spoon in my hand and her face in my stare, I said, "Mom ... they did."

"Hi," I said coming through the door. Angie and Joel were at the table. The smell of soy and MSG filled the air.

My sister met me in the entryway, her brown hair in a ponytail, her red lipstick setting her mouth ablaze. Sheila would have loved her. Reaching for my elbow to direct my attention to her, she said, "We're having Chinese takeout. We have enough. You like egg rolls, don't you?"

"I do, but I just had a hotdog from a street vendor. And before that, I had Mom's minestrone. 'Good for the liver,' she says. So, I'm full for now."

"Okay ... but if you change your mind, I'll leave a couple in the fridge."

I was walking to the guest room where I slept when Angie shouted from the dining room, "Oh, Bryan. A bundle of mail came for you! It looks like someone forwarded it from Yemen. It's on the coffee table."

"Really?" I asked.

Walking into the living room, I saw the worn bundle on the table, envelopes wrapped in a red rubber band. Beside it was a small box addressed with a Sharpie. I tucked the bundle under my arm, opened the window, and stepped onto the fire escape.

I sat on the beanbag chair. It whistled. The air outside was cold and damp, so I brought my legs up to my chest and wrapped my arms around them. With my right hand, I pulled the first few envelopes from the bundle. They were all professional letters, licenses to be renewed, fees to pay, a certifying exam to take.

I laid those letters down and picked up another one. It was a white envelope with tan stains around its edges as if someone had dipped it in tea. Its corners were dog-eared. The Arabic in the postal seal was clear, "Postal Service of The Republic of Yemen." Someone had mailed it within the country.

The return address, printed roughly in pencil in both English and Arabic, read:

Maritza El Haddad
Raqm 1, Sharie Jabbar
Haydan, Republic of Yemen

It was addressed simply to "Bryan, IRC, Sana'a." Yet it had found me in New York. Dorothy knew a letter addressed to "Bryan" from Haydan had to be for me.

I hastily ripped it open.

Dear Doctor Bryan,

I am writing for my mother, Mona. She wanted me to tell you she is sorry that she brought my father the gun. She did not know that he would try to shoot you. My father was once a good man. He listened to Abdul's foolish talk. What he tried to do was wrong. Our hearts were so broken with Alam's loss, he turned bad. Now our hearts are broken with my father. Please forgive me. Please forgive my father.

The Americans traced the ship back to my father. They came here and questioned us. When my mother told them that Abdul was behind my father becoming bad, they came in helicopters into the compound in Huth during the night. They killed Abdul, his wives, and five children along with other men.

It is good for me they killed Abdul. He was arranging a marriage between me and a sixty-year-old cousin. Now my mother wants to send me

to New Jersey to live with another cousin, a good cousin, to escape this war.
He's a chemist there. He has a daughter my age. I will see you again, in
America, perhaps?

We also have sad news. The Saudis bombed our beautiful old home
when mother and I were shopping in Sa'dah. It was drafty and damp … but
I loved it. The bomb destroyed our house and killed Ghada, my sister
Nadira, and our neighbor. It is rubble now, and Ghada and my sister are
gone. We are still living in Haydan in a much smaller house and may end
up in the camp if we can't afford to live here. Now, we are living off the
proceeds of selling Father's truck.

Mother also wanted you to know that Raziya, who you call Rosie, is
doing well. She lives in Sana'a with her children. She came out of hiding
after Abdul died. She visited us here, looking for you.

But I do have hope again. I can laugh because I know this war will
end for me. It has to.
Sincerely,

Maritza

Tears filled my eyes until they tripped over and ran down
my cheeks. I stroked the page with my wet finger. I never expected
to hear from Jabbar's family. He really *was* a good man—once. But
he'd been swept away by inconsolable grief.

I held Maritza's letter close to my heart, elated. "She can
laugh again! That's all that matters," I whispered.

Someone Irish, I believe, said, "Our revenge will be our
children's laughter." The giggles of Yemen's children were the
millstones of God's revenge, the real stones of Yemen.

I looked down at the street below and noticed an old man
walking a little white dog. A Bolognese, perhaps? It started to sleet.
His umbrella opened above their heads, deflecting the ice.

I looked at the remaining letter in the bundle. Oddly,
someone had mailed it from New York to Yemen, and then it had
found its way back from there. The return address embossed in gold
lettering was "The Mennonite Central Committee."

I opened the envelope and pulled out the formal-looking letter.

Dear Mr. Rogers,

It has come to our attention that you have recently returned from Yemen. We also understand that you have gained fluency in the Arabic language. We have spoken to Dorothy Robinson with the IRC in Sana'a, and she gave us a glowing report about your service.

We are looking for a highly qualified physician or physician associate for our refugee clinic in the village of Sayqat al Amir. It is in the government-controlled southeast of Yemen, well removed from present areas of conflict. However, the needs of the people are just as great as those who live in Haydan. It is an arid area of mountains, however, the village itself is in an oasis.

Please consider this opportunity. We are looking forward to hearing from you.
Sincerely,

Robert D. Jamison, MD
Medical Director, Mennonite Central Committee's Near Eastern Division.

I stood up, envelope in hand. I walked back to the railing. The man and his dog were now gone. The sleet had turned to rain. My eyes followed each drop from my sixth-floor landing down to the ground where my tears had fallen.

I spoke into the damp air. "Dad, what should I do? Can I do this?"

The little yellow box intrigued me. It was from the Sana'a office. Had I forgotten something?

I tore the box open, and to my amazement there was my watch. My dad's watch. I put it on and fastened the clasp. Dorothy had wrapped it in a handwritten note.

Bryan,

Without a clinic in Haydan, we expedited the solar pump and water system to cut down on cholera. They sank a new pipe into the aquifer. When they pulled the old pipe up, the watch came with it. A miracle, perhaps. Take care.

P.S. Everyone was asking Nabil, who supervised the new pump installation, "When is Dr. Bryan coming back? We miss him ... we love him."

Sincerely,

Dorothy.

I rotated my wrist to look at the dial. My jaw dropped. It read 10:28 A.M. It had stopped on that time again, the precise moment of Dad's death. *What the hell? How can that be?*

I felt his presence and those familiar words in my ears, the words he'd said to me as a boy anytime I met a formidable challenge. "Son ... you can do this."

Acknowledgements

It takes a village to write a book. I am indebted to that community of people who made *The Stones of Yemen* possible. To Kevin Brown and Eric Holden for reading the first draft and giving my creative energies some better direction. I want to thank those ten people who were later my beta-readers, you know who you are. I want to thank my editor Carrie Cantor for her invaluable work in corralling my many words into understandable sentences. I want to thank Brian Backman and Dave Mittman for their willingness to read a late draft and give me their valuable impressions and comments. I want to thank my oncology nurses who were able to work around my laptop and note pads to stick me with their needles and tubes. As always, I want to thank my family for their patience and unyielding assistance. Lastly, I want to thank my readers for whom I write. Thank you for trusting me as your guide—out front with a torch—as we took this enthralling journey. I hope my book brought you joy, entertainment, and thought. If so, I hope you can recommend *The Stones of Yemen* to your family, friends, and colleagues.

About the Author

J. Michael Jones grew up in Tennessee's Appalachian Mountains. He completed a degree in psychology and biology at East Tennessee State University, the Physician Associate program at the University of Kentucky, a Master of Medicine-neurology emphasis at the University of Nebraska, and a degree in Arabic from the American University in Cairo. He lives with his wife Denise in Washington State's San Juan Islands.

Personal Experiences that Influenced the writing of *The Stones of Yemen*

As a physician associate student, Mike worked in Abu Dhabi, and the Burami Oasis of Oman, where he met Denise. From there, he hitched a ride on a plane to Rawalpindi, Pakistan. In Pakistan, He hitchhiked into the Afghanistan's Khyber Pass, where he worked in a refugee camp. After returning to the states, Denise and Mike were married and settled in Ann Arbor, where Mike took a position at a headache treatment center. While in Ann Arbor, they became a host family to Yemeni students for two years.

In 1987, Mike and Denise returned to the Middle East, working in Cyprus and then Cairo, Egypt. While working in the Village of Garbage outside Cairo, Mike finished a degree in the intensive Arabic program at the American University in Cairo. After two years, Mike and Denise were preparing to move to Sana'a, Yemen, but due to illness of their son, they returned to the states, where Mike took a position with Mayo Clinic as a headache specialist. They eventually moved to the San Juan Islands   in

Washington state to finish raising their five children. There, Mike was the founder and owner of the Pacific Rim Headache Center.

Mike returned to Pakistan to assist in earthquake relief in 2005 with a group of medics from New York City (NYC-Medics), many of whom had worked in the 9/11 disaster. In 2012, Mike went to Nepal and offered medical assistance in remote Himalayan villages and in 2015, he coordinated the association of the NYC Medics and Himalayan Healthcare for relief work after a major earthquake crippled Nepal.

On Writing

Mike began writing professionally in the 1980s, publishing over thirty articles in journals and magazines. He began writing non-fiction books in the 1990s. In 2019, while he and Denise were training for a trek across Greenland, Mike became suddenly and seriously ill and was diagnosed with Multiple Myeloma (bone marrow cancer) with related renal failure. His career as a physician associate suddenly ended. At that juncture, he became a full-time writer, shifting to fiction. He is the author of A *Kernel in the Pod, Butterflies in the Belfry, Why Your Head Aches, The Waters of Bimini, Christiana Athena, Ristretto Rain*, and his best, *The Stones of Yemen*.

Made in the USA
Las Vegas, NV
03 February 2023

66837979R00213